I0739403

Becoming
A novel

Cheryl Cranick

Becoming: A novel

Copyright © 2015 by Cheryl Cranick

All rights reserved.

This book is a work of fiction, inspired in part by experiences from the author's life. Any resemblance to places, people, or events is coincidental or a fictionalized composite. This work should not be considered a replacement for medical advice by a qualified health professional. The author strongly recommends readers in crisis seek treatment by a health care provider.

Cover photo credit: Sean Flynn
Author photo credit: Betty Cranick

ISBN 978-0-9963314-0-1

For my parents

In the spring of 2013, I self-published a novel I had been drafting for five years. With the support of family and friends, I decided the story simply needed to be read—no matter the size of its audience. I was grateful for the readership it found. However, less than six months after self-publishing it, I had the opportunity to make modifications and share the manuscript with the traditional publishing industry. I decided to try, which is so unlike me. I worked with industry professionals to prepare the novel for its presentation. Some major changes included hiring a professional designer to craft the front cover art and also coming to terms with the idea of changing the title. A small number of copies are in existence of a novel titled *Fabulous And Talented*. That is the earliest printing of *Becoming*. Renaming this book was a daunting experience, in part because I had come to know it by its name. However, being challenged to reexamine the title has resulted in a new identity that I love.

For three reasons, I consented to the title change. From a business perspective, the manuscript needed somewhat of a unique presence. Secondly, the original name did not resonate with certain people—even my attempts to force the issue with the original cover design: the "F A T" was not obvious. Therefore, it needed rethinking. Third, and most important, even before I self-published the novel the first time, I was wavering on the title. My intention with this novel was a story that discussed mental illness, body image, and the journey to professional success. As I prepared it for publication, I was increasingly concerned that mental illness—one of the major themes—was not expressed in the title *Fabulous And Talented*. This novel is about a young woman's development: who is she becoming as a person, who is she becoming as a professional, and also her concept of beauty. Therefore, what a more fitting title than *Becoming*?

A final change to this novel edition was sparked by the advice of an agent with whom I spoke. I was told the story needed more pain. I suppose when I began this novel in 2008, I was not yet completely public with the idea of living with mental illness, mostly the admission of such darkness. There were certain experiences and scenes I was unwilling to write at the time. While this novel remains a work of fiction, there is no denying I lent many of my own feelings, and some of my experiences, to the character as I crafted her unique life. Therefore, this new edition shares more sorrow. Its truth is a composite of my truth.

CHAPTER 1

She hated nights like this. The nights that made the days hard because the nights never came. She lay awake, fetal, aching, as warm tears trickled down from the outside point of one eye.

Her room was black and small like a prison. How fitting that the walls were cinder blocks.

Her mind ebbed from one thought to another. They didn't stop. They never did. They kept her up and exhausted her. She wanted sleep. She wanted silence. She wanted to stop thinking. Claire reached out into the darkness, feeling along the surface of her desk that doubled as her nightstand. There was little space for more in the room. She was searching for her pill bottle. She found it by touch and twisted the top off, fished out a small tranquilizer, and let it dissolve on her tongue.

Moving onto her back, Claire's stomach still churned, her chest pounded forcefully; blood pumped to a drumbeat in her ears. Was she dying? Was this a heart attack? Could that happen at nineteen? Could anxiety do that?

Tears burned from both eyes now, spilling over and trailing down her face to her ears. Claire couldn't catch her breath, and as she labored, her heart felt short, sharp jabs of pain.

She *was* dying. God, thank God. Could she be? She was terrified and yet relieved. Then she wouldn't have to do it. She wouldn't have to think about it or want it anymore. She wouldn't be the crazy girl who killed herself. The spoiled, crazy girl who hated living—hated having loving parents, hated being at a private school, hated seeing her own reflection. The one everyone called *perfect* even as she secretly contemplated ways to die—in her happy home with her enviable family.

If her heart were on the verge of collapse, she would just

die naturally—and be dead—and be gone, away from having everything and feeling nothing but self-hate, guilt, and worthlessness. Her mother wouldn't be as sad if she died that way. People wouldn't think she was bad or selfish if it wasn't suicide.

The thoughts jumped again—to the picture show of the day and then tomorrow, and yesterday—school—her future—the mounting list of everything threatening to unravel her. She almost laughed—*threatening to?* She was unraveled—she came here broken.

Claire shifted her body to her side again and curled up, clutching her rotting stomach. She pushed the bottoms of her fists into her head and her eyes. She wanted to stop the hurt and the tears. But it didn't help. She dug her fingernails into her hands to feel pain, hoping to divert her thoughts for a moment. Then her hands relaxed and cradled her face, covering her shame in the darkness. She sobbed into them for a few moments more. Her breath was still shallow.

The pill wasn't working, so she took another. That was four.

If the heart attack didn't kill her, maybe the drugs would.

She knew she had to call him tomorrow. She had to tell her dad she had been wrong. He had been right. She hated it here.

Tomorrow, she vowed—or if sleep never came, then she'd call him when the second half of today lingered on.

She couldn't recall when she finally fell asleep, but when she woke, she was groggy. She looked at the clock, which had last read 2:49 a.m. Now it was nearly noon, even though her dorm room was still blackened from her lined curtain at the window. Everything ached—her head and her body, and even her jaw was in pain from clenching it in her sleep.

She had slept through her morning class again—her one obligation for the day. She rolled over, pulled the covers in place, and went back to sleep. Somehow, sleep always came easier in the daytime, as though her mind wanted her to escape life. Or maybe it was the exhaustion.

It was after four o'clock before she rose and bothered to shower. Depression never seemed to keep her from that. She cooked boxed mac and cheese in the electric boiling pot her mom had bought her. People watched her in the dining hall. She couldn't go there. She never went there. Not that she actually wanted to eat, but her headache wouldn't subside and her stomach grumbled. The salty fake cheese on the soft noodles soothed her.

She tried to ignore the growing belly under her t-shirt. She always thought she was fat growing up—even when she wasn't. Now she was. She blamed the meds for that—meds that did nothing but make her fat. She ate another spoonful of the food—and another and another until she had consumed the four servings herself. Then she laid on her bed contemplating vomiting, watching the television sideways, which hurt her eyes.

She was waiting for her dad to come home from work so she could call him. She could wait until winter break just a few weeks away to talk about this, but she couldn't wait any longer. She needed his permission. She needed his blessing. She didn't trust any choice she made alone, and her mom just seemed to coddle her.

When she knew dinner was over at home and he would be watching the news, she dialed the number and clutched the phone as it rang.

The moment he answered, she couldn't speak.

Her father was a loving man. Despite his reserved demeanor, he adored his daughter. She knew that. He only wanted what was best for her. They had always been close.

But he was a realist and she was not. For Claire, since life barely mattered anymore, she clung to her passion. To her father, creative writing was folly. It was a pastime but not a career. He had pushed her towards majoring in education; in her heart Claire knew what a horrible teacher she would make.

"Claire?" he asked. "Are you there?"

"Hi," she replied sheepishly. She felt flustered and confused.

He waited through her pause, sensing she needed the moment. "I can't stay here, Dad," she finally confessed. "I want to come home, Boston or New York. And I want to write." She waited in agony for his answer.

He sighed, as she expected he would. But then he surprised her. "It's probably a good idea, Claire. Coming home, I mean."

She held the phone away from her mouth while she breathed rapidly, trying to calm herself. Then the emotions came again—tears of confusion and relief. She had prepared for a fight.

A thousand miles away, John Kelly sat in Claire's childhood home in Connecticut, relieved that his daughter had changed her mind. He still didn't understand depression, even as his wife told him to be patient. Some days, Claire was the outgoing, happy girl he knew. Other days, she shifted so quickly to crying or anger, and he never knew what had changed. It unnerved him. Some days, she reminded him of his mother. That hurt him most of all.

"Find a new school," he said. "Find a major you *like*. Just make sure there's a future in it. OK?"

Claire bit her lower lip, trying to fake a calm manner. "OK," she whispered.

"I'm not trying to be a bastard, Claire. Dreams are great. They're just hard to come by sometimes. That's why you need something to fall back on."

She tried to contain her composure. "I know." Then she paused. "Love you, Daddy."

"Love you, too, kid."

It was that easy, despite Claire always allowing things to be harder than they should. When she placed the phone down, she rested her forehead to her bent knees at her chest. She clung to them, rocking and breathing slowly as her anxiety dissipated. She thought and wondered and hoped and prayed. Then she reached for her computer.

With the approval she shouldn't have needed but couldn't live without, Claire turned her attention to the research she had been avoiding—finding the place where her creativity and her father's realism might merge. She knew the fields she didn't want, but in the weeks of her research, one career option kept popping up. It initially intrigued her, but soon Claire found herself tied to it. At the end of spring, she returned to New England and enrolled for the fall at Adams University. It was a private school on the outskirts of Boston. She chose it for the small classes, respected communications program, and industry connections.

Eight months after her call, she sat in her new dorm room for the first time. She had a new prescription that her doctor assured her would end the depression symptoms and the weight gain. By her bed sat a textbook on copywriting.

She only hoped they were both right this time.

After saying goodbye to her parents and promising them she would be fine, Claire had unpacked her bags and nested. Then she took a deep breath and tried to convince herself she could survive here.

Tomorrow she would meet her roommates, but she was nervous. Claire had called them during summer break, after she received her housing assignment. The first time they even knew she existed was after opening their own housing letters. The girls had a fourth roommate picked out, but she flunked out of school and never told them. This left an empty spot for a shy transfer student. The change didn't seem a welcomed one.

Leigh had been the most agreeable on the phone. When Claire called, Leigh shared some basic details about her and the other two. Jane was bringing a TV, Leigh said, and she had a couch.

"I have a mini fridge if you want it," Claire had offered.

"Yeah, sure. That'd be great." Leigh sounded sincere. Maybe

Claire would have one ally.

Still, Leigh was one of *them* and Claire was not. Since Claire would be arriving two days ahead of them for the transfer student orientation, Leigh let her know immediately the claims already made in the room. It was an open floor plan, Leigh said. "We agreed last spring that Sam, Jane, and me were getting the spots by the windows. So..." Leigh paused.

Claire wondered if the girls came up with this scheme once they learned about Claire. If not, their original fourth must have been on the bottom of the friendship ladder. But for the sake of peace, Claire agreed to respect their wishes.

The other two calls were less successful. Jane seemed distant, as if Claire had interrupted a busy day, and Sam was downright rude. "Look, I gotta go," Sam had blurted out just two minutes into the conversation.

"Uh, OK, sure. See you in a few weeks," Claire said cheerily.

"Whatever," Sam said and hung up the phone.

Claire had taken a deep breath and sighed, staring determinedly ahead. This is going to be fun, she thought. But inside her chest, the fear was churning.

Now Claire was there, in the corner they said she could have. She was tired from orientation. But at least she had some idea of campus and her classes. She had her textbooks and had met a few people.

Claire brushed her teeth in the room's private bathroom. She tapped the brush in the air a few times, scattering the water on the porcelain bowl before returning the cap and tucking it in her shower caddy. She imagined her personal items would always stay personal from the roommates. She had the big closet after all—another delightful surprise Claire found in what she assumed would be a spartan place. It was a full walk-in, with room for all of her things, including her dresser. Maybe the fourth roommate had more clout than Claire assumed.

She placed her caddy by her dresser, but as she turned to leave the room, she caught her reflection in a long mirror resting against one wall. She stared skeptically as she rotated slightly and studied her profile. She tugged at her oversized tee—which was not so oversized thanks to meds and stress eating. She pulled down the inseam of her shorts, which rode up unladylike between her legs. She lingered for a few moments in front of the mirror as her disappointment grew, before she shook her head, bit her bottom lip to force away the tears, and went out to her bed.

That was Claire, always dwelling on the negative. Under the covers in the darkness she tried positive coaxing. "This program's going to be amazing!" she said aloud. "Claire, this school is ranked *fifth* in the country for your program. It's right this time." She was grateful no one could hear her. They might assume she was crazy. "Once you get comfortable, you'll make friends, you'll go out, maybe even find an exercise buddy—or at least force yourself to go. The meds will work, too. The weight will come off. Dr. Edlson said so." Her voice was no longer audible. The words were mostly in her head. By the time she tried to convince herself she would be back to her old size six or four by next summer, Claire was wiping away the hot tears that now trekked down the curve of her face, already soaking her pillow.

After a restless evening, she fled the room before ten that morning in hopes of avoiding the roommates a little longer. She knew meeting them was inevitable, but she craved a few more hours of her imagination pretending this year would be a pleasant success.

Leigh opened the door and smiled, seeing the beds by the windows were untouched. She glanced over at the fourth bed, made up neatly with a purple comforter, and she suddenly remembered why Alyssa had not fought for a window. Their new roommate, Claire, had positioned her space in the corner nook, with her bed and her desk shielding the massive walk-in closet. After the windows and private bath, the closet had been one of the room's major attractions.

"Damn it!" She pursed her lips. But it was too late now. Where was Claire going to put her bed if not there? She couldn't believe Alyssa flunked out. What an idiot! Leigh avoided thoughts of her own grade point average, which thankfully had been higher than both Jane's and Sam's. But that wasn't saying much.

The other two arrived soon after Leigh and quickly realized a glaring problem with their new roommate: Alyssa had promised to share the walk-in. Leigh unhappily but quietly hung her clothes in the small closet by her bed, but Jane and Sam swore aloud as they shoved their clothes into the third, exceptionally long, narrow closet.

This, they thought, is not going to last!

Claire purposefully returned late, after enjoying a quiet dinner alone. She had left campus to explore the city and found a charming local coffee shop just down the street. When she finally convinced herself to come home, she opened the dorm door nervously. The girls were out and the once orderly space was in complete disarray.

"Oh, God," she grumbled, surveying their mess. Their trail of debris covered a large section of the open room and spilled into Claire's tidy corner. She wondered what moron at Residential Life overlooked the compatibility boxes she had selected on the roommate personality form.

Neat? *Check.*

Organized? *Check.*

Requires quiet to study? *Check.*

Nervous wreck? *Double check.*

OK, so that last one was not on the questionnaire, but it should have been.

The pile of high heels tossed at the bedside, the shimmering tube-top slung over the desk chair, and the overflowing box of makeup on the dresser meant one of two things: her roommates were either partiers or professionals. The second scenario seemed highly unlikely, but she feared the first more. What was the year going to be like rooming with three girls so clearly unlike her?

Claire opened her mini fridge and got an inkling of an answer. Next to her half gallon of milk and orange juice, someone had stashed a six-pack of beer. She shook her head and closed the door. It could be worse. They could be smokers. She looked around and saw a lighter haphazardly thrown on a bedside table—so much for that.

Claire tried for a moment to focus on the future. She was excited to be starting class the next day. She was a nerd. So what? Nerds can still be cool. Unfortunately she was not cool. She was just Claire: quiet, except when loud; attractive, but a little overweight; smart, but self-loathing; creative, but paranoid; doting, but shy. She was far from average. But sadly average was what she longed to be.

Claire missed her friends from home, the ones who had known her for so long that they continued to love her despite her new self. She never found similar friends at her first school—another reason on her list of reasons to leave. Now she was completely lost again—one in a sea of many.

She wanted to lay down and wait for the hours to tick away until tomorrow. Tomorrow she would be busy; tonight she was lonely.

The dorm building was surprisingly empty. Her classmates were probably at some local hot spot where Claire would never go—certainly not without the right outfit to cover her newly expanded body. In high school, she thought she was fat. She wasn't. Now she was a size ten, still pretending to be a size eight. She would have spent more time worrying about that if she had not been preoccupied worrying about everything else. Anxiety was a nasty pastime. It devoured so many minutes of her life until those minutes fused into lost hours and days of worry. She kept hoping the right prescription drug would make it all better; she was still waiting.

Claire bent down and collected the few items belonging to her roommates that had crossed the invisible line of her personal space. She briefly considered laying down an actual line on the floor with tape or a black marker, but she figured that would make a bad first impression. No, she would just relocate the shirt, magazine, notebook, and shoe back to her roommates' territory. She didn't know where to put them, but considering the mess, she figured anywhere was fine.

She looked in the bathroom and found its built-in shelves littered with hair products, more makeup, mismatched towels, and other random beauty supplies. Various shampoos and conditioners cluttered the limited open space in the shower stall. "At least I have my closet."

Claire looked at the sink she had scrubbed the day before and saw it now had smears of toothpaste in various spots. "Jeez, they're disgusting," she said as she cringed while wiping away the mess with a tissue. She then vigorously washed her hands with soap and hot water before showering. When her roommates came back, she would be without makeup, styled hair, or real clothes.

"They're not going like me anyway," she said to her reflection, dabbing lotion on her softly scrubbed cheeks. "Why bother dressing for the occasion?"

Once she dried and dressed herself, she was snuggled under her covers with a textbook. She figured she either could read for pleasure or get a jump on her homework. *Fundamentals of Human Communication* sounded interesting enough. She was three chapters in when she heard a key slip into the door. It was just after eleven that night. She had wondered how late they would stay out. Perhaps they had a self-set curfew. She could only hope.

Her roommates were giggling and chatting about some guy when they entered the room a little too loudly. Only one faced Claire, who was sitting propped up in her bed. Claire nodded and waved.

"Hey," she said quietly.

None of them replied.

"I'm Claire."

"Yeah, hey," said Leigh. "We wondered where you were."

The somewhat friendly tone surprised Claire. She smiled at the other two, who also responded with pleasant waves. Wow, thought Claire, maybe I've misjudged them. The tallest of the girls headed through the room, tripping on the throw rug before she fell to the couch and slung her forearm across her brow.

OK, maybe they were not so much nice as a little drunk. But if they were going to be partiers, at least they were nice when they partied. Maybe Claire could handle this.

"I'm Leigh," said the one with fair skin and short black hair. "And that's Jane and Sam." The other two were blondes with deep golden tans. Jane looked up briefly from unfolding her bed sheet to smile faintly, and Sam raised her hand above the back of the couch.

Leigh noticed Claire with a textbook in her hand the night before school even began. She raised her eyebrow. "Is that for fun?" she asked sarcastically.

Claire smiled. "No, I just figured I'll be reading it sometime soon. I have the time now, so why not make my load lighter?"

Leigh instantly knew their roommate was an outsider.

"What's your major?" Leigh asked.

Claire closed the book, marking the page with her index finger. "Communications and advertising, but I'm also considering psychology."

Leigh nodded. "Which one would you do?"

"Well, I'd do both."

Leigh paused, mentally confirming her initial assessment of Claire. "*OK*," she said slowly nodding her head; her tone exaggerated and her eyes widely staring sideways in confusion, contemplating whether her new roommate was nuts or just pathetic.

"What about you?" Claire tried hard to sound upbeat.

"Uh, well, I'm early childhood ed, Jane is art history, and Sam is dance."

"Oh, cool!" As the words came out, Claire realized they sounded pitiful in their saccharine excitement. She wondered what her father would think of the roommates. "Jane," she called out, "are you an artist as well?"

Jane was in the bathroom; Claire could hear the water running. She heard Jane spit and then respond casually, "Pottery mostly, but I also paint."

"That's great." Claire couldn't seem to stop the conversation; she also couldn't go throw up in the bathroom. She contemplated dashing to the closet and hiding till their intoxicated bodies fell asleep. But Claire continued because she was incapable of silence. "I'd love to see your work sometime." Claire clutched the edges of the book cover, gripping tightly to push out her mounting tension.

Shut up! She told herself. They don't care. They don't like you! Why can't you stop talking?

The new pills should be working. It had been long enough. Why weren't they working?

Jane flipped off the bathroom light. She exited through the hall and gave Claire a weak, disinterested smile as she passed. Claire knew they all wished her gone. She also knew she would never see any of Jane's art. Frankly, she didn't care. Claire nearly asked Sam what type of dance she preferred, but she literally bit her tongue to stop herself. She could taste the blood in her mouth. It provided enough distraction to breathe and unclench her hands to open her book again. She read the same few lines over again at first until she could remember where her saturated mind needed to focus.

The book. Communication. Come on, Claire!

When she reached the second page of the chapter, her attention seemed to click back on. Her wandering thoughts tuned out the girls.

Sam was the first to fall asleep, cuddled in her freshly made bed while still wearing her party clothes, which stank of cigarette smoke. Claire could hear her snoring quietly. The other two followed soon after. It was nearly midnight by the time Claire finished the third chapter. She set a card between the pages to hold her place and reached up to turn off her lamp.

Her senses were wild. Her tongue ached. Her eyes were as wide awake as her brain. The room's silence was screaming, reminding her she wasn't home, and even worse, she wasn't wanted. She opened the drawer by her bed and carefully pulled out a pill bottle, downing the tranquilizer dry. It was the only thing that could stifle the activity whirling around her head. Soon the loud silence lessened to just silence, and quiet snoring across the room. Claire craved something for white noise besides her roommate's sinus problem, but once the drug kicked in she was calmer, enough to drift off in the room filled with strangers.

CHAPTER 2

Claire's alarm woke her a little after eight that morning. She lifted her hand and tapped the snooze button before rolling over and tugging the covers to her face. She felt groggy and nauseous, and wondered if her bout of nerves was from fear or excitement. Whatever the cause, she sensed again that she might throw up. Claire never really learned how to handle change or new experiences. She felt out on a limb in Boston, wondering if she should have just stayed down south where she at least had a few friends—or better yet, if she should have stayed home.

She groaned quietly under her covers, closed her eyes, and tried to calm herself by controlling her breathing. She worried that the alarm might sound again and wake her roommates. Now, unable to sleep, she pushed the quilt away and sat up. Claire turned off the alarm and went to the spacious closet that was all hers. She pushed the door shut and undressed, then slipped into her robe and grabbed the handle of her shower caddy.

Her roommates were still sleeping while she finished her shower and dressed. She ate a small yogurt from the fridge, quietly gathered her things, and left, gently pulling the dorm door shut behind her.

Claire was thankful now for the free time she'd had the day before. Confidently, she made her way across the sprawling campus to her first class. She was in her seat almost twenty minutes early. As others started arriving, she looked up occasionally from her textbook so as not to seem unapproachable, but she was a little too nervous to talk to anyone. When the professor entered, he set his briefcase onto the desk and hit the gold tabs to open its lid. He glanced at the wall clock and continued rifling through his papers. His eyes turned to the clock again and he walked toward the door, reached for the handle, and began to pull it closed. Just before the door clicked shut, a petite brunette appeared in the frame and slipped in.

"You're late, Ms. Mills."

"Sorry, Mr. Murk."

The girl waved quick "hellos" to a few students in the class. She surveyed the room for available seats and found that the only one was next to Claire. Ms. Mills pulled off her messenger bag and dropped it under the desk before settling into the uncomfortable wooden chair.

The professor returned to the front of the room and flicked on the projector for his PowerPoint™ presentation. Oh, how Claire loathed PowerPoint. Sure, it was a useful enough tool, but professors' dependency on it bordered on obsession. As he outlined the course, Murk touched on another of Claire's pet peeves: the group project. "Advertising agencies are about teamwork," he said. "By the end of my class, all of you will be experts at it." He paused. "I've found the most effective way to teach this is to assign your teams."

The class groaned.

"I know, I know," he said sarcastically. "But in the real world, you don't always like or know the people with whom you have to work, so you may as well get used to it now."

He handed a paper stack to a girl in the front. She took one and handed the rest back.

"These are the groups. I broke you down randomly from the roster and assigned each group an industry. As a team you will pick your product from that industry, and by the end of the semester you will develop an integrated campaign and present it to the class. I expect genius from each and every one of you. If you don't like public speaking, I suggest you learn to like it. In advertising, impressions matter. Everyone will be watching… especially me."

Claire found her name on the list along with two other female names and one guy: Alexis Jester, Erik Quinn, and Kimberly Mills.

Mills—wasn't that the name Murk called the girl who was late? Claire was nervous. If it was the same Kimberly, was she a slacker? Group projects were hard enough.

"OK, now that you know who's in your group, let's meet them. You know the drill. I want everyone to go around the room and say their name, where they're from, their major, and what aspect of advertising they want to pursue, if advertising is their major. Look around as we go and note your team members, if you don't already know them. We'll have time at the end for brief group meetings."

As the class exercise began, Claire learned that Alexis was the tiny girl in the back of the room, Erik was the cute guy with shaggy hair, and the girl who had been late was indeed Kimberly, who went by Kim. She seemed nice enough, Claire thought.

Kim turned to Claire and smiled. "I vote we stay here and make Alexis and Erik come to us."

"Sounds good to me," Claire said smiling back and nodding her head. She already felt more comfortable with Kim. Eventually, Claire would learn Kim always ran a few minutes late but she never failed to complete anything.

"Come here," Kim said as she wagged her hand impatiently at Erik and Alexis. There was little the group could do at this point, but they did manage to formally introduce themselves and exchange email addresses and phone numbers.

The team meeting ended abruptly and as they packed up their bags, Kim turned to Claire. "Do you have any other classes today?"

"Uh, yeah," Claire said. "I have a writing class at two o'clock. What about you?"

"My math elective is at one thirty."

Claire was not sure what to say, so she just nodded.

"It's almost noon. You wanna grab something to eat?"

Claire could see the chic young woman sizing her up, and Claire was intrigued by the prospect of getting to know Kim better.

"Sure, that sounds great." Claire tried not to appear too eager. She would never admit it out loud, but Kim intimidated her. Everything about Kim suggested she was popular. She was attractive, slim, and outgoing. Claire shifted her shirt a bit uncomfortably.

Kim slipped the strap of her messenger bag over her head and positioned it across her chest. "Let's go."

Claire pushed her notebook quickly into her bag, slung it on her shoulder, and followed.

"Later, Mr. Murk."

"Have a good day, Ms. Mills."

"Bye," Claire said in a hushed tone as she left.

The girls ended up at a small deli. Kim got a salad and Claire ordered a turkey sandwich. Claire wanted to be good about her food, but a few pieces of lettuce would not sustain her. As they ate, they fell into a comfortable conversation. Kim grew up near Boston, so she knew the area well. This was her second year at Adams University. She was majoring in business, and this was her second elective in the communications department. Claire learned Kim was the only child of an accountant and a dentist. Claire talked briefly about her life, her parents, and growing up in Connecticut.

"What time is it?" Kim asked suddenly.

"Just after one o'clock."

"Shit, then I have to run," Kim said. "I need to buy my stupid book before class. I tried to get it the other day and they didn't have it in yet. And from what I hear, this professor assigns shit on the first day." Kim shrugged disapprovingly. "Who does that?"

They left the table, tossed their trash near the door, and headed out into the sunlight. Kim stretched her back slightly, pushing her face up to the sky. "It's so nice out," she groaned. "What a waste spending the day in class."

Claire half smiled at her, still worried about Kim's dedication to her studies. They walked and talked for a few minutes more until they parted.

"Have fun," Kim said as she walked backwards toward the bookstore.

"Yeah, you too," Claire said. "Though I think I'll be enjoying mine more than you will yours."

"But it's *writing*." Kim wrinkled up her nose.

"Yes. I love writing."

"Good, then you're our team copywriter."

Claire beamed. "Perfect."

She waved goodbye and headed off in the direction of her second class. She was going to be early, but at least now she felt a little more welcomed in Boston.

CHAPTER 3

Two evenings later Claire returned from class to find her roommates tossing clothes on the floor as they tried to decide what to wear. She pushed the door aside, fighting against a boot that had become wedged under it. They looked up at her, momentarily acknowledging her existence.

Claire didn't bother to say "hello," but nodded recognition when her eyes met Leigh's. Leigh reciprocated. Claire dropped her bag by her desk and slipped off her shoes. She wanted a shower to wash away the long day. At least she only had one class tomorrow and it was not until noon. Tonight while her roommates were out, she would enjoy an evening alone with a movie, a bag of cookies, and a stiff glass of milk.

Claire saw Leigh talking quietly to Sam and Jane. She pretended not to notice, walked to her closet, and put on her robe. When she came out with her shower caddy, she was shocked to hear Leigh speak.

"You wanna come out with us tonight?"

Claire just stood there with the plastic container in her hand as her roommate's words slowly registered. She didn't *really* want to go with them, yet she was somewhat touched by their apparent offer to include her. Maybe they didn't really like her, but maybe they could *learn* to like her. If she said "no," what was she actually saying to them?

She finally shrugged and stammered out, "Uh, sure." She paused, still trying to decide if this was an awful decision. "Where are you going?"

"A party with some people we know."

Claire nodded her head. Wonderfully vague, she noted, but she had already agreed. Her mouth opened slightly as she continued nodding. She smiled. "I'll get ready."

Claire didn't have anything good to wear. She still needed to take a quick shower, but she wouldn't waste time washing her hair. She glanced in the mirror and it looked fine, so she stuffed the strands under a shower cap. Then she quickly scrubbed her face and cleaned her body with a coconut wash. Back in her robe, she walked down the small hallway and into her closet, where she clicked on her curling iron.

The girls were in tight outfits, lining their eyes and cheeks with makeup. Alone, Claire slipped into a fresh pair of panties and a black bra. She pulled from the hanger her favorite black pants, embroidered with black thread at the base. She had loved them in high school, often pairing them with any cute top short enough to graze her slim midriff.

As she hoisted the pants up over her hips, Claire whined inaudibly. Her panty line and rolls were obvious, the button would not close, and the zipper was completely hopeless. There was only one possible fix, but there was no way she would ever step outside in the open room with her roommates and lay down on her bed to attempt to coax it into place. If she tried, she would probably tear the seams anyway. Angrily, she slipped off the pants and pulled out another black pair; a simple design she had just recently bought, with a pressed line down the center of each leg. This pair barely fit. If the cloth hadn't been sort of stretchy, it definitely wouldn't have budged. She matched it with a navy blue shirt that clung a bit to her body. She pulled at the fabric, hoping to widen its shape enough to hide the bump peeking over the top of the pants. But she was not going to argue with a pair that buttoned. She didn't have any others to try.

She picked out a pair of black leather sandals with a wedge heel. These also were a favorite from high school. Her toes poked out more awkwardly than they used to, and Claire worried if even these would eventually be too tight. Fastening them into place around her ankle, Claire hit her hair with a burst of heat from her hair dryer and several spritzes of spray before smoothing the wild ends with her curling iron. Finally, she lined her face with a diluted evening look of makeup.

Her last touch was locking a silver chain choker necklace in the center of her throat. She paused sadly after she clipped it in place. Some women lived by the number on a scale, the size of a favorite outfit, or the dimensions of a ruler. For Claire, it was the simple bone at her collar that used to frame her figure so delicately. It was one of the first things she noticed when the weight amassed. Now it was sinking slowly into her skin.

She could hear the tapping of her roommates' heels as they wandered around the room. They were nearly ready. She could not avoid them any longer. Claire finally turned and lifted her eyes up, staring face-to-face with her image in the long mirror on her wall. She had done a good job—considering what she had to work with. She was always too hard on herself, but as she glanced up and down at her figure, she was brokenhearted.

This was not what Claire Kelly looked like. Claire Kelly was lean and fit. Claire Kelly didn't toss an outfit to the side because it wouldn't zip. Claire Kelly wore a size six comfortably, sometimes a four—hell, even a two—depending on the brand.

As the inner conversation flowed through her mind, she remembered the shaming dialogue it replaced from just a few years ago in high school, before the meds: God, you're so ugly. Your hips are horrible—you can't even wear pants that fit right. That ass! Why can't you get rid of that fat below your belly button? Two hours isn't enough on the treadmill. How are a thousand sit-ups not doing anything? A size six is pathetic. You're so fat. No wonder you're single.

It was never enough. She was never good enough.

She tabbed a tissue on the inside point of each eye and felt the painful tingle inside her nose that came on with emotions. She would give anything to be a six again. The pants she wore now were an eight and almost painfully tight. She pinched the stomach roll she could see beneath the fabric. If she stood up straight, it sort of disappeared. But it was still there. She tugged at the shirt again, continuing to stretch out the material. She stopped when it sounded as if a stitch snapped.

She clenched her fists trying to sharpened her attention. She stared in the mirror and saw what hurt her the most. It wasn't her flabby stomach, her fluffy arms, or her pudgy feet; it was her face. She couldn't hide it behind anything. She gently touched her cheek with the back of her hand so as not to smudge her makeup. As she tilted her head, she grabbed the wedge of skin forming under her chin and then closed her eyes tightly, trying to suppress the tears.

Her chest burned as she felt the wave of hatred ignite. She wouldn't have minded getting fat so much if it had spared her face. Everyone had always told Claire she was beautiful, and sometimes she believed them—but she couldn't see it anymore.

She finally took a deep breath and snatched another tissue from her dresser. She leaned into her small mirror and touched up a few spots of her makeup. Then she left the tissues on the dresser in her closet and headed out to the main room, this time hoping that if she couldn't see the fat girl in the mirror, she might stop crying.

She appeared to be assertive, even if she didn't feel it, and her roommates seemed surprised she could look that good. Claire sat on the end of her bed, fiddling with her fingernails until the girls announced they were officially ready to go.

She followed them out the door and downstairs to Leigh's car. Claire wondered if she should offer to drive, but then she realized she could always take away Leigh's keys or call a cab for herself, but she had no interest in washing away their vomit stains. She relented and climbed into the back seat of the small car.

Claire watched the road, trying to memorize the route. The party was not far from campus. It seemed to take more time to find a parking spot on the residential street; luckily, the tiny vehicle slipped into a small space just before the part of the curb marked for a fire hydrant. Leigh reminded them to lock the doors before they headed toward the house where speakers were blaring with loud music. Claire trailed behind, wondering once more if this evening would end in disaster. Men catcalled as the roommates passed, and the girls flirted back, oblivious to the inherent insult of the boys' behavior.

The party had spilled out onto the lawn, and Claire's impression of the evening worsened by the minute. She followed her roommates up onto the porch and into the messy living room. Claire could tell boys lived here. The furniture was ratty and the wall art borderline offensive, but she decided to excuse these college boys for their decorating faux pas.

Her roommates fell quickly into conversation with friends or acquaintances—or perfect strangers, for all Claire knew. They comfortably took drinks from the countertop and danced casually to the music.

"Here," said Leigh, handing a red cup to her. Claire thanked Leigh for it and pretended to drink and swallow. Either she was too cautious or too boring, but she didn't trust a drink she hadn't poured herself. Plus, she hated beer. As the girls spread out through the room, she looked for a bathroom. Claire expected it would be utterly disgusting, but it was only somewhat disgusting. She decided whatever came out of the faucet would be preferable to drinking beer, and she was desperate to have something in her hand.

She walked out of the bathroom and heard noises coming from the room next door. She tilted her head slightly, trying to see what was so amusing. Suddenly, a random boy who knew the secret called out to her. "You gotta see this!"

Claire looked behind her shoulder, not realizing he meant her. She walked cautiously into the room and peered between the crowd. She was suddenly very curious. A young man with shoulder-length hair sat on the bed. Beside him was a large aquarium. His hands dangled inside the glass box touching something. Finally, he pulled it out. Claire's eyebrows rose skeptically as she stared at the young man's baby alligator. It could not have been more than a foot long. He held it by its tail with one hand and beneath the throat with his other. Bystanders leaned down to feel its back; girls giggled as they barely touched the skin before pulling their hands away.

Claire tried to remain cool. She wondered if this genius had a plan for his pet once it grew up. She took another look at him and decided he did not. She turned away and nodded and smiled at another stranger, who was enthralled by the creature. Claire was slightly amused by the idiocy of her classmates and slightly concerned about the apparent limitations of the school's admissions team. Maybe they were the ones who processed the housing paperwork, too.

Claire ducked out and returned to the living room. She wondered how she could pass the time until her roommates would be ready to leave.

I should have known better than to come, she thought. Claire stared at the room's shadows, holding on to her plastic cup of tap water. She wished she had stayed at home, enjoying a glass of milk and a bag of cookies.

She longed for someone to talk to, but she didn't know anyone. She finally sat in an unoccupied chair at the far end of the room and watched the partiers come and go. This was only the second college party she had ever attended. The first was at a frat house her freshman year at her other school. She might have had only a sliver more fun there, and only because she went with a group of actual friends, which meant she had people to talk to. Here, she felt alone in the chaotic din, impatiently waiting to leave.

Then, through the crowd, she recognized a familiar face. It was Erik Quinn from her advertising class. She had barely spoken to him when the team met, but she was outside the classroom now. She stared at his charming face and her heart raced.

Please make him look at me. Please have him come talk to me, she begged the Universe.

And he saw her. Claire smiled and waved slightly, not wanting to appear as desperate for human contact as she felt. She never dreamed it would be Erik.

She wondered if she should get up and go talk to him. But boldness was out of character for her, so she waited as the long seconds passed. He smiled back and nodded his head, and then he paused to talk to someone. When the crowd shifted, Claire saw who had stopped Erik in his tracks. She was tall and thin, wearing a small red dress that hugged every curve of her tight body.

Claire waited for Erik to look up at her again, but he didn't. She waited for his conversation to end and for him to come over to her, but he didn't. All Claire got from him was a smile and a head nod. She sat there alone and dejected for the rest of the night, until Leigh found her. Leigh was definitely tipsy and friendlier than she had ever been. Claire tried to smile but she couldn't fake it anymore.

"Are we going soon?" Claire asked flatly.

"Yeah!" Leigh said loudly over the music. "We've been looking for you."

"I wasn't really that hard to find."

Claire stood up from the chair and left her now-empty water cup on the table in front of her. She followed Leigh, who led her to Jane and Sam. The three girls locked arms and stumbled out the door together. At first, Claire followed them, but when it became obvious that they had no sense of direction, she quickened her pace and guided them back to the car.

Leigh fumbled to pull her keys out of her purse. Claire let Leigh find them and then took them.

"Hey!" Leigh shouted. "Those are mine!"

"Get in the car," Claire said.

Leigh whined for a second more but gave up the fight easily and tumbled onto the backseat. Claire followed the same path she had watched Leigh drive earlier that evening. She was halfway home when she heard Sam mumble something.

"What?" Claire said glancing over her shoulder.

Without warning, Sam vomited on her own lap. She also hit her purse, her shoes, and Leigh's passenger seat.

Claire groaned. "And that's why I didn't bring my car," she muttered quickly under her breath. She hit the button for the windows as the putrid warm smell instantly filled the small vehicle.

She drove the few remaining miles back to the dorm parking lot and turned off the engine. She got out, opened the girls' door, and backed away. "Come on," she ordered impatiently.

The three moaned slightly and popped their heads up to look around.

"Where are we?" Leigh asked.

"Home."

"I don't live here," Jane whined.

"Yes, you do." Her tone was rougher.

Claire would have left them there, but she felt somewhat responsible for their well-being. She finally coaxed them out of the vehicle and left the windows cracked slightly to keep the smell from infesting the interior. But after she led them back to the room, she never went down again to wash out the seat fabric. Her responsibility ended at the door.

Sam lingered in the bathroom only long enough to splash water on her face to wash away most of the vomit. She didn't even brush her teeth. The other two went directly to bed. Claire

removed her own clothes in her closet and noticed the nasty
indent the tight waistline left along her stomach. She shook her
head but wasn't surprised by the sight. She waited patiently for
Sam to get into her bed and then took a shower to wash away
the evening. When she stepped out of the steamy bathroom, she
found her roommates sleeping soundly.

The next morning, Claire rested on her pillow watching
the clock turn to twenty past nine. She knew all three of her
roommates had classes today; Sam's was at ten o'clock. Sam's
alarm had been chiming for the past fifteen minutes. Finally,
Claire heard rustling by the window. Out of the corner of her eye
she saw Sam toss her covers aside. With ratty hair and a face half
streaked with makeup, the gruff girl stumbled off the mattress and
into the bathroom. She showered and dressed, groaning the whole
time. Then she scanned the room. Claire wondered at first what
she was looking for. Finally, she saw her roommate pick up her
purse, which had been in the line of vomit the night before. Sam
held it for a moment and then swore. She reached for the wallet
inside and tossed the stained bag to the ground when she left.

Claire rolled over and went back to sleep. She had set her
alarm for eleven o'clock to recoup some of the time lost the
previous night. When she woke again, she sat up in bed, stretched
her arms out wide, and glanced forward. She was not completely
surprised to see all three roommates, Sam included, snoring
quietly in their beds. She also noticed not one had an alarm clock
set.

After class and a late lunch, Claire returned to a furious Leigh.
The roommate knew Sam had been the one who threw up the
night before, but she blamed Claire.

"What'd you expect me to do?" Claire asked defensively. "Go

down with a bucket of water and scrub? It wasn't my vomit."

"I don't know…at least you could have cleaned it with *something*!"

"It wasn't my car. It wasn't my responsibility."

"I can't believe you'd say that!"

Claire stared at her dumbfounded. "I can't believe you're saying this. I don't even know why you invited me. I'm beginning to wonder if you were just looking for a designated driver."

"We felt sorry for you."

"Don't," Claire said flatly, as she walked toward the door with her purse. She grabbed the knob in her hand and paused in the frame, glancing back at Leigh before she left. "I don't clean up after you here. What makes you think I'd clean up after you anywhere else? If you need someone to blame, blame Sam. You can follow her trail of guilt all the way to the puke-stained shirt that's still laying on our bathroom floor a day later. And, if I'm not mistaken, that shirt belongs to Tara from across the hall." Claire turned and slammed the door as she left.

That ended any future relationship for the four. They reverted to simply being roommates, nothing more—maybe less. The girls never again offered to take Claire out partying with them; they barely spoke to her, in fact.

Their first impression of Claire had been right. She wasn't one of them.

Chapter 4

The weeks of that first semester ticked away, and Claire, despite her rather uncomfortable living arrangement, fell into a new routine. She avoided her dorm as much as possible, but otherwise tried to stay busy. She attended lectures, explored the city, and did her reading alone in coffee shops—her favorite was Solace. She gradually concluded that the degree would be worth it. That is, if her philosophy class didn't kill her first. But her core coursework redeemed even the worst moments of her first semester. Writing clearly was her favorite class; she had gotten her major right.

Professor Janet Ellis had nearly fifteen years of advertising writing experience and she had taken a liking to Claire. Seven years earlier, Janet successfully juggled a new infant and a career in Manhattan, until her husband was offered a promotion in Boston. She agreed it was the best move for her family, and took a four-year hiatus from her job to raise their daughter while her husband put in long hours as a surgeon. Once Alice started school, Janet took a freelance gig that restarted her career. Less than two years ago, she added the line of "professor" to her resume.

This was only her third semester as a lecturer, but she appreciated the challenge. She particularly enjoyed mentoring young people as they attempted to decide the rest of their lives before they were old enough to legally drink. Janet thought Claire was an exceptional student with a real writing talent. What impressed her the most was Claire's ability to take direction. Janet believed with a little more coaxing and the right connections, Claire had a real chance in the advertising business.

Janet stopped Claire at the door as she left class. "I really liked the tone you took with this project," she said. "You're obviously reading that optional book on influence."

"Oh, yeah. I did," Claire said nodding. She was glad Janet had noticed. "It's really interesting. Why isn't it assigned?"

"I'm not supposed to overload you guys," Janet shrugged. "But I hoped if I included it on the syllabus maybe one of you would read it."

Claire laughed. "I guess I'm the nerd."

Janet smiled, noting the self-deprecating tone to her student's voice.

"And people always tell me overachieving is a bad thing." Claire grinned.

Janet held up her index finger in caution. "It's only a bad thing if your motive is to escape living."

Claire chuckled again, this time softer, but said nothing. Did Janet sense that was her problem?

"Well, keep up the good work. I see great potential."

Claire took a deep breath. "Thanks."

"By the way, what are your career goals?" Janet asked. "I mean, besides being a copywriter. Do you plan to stay here? I have some connections here in Boston, more in New York, if you're looking for real-world experience."

"*Really?* That would be awesome."

"I might wait till you get closer to graduation; maybe next summer or your last year. But there definitely are firms to check out around here."

Claire nodded. "That would be great."

"You're a junior, right?"

"No. I'm a sophomore."

"Oh? Wow! I thought you were older. But I guess a year isn't that big of a leap." She shrugged again. "Anyway, keep doing what you're doing. Anything I can do to help, just let me know."

Claire was bursting with excitement at the thought of her very own mentor. She thanked Janet and left the classroom, glancing at her watch as she went. Murk's class had been canceled this morning, owing to a scheduling conflict. But he strongly suggested they use their time wisely with team meetings. Their presentations were due the following week. Somehow Claire had convinced her group to come together for one last practice session. She headed to the library to meet them.

They had developed a solid campaign. To date, Murk's comments had been generally supportive. He had asked them to focus on the tourism industry, and they created a plan to stimulate travel to Mexico. Murk was intrigued by their choice, given the hurdles of crime and competition. Kim had promised her group that Murk routinely demanded more out of his students, so the added challenge of their choice would matter to him—if they presented a strong campaign.

"He wasn't kidding when he said he'd be paying attention. And I want a good grade on this," she said.

Claire concurred, and the group agreed the topic was one on which they could all find common ground. Alexis was the only team member who had never been to Mexico, but she was also the least productive. Kim was a natural leader, Erik invoked a necessary sense of humor, and Claire supplied the infusion of creativity essential for success.

They wondered why Alexis was even in the class. She wasn't a business or communications major, and it showed. She didn't even try. They all planned to enact the only revenge possible when they filled out their individual group evaluations at the end of the semester.

Claire glanced sideways at the library steps and saw Erik heading in her direction. He walked with his messenger bag slung across his chest under his head of shaggy hair. She waved to him and waited until he caught up.

"Hey," he said. He reached for the door and stood aside to let her pass.

Claire's heart pounded, but she managed to disguise her

excitement with a cool smile. "Hey," she replied. Erik had never mentioned seeing her at that party early in the semester, and neither did she. But since then they had developed a casual friendship, at least in class.

With the meeting in mind, Claire had meticulously selected her outfit that morning. She always took extra care if she thought she might see Erik. She wore a basic black empire waist dress designed to conceal a body. She matched it with a long, pale-pink sweater—which gave a touch of color but added to the undefined figure outline. The total effect was a well put together Claire. She had impressed herself, yet Erik barely noticed.

No harm, she thought. She considered him not looking at her body to be the triumph of the day.

Claire followed Erik to the elevator and they rode to the third floor in silence. He selected a quiet table tucked away behind the stacks. Claire set her bag on the chair beside her and began digging through her purse for her cell phone; it had vibrated only moments before. When she found it among a sea of personal belongings, she noticed a missed text message. She read it, shook her head, and looked at Erik.

"Guess who's not coming?" she said with a whimsical tone to her voice.

"Again?"

"Again."

"What a bitch," Erik muttered quietly. He caught himself after realizing he probably shouldn't have said that. "Sorry," he said casually, shrugging a shoulder.

Claire raised her left eyebrow and gave him a half smile. "For what? Forgetting to put the word 'lazy' before it?"

Erik chuckled softly, realizing how much he actually liked Claire. Not *liked* liked—just that she was pretty cool. Leaning back in his chair, he covertly stared at her as she navigated the files on her computer. He let his eyes run down her body and realized he couldn't see anything through her outfit. Erik tilted his head slightly, half paying attention to whatever she was saying. If he was honest—just to himself—he had to admit that Claire was rather attractive. He had probably noticed it before, but never really realized it until now. Actually, he thought, she'd be pretty hot if she wasn't fat.

It then occurred to Erik that he had been nodding his head randomly at her but saying nothing. He must have looked like an idiot. "Where's Kim?" he asked finally, glancing at his watch. He hoped to convince her he had been listening.

Claire scrunched her face and stared at him as though he had said something stupid. "I just said, 'Kim's late as usual.'"

Erik shrugged it off. "Sorry. I was thinking about something else."

Claire nodded, wondering what was going through his mind. Then she wondered if she really wanted to know.

"What the hell's up with that girl?" Kim called loudly through the library, obviously referring to Alexis's text message. Kim didn't care if she disturbed people. Claire and Erik turned and saw Kim scowling as she held up her phone.

"Are you surprised?" Claire asked sarcastically, feigning shock.

"No," Kim lowered her voice and rolled her eyes as she tossed her bag haphazardly on the floor. The bag landed hard on the thin carpet. Claire hoped, for her friend's sake, that Kim didn't have her laptop with her. The two had grown close since the start of the school year, and Claire now found Kim's chronic lateness, loudness, and carelessness endearing.

Kim pulled a chair out from the end of the table and slumped down into the seat. She rested an elbow on the table, turned to Claire, and began motioning for her to get started. "Let's see the presentation," she directed. Kim knew what she wanted done, by whom, and when. She was definitely future management material. Claire pulled out copies of the script and slid them across the table to Kim and Erik, the team's spokesmen. Then Claire turned the screen toward her group mates and hit the start button. She watched as they ran through their assigned lines, ones they already had read many times before. They had taken her suggestions to heart. Erik toned down the sarcasm, which had overpowered his previous reading, while Kim slowed her pace and stayed more on script.

"I really like that font change," Kim said after delivering the final line of the presentation.

Claire disagreed; she thought the new typeface was a bit immature and difficult to read. But if they were willing to compromise on her suggestions, she could accept theirs.

"I really think we're ready," Claire said nodding with a look of confidence.

"Me, too," Kim said.

Erik shrugged. "Yeah, it works."

"All right then," Claire said. Erik looked bored and seemed eager to leave. "I guess we're good to go?"

Erik grabbed his bag and nearly leapt out of his chair. "Text if you need me," he said as he headed to the elevator.

"Bye," Claire called after him. She turned off her laptop while Kim fiddled with her phone, which had just received a message. She tapped away at the keyboard for a moment without looking up. "You interested in dinner?" Kim asked.

"Yeah, sure, I guess," Claire said slipping her laptop back into her bag. "Where?"

"My friend, Kyra, and her friend, Jill, want to go off campus for Italian."

Claire had met Kyra once before during another dinner out with Kim. Kyra and Kim were both business majors and floor mates in their dorm. Both were pretty, thin, and driven. Kyra was nice enough, but in the car on the way to the restaurant, Claire was more drawn to Jill.

"So, Marian is from this area," Jill said referring to her mother by her given name, "but I actually grew up in Colorado. Marian went out there for college, married Donald, had me, and never came back."

"So, what's your major?" Claire asked.

"Psychology. I'd like to do my graduate degree right after— probably in *educational* psychology." Jill said the word sarcastically.

"And you seem thrilled about it," Claire said with a smile.

Jill rolled her eyes. "That's what Marian and Donald want me to do. They're poster children for 'helicopter parents.'"

Claire smiled while Jill's face remained rather serious.

Jill shrugged. "I'd rather do clinical psych and work with adults."

Claire remembered how her own father had pushed education on her, too.

"What about you?" Jill asked. "What's your major?"

"Communications, focusing on advertising and copywriting."

"Oh, cool," Jill said. "Hey, Kyra, can you turn down the AC back here? I'm *literally* freezing."

Claire smiled again. Jill seemed to be easygoing and funny. She also looked a lot like Claire. She had long, dark hair, deep-set dimples when she smiled, and she was a little bit overweight. Claire related to her instantly.

The four squeezed into a booth in the North End for Italian. Claire loved pasta and tried not to apologize for it. She ordered a large plate of lasagna, which she was thoroughly enjoying, much to Jill's envy.

"God, that looks so good," Jill said studying Claire's plate. She looked down at her own dish. "I thought this would be good, but the potato in it…ick."

Claire laughed. "Yeah, I had that once in high school on a school trip to Italy. So you *know* it was the real deal. But I didn't like it, either." She smiled wide. "I did warn you."

"I know," Jill shrugged. "But I like trying new things."

"You want some mussels?" Kyra asked.

"Ick," Jill responded more forcefully while cringing.

"Oh, you most definitely were not born in New England," Kyra laughed.

"No, I was not. I was wonderfully landlocked."

Claire cut off a sizable piece of her lasagna. "Here," she said offering it to Jill on a bread plate.

Jill waved her off. "No. I am not stealing your dinner."

"Oh, come on. I can't eat all of this myself, and I don't like leftovers."

Jill eyed the dish again, considering the offer. She shrugged. "Oh, *OK*," as if she was doing Claire a favor. She took Claire's plate, and pushed aside her gnocchi to make room for the lasagna. She took a bite and closed her eyes. "Mmmm."

"Good?"

"Uh-huh." She offered the girls her plate of gnocchi. "Want some?" she asked smiling.

Claire wrinkled up her nose. "No, I'm good. I'll steal some of your dessert later."

Jill shook her head. "No, we should go to that gelato place down the street. It's fantastic!"

Kyra shrugged, "Sure," while Kim pushed around the rest of her salad, having only eaten a third of it.

At least she ate her greens, Claire thought.

At Jill's instance, they did go for gelato. Claire and Jill each ordered medium cups and enjoyed every bite. Kyra ordered low-fat mango gelato in the smallest available size, but barely ate it. Even Kim couldn't help her finish it. Claire smiled at the pair, wanting to point out mango is a fruit. It was guilt-free, sort of. But having only met Kyra once before, she wagered it was unwise to start teasing yet.

It was days later before Claire learned the real reason for the dinner; she had been interviewed, so to speak. Housing requests were due soon and the best campus apartments filled up fast. Kim, Kyra, and Jill planned on a two-bedroom place, but they needed a fourth.

"So…are you interested?" Kim asked eagerly, as the two left Murk's final class after acing their presentation.

"Of course!" Claire exclaimed. Next year's housing assignment had been the least of her worries. She was thinking about this year's roommates. She had mentioned only a few of her roommate woes to Kim.

"Good," Kim sighed. "Now, the only bitches you'll have to put up with will have wanted you from the start." She chuckled softly and elbowed Claire in the side.

Claire smiled back, relieved that at least some part of her life was coming together. But it changed nothing for her current situation. Christmas break would provide only a slight reprieve from her roommates before she had to return to another four months in purgatory.

CHAPTER 5

Claire hated her roommates, but she never imagined they would go so far—until she came back during her last week of winter exams to find Sam in her closet. The dorm room was unfit for privacy, except for the doors on the bathroom and her closet. The lines dividing the space were naturally theoretical, but nonetheless, the girls had observed unspoken boundaries all semester. Claire had no reason or interest to invade their area, and to her knowledge, she had no reason to believe they'd violated hers. So seeing Sam loitering among her things inside the walk-in was enough to enrage even the calmest person. "What the *hell* are you doing?" Claire demanded, her face tightened to a look of utter disgust.

What made it worse was the casualness Sam displayed. She turned at her own pace, as though she had been waiting around in the closet for Claire to arrive. She exited it slowly. "We've decided it's not fair for you to have this," Sam said.

"*What?*" Claire exclaimed, shaking. Her nostrils flared in frustration.

Sam stepped between Claire's desk and bed, meandering back to the center of the room. "Before Alyssa left, we were all going to get to use it," she said dismissively.

Claire shouldn't have been surprised, but she was. "So what? Alyssa's not here, and she didn't leave; she was *thrown out.*" Claire pointed a finger accusingly at her roommate. "And I was nice enough to take this spot and let you all keep the windows even though I got here first." She paused for a breath. "It's not my fault this little corner happens to have the big closet. You can't have *everything* in here. Get out of my space!"

Sam laughed. "*Your* space? This whole room is *our* space. *You're* in our space."

Claire stared at her for what seemed like minutes, but was barely five seconds. Then she turned—bag in hand—and stormed out of the door, slamming it behind her.

She had never been to an RA's room before, but Claire had received phone calls from several of them on duty during the semester—asking *her* to ask her roommates to tone down their gatherings. The RAs knew Claire was never part of the ruckus, but that didn't stop them from dialing her extension when the roommates took the door off a closet for beer pong. Claire would relay the warning, but the girls never minded her comments and the RAs never followed up. Now Claire was determined to make at least one of them earn the free housing privilege.

Anita was nice enough. She was a senior physics major. Claire only hoped she would be somewhat skilled in managing conflicts. Claire pounded loudly on her door, fidgeting and hyperventilating, and feeling as though she might pass out.

"Hey," said Anita casually once she opened her door. She could tell the student on the other side of her peephole was not pleased. She hated this part of the job. She was trying to study for her last final, not deal with whatever crisis an underclassman was having. So what if she was on duty? But when she opened the door and saw Claire, she vaguely placed the student with the room and wagered the girl's complaint might be justified. She was well aware of the three roommates.

"*I—want—another—room,*" Claire said angrily, dragging out each word to form one droning sentence. Her chest was tight.

"Come in," said Anita, motioning with her hand. Claire glanced casually around the room, noting nerdy science posters and mug on the desk; all making bad puns. Anita peered at Claire through black rim glasses, her hair pulled back in loose pigtail braids. She was wearing a faded green Pi shirt and black yoga pants.

Claire sat down hard in the chair by Anita's unkempt bed,

letting her bag hit the ground. She had momentarily forgotten about her laptop inside and groaned quietly once she realized how hard it hit.

"What happened?"

"I've been putting up with their bullshit all semester. I put my stuff where they told me to put it last summer, before I even moved in. But that corner has the big closet."

Anita scoffed under her breath.

"What?"

"Women and closets."

Claire wrinkled up her brow. "I would have gladly used any damn closet in that room. But that is my space. I don't want them there."

Anita held up her hands. "Look, I understand. I'm surprised you lasted this long."

Claire tried to control her tears, but she couldn't as they burned her face. Her depression had been generally suppressed by her meds, but sometimes things bubbled over and she couldn't stop the flood of emotions. She just hated crying in public.

To her credit, Anita handled the situation with grace, simply handing Claire a box of tissues.

"What am I supposed to do?" Claire asked whining through her sniffles. "I can't do another semester." She thought she might vomit.

Anita pulled out her desk chair and sat down, facing Claire.

"The problem is we have a bit of a housing crunch," she said flatly. "There just really aren't that many rooms available."

Claire groaned.

"Look," said Anita, "there are a few options. Unfortunately we don't have any singles left. But I know a couple of other girls who are also having problems." She paused to collect her thoughts.

Claire had slowed her tears and tilted her head. She wished Anita would just tell her what she was thinking.

Anita looked skeptically at Claire. "Are you religious?"

"No."

"Do you have a problem with religion?" Anita asked without judgment.

Claire shook her head. "No."

"Do you worship the occult?"

Claire laughed aloud. "What do you think?"

"You never know," Anita shrugged.

"That answer would also be a *no*."

"OK. We've got a situation on another floor, where a very Christian girl and her Goth roommate are having issues of their own."

Claire smiled softly and nodded her head.

"They're complaining," Anita said opening her right palm. "You're complaining," she added, opening her left palm. Then she crossed her arms. "Housing could switch you two."

"Who would my roommates get? The Christian or the Goth?"

"Which one would you want?"

"I dunno. The Christian, I guess?"

"Done. I'll talk to my boss in the morning. She'll be happy to have that situation handled."

"When can I move?"

"Well, we'll talk to the girls in the other room and make sure they are OK with it. Maybe you can get in there before break."

"What about my roommates?"

"You let me worry about them." Anita smiled and chuckled lightly. "I have a feeling they'll miss you when you're gone."

Claire smiled with her, but it only masked the worry wrinkles on her brow; the creases at her eyes were anything but jovial.

Anita smiled softer then, stood, and rubbed Claire on the shoulder.

"Feel better?" Anita asked.

Claire took a deep breath. "A little." She left the RA's room somewhat calmer than when she came. Her rattled mood didn't completely subside for a while, and she spent the next few hours at Solace trying to center her mind.

Though distracted, she read for pleasure, drank a coffee, and watched customers—anything to avoid going back to her dorm. When she finally returned, she was relieved to discover that Sam and Jane had already left for Christmas break. Leigh said very little to Claire that night. It was obvious she knew about the blow up. Leigh was gone the next morning after her final exam.

Claire received an email by ten o'clock to say the other roommates had agreed to the swap. She visited Housing that afternoon and completed the transfer paperwork. Claire had planned to return to Connecticut as soon as her final exam ended, but now she thought better of it. She would make the move immediately while anger fueled her. The change would be a complete surprise to her roommates.

Claire simultaneously switched places with Layla, who, despite her dark makeup and facial piercings, didn't seem so bad. But Claire knew the roommates were going to hate her. She wasn't a pushover.

Though hopeful, Claire remained cautious as she smoothed her purple comforter on her new bed. But Layla's sly smile and sarcastic parting words lingered in her mind: "Rebecca's *all* yours."

Claire endured the weeks of winter vacation fighting the unknown of it, trying to ward off her growing unease. How could Rebecca be worse?

She and Rebecca met the day before spring classes resumed and her first impression was positive. But during the next few weeks, Claire began to wonder again.

"How are things?" asked Emily gently. Her mother rushed to answer the phone whenever Claire called, but tiptoed when she answered.

Claire shrugged. "I don't know. Better, I guess. I went from roommates who were out drunk till 2 a.m. to a girl in bed by nine. It could be worse. But I feel weird, like I'm keeping her up when I'm reading at midnight. I hide under the covers now. She's made a few comments."

"Do you have to work so late?" asked Emily, her motherly tone naturally kicking in. "You really should be getting more sleep."

"Jeez, Mom. I don't need you criticizing me, too," Claire snapped. A moment later she felt bad about it. "Sorry," she said meekly.

"It's OK. I didn't mean to upset you." Emily could sense Claire's curtness wasn't actually her fault. Smaller things than this set her daughter off. "Are you still taking your pills?" She wondered if that might be the real cause.

Claire groaned. "Yeah, Ma. Though Rebecca thinks I'm crazy."

"Why would you say that?"

"She's made comments about that, too, stuff about will power and pharmaceuticals being a sign of personal weakness."

"She doesn't know what she's talking about. You know that has *nothing* to do with it."

Claire was quiet for a minute, because *weak* was exactly how she felt most days. "It doesn't matter," she said dismissively. "She doesn't say it anymore."

"Maybe she's smartened up."

"No," said Claire. "I hide them now. At least she stays out of my drawers. I guess that means this room is better than the other one. And it's only a few months more. But you know, some days I wonder why I didn't just pick the Goth."

CHAPTER 6

After surviving a semester with the roommates and a semester with Rebecca, Claire was grateful to start her junior year fresh with people who actually wanted her around. Despite knowing Kim longer, Claire found that she and Jill had more in common. From the beginning of the semester, they decided to pair off in one room, with Kim and Kyra across the hall.

Since their busy third-year schedules took them in opposite directions with varied hours, one night each week they came together, to catch up at a family dinner. Claire, unlike her roommates, enjoyed cooking, so she often shopped for the food and prepared the meals. Unfortunately, finding things that Kim and Kyra would eat could be a challenge. But both girls had tried Claire's chicken Caesar wraps before and loved them. In fact, Kim had requested them for tonight's dinner. Kim excused the calories by reminding Kyra that Claire made the dressing from scratch, so it was better for them. Jill also liked the dish, but she avoided the kitchen whenever Claire pulled out the anchovies. Just the sight of the small tin can of "oily minnows," as she called them, made her queasy. But Jill had no problem eating the dressing as long as she had not personally seen Claire prepare the ingredients.

Claire had checked the fridge that morning to determine what she might need to purchase later at the grocery store, where she stopped after her last class. She was scanning the store shelves, unsuccessfully, looking for Dijon mustard, and becoming increasingly frustrated.

"Finally!" she grumbled when she spotted it. She grabbed the jar and added it to her growing pile. Claire wished she had taken a basket or a cart, but she had only intended to pick up a few things. Now she worried she might drop everything. She had slipped three boxes of macaroni and cheese and brownie mix behind the package of flour wraps. If only she had two more hands, she thought. A basket would have been a far simpler solution.

As she stretched her arm out to fetch the last item on her list—the plastic container of baby greens—she felt items begin to slip from her grasp. She left the greens on the shelf and quickly hunched over to stop the mortifying experience of it all crashing to the floor.

"Whoa!" she heard a man exclaim. "You got that OK?"

Claire was still fumbling with her items when the man held a black plastic shopping basket under her pile. "Here, drop them in."

She was about to say, "no, thanks, I'm fine," when she glanced up and saw a familiar face.

She smiled awkwardly. "Erik, hi!" She said it more enthusiastically than she intended. She hadn't seen him in nearly a year. The two were well into the second semester of junior year.

He pushed his messy hair aside. "Hey."

Claire had wrangled most of the items when a can of chocolate frosting slipped free and hit the floor with a *bang*! She stared at it, hating it for falling, but grateful it hadn't broken. She hoped Erik would think she was baking a cake, not planning to eat the confection right out of its container with a spoon. By the end of the week, the frosting would be gone. Was that obvious to Erik?

Claire tried hard to watch what she ate, but when the stress of school and life got to her, she found it was easier to soothe her anxiety with something sweet. Unfortunately, this obsession was becoming something she couldn't hide behind closed doors. Every mirror made her more depressed.

She pulled down on the hem of her shirt the best she could with loaded arms, hoping she still remained invisible to him. Maybe he didn't notice.

"I think you need this," he said pushing the basket closer to her.

She hesitated. "I'm…fine."

"Take it anyway." He stooped slightly and swiped the mound from her arms into the basket. "There's a stack over there. I'll just go get another one."

"Thanks," she said, finally consenting.

Erik stood silently for a moment, staring at Claire. He turned as a woman waved her hand quickly. Claire assumed it was either a friend, or probably a girlfriend. But Erik didn't elaborate. "Well…I gotta go. See ya later," he said with a lame gesture that was probably intended to be a wave.

Claire wanted to say something else to him, but she was tongue-tied. She felt her heart pounding as it always did around Erik. She was supposed to be so skilled with words, but he always left her with nothing to say. She sort of waved back and watched him collect another basket and head down the chip aisle, the musk of his hair gel still lingering in the air. Dejected, Claire reached for her greens, shoved them in her basket, and went to check out.

When she arrived back at the apartment, Kim jumped up from the couch. "I'm starving. You start cooking. I'll put the stuff away." At the bottom of the bag, she pulled out the can of frosting. "What's this for?"

Claire looked up from her mixing bowl and smiled sheepishly. "Medicinal purposes."

Kim raised an eyebrow, shaking her head. "You gotta be careful."

"Of what?"

Kim held up her hand in defense. "Look, I'm just sayin'. You don't want to get—"

"What?" Claire pressed, her tone sharper. "*Fat?*"

"It's just—"

"What?" Claire repeated, with a smile that in no way expressed pleasure. It had a sadness to it.

"Look, you know I love you. And I know you're beautiful. But…"

"I know," Claire said quieter this time. She diverted her eyes to the bowl of food. She said nothing more because all she could think to say was: it's too late.

Kim knew Claire had bought several new outfits. She went from designer labels to mid-level brands because she was so upset about buying things in a size twelve. Claire had never in her life been a size twelve. She had never been a double digit. But what she really didn't want to admit to Kim was that she barely fit into those pants. She only bought them because she couldn't bring herself to buy a size fourteen.

"Are they gone?" Jill asked entering the kitchen with her eyes covered.

"What are you talking about?" Claire asked still bothered by Kim's comments.

"*The anchovies*," she said as though the question was a stupid one. "Are they gone? I think I can smell them." She wrinkled her nose in disgust.

"Anchovies?" Claire asked, now more playful.

Jill pulled her hand down from her eyes and smiled. "Exactly," she said, grateful for the ruse. She plucked a piece of cooked chicken from the plate and popped it in her mouth. "When are we eating?"

"Anytime. It's pretty much done."

Out of the corner of her eye, Claire watched Kim stash the frosting, the brownie mix, and the mac and cheese up on the shelf in the pantry. To her credit, Kim said nothing more about it, and Claire felt somewhat at ease by the end of the meal.

After she washed her plate, she left the girls to do the remaining dishes while she scurried to her room to grab her phone. Claire had heard it ding during dinner, indicating a new email, but vowed to stay disconnected until family time was over.

Once she picked the device up from her bedside table, she felt the nervous excitement bubble, realizing it was the message she had hoped for. Her former writing teacher, Janet Ellis, had connected her with a small, local advertising firm, which Janet said might be in need of a copywriter intern for the fall. It was probably premature to approach the company in April, when the internship would not begin until August, but Janet said it was not completely inappropriate to at least inquire.

In his reply email, Jack—the firm's creative VP—complimented Claire on her portfolio. Unfortunately, he said it was too soon to secure internships for the fall. In the email, he thanked Claire for her interest, but offered no indications or promises.

She slumped her cheek onto her fist, her elbow pressed hard on her desk. Claire had been really excited about this opportunity. Even though she had not been rejected, she felt discouraged.

Kyra was setting the clean dishes back into the cabinet when Claire tapped her hip, asking her to move aside. Claire was trying to pull open the silverware drawer. Kyra watched Claire reach to take out a spoon and then rummage through the pantry.

"What are you doing?" Kyra asked when she finally realized Claire was now tearing off the foil from a can of frosting, with no cake in sight.

Claire glanced at her once, then grabbed the can of frosting and shuffled out of the kitchen in the direction of her room.

Kyra looked at Jill, who looked back at her and shrugged.

"I heard her phone make a noise during dinner," Jill said. "Like it does when she gets a new email. Maybe it was bad news." Jill dropped the towel on the counter and left in pursuit of Claire. She found her friend curled up in bed with the can of frosting, watching a sitcom on her laptop.

Jill leaned against the door and sighed. Claire's depression had been fairly tame lately, but then again, things had been generally going her way. It was stress that broke her good moods.

"Everything all right?" she asked.

Claire barely looked up from the screen. She could have watched the show with her eyes shut and still been able to visualize nearly everything in every episode. She was not afraid of breaking eye contact with the screen and missing something. She was afraid of making eye contact with her friend and crying. She shrugged and consumed another heaping spoonful of frosting. She had made the mistake of buying the whipped kind, so it did little to suppress her sadness, but she ate it anyway because she couldn't stop.

"I don't think they're working." Claire's voice quivered through the phone the next day.

Her mother was completely caught off guard by the call, having almost missed the phone ringing as she dragged groceries into the house. Claire was supposed to be in class. Hearing her daughter's tone and imagining her face forced Emily into a chair at the table, her free hand massaging her temple while she hopelessly listened to her little girl weeping through the phone. Ice cream softened on the counter and her back car gate was still open with the last three bags. "What's not…the new pills?" Emily asked.

Claire nodded then wiped snot on the sleeve of her shirt. Nothing mattered anymore. "I'm really happy sometimes, then something will happen and I'm a mess." She was quiet, then whispered, "I've missed some classes lately. I just can't go." The sentence was laced with guilt. "Some nights I'm up really late; I just can't sleep. It's like my mind is on fast forward through all of the things I'm supposed to think about for the next week. It just goes on and on and on. I can't stop it. I'm taking more of those tranquilizers than I probably should be."

"Well, what does the bottle say? Are you taking more than that?"

Claire was silent. "A couple of times."

"All right, well, you know that's not good for you."

She said nothing.

"Claire?"

She was curled on her side, facing the wall. She continued whispering even though she wanted to scream. "I still think about it. A lot lately." She didn't even cry at the thought—she was nauseous and a headache was mounting.

Emily didn't need to hear the word "suicide" to know Claire's meaning. She used it too many times in high school. Too many times Emily debated calling a hospital, bringing her daughter in, and leaving her there—until she was better. But Emily and John feared what that label would do to Claire's future. Instead, they let their daughter gamble with her life and suggested more covert options—the family doctor, a personal therapist, medications— it didn't matter the financial cost. They were fortunate in that sense. Emily wiped her own tears. "Are you writing it down still? Tracking what happens? Looking for patterns? Remember, the doctor said that could help."

"Yeah, a lot of poetry, but I'm not sure how that helps. It gets the thoughts out sometimes, so I guess that's good."

"Are you eating?"

Claire snorted softly as she laughed—harsh and self-deprecating. "I have almost nothing that fits. So, yeah."

"Things that aren't nutritious?"

"Is brownie mix nutritious?"

"Be serious, please," Emily pleaded.

Claire closed her eyes, imagining her own face as its former self. "Do you even remember?"

"What, sweetie?"

"How I used to look? You know…when I thought I was fat. I wish I was her again."

Emily couldn't say anything. She knew nothing she said would make her daughter better. She took in a breath and went to respond.

"I think the girls are home," Claire interjected quickly.

Emily felt like the worst mother in the world, relieved by being saved from speaking. "Uh, OK, I can let you go. Go do something for yourself or something with Jill. Just get out for a little while. Maybe that will help."

Claire's gut was in knots, knowing how badly she hurt her mother each time she called like this. But she was desperate to say these things to someone—anyone—to prevent being the only one who knew them. Unfortunately that burden fell to Emily, but she wore it well.

Claire sniffled and vowed to her mom that she was as well as could be expected, and yes, she would try to do something fun with the girls. Secretly, Claire wanted to dig a hole outside and bury herself in it. She told her mother goodbye and parted with an "I love you, too," before hanging up. Her headache was a growing beast inside her forehead, pounding its fists. She pushed her fingers against it in a pathetic hope of calming it. Then she lifted herself out of bed and snatched a painkiller off her desk. She debated taking a little yellow anxiety pill, too, but she already had three in her.

She opened the closet to grab a zippered sweatshirt, but as she went to close the door, dangerously she allowed her gaze to linger on the long mirror hanging inside.

Who was that girl? She was fat. Fat everywhere. Her fingers looked ugly and bloated, so much so that the sapphire ring from her sixteenth birthday no longer fit. Her thighs appeared to be fused together. In the heat, they rubbed and it hurt. Her shirtsleeves could no longer fit her arms. Her torso was massive. The silhouette of her figure no longer indented between her breasts and her belly button. And her cup size was a DD. But sadly, the most telling changes had occurred in her face. Her checks rose out beyond her eye sockets, creasing terribly whenever she smiled. Her neck—once so thin she could barely pinch one bit of skin between two fingertips—had tripled in size. She could now easily grab a fistful of flab. Even her nose looked distorted.

The only remnants of Claire that remained were her eyes and her smile. But those happy eyes now hid in shame and the smile rarely came. It was an odd, surreal experience; she could see the weight reflected but she almost didn't believe it.

After a moment, Claire slammed the closet shut, locking the fat woman inside with the size fourteen clothes that didn't fit.

Jill opened the bedroom door as Claire was pulling back the covers on her bed. When Claire looked up, her face was blotchy red and her eyes were puffy.

"Oh, Claire!" Jill exclaimed. "What's wrong?" She ran to Claire, who sat back on the mattress and her face fell into her hands. She sobbed—mortified to be seen crying, even in front of someone she loved.

"Sweetie, please…" Jill knelt by her friend, gently stroking her hair. "Talk to me."

Claire wailed softly, but turned her face up as Jill touched her chin. Claire looked everywhere except her friend's eyes.

Jill bit her lip and scrunched down somewhat, following Claire's wandering gaze until she drew her attention. As their eyes met, Claire's crying flowed hard again and Jill sat helplessly, fighting back her own tears.

"Claire, I think you need to talk to someone. You know I'm always here for you—but…maybe it's that bad."

Claire wiped her face with the back of her hand, rolling her eyes in the process. "I've *had* therapists. Shitty ones. The one who tried to blame my parents. The one who tried to blame me. The one who let me tell my whole damn story—suicidal thoughts and all—just to tell me she didn't have appointments that would match my schedule."

"I know. But finding a therapist you don't hate isn't easy. It should be but it's not. Have you tried the school counseling center?"

Claire shook her head. "I've only done private practice."

Jill shrugged. "Would it be worth trying?"

Claire shrugged dismissively, using her sweatshirt to clean the snot from her upper lip. She sniffled. "I don't know. Maybe."

"Would you promise me you'll try it…at least once?"

Claire looked at Jill and saw fear. It was the same fear she saw in her mother's eyes.

Claire brought pain wherever she went, it seemed. She closed her eyes to avoid seeing the fear, and eventually nodded. "Yeah," she said.

The following morning, Claire called the center. She specifically requested an appointment with Heather Tofitt, MSW. Claire had met Heather her first year during the transfer student orientation. She had been inviting and kind, and encouraged Claire to stop by anytime she needed to talk.

Claire wasn't surprised that Heather didn't seem to remember her. Heather must have seen hundreds of students each year. When Claire mentioned their first meeting, Heather did a poor job of pretending to place the conversation.

"Oh…yes, of course," said Heather. "How have you been?"

The compensation almost made Claire smirk. "OK, I guess."

"Great. And your transition here has gone smoothly?" Heather asked, pen and pad in hand.

"Well enough. I had roommate issues the first year, but I live with really great friends now."

"Super. And classes are going well?"

"Yeah. That's never been a problem."

"Wonderful. So…how can I help?"

Claire took a deep breath. Filling in a new therapist was always a chore. What to bring up? What to leave out? She usually started with her diagnosis.

"And that is?" asked Heather.

"Depression. Anxiety. The doctor suspects possible OCD as well."

Heather wrote. "And you're receiving treatment?"

Claire discussed her medication history and weight gain.

Heather seemed far more clinical and distant now versus the day she conversed with Claire in the auditorium.

Then Claire used the "S" word. She always said it with underlying nervousness that it might trigger a reaction she couldn't reverse. She always said *suicidal* with as much stability as she could muster. So far, it had never once ended in a hospital order.

Heather too, just wrote and probed with a few simple questions.

Claire stared back at her therapist wondering: Did Heather not believe her? Did they all think Claire was joking or exaggerating or doing it for attention? What happened when it was no longer just a word or a thought? *What then?*

Claire went to speak again but was suddenly interrupted. In her three years of off-again-on-again therapy sessions, never *once* had a phone rang.

But Heather's did, and to Claire's amazement, Heather held up her finger. "Just a moment," she said, and answered it.

Claire's pondering about the day of her eventual suicide halted as she stared stunned at Heather chatting.

"Yeah, OK. Sure," said Heather casually. When she set the phone back down, she turned. "Just a second," she said to her computer screen—though the comment was meant for Claire.

Claire was speechless. She was appalled to realize Heather was writing an email. She wanted to scream at Heather or get up and walk out, but she was too polite or shy to do either. So Claire just sat there silently as Heather typed.

Her depressive thoughts didn't even matter to her counselor.

Claire felt stupid and was still baffled why nobody cared. Did she play *normal* that well?

When Heather turned back to Claire, Heather seemed aloof. "Sorry, Claire, you were saying…"

Claire could remember nothing of what she had been saying or what she intended to say. She remembered nothing else from the appointment after the call but that she consented to a follow up. It was one she never meant to keep. Heather had trampled on Claire's trust and left her feeling violated.

"How'd it go," asked Jill gently when Claire arrived home.

Claire shrugged. "I don't know." She assumed Jill would claim the blame if Claire was honest.

Two days later, Claire canceled the appointment. She never saw Heather again. But what made Heather the worst therapist Claire had ever known was not that she answered a phone call or sent an email during the session—it was that she never bothered to call or follow up. She never took the time to make sure Claire was safe. And worst of all, she nourished the thought in Claire's mind that she was indeed worthless.

Chapter 7

At the start of her final fall term, Claire moved back in with the girls. She shoved a makeshift wardrobe into her closet, low-end pants and shirts that she never figured she would buy. She loved her brands, but refused to waste money looking good when she didn't feel good. Now, she bought clothes to fit a body she hated, versus sculpting her body to fit the clothes she loved.

The closet included some professional outfits—enough to mix and match two days a week for her internship. After a follow-up email at the beginning of the semester, Jack agreed to meet her. When she arrived at McGill, Inc., she was suddenly not so sure she wanted the experience anymore. But she was too polite to refuse the offer, especially after making such a big deal about working for the firm. She accepted the unpaid position, hoping it might somehow lead to something. There she went again, expecting everything from something small. She soon began to wonder if going small would ever get her anywhere.

Unfortunately the creative firm was not as grand as she hoped. Claire always imagined writing major campaigns for national brands in a bustling office twenty stories in the sky, where her view could help inspire her creativity. Instead, she went to a two-story building that resembled a house, where desks lined the outside of a single open room. Her view was a dingy brick wall. It was stale and exceedingly gloomy. Claire sat quietly in meetings and did a small amount of work on projects that she considered dull. Although the team actually used a few lines of copy she developed for two of its clients, Claire went into the job twice weekly believing it provided little insight to advance her knowledge of the field. But she stuck it out because she couldn't see any reason to leave as she had nowhere else to go.

⚜ ⚜ ⚜

Claire left her classroom building one unseasonably warm October afternoon. She pulled her bag forward and fished out her phone. She had set it on silent—not vibrate—as she always did for class. Now she wondered what had happened in the past fifty minutes during her math elective. She dragged her finger across the screen and saw the notice for a new email. She touched the button and was not too surprised to see it was from Janet. Her former professor periodically checked up on her nearly two years later. They had even gone for coffee a few times.

Regrettably, Claire had been honest when Janet asked her how the internship was going. Claire tried to come up with a creative way to shield her feelings about the experience, but the minute she sent the email, and then reread the message, Claire wished she had not pushed send. It had been nearly ten days and Janet was just now replying. Claire flinched slightly as she opened the message and squinted through nervous eyes as she read.

Sorry about the job. I've only done a little work for them. I stopped by the other day and was pretty surprised to see you weren't far off in your assessment…no matter how much you tried to sugarcoat it for my benefit. :) But Jack had nothing but good things to say about you! Let's have coffee this week. Maybe Wednesday around 2? I want to talk to you.

- Janet

Claire was nervous, wondering what Janet wanted to say. Was she going to try to dissuade Claire from pursuing a copywriting career? Janet had agreed with her about the firm's shortcomings, so maybe Claire had nothing to worry about. But she worried anyway. She always worried.

Two days later, with just eleven days left at her internship—not that she was counting—Claire pushed open the door to Solace. She ordered a big, frothy iced drink with a mound of whipped cream on top. She did not question the sugar or the heavy cream or the calorie count of this little glass of heaven. The semester's end was only a few weeks away and Claire had deadlines to meet.

She shoved the straw down into the cup and sucked up three massive gulps. As she swallowed, she felt her stress begin to dissipate. She found one of her favorite big chairs empty and nestled into it, breaking off a piece of the chocolate chip cookie she also bought. Claire had forgotten to have lunch today and her stomach was grumbling. She quickly popped big pieces of cookie into her mouth, trying to finish the whole thing before Janet arrived.

Suddenly, she glimpsed Janet opening the door. Her former professor scanned the room and saw Claire waving from a pair of chairs in the far corner. She smiled, waved quickly, and then pointed toward the counter, following with a gesture as though she were drinking from an imaginary glass. Claire smiled and nodded, indicating she had gotten the message, secretly thankful she had a few more minutes to cram the rest of the cookie into her mouth. When she was done, she wiped her fingers on a napkin and left her notebook on the chair while she went to throw out the evidence.

With a black coffee in hand, Janet sat down in the seat Claire had been saving with her coat.

"Hi," Claire said smiling.

"Hi." Janet's soft, hesitant tone implied a lingering sense of guilt. Claire's heart raced as she wondered what bad news Janet was about to tell her.

"How's school?" Janet asked.

"Fine."

"That's good."

Janet took a slow sip of coffee and swallowed, while Claire sat impatiently on the edge of her seat. Janet placed the cup in her lap, her two hands wrapped around it. She looked up and her eyes met Claire's.

"I'm really sorry this internship didn't turn out to be something greater."

"Oh—" Claire tried to stop Janet from apologizing, but Janet persisted.

"No, I feel bad. I'm the one who recommended McGill. They seemed pretty good on the phone and through digital channels. I've only ever met Jack out on lunch meetings."

Claire shrugged. "It's not that bad, it's just not exactly what I was looking for. I guess I want something bigger."

Janet nodded her head. "Right, I understand. And I called one of my old colleagues in New York the other day to sniff around for some opportunities there."

"*Really?*" Claire asked excitedly. She sat up straighter, inching forward. Janet smiled, feeling as though she was making up for her previous disappointment. "Dan is a finance guy at a firm in Midtown, but I asked if he had any ideas. Have you ever heard of Marshall's Creatives?

Claire thought for a minute. "Maybe." She hadn't.

"They're a pretty big, well-known agency in Manhattan, with a growing client list. They started in Seattle—that's where Chip Marshall is from. He decided to take his small firm big league about eight years ago; moved to New York, and has been winning awards and wooing clients ever since."

Claire jotted the name down on a pad. "I'll definitely go look them up." She was slightly apprehensive about the thought of moving to New York City. She felt her nerves jitter and her stomach churn. But damn it, if she wanted a big-time career she could not be afraid of a big-time market.

"Dan told me his daughter wants to be an art director someday, so he's been looking around for opportunities for her. About four years ago Marshall started an associates program. It's sort of like a full-time paid internship program, where they bring in bright young talent. They have different divisions where you can work,

and after a year they hire the best candidates. But even if you don't
get a job with them, it's great experience that can lead to other
prospects outside of Marshall's place."

Claire was slowly beginning to forget about her fear of New
York as she imagined herself twenty stories up, looking out on
the city as she crafted an award-winning campaign late into the
evening. She felt some of her cynicism and doubt melt away as she
suddenly realized she was perfect for this.

Janet watched the excitement spread across Claire's face. She
smiled, but held up her hand in caution. "It's competitive. I want
you to remember that."

Claire nodded.

Then Janet smiled. "But I think you have a real shot. The
portfolio you put together for McGill was fantastic. You should
add in any work that you're proud of from there. You may
not like the internship but it's still agency experience. In your
application, be sure to highlight your program at AU, including
specific coursework that relates to the industry. That matters. And
definitely talk about the student awards you've won."

"Absolutely."

Janet was a bit hesitant as she stared at Claire.

"What?" asked Claire nervously.

"The application is due next week."

Claire gasped quietly. "*Next week?*"

"I'm afraid so." She paused. "But I know you can do it. I already
looked at the application online. It's not that involved. It's a bit
of personal background. You know, name, address, phone number,
that kind of stuff, and then a resume and short cover letter
outlining why you would be a good candidate for the program."

Claire looked at her doubtfully.

"You're a writer. I think you can write that."

Claire smiled.

"Plus, your portfolio is already done, and it's digital. That's the
hard part."

Claire nodded her head. Janet was slowly putting it into perspective for her. She was a writer. She could do this.

"Besides, a week is a long time. And if I know you," said Janet, "even though this is the end of the semester, I'll bet you have everything already done."

Claire smiled. "Mostly done."

Janet nodded. "A little cover letter. That's all."

Claire took in a breath. "You're right." She smiled. "Thank you so much for this."

"No worries. I just hope it turns out to be everything you wish it could be."

The statement almost sounded like a warning. And Claire realized only a few months ago she had built McGill up in her mind, which had proven to be a disappointment. But this prospect seemed different somehow. Maybe it was Janet's description of a firm with ambition, maybe it was the words "award-winning," maybe it was New York, or maybe it was just Claire's imagination going wild. But whatever the cause, she began to let her expectations paint a picture of perfection for a golden road of opportunity toward a shimmering future.

Janet took another sip of her coffee, looking over the lid at Claire, whose mind was obviously wandering.

"I'd love to stay and chat but I have to go pick up my daughter from school. And I imagine you're already crafting a cover letter as we speak." She smiled.

Claire laughed softly. "Pretty much."

Janet nodded. "Let me know if you want me to read it," she said.

"Definitely," Claire replied confidently.

The two walked out side-by-side and parted at the door. "Thanks again," Claire said.

"Anytime."

Claire scurried home to the apartment, slid the key quickly

into the lock, and slammed the door shut behind her. Jill was sprawled out on the couch watching TV. She jumped at the commotion and watched Claire zip by her to the bedroom.

"Are you OK?" she called out.

"Fine."

Claire didn't seem hurt or sad or scared or upset. In fact, she sounded sort of excited. But Jill knew her roommate had been nervous about her coffee date today, so she began to wonder what the hurry or the worry was all about. Jill found Claire sitting cross-legged on her bed with her laptop balanced on her knees.

"Is something wrong?"

Claire looked up from the screen, barely noticing her friend was in the room. "What? Yeah, fine. Why?"

"You just seem…" Jill stared at her "…I dunno."

Claire laughed. "That's eloquent."

"You know what I mean. Are you OK?"

"I'm fine," she said, playfully annoyed.

Jill pulled out a chair at her desk. "Then what's going on here?" she asked. "What happened with your professor?"

Claire quickly explained.

Jill's brow knitted skeptically. "This isn't going to turn into another McGill, is it?"

"No. This is a big firm—in *Manhattan*," Claire said as though its location instantly guaranteed it would be incredible.

"Look, I'm just sayin'. Boston isn't a dot on the map and you ended up at a dead-end."

"Yeah, I know. But I just feel this could be it," Claire said, staring up at her with eyes that were either hopeful or pleading. Jill couldn't tell which. "It's practically a doorway to success."

Jill shrugged. "Well, then, that's awesome," she said. "I'll leave you to it." Who was she to dash a dream?

❖ ❖ ❖

Janet had been right. Once she started writing the cover letter, it practically wrote itself. Claire had a million reasons why she wanted to be a copywriter. The trick was picking the best ones and highlighting them. After all, her cover letter was the first writing sample the firm would have from her. She wrote and rewrote for nearly an hour. When she finished, she walked away from her computer for dinner. She needed to let it rest.

Claire's second review of the letter renewed her confidence in herself and her odds of being selected.

"Hey, Mom," Claire said when she called after dinner.

"Hi, sweetie. How was the meeting with your professor?"

"Actually, kind of amazing." She explained what the fuss was about. "I emailed you the letter. Would you read it?"

"Of course. I'll do it right now," Emily chimed back.

A few minutes later, Claire's phone rang. It was her mother calling back.

"I love it. I think it sounds perfect."

"So, it's good?" Claire asked.

"It's great!"

Claire smiled at her mother's overcompensation.

"And your portfolio is done?"

"Pretty much. I just have to link up the samples from McGill. I wrote a little caption to go with that stuff. I'll send you it all when it's done."

"I have a good feeling about this," Emily said excitedly. Her mother could not see her daughter's smile through the phone, but she sensed Claire's elation.

"Me too," Claire said. She was almost giddy at the thought. She still had no idea how much this was all going to cost, where she was going to live, if she was going to have a roommate, and so many other concerns. But she soared on her fantasy, devising a perfect scenario in her mind.

Emily was silent for a moment. She had many of the same questions as Claire, but she figured now was not the time to bring them up. Tonight she just had one. "Are you sure you can handle New York?" she asked. "I know you are doing well in Boston. Better than well—great! But…"

"I know," Claire groaned, annoyed her mother would shatter the daydream. "I guess I'm just going to have to be OK with it."

The response was weak, but it made Claire feel better to have some type of answer, and it made Emily feel better to get Claire thinking about the important details. They chatted for a little while longer, until Claire said she should probably get back to work on the application.

Claire finalized her portfolio, reread her letter, and double-checked all of the requirements before sending it off to Janet for review. She was not going to waste the offer. Then she closed all of the pages on the laptop and shut the computer itself. She could hear the television in the living room and realized she needed a break from thinking.

The next afternoon, with Janet's blessing and everyone else's support, Claire filled out the online application, pasted in the link to her portfolio, and uploaded her letter and resume. She read and read and reread the review page. Then she hit submit and it was gone.

She sat on her bed staring at the pop-up page that said the application was successfully submitted. She heard her phone ding, reminding her an automated email response had been generated. The funny thing was, now that it was sent, she was more nervous than before. If she was rejected, she was a failure. If she was selected, she had to move to New York. Both outcomes scared the hell out of her.

CHAPTER 8

Beep! Claire laid on her horn in protest.

She had finished her classes for the week and had stopped off at the store for a few things before heading home. But when the middle-aged man in his beater car pulled out quickly in front of her, Claire fumed. People had cut her off before; sure it made her mad, but it didn't stick with her—usually. Yet, the past few weeks had been nerve wracking as she waited to hear about the program. She was more impatient and anxious than before she had even an inkling of a prospect. Now, she felt she had more to lose. Such was the trouble with trying.

But seeing that car now, traveling straight in front of her—just another jerk taking a short cut in life—was almost more than she could bear. Claire would have used the word *annoyed* if only it would describe her feelings. But it didn't. It couldn't. She was hovering in a growing state of anger and frustration that she almost couldn't control.

As he tapped his brakes, she breathed heavier and became more agitated. She could see him look up at his mirror. Why did he bother watching the road when he did not respect the rules of the road? Her fingers tapped rapidly on her steering wheel. Her heart beat faster. She started shaking and gripped the wheel till her knuckles ached. She took a deep breath. "AAAHHH!" She screamed the piercing bellow inside her car.

It did little to release her tension.

Her severe reaction to this stranger's behavior scared her. Her anger and explosiveness had intensified. Less than an hour earlier she had been laughing in class, joking with her friends. She smiled at people she did not know as she walked to her car. But in an instant it was gone. As if she didn't have enough to concern her—

now she was consumed by her emotions. She didn't know which was worse: that she couldn't really explain why it was happening or that she had no idea when it would stop.

She reached over to the passenger seat and felt through her purse without looking at it; such a state of fixated panic demanded her last drop of concentration. Her attention was locked on the car in front of her, yet she felt wildly distracted. She finally gave up her search after finding nothing; swearing once, she pounding her fist on the console in protest. She would take a yellow pill once she got home.

She wondered if relief would come naturally when she turned down a different street from him, but it didn't. She could almost see the memory of his bumper through her window. She could almost see his face peering backward through the mirror.

The sad thing for Claire was that he probably had no idea what he had done. Or worse, he didn't care. Either way, he could never imagine the eruption flowing through her veins now, which left her shaking and gasping slowly for air. This kind of thing did not happen all the time, but it happened enough—increasingly, usually spurred on by things that didn't really matter in the long run. But for Claire, in each instance she felt trapped and helpless in a haze of frustration.

She turned into her driveway and took the closest spot she could find that allowed her to stop her car immediately and find a pill. Before she even turned the car off, she pressed her foot hard on the brake and roughly hauled her purse to her lap, rooting through its center pocket.

"Where the hell…?" she said angrily as she searched. When she found the small pillbox, she instantly felt a little calmer. She gathered sufficient saliva in her mouth and swallowed the pill dry. As she did, she remembered the incident a few years ago when she experienced a 48-hour panic attack that triggered her first anti-anxiety prescription. Once the pill finally made its way down her dry throat, Claire put the car in park and turned the engine off. She leaned back into her seat and closed her eyes.

OK, calm down, she thought, as her heart continued to beat hard, her fingers twitched without her consent, and her breathing labored.

She sometimes wondered why she even bothered taking her medication. At last count she had passed the 200-pound weight mark and she still was not emotionally stable. Something was not working. She knew some people gave up or resorted to other means of treatment to stifle their feelings, and she supposed she could sympathize on some level. But she preferred sugar. So maybe it was her fault.

She sat alone in her car waiting for the pill to work. She felt slightly lightheaded and sick to her stomach. She didn't know whether to blame the drug or her surging emotions. She finally opened and closed her eyes a few times slowly, rubbed her temple, and grabbed her bags from the passenger side.

As she climbed the steps to her apartment, she felt sick and dizzy again. She was not in the mood for friends or roommates tonight. She wanted to take a hot shower and slip into bed. She silently thanked her obsessive work ethic. She had completed the paper due tomorrow for her sociology class more than a week ago. At least she had something going for her. Maybe her life was not so out of control. When she got to the apartment, she promised herself she would not take this out on the girls.

Jill looked up. "Did you get my cream cheese?" she asked benignly.

"Yeah," Claire said. She didn't mean to be so gruff.

"What's with the mood?" asked Jill.

Claire didn't look up as she hauled the bags to the counter. "Just aggravated. This moron cut me off."

Kim was rummaging through her purse. "Some people just shouldn't be allowed to drive," she said.

Claire breathed out. "Exactly."

"Well, don't let him ruin your night," Jill said. She walked over to Claire. "We're thinking of grabbing something out for dinner. You game?"

Kyra came out from her room, pulling her hair up into a loose bun on her head.

Claire looked at her friends and just felt like crying. They were content and comfortable, and she was a wreck. She knew she should go out and let the day just melt away—so long as she didn't have to drive. But she could not bring herself to be happy because she knew she would have to work at it.

"Nah, I'm not really hungry."

"Oh, come on," groaned Kim.

"No, you have to come!" Jill protested.

Claire shrugged uncomfortably. "I have such a headache—probably why I'm so agitated." That was a lie. "I really would be awful company." That was not a lie.

Jill moved to comment.

"And I could use a little quiet time here just to myself," Claire finished quickly.

Her roommates studied her. They knew the statement was insincere. But if Claire was going to be a raincloud, they didn't want their evening destroyed. Claire was not one to be helped if she didn't want to be.

"Suit yourself," Kim said flatly. She was not going to fight with Claire anymore. Sometimes she wondered what the hell Claire's problem was. Sometimes she was really cool and other times she was a major pain in the ass.

Jill gave Claire an exaggerated sad face and hugged her gently. She leaned down in Claire's ear and whispered. "Now I'm going to have to go to some lame healthy place to eat with them."

Claire grinned and rested her forehead against Jill's.

"If they even suggest sushi," Jill warned, "I'm blaming you."

Her comment was over-the-top in its hushed sarcasm. Claire chuckled softly, appreciating her dear friend's attempt to change her mood; but as Jill pulled away slightly and winked, Claire had to fight to stop from crying as she smiled. When she saw the door close, the hot tears began driving down her cheeks. She hyperventilated. She hurled her keys across the room. They just missed knocking over Kim's vase. Claire leaned her elbows hard on the counter and pounded her fist in anger at not knowing what had caused this. So what if she had been cut off? Why couldn't she shake it? She rested there sobbing for minutes. Then she took a deep breath as she lifted her body upright again. She rubbed the wetness from her face and reached for the bags. She threw the perishable items into the refrigerator and left the rest on the counter. She cursed herself for having passed on ice cream at the store.

I try to be good, she thought.

She left her shoes by the door and slowly started shedding her clothes as she headed toward the bathroom. Even more than chocolate, she craved a shower. Her face was red and warm. She yearned for the calming power of water rushing down her body to take some of the tension with it.

She opened the cabinet and reached for her face wash. Lying beside it was the razor for her legs. Claire found herself internally debating whether the blade could do any real damage to her life if she tried.

I'd probably even fail at that, she thought, as she slammed the mirrored door shut. She was lucky she didn't break it.

She turned on the shower and let the water heat up for a moment. Then she stepped inside the foggy box and stood under the flow in a lifeless state, staring through the warm mist at the bland beige stall. She blinked away drops of water that sought to burn her eyes. She draped her forearm on the wall and leaned her weary head in the curve of her elbow. She wished she could just stay there forever.

When she realized the shower would do no more good for her, Claire turned the knob off and pushed open the door. She dabbed herself dry and streaked her hand across the cloudy mirror. Even through the marred view, Claire hated what she saw. In disgust, she groaned and turned to leave the bathroom. Once she had slipped into some clothes for bed, she hung her soggy towel on her door and ventured back into the kitchen. She searched and searched, and then cursed living with healthy eaters—and Jill, who preferred salty treats. If she were not shiny and clean now, she would go out immediately for ice cream or brownie mix. But she couldn't be that obsessed. Instead, she pulled out a yogurt and sat to watch TV alone.

Hours later, having expected the girls ages ago, Claire was tired enough to try to sleep despite it not even being ten o'clock yet. She left a few lights on in the family room and headed to her room. Rest came slowly as she tossed and turned, thinking about the application, school, the driver, and chocolate. By the time her roommates returned, Claire was asleep.

Later that night Kim heard a key rattle in the lock and looked up from the couch, perplexed. She had been staring at the ceiling in her own room and hoped watching a show might help her fall back to sleep. As far as Kim knew, all of her roommates were accounted for in their own rooms, dreaming. Jill and Kyra had gone to bed shortly after coming home from dinner and Kim had seen a lump under Claire's sheets. So the moving knob sent fear through her. Kim was amazed when the front door opened and Claire walked in with a grocery bag in her hand.

"Where were you?" she asked stunned, glancing sideways to see the clock. "It's nearly midnight," she whispered quickly.

"I ran out for a minute," Claire whispered back. "I just went down the street."

"It's almost twelve o'clock," Kim scolded. "*In the morning!*" Her voice rose. "What did you need so desperately?"

Claire avoided eye contact and turned toward the kitchen. "Nothing."

Kim was far from shocked to see Claire pull out a box of brownie mix and a carton of chocolate ice cream. "*Nothing?*" Kim whispered angrily, her face scrunched up in frustration. "Are you making brownies now?"

Claire didn't answer her. But Kim knew the answer was "no." Claire would be making brownie mix and storing the raw batter way in the back of the fridge in a plastic container. This was not the third or even the fifth time Claire had done it. Kim was not one to lick the bowl; frankly, she wasn't even that big into sweets. But the thought of keeping the mix prepared and uncooked for days was a little sickening.

Kim sensed the shame on Claire's face. She watched Claire tuck the box in the back of the pantry and pass by on her way to her room, with a spoon and the ice cream instead.

"Night," called Claire as she passed without looking.

"Goodnight," said Kim slowly, watching her roommate scurry away.

Claire loved Jill but hated sharing a room with anyone. She would have preferred sitting on the couch, but she couldn't eat with Kim's judgment staring her down. At least Jill was asleep. Claire climbed into her bed in the darkened room and pushed her headphones into her ears. The other end was stuck in her laptop. She dug her spoon deep into the hard ice cream, fighting for small clumps to break free from the mass.

Kim didn't understand what it was like to stress eat. If she was ever rattled, which she rarely was, Kim did the opposite of Claire. Kim worked out. Claire couldn't find the will or the time to exercise. Instead, she went out to the store at midnight and bought ice cream and brownie mix.

Claire knifed the ice cream again with her spoon, but the dessert was mostly frozen solid. She pounded it over and over, getting increasingly frustrated by the task until she finally got another scoop. She slipped the cool spoon into her mouth and tried to savor the bite. She couldn't help but begin to worry about the calendar. She was concerned that, in a little more than a week, school would break for Thanksgiving, and then it was almost Christmas vacation. Time was running out and so was her patience. It had been more than four weeks since she had submitted her application. Claire was beginning to panic. She had already begun planning her life in New York. She had even selected a few neighborhoods she might be able to afford, with a little help from her parents. She had her heart set on going, but Marshall wasn't calling.

She separated another mouthful and ate it, yet as she let her mind wander to the possible outcomes of this scenario, she began to feel a little sick. She batted away a few tears as she paused to consider whether the ice cream was worth the fight. She decided it wasn't. Instead, she pushed the top back into place and held the spoon between her lips. She tiptoed away from her bed, hoping her constant movement was not enough commotion to wake Jill.

She turned the knob of her door and looked down the hall. The living room was quiet and dark; Kim had gone back to bed. Claire ventured out from her bedroom to put the ice cream in the freezer. Now that she was alone, as she first expected to be when she ran to the store, Claire didn't feel so guilty. No one was there to watch her eat. She reached into the fridge for eggs and pulled a measuring cup, bowl, and oil from the cabinet. She mixed the wet ingredients together, grabbed the brownie mix box off the shelf, tore open its lid, cut the bag, and poured its contents into the liquid. Then she stirred the batter by hand with a spatula. She tasted it with a spoon before scraping the mix into a plastic storage container. Claire poured herself a tall glass of milk and stood in the kitchen, leaning against the counter, scooping mounds of chocolate into her mouth. Each spoonful calmed a nerve, yet she almost didn't taste the sweet treat because she ate it so fast. Maybe if she made herself sick from the brownie mix, she could blame the storm in her stomach on dessert instead of fear.

She didn't know how much she had eaten, but she finally began to feel like she might throw up. It was time to stop. Claire pushed the lid onto the plastic dish and dug out a spot for it way in the back of the fridge. She suspected she did not need to hide it from her roommates' temptations, just their criticism.

She lingered in front of the sink as she gulped the rest of her milk. She swallowed hard and it hurt her throat. Then she placed the cup quietly into the sink and turned to leave the kitchen, shuffling slowly back to her room.

It seemed to have worked. As she lay in bed, tossing and turning, she still felt sick, but all she could think of was overeating, not underachieving. The night was a long one, but somehow Claire managed to fall asleep without throwing up.

When she woke in the morning, she could barely remember the night before. She didn't feel sick or worried. She didn't feel anything at all. It was a Friday and she did not have class on Fridays. It was well past ten o'clock and she had no sense of urgency to get up. She was curled in a ball in her bed, wondering if, maybe, she could stay there all day.

Claire reached for the phone on her nightstand and clicked the email icon. She already had eleven new messages. Most of them were junk. Two were school-related. One was from her mother. But as she lightly touched the check box before each throwaway message, intending to delete them, she paused as she skimmed an unfamiliar name. A *Chase Donaldson* had emailed her, regarding *Your Application*. Claire sat up quickly in her bed and pushed the message to open it.

It was not a form rejection letter. She scanned the paragraphs, becoming increasingly more excited. *Impressed by your portfolio*, she read. *Highly qualified candidate. Schedule a phone interview next week.* Claire was bursting with excitement—and to think she didn't want to get up today!

The email was sent about thirty-five minutes earlier. To avoid seeming too eager, Claire waited to respond. She climbed out of bed and went to take a shower. When she came back, she was wrapped in her hot pink robe with her hair still up in a big twisted towel. She sat at her desk and opened her computer. Navigating to the email, she reread the message on the larger screen. Chase Donaldson's email signature listed his job title as Junior VP of Creative Services.

She pulled the computer closer to the edge of her desk and hit reply.

Dear Mr. Donaldson,

I am free for a phone interview next week. Please let me know what days and times work best for your schedule. I look forward to speaking with you.

Sincerely,

Claire Kelly

She sat wondering if the email said enough. But she didn't want to say too much either. She could sit there obsessing about each word or the length of her paragraph, but the more she changed the lines, the more chance she risked making an error. Instead, she pushed send.

Then Claire turned from her computer and went to get dressed. She pulled out a clean pair of cozy gray pants and matched it with a teal long sleeve shirt. She had no plans to leave the apartment today. She certainly had a few projects to catch up on from the comfort of her couch.

Less than ten minutes later as Claire was pulling her hair into a ponytail, her phone dinged again. Her computer was still open on her desk within reach, so she checked it there instead. She was shocked to see an email reply from Chase.

Hi, Claire,

Thanks for getting in touch so quickly. Since there's the long holiday weekend coming up, can you do any time on Monday? Late mornings are usually good for me, after 10 a.m.

Chase

Monday! That was only a weekend away. But she would rather get it out of the way before Thanksgiving. It would break the suspense. Besides, they had to narrow their candidate pool sometime. Claire didn't have class on Mondays either, so it was perfect timing. But as the idea of the interview became more formalized in her head, Claire was nervous again. She took a tranquilizer to calm down and gave the situation a ten-minute break before hitting reply.

Hi, Chase,

Would Monday around 1 p.m. work for you?

Claire

She realized after she sent the message that their conversation had become increasingly more casual, and she became increasingly more curious. She wondered what he looked like, so she typed into her browser: Chase Donaldson, Marshall's Creatives. His company profile popped up on her screen. He was an attractive man in his early thirties, with messy dark hair—a look that probably took him an hour to achieve—a suit but no tie, and a line of bright white teeth. His bio was a bit thin, but she learned he went to a pretty good school for business and he was from New Jersey. He liked soccer and baseball, and his hobbies included rock climbing and running marathons.

He was a really attractive athlete. Was he a jerk? She shook her head at her snap judgment, figuring Chase had many endearing qualities and was just as easily a saint.

She loitered around her computer for another fifteen minutes, surfing the web and wasting time, but he did not write back. She shut the computer and went out to make something for breakfast. He didn't respond until after lunch, but Monday at 11 a.m. it was. He confirmed the appointment and her cell phone number in the message. She wondered if she should confirm his confirmation. It almost seemed repetitive, but she figured it could not hurt. She replied, telling him again that she looked forward to his call, and yes, the number he listed was the correct one to call.

She dialed her mother to tell her the good news. Emily was excited for her daughter, though her absolute faith that the job would become Claire's failed to serve as a self-esteem boost. It just made Claire more nervous. She finally told her mother she had to go and shuffled out to the living room to watch television.

She could have emailed Janet, but she figured she would wait to see what came of the call. She could have brought her computer and done research for her last paper. She could have done a lot of things. But she watched a marathon of sitcom reruns instead. It was the only thing that did not require her to think. Her mind worked too much as it was.

Even if only for a few hours, she wanted to just give it a rest.

Chapter 9

The clock seemed to linger at 11:01 a.m. Claire sat cross-legged on her bed, leaning against the wall, waiting for the phone to ring. Fortunately, her roommates were out. This was the first real job interview Claire had ever had and she was nervous. She had already taken a tranquilizer to calm herself down.

Her eyes shot back at the clock: 11:02 a.m. Then her phone started ringing. She let it ring three times before she answered the call. She took one quick, deep breath and spoke calmly. "Hello?"

"Hi, can I speak to Claire?" His voice sounded as attractive as his photograph. She felt herself visualizing what he looked like as she listened.

"Yes. This is Claire," she said trying to control the pitch of her voice. Sometimes she felt it rising too high.

"Hi, Claire. This is Chase Donaldson from Marshall's Creatives." He seemed collected, soothing, and self-assertive. Claire knew the type: popular but nice, the jock who stopped to help you pick up your books if you dropped them. Her heart raced as they spoke, and she instantly knew she had judged him too quickly. He was not a cocky jerk. He laughed readily and was quite complimentary.

"I loved your website," he said. "You didn't make that, did you?"

She smiled, as if he could see her through the phone. "I did. I took some web design classes here at Adams," she said confidently.

"That's awesome. I was looking over the candidates and some of them had things online. Not as many as I'd like to see, but some. But, wow…nothing like yours."

Claire was beaming. "I'm happy you liked it."

"It was fantastic. It's great to see a word person so comfortable with technology. We like to hire people who have a wide range of skills."

Claire nodded until she realized he couldn't hear her nod. "Of course," she said. "I expect it's becoming required by most firms."

"Pretty much." He paused. "So, I see your grades are *awful.*" He drew the last word out slowly, sarcastically.

She laughed. "Yeah. I hated philosophy. That's the B."

"I was wondering what messed up the 4.0." He was quiet for a moment. "That must have pissed you off, huh?"

She was shocked he would be so informal with her, but she smiled. "Yes, it did."

"Good. We like people who demand only the best from themselves."

Claire was relieved her honest response had been well received.

"So, what are your thoughts on working in New York?"

She shrugged. "I'm fine with it. I mean—it might take me a little while to learn my way around."

"Nah," he said. "I think you'll be fine. But I'm a great tour guide, if you need one."

The comment came out as more of a flirtatious offer than a casual jest, and she had to admit she was flattered.

"I'll keep that in mind."

"Good." He paused. "Anyway, I think you're a great candidate for the program. The samples on your fantastic website show a lot of potential. I also like that you have some agency experience."

She began to nod again, smiling. Then she caught herself. "Thank you—a lot. Really, I appreciate it."

"I'd like you to come in for an interview after the holiday, if you're free."

Claire almost couldn't contain herself. "Just name the day." She didn't bother to look at a calendar. If she had plans, she would break them. He suggested a date, which she agreed to, and then he promised to send a confirmation email before he said "goodbye." Claire's phone disconnected and went black. She sat there trying to determine Chase Donaldson's true character. She wondered what he really thought of her. She tried to decide whether he was that impressed by her website.

"Stop it," she said out loud to herself, shaking her head to control her thoughts. She had to stop overthinking everything.

As she tossed the phone on her pillow, she heard the bedroom door creak as it opened. Jill's eye poked through the crack.

"Yes?" Claire asked playfully.

"Are you done?" Jill whispered loudly.

Claire smiled. "I wouldn't be talking to you if I wasn't."

"Right." Jill pushed the door open more and walked in, staring inquisitively at her roommate.

Claire mirrored back an exaggerated version of the expression.

"*Well?*" Jill asked impatiently and wide-eyed.

"Well, what?" Claire asked smirking.

Jill huffed. "Well? How'd it go?"

"What?"

"Oh, come on! The interview."

"Oh! Right. It went well."

"Just *well?*"

Claire beamed a bit.

"More than well?" Jill asked hopefully.

"I'm going there for an interview after Thanksgiving."

"To *New York?*" Jill was nearly squealing now.

"Uh-huh."

Jill leapt towards Claire and tossed her arms around her friend. "I'm so excited for you!"

Claire tapped her hand lightly on Jill's back as she acknowledged Jill's support. "Thanks," she said, almost whispering.

"Can anyone help?" called Kim's voice from the hall.

The girls looked toward the door and then pulled away from each other and scurried to the kitchen. They found Kim tangled with her purse and shopping bags, trying to pull out her keys.

"Claire got the second interview!" Jill called loudly from the hall.

"*What?*" Kim burst out, dropping her bags. She didn't even notice but instead stepped over them quickly as Claire was nodding her head and smiling. "That's awesome!" Kim said hugging her. "I knew you'd get it."

Claire smiled weakly. "I don't have anything yet."

Jill and Kim looked at each other. Jill rolled her eyes slightly; Kim had to bite her tongue not to comment. Sometimes Claire's negativity pissed her off. She just shook her head.

Claire sensed their annoyance, but she couldn't help the overwhelming dread that was beginning to form. She couldn't place exactly why she was washed with a sense of tension, but she was suddenly very aware of the fact that she had to go through with this. And if it did work out, she would have to move to New York. She was not quite sure she could handle it. She could only shrug her shoulders. "But I guess the interview is a start."

Jill smiled. "Exactly."

Kim pulled in her lips slightly and nodded her head. She was not going to bother saying anything else. She just stooped down and picked up her bags so she could close the door. But as she slipped her purse up over her shoulder, she paused. "Do you want to do anything to celebrate?"

Claire shrugged. "Maybe, if I get it," she said flatly.

"Don't you mean 'when'?" asked Jill.

Claire scoffed gently under her breath. She sort of nodded. No, she had meant "if."

"Suit yourself," Kim said as she toted her shopping bags off to the kitchen counter. That's the last time she would bother.

Claire finally pulled away from Jill and went back to their room while Jill helped Kim put away the groceries.

They never did celebrate. In fact, they never brought it up again. Claire felt almost too sick to even eat dinner that night, and she could not decide if the tension was because of the interview, a possible move, or the fact that she had set her friends at arm's length—again. Somehow she shifted between being engaged and enraged, loving and distant, calm and unsettled. Somehow, they put up with her. Yet, sometimes their patience ran rather thin.

Kim went to bed without comment and Jill came in to find Claire curled up in bed. Jill settled under her covers but the room was a bit too chilly, meaning sleep would not be as simple as she hoped. Jill was aggravated when she woke again, well before dawn. She pushed her covers aside and slipped out of bed. She had been so comfortable under the blankets where it was warm, but she could not wait any longer. She turned the knob of their bedroom door, cringing slightly as the metal creaked. She didn't want to wake Claire. She pulled the door open just enough to slip out into the dimly lit hallway. They always kept a nightlight on, but Jill turned her head as she realized the area was brighter than usual. She could see the floor lamp was on in the family room and heard fingers tapping away feverishly on a keyboard. Neither Kim nor Kyra could type that fast.

"Claire?" Jill called quietly before she could even see clearly, blinking her still-tired eyes to dull the unwelcome light.

Claire turned quickly at the sound of her voice. "Hi," she whispered. "Did I wake you?"

"No," Jill mumbled back. "What are you doing up?" She glanced at the clock. "It's almost four in the morning. What time did you go to bed?"

"Well, I tried, but I couldn't asleep." She took a sip of water from a green coffee mug.

"What are you working on?"

"A paper."

"Why now?"

"I told you, I couldn't sleep."

"Are you worried about it? I mean, is it due soon?"

Claire smiled sheepishly. "No."

Jill smirked. "When's it due?"

"In about two weeks."

"And when was it assigned?"

"Four days ago."

Jill pulled in her lips and nodded her head slowly. "Right."

Claire shrugged. "It's better than staring at the ceiling."

Jill agreed. "I guess so. All right, I gotta pee." She started to turn. "Go to bed sometime tonight, OK?"

Claire smiled. "Find the off switch for my mind and I will."

Chapter 10

Claire sat in a corner chair at Solace with a book in one hand and a cookie in the other. She was nibbling at it, hidden behind the pages. When she popped the last bite in her mouth, she rubbed her forefinger and thumb between a brown napkin, never looking up from her novel. Blindly, she reached for her coffee, but she missed twice and finally pulled her attention away from the story long enough to find the cup. As she paused to take a sip, she noticed a familiar face at the end of the bar waiting for a drink. She hadn't seen Erik in forever. She was sorry to see he had cut his hair a bit. She liked the shaggy look on him. He loitered around, looking at nothing in particular. She caught his glance and he smiled slightly. She had never once in her life gotten more than a comfortable grin from him. Claire wondered if it was her fault that he never really smiled wide, or whether that was just Erik's way. Nevertheless, once he grabbed his cup to go, and stopped to lighten it with cream and sugar, she felt her breath catch as she realized he was walking toward her.

Relieved the cookie was gone, Claire discreetly pushed the plate out of reach beneath the leaves of a plant. She touched her face to be sure no crumbs lingered. Then she leaned back in her chair and tried not to look as nervous as she felt.

Unfortunately, it was not so much that he was coming to see her as he was passing her on his way out.

"Hey," he said tilting his chin ever so slightly in her direction.

"Hi," she replied.

The chair beside her was empty and she wondered if he would stop for a chat. Instead, he stood there quietly.

Finally, Claire broke the silence. "Just one more semester," she said enthusiastically.

He nodded. "Yeah."

"What's next for you?"

He shrugged. "Law school."

Claire almost couldn't control her bugging eyes. *Erik—a lawyer?* At least she didn't laughed out loud. "Law school? Wow," said Claire, trying to cover for her stunned reaction. "I had no idea you wanted to be a lawyer."

"Yeah. My dad's a lawyer. He's really pushing me. I dunno, I guess it could be cool." He took a sip from his drink and swallowed.

"Huh…great," Claire said weakly.

He gestured toward her with the cup in his right hand. "What about you?"

Claire shrugged, smiling. She couldn't stop the nagging feeling drilling away about the interview. She couldn't get over the fear of failure if she didn't get it. But somehow, having nothing to say seemed worse than the truth.

In her head, she just kept thinking: what if it doesn't work out? But suddenly she heard herself say, "I have an interview for an associates program at an ad firm in Manhattan."

"Wow. New York? That's cool." He took another sip. "Doing what?"

"Copywriting."

He nodded his head. "That's cool," he said again after thinking a moment. "I could see you doing that."

Claire smiled deeply at the compliment. At least some people had faith in her. Well, not really faith so much as recognition of her talent, perhaps?

"So, no grad school for you?" He smirked.

"I don't think so. I'm ready to be done with school."

"*You?*" he said quickly. "I never expected to hear you say that."

She laughed softly. "Why's that?"

"I dunno. It just seemed like you love to write. You love

projects." He shrugged. "I thought you loved school."

"Well, I do love to write. And do projects. And I like school. But I'm so ready to get out into the real world and start working."

He nodded his head, seeming rather disinterested now. He glanced down at his watch. "Oh, you know, I gotta get going."

Claire smiled slightly. "Sure."

"Good luck with your interview."

She smiled wider, appreciating the sentiment. "Good luck with law school," she said, genuinely this time.

He sort of laughed under his breath. "Thanks."

She watched him walk out of Solace, figuring she would probably never see Erik Quinn again. But she didn't pause too long. He didn't want her anyway.

She lingered for another thirty minutes sipping her coffee and trying to finish a long chapter of the book. Then her phone vibrated with a text message. She looked down and saw it was Jill.

"Shit," she grumbled. She had told her roommate she would be home fifteen minutes ago. Claire might not be planning on grad school, but she had promised Jill she would help her study for the graduate entrance exam. Jill was panicking about taking the GRE. She didn't like standardized tests. Claire offered to help quiz her, hoping to ease her friend's fears.

She slung her coat over her shoulders and stuffed her book in her bag. She brought her cup up to the front counter and left it behind before quickly weaving through the mess of customers, typing a fast reply: *Sorry! I'm coming!* At least, they only lived around the corner.

She stumbled through the door, apologizing again. Forty minutes later, Claire was leaning over the prep book, still trying to put the deceiving GRE math problems into perspective for Jill.

"Agh!" Jill groaned as she leaned back on the couch. "This sucks. You're so smart not going to grad school."

Claire smiled at her. She closed the book and set it on the table. "Enough for one night?"

"Yeah, I guess so. I can't believe I have to take this stupid test."

"But at least you'll have it done."

"At least the first round," Jill said.

Claire looked at her, confused by the comment.

"You think I'm going to get a good enough score the first time?" She scoffed at the thought.

Claire shook her head. "I think you'll do fine."

Jill rolled her eyes. Claire sounded like her mother. "So, when are you going home for Thanksgiving?"

"I figure I'll leave tomorrow at three o'clock after my last class," Claire said. "We're just doing a quiet thing at home."

"Lucky you. I have a holiday weekend flight to Colorado *and* a massive extended family dinner with everybody. I wish I could just stay here."

"How do you think that would go over with your parents?"

Jill smirked. "Not well."

Claire smiled and nodded her head. Jill had filled in the past few years with many interesting stories about her parents. Claire almost didn't believe them until she met Marian and Donald in person. They were mostly nice people who somehow missed the fact that their only child had grown up. She wondered how on earth comfortable Jill had come out of that overbearing huddle.

Had it not been for the calming presence of her mother in her life, Claire probably wouldn't have survived this long. Emily Kelly was her rock, her therapist, and her cheerleader, as well as her shoulder to cry on. Her father, John, was quite the opposite: practical, straightforward, and usually quiet. Claire loved her father, but sometimes she had a hard time connecting with him. They bonded over political conversations and current events, but somehow, when the conversation turned personal, John's comments often offended Claire. Not that he ever really meant to offend. But he always seemed to anyway.

If the fears rattling around inside her head were not already disturbing enough, Claire's father would point them out. Still, things appeared to be going well for Claire, so unlike Jill, Claire looked forward to going home for Thanksgiving.

Besides, her dad was unlikely to say anything she hadn't already thought herself.

Her mother greeted Claire with a big hug and told her how much she had missed her. Claire had been so consumed by school, and so preoccupied with her future, that she almost didn't realize she hadn't seen her parents in months. But the funny thing was, because she talked to her mom nearly every day, it didn't seem that long.

"I'm so excited about your interview!" Emily said as she hugged her daughter. She did not say, *I'm so nervous about you moving to New York.* She kept that thought to herself.

"Thanks, Mom," Claire said.

Her mother stared at her for a moment in wonderment. "Aren't you excited?" she asked.

"Yeah, of course."

"You're not acting like it."

Claire shrugged. "Well, I have an interview. Not a job."

"OK, that's true. But you're a shoo-in."

"I am?"

"Are you OK?"

Claire looked at her mother skeptically. "Yeah, why wouldn't I be?"

"I don't know, you just seem…lost."

Claire laughed uncomfortably. "I know exactly where I am. I'm on track."

Emily softly rubbed Claire's back. "Really? I mean, because sometimes you're good and sometimes you're—"

"Mom, I'm *fine*."

"Are you taking your medication every day?"

Claire groaned. "Yeah, Mom. And they're obviously doing a *splendid* job. I mean, look at me." Claire waved her hand lavishly down her body. "I'm dandy and so damned dainty."

"Claire," Emily sighed. Of course she had noticed her daughter's weight gain. How could she not? Claire's clothes didn't fit, and her poor face and fingers were so puffed out they almost looked painful. It broke her heart to see Claire like that. She had even discussed the issue with her own doctor. He said Claire's type of anti-depressant could do that.

She let Claire go to her room and unpack without saying a word. By the time Claire came back, her father had arrived home. He was standing in the kitchen when he saw his daughter descend the stairs. He did a double take. *What had happened to his little girl?* He smiled, hugged her, and noted the arm span now required to get around her. John had never interfered before in Claire's upbringing, but now he wanted to turn to his wife and say, *No dinner for Claire, tonight!* Instead, he left the room to change out of his suit.

Claire picked at the food as her mom spooned the meal into bowls. Everything was mostly healthy, though Emily suddenly regretted making cheesecake for dessert. She couldn't tell her daughter not to eat it, but she really didn't want her having dessert. Of course she would never deprive her child of food. But all she could think about were the medical complications associated with severe weight gain. Her father had died early from heart disease. Her husband had diabetes. And, now her daughter weighed God knows what. Emily didn't know what to say. She just smiled weakly.

"Here," she said handing Claire a bowl. "Put that on the table, please."

"Sure," Claire said.

When the table was set, the family sat down and ate in relative silence. Claire usually carried the conversation—when she was in a good mood. Claire was not in a good mood today. Her father asked about the interview in New York and Claire filled him in on the details. John nodded and congratulated her for advancing that far.

Claire finished the last bite of her dinner and brought her plate to the counter. "Who's for cheesecake?" she asked pulling the lid off the dish.

Her parents looked at each other nervously. Her father suddenly wished dessert didn't even exist as a concept.

"Maybe we should wait," Emily said shrugging her shoulders.

Claire scowled. "Fine. I'm not." She sliced off a generous helping for herself. "I'll be in my room," she said. Apparently her apartment was not the only place she had to eat in hiding.

Claire ate her cheesecake while she watched television. An hour later, her mother tapped lightly on the door. "Can I come in?"

"Yeah."

Emily pulled out Claire's desk chair and sat down.

"Are you nervous about the interview?" she asked.

Claire smiled. "Mom, I'm fine. I know what you're doing."

"What?"

"I got fat."

Emily winced.

"I did. It's obvious. And it sucks," Claire said.

"Are you eating healthy?"

"Sometimes. What food group does frosting belong in?" Claire asked sarcastically.

Emily rolled her eyes slightly. "That's not healthy."

"I eat when I'm stressed. And sometimes I eat because I'm hungry, even when I've already eaten. It's weird. Sometimes I can't stop."

"That was a pretty big slice of cheesecake."

Claire smiled. "It was good, Mom."

"That was a pretty big slice."

"I know."

"So, should we make an appointment? Talk to your doctor about all this?"

"Not now. It's a holiday. Maybe over winter break?"

"Do you feel the meds are doing anything for your depression? What about that supplemental one that's supposed to help with the weight gain?"

Claire shrugged. "Obviously that one's not helping. The other one…I don't know. I feel OK, sometimes. And sometimes I'm so depressed I just don't want to do anything. But I do everything, anyway. But then it's weird; sometimes I'm really good. I mean…I got really excited about the interview in New York. The guy—Chase—he loved my website and samples. I mean, *loved*."

Emily smiled. "Of course he did."

Claire nodded. "I guess it's…I dunno…"

"Maybe there's something else going on?"

Claire shrugged. "Sometimes I just want to go off them. You know, when I'm feeling better."

Emily shook her head. "That's because they're helping."

"What about when they're not?"

Emily stared at her. "We'll have to do some investigating. We're the ones who figured out the depression."

Claire nodded.

"What can I do right now?"

Claire looked at her mother almost shamefully.

"What?" Emily asked nervously.

Claire's eyes suddenly welled up with tears.

"What is it?"

"I need a suit," she said diverting her eyes to the floor. "I don't have anything that fits for my interview."

Emily moved from the chair to the bed and slipped her arm around Claire. She squeezed her tight in a single-arm hug. "You know I love shopping." She smiled. "And I love *you*."

Claire sniffled and smiled as her mother kissed her on the temple. She nodded and managed to whisper, "I love you, too."

Claire was the one who suggested the outlet stores. She wanted an outfit that she didn't mind parting with. When she was thinner, she loved shopping. Now she refused to spend her parents' money on something she had no intention of keeping. This hell could not last forever…could it?

"No," said Claire as her mother held up a gray, two-piece skirt suit. "I want something black. Black hides everything. And no skirts."

"OK," Emily said. She put the suit back on the rack. "What about this?" Emily asked holding up a black pinstripe suit.

Claire wrinkled her nose. "I don't like pinstripes."

"All right," Emily said. Her mother was nothing if not patient. But she had dealt with Claire for twenty-one years. She had learned compromise.

"This?"

Claire paused and studied the outfit. It was almost boring, but it was pretty much what she was looking for. It was a no-frills basic black pants suit. Claire shrugged. "Yeah, that's a good possibility. What size is it?"

"Well, this is a two."

Claire narrowed her eyes slightly in contemplation. "I don't think that will fit," she said sarcastically.

Emily smiled. "I was just holding it up for approval before I bothered searching for your size." She set the suit back on the rack and began pushing through the hangers. "What size do you want?"

Claire came over and hovered behind her mother. "I dunno,"

she said weakly. She sort of knew, but she really didn't want to say.

"Well, we can bring in a few different sizes. What, a twelve?"

"Maybe," said Claire meekly, which she quickly followed with, "and a fourteen."

Emily didn't flinch as she pulled out the two sizes. She had been lying when she suggested the twelve. Claire only hoped the fourteen would fit.

It didn't.

Claire's heart sagged as she tried desperately to fasten the buttons of the pants over her stomach. They almost closed. But almost didn't count. The suit jacket was not much better. It fit up over her arms, but she could barely move once it was in place.

"So, we'll get a sixteen," Emily said hopefully.

That number made Claire sad. She took a deep breath and closed her eyes. The very idea of a size sixteen outfit was enough to make her cry.

Emily laid her hand gently on Claire's arm. "Claire, no one has to know the size unless you tell them."

Claire stared at her.

"Think about it. If you see a thin girl who's, say, a size four, but she's lying to herself and trying to fit into a size two, then she looks silly and *fat* in her tight outfit. If you're a sixteen and you wear something that fits you well, it looks good, no matter what the number is."

Claire didn't really believe her mother but she appreciated the sentiment. And she supposed the logic kind of made sense— though *good* was probably a bit of an overstatement. But if Claire was willing to try on a fourteen, what was the difference between a fourteen and a sixteen? Ten pounds was not earth shattering when the overall baggage was 80-something pounds.

She nodded her head and relented, mostly because she had no other choice. But while she waited for Emily to return, Claire began to worry that she might have surpassed the size limit for real stores. That was her greatest nightmare. Well, maybe not her *greatest*, but close to it. When Emily finally knocked quietly on the dressing room door, she held two suits that only slightly resembled the first.

"They didn't have it in a size sixteen in the other style. But these are close to it," she said carefully.

Claire stared at them, wrinkling her face ever so slightly. Finally, she took one. "I don't want either, but I didn't want the first. I guess a black suit is a black suit."

Emily smiled. "That's the spirit."

Claire rolled her eyes. She pulled the pants off the hanger and stepped into them. To her dismay, they fit.

"Look at that," said Emily excitedly, as though it was an event worth celebrating.

"Mom, you have *no idea* how elated I am," Claire said.

It was a beautiful suit. Too bad it was a size sixteen. Claire slung the garment bag over her arm and followed her mother out to the car. Emily asked if she needed anything else, but Claire said she was officially "sick" of shopping.

"Bite your tongue," Emily said.

Claire smiled, appreciating her mother's newfound sassiness.

"I'm tired," she whined.

"Oh, Claire! Where's your female gene?"

"Hidden in the back of my closet with all of my skinny clothes."

Emily smiled gently.

On the drive home, Claire thought about the interview. She was suddenly calmer and even a bit more hopeful. Perhaps her reservations had been about having nothing to wear. She might still be nervous, but at least she would look as good as possible. She only wished the suit could hide more of the weight. But dark fabric was not a miracle, just a patch.

Her father was home when they arrived. Claire passed by him in the kitchen, holding the garment bag behind her. Generally,

John paid little attention. He could care less about fashion. But he mentally noted the purchase.

It was not the expense that bothered him. It was what the need for new clothes represented. He said nothing about it, but it kept him up for hours worrying. Well after two o'clock that morning, John could feel his body shaking. He was having a diabetic reaction. He needed food. He slipped out of bed, and as he pulled his bedroom door open he noticed a faint light coming from the kitchen. Since his wife was sleeping beside him, he sighed, realizing it was Claire.

He found her seated at the kitchen counter eating a bowl of fresh fruit. Claire poked at the berries with a fork. She speared them on a single prong until not another berry could fit. Then she slid them off the line, one-by-one, with her teeth.

Claire jumped when he entered the room. "Hi, Dad," she said catching her breath.

"Sorry I scared you," he said quietly.

"No, it's OK." She shifted in her chair as she counted out another line of berries. She watched her father pull out a bag of crackers and spread a dab of peanut butter on three, eating them as he went.

"Blood sugar?"

He nodded as he pulled out a cup and the pitcher of juice, and poured himself a glass. "Can't sleep?" he asked.

She shrugged.

"Worried about something?"

"Always," she replied sarcastically.

He grinned. "Did you get a new suit for the interview?"

She looked at him. Since when did her father care about her clothes?

"Uh…yeah."

"You needed one, huh?"

She stared at him, her brow slightly furrowed. "What's that mean?"

He lifted the glass to his lips, took a long sip, and swallowed. "Come on, Claire," he said, "I have eyes." He looked at her, hoping for a response. Finally he said, "You look different. You've been looking different for a while. I almost can't believe it sometimes."

Her back tightened a bit and she scowled. "Thanks, *Dad*," she said sarcastically.

He shook his head. "I'm not trying to be mean. I'm just saying…look, you're a beautiful girl. But…"

She scoffed at the backhanded compliment.

"…you gotta watch it. I don't want you getting diabetes like me." He sighed.

Claire frowned in panic. She had never thought of that. Not once. Now she had something else to worry about.

"And you have to be careful." He paused.

Her eyes narrowed, waiting for the next ball to drop.

"Claire, I'm gonna tell you something that a father's not supposed to tell his kid. Dads are supposed to say everything's always perfect and everyone's always nice."

She stared at him just wishing for him to shut up.

"I wish life was fair but it's not. I've been in the workforce long enough to know it. Fair or not, it seems people who are thin and attractive just get further than those with talent alone."

Her face fell as she listened. She already thought these things. Hearing them made them real.

"And you, kid, have talent… You have looks, too. It's just a little hard for others to see it."

She couldn't look up. If she did, she might cry. Why did he have to say it? She just nodded her head weakly, hoping if she pretended he wasn't there, then maybe he would go away.

John finally picked up his glass and placed it by the sink. "Goodnight, kid," he said as he left her at the counter to count her berries.

Claire was suddenly sick at the thought that everyone could

see the fat girl in the mirror. She was no longer a figment imagined on a depressive day when Claire was young, thin, and anxious. That girl had escaped and was running free in the world.

Claire ran to the sink to catch the vomit that began to surge. Her stomach was as wild as her mind, and after the berries splattered her mother's clean black stone sink, she used the edge of the counter to keep from falling from the sudden dizzy spell. She tried to stop her inner scream from coming out and waking the house. Even pounding fists against the granite would probably just break her hand. Instead, she wrapped her fingers tightly into themselves and let her nails dig deeply into her palms as she slunk to the floor in a silent cry. Her jaw ached as she clenched her teeth and her painful fists pressed into her face.

Her heart fought back, pounding so forcefully inside her chest that she heard the whooshing blood in her ears. A weak whine escaped through her lips as Claire felt her body about to erupt. She flattened out her hands and her fingertips began to roughly rub against her temples, in rhythm with the beat of her heart. She stared ahead at the clean floor, smelling the faint odor of the bleach her mother used. Claire thought about it down her throat. Then a brilliant idea came to her and her eyes shifted up towards the fridge across the way. It seemed so massive from her vantage point.

Her hands fell to the side, and as the lesson from biology class mingled with that from her television watching, a faint hope came to her. She used her sore palms to push herself up and she went to the fridge. She pulled open the door and let her hand follow its own will. Reaching to the container her father kept in there, Claire went past the pierced vials and plucked out an unused, still full insulin pen, a self-contained syringe conveniently packaged for delivering the fast-acting liquid to treat John's diabetes. A synthetic imitation of what already existed inside her; untraceable and lethal in a high dose for someone with a working pancreas.

She felt relief mixed with guilt as she stole the pen and a needle from his stash. She knew he'd never know. She tucked them inside her robe pocket, washed the vomit from the sink so her mother would not wonder, and left the berry bowl—half full—by John's cup.

She then scurried up the stairs quietly with the pen—what gave her father life could give her death. Its versatility almost made Claire smile, and she felt calm. In her room, she hid the pen. Her mother was not one to snoop but she sometimes still cleaned up. Claire placed the back-up plan in her computer case, somewhere her mother would never go.

Claire's goal was not to die tonight. She would give New York a chance. But her nerves were suddenly quieted—faster than a tranquilizer could have done.

Chapter 11

The train jostled slightly as it rattled down the rails from Boston toward New York. Claire had been awake since just after five o'clock that morning. Worry woke her, after keeping her up well past midnight. She had huddled under the covers for another thirty minutes, trying to avoid the day. She finally slid out of bed, exhausted but wired. After a quick shower and a much-deserved cup of coffee, she had pulled out her new suit, grateful for one less burden. At least she had taken her time today. Knowing she was not going to be late for the interview kept her calmer, though the tranquilizer likely helped as well. She boarded the New York-bound train early, and when it left the station, she stared out the window watching the rain blow past the pane. Of course it had to rain today. She had intended to wear her suit on the train. Emily suggested she bring it with her and change there. That sounded like too much work until she saw the sky. Now her suit sat next to her in its garment sack. Claire checked her bag again to be sure she had her portfolio as well. Of course she did. But she knew she would check it ten more times before the meeting.

She glanced down at her watch hours later. Claire could feel her heart pounding again. Her nerves were getting the better of her. She closed her eyes trying to block out the bleak view through her window, but all she could do was visualize the rest of the day. She had no idea what to expect and that scared the hell out of her. Then the thought hit her: if this all worked out, she would be living one day after another without knowing what to expect in a terrifying city. Her heart began beating faster as she wondered if she should pursue the program at all. She breathed deeply, over and over, in hopes of reining in her anxiety, while thoughts raced through her mind like a picture show. Suddenly she realized the pictures were memories. She remembered feeling the same way before she went off to college for the first time. She remembered experiencing the same apprehension when she transferred to AU, thinking Boston was too big. And then she stopped to consider how many times she had lived through that feeling.

Claire opened her eyes and stared out the window again. Fear of failure kept her from asking too many questions. She finally blinked, returning to reality. She could see her reflection faintly staring back at her through the spotted glass. For a moment, she had almost forgotten where she was. But the quiet rumbling of the train was a gentle reminder. Maybe her existential pondering was a side effect of exhaustion.

She checked her watch again and tried to breathe. One thing at a time, she thought. Wise words. But telling Claire Kelly to live in the moment was like telling a bird not to fly. She turned back to the ebook in her hand, flipping through the virtual pages but not really focusing on the words. She glanced up again at the window and could see the outline of the city hidden in fog. Her heart beat faster. Claire finally just held the button down and turned off the machine. It was not worth pretending to read anymore. She knew once she was in a better frame of mind, she would be flipping back page after page to the last spot where she actually recognized the plot.

Someone made an announcement over the speaker. The train was on schedule. It would not be long now. As the minutes ticked away, the train slowed down before pulling into the station. She collected her bags, checking again to be sure she had everything, and then followed the line of passengers to the door. Once outside—under the shadow of the New York skyline—she hailed a cab. She was not going to risk getting lost. She only had two hours, after all. She rattled off an address that meant nothing to her.

She sat rigidly in the back seat, watching the city pass by. She had been to New York before on school trips and a few times with her mother. But she still considered it a different world. She could feel her heart beating faster as she, once more, contemplated having to learn her way around. She laughed softly under her breath as she remembered Chase's offer to be her tour guide. But she assumed he was just teasing.

"Is it much longer?" she asked politely.

"Nah, just a few minutes."

The cab driver never asked why she was here and she didn't chat. She just turned back to the window and watched the city. Marshall's Creatives took up two stories in a skyscraper: floors twenty-one and twenty-two. Claire reminded herself to note the view when she got there. With any luck, it would be a view she would experience every day—and probably even some nights—as she made advertising magic.

She took another breath and suddenly felt a surge of confidence. She was finally getting excited. This was all becoming very real and she had a good feeling about it.

"We're here," said the driver as he tapped his blinker and pulled out of traffic.

"Which one is it?" Claire asked as her eyes searched the buildings.

He could tell she was a newbie. He smiled slightly as he looked at her from his rear-view mirror. "That one," he said, pointing through the glass, leaving a small smudge on his window.

Claire tilted her head in the direction he had pointed and looked up. She took another breath. Then she paid the fare and grabbed her bags.

"Good luck," he said. She reminded him a little of his daughter.

She looked at his eyes in the mirror and smiled. Was she that obvious? "Thank you," she replied.

The weather was just a slight mist, but Claire scurried as fast as she could toward a bit of cover. She decided to go into the lobby to verify she was in the right place, before finding somewhere to spend the time until her meeting. She found an office directory just inside the second set of doors and scanned down to floors twenty-one and twenty-two. She was indeed at the right building.

She turned; she could see through the glass doors that the rain had picked up a bit. She reached inside her bag and pulled out a small, collapsed umbrella. She unsnapped it and extended the neck out, but she waited until she was past the twin set of doors before she opened it. She stared through the gray haze, looking for somewhere to go until her meeting. After a few blocks, she noticed the familiar Starbucks sign and darted in. She shook her coat slightly and tapped her relaxed umbrella on the doorframe to scatter the rain. The room was rather full.

She ordered a fancy coffee and a plain bagel.

"Toasted?" asked the man behind the counter.

"Nope. Nothing."

"OK." He pulled out a pair of tongs and slid the meal into a paper bag. She paid and took it to the end of the counter to wait for her drink, standing off to the side between all of the New Yorkers. When her drink was called, she grabbed the cup and scanned the room for a seat. The day was looking up as she noticed a woman about to leave. It was a big chair nestled in a corner, perfect for waiting.

She placed the damp umbrella and her bag by the chair. She folded her suit in half and put it on top. Then she peeled her jacket away from her body and laid it upside down on the chair's back. The room felt a little chilly, but she was not going to sit in a wet coat. She rubbed her bare arms and drank her coffee. No one seemed to notice her as they worked their wireless devices, talked on their phones, or read their papers. So this was New York? It was a place where someone could get lost and be invisible. If she was admitting the truth, Claire liked that about the city. She preferred being overlooked. She was a behind-the-scenes kind of person. But as she tore a piece of bagel off and ate it, she hoped she would be able to stand out today in her meeting.

Claire wondered how many people would be interviewing for the position. She figured it couldn't be that many at this stage. Why would Chase waste his time with people he wasn't serious about? Why would he make her come all this way?

She chewed on the doughy bite and swallowed. She should probably be eating a proper lunch, but she figured it would not sit well if she did. Her nerves were churning. She thought about taking another tranquilizer but decided against it. She didn't want to be dazed during her meeting.

She checked her watch. She now had a little more than an hour to go, if she wanted to give herself time to get back to the building and up twenty-one stories. She took another sip of her coffee, pulled out her phone, and called her mother.

"Hi, sweetie!" Emily said. "Are you there?"

"Yup. I took a cab to the building and now I'm at a Starbucks a few blocks down."

"That's good. I've been thinking about you. Is it raining there?"

"Yeah. It's been raining since I left Boston."

"It's raining here, too. How was the train ride? I was a little worried you might not get up in time. Honestly, I almost called. But I didn't want to bother you."

Claire laughed. "I meant to call you on the ride, but my mind just kept wandering."

"At least you stayed busy."

"Yeah, freaking out."

Emily smiled. "Are you better now?"

"Not so much better as getting more used to the whole thing. I think knowing where I'm going today helps. So does knowing I'm just five minutes down the street from the office."

"I'm sure."

"I'm relieved I took the earlier train, even if it did put me here well before my meeting."

"Well, I would have strongly suggested against it if you had wanted the later one. What time is your train home?"

"They have a three o'clock, but I couldn't get a ticket on that. So it was 2 or 4 p.m. I don't know how long this is going to last, so I opted for the four o'clock train."

"That was probably a good idea."

"Yeah, I just don't know how I'll occupy myself until then."

"Have you actually eaten anything today?"

"A yogurt for breakfast and a bagel now."

"That's nothing. You should have an early dinner after your meeting. What time do you get in?"

"Around eight."

"Definitely have dinner before you get on the train."

Claire and Emily chatted more about the trip, the weather, the program, and even a few comments about Christmas break. As Claire glanced back down at her watch, she realized she had about forty minutes until she officially had to be at Chase's door. She still had to change into her outfit and arrive early.

"Well, I should probably go change. I think the bathroom is free."

Emily smiled. "Brought your suit instead?"

"Yeah. You were right. You're always right."

"I'm a mother. That's what I do."

Claire laughed softly. "OK, thanks for occupying me."

"Call me after to let me know how it went."

"I will."

"I have a really good feeling about this," Emily said.

Claire was not so sure. But if Emily was always right, then she would take the vote of confidence. She told her mom she loved her before hanging up. She ate the last bites of her bagel, washing it down with coffee. Then she went to the bathroom and was relieved that it was indeed free. She hung her suit on the door and took her heels out of the bag. She stood on her sneakers as she removed the pants from the garment bag and maneuvered out of her damp clothes and into the dry suit, trying desperately to keep her body from falling or anything from touching the bathroom floor.

As she was stowing her clothes into the bag, someone knocked.

"Just a minute," Claire called. She turned to the mirror to check her makeup. She ran her hand along her chin, hoping she didn't have foundation lines. She wiped away a small streak of eyeliner from under her eye and pushed a strand of hair back into place. Then she fished out her mouthwash and swished the minty liquid around in her mouth for thirty seconds. She spit and rinsed away the mess, and finished off her look with a swipe of tinted gloss on the top and bottom lip.

She looked again at her reflection. Claire didn't really like what she saw, but that was beyond her control. Here and now, regardless of weight, worry, and water, she was ready. She took a breath and unlocked the door.

As she walked past the line, she noted a crowd forming. The rain had picked up. She was so relieved she had brought her umbrella. Her umbrella! She had left it by the chair.

"Sorry," she said as she reached by the woman who now occupied the seat. "I think I'm gonna need this."

The woman just stared at Claire as though she was irritating.

Claire smiled back. She began to fear she might be too polite for this city. She supposed she would just have to get over that. Given enough abuse, she could learn to be a New Yorker, too.

Claire pushed open the coffee shop door and stepped into the storm. She still had twenty-five minutes until her interview; just enough time to walk the five minutes to the building, take the elevator, check in with someone, and wait.

She made her way through the crowd, fighting to find airspace for her umbrella. Once inside, she tapped her umbrella several times to dry it. She carried it with her to the elevator and waited with three other people for a ride to the top. They were stopping at floors seven and sixteen. Hers was twenty-one. The last moments allowed for quiet contemplation. She checked her face again in the mirrored walls. For a drowned rat, she didn't look too bad. Finally, the machine dinged and the doors parted. She was met with a long reception desk, behind which an attractive young blonde sat wearing an earpiece. The woman tapped the earpiece, fielding calls, as she signed for a package delivery. She quickly turned to her computer, typing furiously, assuring the person on the other end that she had set up the appointment.

Claire looked down at her watch and noted she was still fifteen minutes early. That was probably too early. Was she making a bad impression by getting there so far ahead of time? Then she wondered if Chase was even there. It was lunchtime after all.

She saw a small reception area to the right where a man was waiting. He was scrolling down on his cell phone with his index finger. He didn't even look up when Claire sat three chairs from him. She pushed on the contents of her tote, trying to keep them from showing over the top. She verified her portfolio was still there. Claire would have tucked her umbrella inside the bag as well but she didn't want to risk dampening her papers.

The receptionist was flirting now with the deliveryman, having finally hung up from her last call. She smiled, then rolled her eyes, reached her hand to her ear, and started talking again. Claire heard her say, "Good afternoon, Marshall's Creatives, how can I help you?" As she tended to the person on the other line, she shrugged and waved sweetly at the deliveryman.

The elevator dinged again and four men walked off. Two wore suits and two wore jeans and button-up shirts. They were laughing. Claire tried to see if she recognized any faces, but she could only see the backs of their heads.

The receptionist reached up to her ear and clicked off the call. Claire glanced back at her watch. Her interview was in seven minutes. She picked up her tote and her umbrella and walked to the counter. The girl looked at her indifferently.

Claire smiled.

"Uh, hi. My name is Claire Kelly. I have a meeting at one o'clock with Chase Donaldson."

The girl opened a page on her computer to check the schedule. "OK," she said. "Have a seat. I'll let him know you're here."

Claire nodded her head. "Thanks," she said gratefully.

She sat back down by the man on his phone. He still didn't look at her. Claire waited quietly, checking her watch every minute or two. Finally she pulled out her cell phone and turned it off. She checked her watch again. The hand hovered at just before 1 p.m.

"Ms. Kelly," she heard.

Claire looked up. The receptionist was trying to get her attention. Claire stood quickly, grabbing her belongings. "Yes?" she said.

"Mr. Donaldson will see you."

Claire smiled and nodded her head.

"It's down there. The sixth door on the left."

Claire nodded again. "Thank you," she said smiling. She was nervous. She suddenly realized she had been calm for the past thirty minutes or so, but now she could vomit.

She passed first through a large open room, divided by short cubicle walls. She saw glimpses of desks littered with colorful toys and silly posters tacked up around the room. Through a wall of windows she could see the sprawling overlook of the city—though a bit dark today. She smiled, trying to remember the view. Then the walkway narrowed and she started slowly down the hall, counting the doors. At the sixth one, she saw his name on the plate.

She stood outside breathing slowly. Her hand hovered in midair just beyond the wood. She could not bring herself to knock. The door across the way clicked open. It startled her.

Instead of looking like a simpleton hiding in the hall, she instinctive hit the door two times softly.

"Yup. Come in." She remembered Chase's voice from the phone call. She was suddenly even more nervous. But she reached for the latch and pressed it toward the ground. She pushed the door inward and there was Chase Donaldson, looking even more attractive in person than in his online company profile.

Claire tried to contain her nervousness and smiled. "Hi," she said politely as she stepped out from behind the door.

Chase sat at his desk but began to rise as she entered. She noted he paused only for a second as he stood. His face seemed momentarily confused. Then he forced a smile.

"Claire?" he asked.

"Yes. Claire Kelly." She held out her hand. He shook it gently.

"Ah, OK," he said awkwardly. "Have a seat."

"Thanks."

She leaned her umbrella up against the wall, draped her coat on her chair, and set her tote on the floor.

"Thank you again for meeting with me."

"Oh, sure. I wanted to meet you. Your samples were good."

Claire noted his enthusiasm was much weaker now. Her samples were *good?* What happened to fantastic? Great? She would settle for *very* good.

"Thanks for making the trip."

"Of course," Claire said hoping she didn't look as though she was trying too hard.

Chase nodded. "Let's get started."

"Great."

"OK, tell me why you want to work here?"

"Well, I think this is a great opportunity to learn the business from an industry leader. It can be hard to transition into a position after college—even an entry-level one—because there's so much competition for these kinds of jobs. This program will give me the chance to continue to learn, but in an actual work environment." Claire smiled, deeply impressed by her answer. She was breathing now and finding herself uncharacteristically composed and collected. "I think it would be the perfect place to prove myself." She shrugged. "And hopefully work my way up."

Chase nodded, jotting notes on a page. He didn't even give her a smile of encouragement. "And why do you want to be a copywriter?"

"I love to write. Creatively. So I didn't want to be a journalist. I considered at one point going to college for creative writing, but my father said I needed to study something a bit more stable."

Chase actually grinned slightly at that.

"But the more I learned about what a copywriter actually does, the more interesting it sounded. And then I got into a program where I started doing it, and I was both enjoying what I was doing and getting a lot of positive feedback."

Chase nodded, making eye contact with his notes instead of her. Claire hoped that was a good sign. If he was writing things down that meant he cared about what she was saying, didn't it?

He asked her to describe a project she specifically enjoyed working on. She rattled off details about a campaign she had developed for a business in Boston. She almost found it comical that her internship at McGill turned out to be the example she was using for a real job.

Chase nodded and made some notes.

"OK, thanks," said Chase. "Now let me go over what you may or may not know about the program. There are four core services that we offer as a firm. The person we hire as the copywriter associate will work with an art associate. They'll essentially be a junior team working under an experienced writer/artist team here at Marshall's. That associate team will be given actual projects and will work the campaign, under supervision, of course. It's a twelve-month appointment and we pretty much want a firm commitment from the associates we hire. We can't stop you from going somewhere else during that year, but many of our associates are actually hired full time after the year—or at least offered the opportunity. The rest usually leave with really great recommendations. Only a few haven't been successful."

Claire nodded.

"So, do you have any questions for me?"

Claire pulled out her leather case and flipped open to the notebook. "Can you tell me what a typical work week would look like?"

Chase nodded. "Sure." He talked a bit about weekly norms, such as staff meetings and mentoring sessions. He also noted the large blocks of free time the associates were given—left to their own devices to sink or swim. "Associates really are staff members and are expected to carry their weight." He sort of winced when he said it. Then he swallowed. "Any other questions?"

She was getting uncomfortable by his lack of interest. He had been so outgoing on the phone. She didn't need flirting but more than rigid civility would have been nice. Where was the guy who offered to be her tour guide?

"Um," she paused, scanning down the list of questions she had prepared. She seemed to be boring him and she didn't know why.

One more and then I'll leave him alone, she thought.

"What type of professional development is available for associates? I mean, besides the one-on-one personal mentoring and job shadowing?"

"Well, we have outside consultants come in at times to do workshops on new software or the latest-and-greatest practices for trends, social media, that kind of thing."

Claire nodded. "That's interesting." She jotted down a small note in her margin.

Within moments, Chase took in a deep breath. "Any other questions?"

She looked up at him, trying to control the expression on her face. She was beginning to feel as though he wanted her out. Maybe he was just rolling the interview along because he had somewhere to be. She desperately wanted to look at her watch because she feared she had been there for less than ten minutes. But looking at the time during an interview was bad form. Instead, she smiled. "I…guess we've covered everything," she said slowly. "Oh," she turned to the back of her binder. "I brought a print copy of my portfolio," she shrugged, "if you—"

"No, we're good. The digital is fine. Better, in fact."

Claire nodded. "OK…sure. Great." She paused, then closed her book. "Well, thank you again for meeting with me."

"Sure. Thanks for making the trip."

She stood, grabbed her bag, and pushed her book back into it. She set the tote on the seat cushion and slipped her jacket over her shoulders. She reached out her hand to Chase. He thanked her again, shook her hand, and watched her leave.

"Goodbye," Claire said as she walked out of the office.

"Bye," he called.

Claire left confused. That didn't go well at all. She couldn't help wondering what had changed his opinion about her so dramatically as to shatter her confidence of ever being selected. She looked down at her watch. It was barely quarter after one o'clock. The interview had lasted less than fifteen minutes. She now suddenly wished she had an earlier train home. Waiting with anticipation as your companion was one thing, but waiting with disappointment was clearly another.

She pushed her bag up on her shoulder and walked beyond the narrow hallway into the open floor plan. Past her went a tall, handsome guy who was roughly her age. He had pretty boy hair, jeans, and a superhero shirt. He looked down at her quickly as he passed and she couldn't help noticing an exaggerated look in his deep brown eyes.

❖ ❖ ❖

Steve Waters, junior art designer, slipped by Claire, barely making eye contact. But he looked her up and down as she went. His eyes bulged a bit. *Who was she kidding? That suit wasn't hiding anything.*

Chase's door was slightly ajar. He tapped on it as he opened it.

"What was that?" he asked crudely when he got inside.

"Huh?"

"That. What I just passed in the hallway."

Chase scoffed slightly under his breath. "I dunno." He shrugged. "*Definitely* not what I expected."

"You're not gonna hire *her*, are you? I thought you promised no fatties."

Chase shook his head.

"What else you got?" asked Steve.

"There's a few others," said Chase matter-of-factly.

"What about that hottie this morning?" Steve asked, remarking on the first interview of the day.

Chase shrugged. "She's not bad." He paused. "I dunno. Maybe. I've got a few more to talk to. There's a guy coming in later who had some pretty good stuff in his book."

Had Chase been a better man, he would admit to himself that he was lying. But Claire didn't meet all of his requirements. He was looking for more than just substance. He had only called in the ones who had the skills; now he had to narrow down the list. He was hoping for a pretty girl or a funny guy. Claire might have been the best candidate but not to Chase. He actually felt deceived. When he Googled her a few weeks ago, he only found one picture. He wondered now if it had even been her. It was a high school track team photo. That girl had been thin, athletic, and super attractive. He did the math. If that was less than four years ago, maybe it was a different Claire Kelly. It was a common enough name. Who gets that fat that quickly?

❖ ❖ ❖

Claire had only gotten partway down the hall when she realized she had forgotten her umbrella, again. She noticed another person carrying one and remembered she didn't have hers. She turned, aggravated. How embarrassing to have to go back in there. She almost considered leaving it.

The door was open a bit more than she thought she had left it, and then she realized Chase was not alone. That cute guy she had just passed in the hall—the one who had looked at her oddly—was inside the office.

What did he mean by "that"? Was he referring to her? She suddenly felt her stomach drop as she heard him go on.

"You're not gonna hire *her*, are you? I thought you promised no fatties."

She felt her hand shaking as she brought it up to her lips to cover her mouth. Her eyes welled with tears.

"What else you got?" she heard.

When Chase said, "There's a few others," she knew she had heard enough. She turned quickly and hurried as fast down the hall as she could go without running. Screw the umbrella. It wasn't worth the high price of shame.

Chapter 12

She tapped the button wildly, trying to summon the elevator faster. Finally it dinged and the doors opened. She stepped inside and quickly pressed the button for the ground floor, hoping to leave before anyone else could get on. She wiped away the tears and reached into her purse to find her tranquilizers. She slid open the small wooden pill box and fished out another pill as fireflies raced wildly in her stomach. She swallowed it with just a bit of spit as she tried her best to hide her shallow breathing and racing pulse. The prescription said to take as needed. If this wasn't a case of necessity, nothing was. The elevator ticked down floor after floor, with Claire praying it wouldn't open until it hit the ground. She was not so lucky.

A man and woman in business suits stepped on at the tenth floor, as she backed into the corner trying to hide. They only rode with her for two flights. When they got off on eight—having barely paid a moment of attention to her—Claire again hoped for a solo ride. To her great comfort, she reached the bottom alone.

She made her way through the busy lobby and out onto the street. Her heart pounded inside her chest and she found herself fighting for air. She had only just recently learned that a panic attack can feel very much like a heart attack. Had she not known what was happening, she might have been really worried.

The rain fell harder on the pavement now than when she entered the building. This time, without an umbrella, the water ran down her cheeks, diluting her tears. She was thankful to have a real reason that could explain away her smudged makeup. She tucked her bag underneath her coat, wiped the rain from her face, and attempted to hail a cab.

She lost three to pushy New Yorkers, but finally one stopped and she yanked open the latch before anyone else could claim it.

"Penn Station," she said annoyed. She was beginning to fit into this city.

The driver took little notice of his drenched passenger's tone. He just maneuvered into traffic and headed back the way Claire had come only a few hours before.

She could feel the water in her shoes and considered switching them now. But since she planned to put on her change of clothes for the train ride home, Claire figured why not wait until she was completely under cover. She sat soaked as the cab made its way further and further away from Marshall's Creatives.

When the car finally stopped at the station, she pulled out her wallet, paid the man, and left. She pushed her way through the crowd and went to the counter. Claire looked at her watch.

"Are there any seats on the 2 p.m. train?"

The woman asked for her final destination and then clicked her computer keyboard. "Yes," she said.

Claire snapped her credit card on the counter. "One, please."

The woman printed out her ticket and Claire signed the receipt. She had already wasted too much money on the useless trip. More, if you counted the suit. At this point, a few bucks to catch an earlier ride was a small price to pay.

Claire took her ticket and hurried to the bathroom. She wanted out of her wet clothes now. She was starting to shiver a bit but that was probably mostly from her wet shoes, or maybe her nerves? She waited impatiently for a large stall and then quickly stripped off each part of her outfit, beginning at her feet. She found frustration made the process even more difficult.

She heard sounds coming over the speaker for the train schedule and she knew she needed to get moving. She folded the suit over itself and threw it in the bottom of the garment bag, which she then folded poorly and shoved into her tote. She could care less if her portfolio got drenched. She considered throwing it out in the street.

What did it matter? She was fat and that was all he saw. Bastard.

He didn't care that she would have been an outstanding associate for the program or an invaluable member of the team. Her father had been right; she just never expected it would happen.

She stared at herself in the mirror as she quickly washed her shaking hands. What was she going to do? She was thin, deep down. She had been thin her whole life. Yet now all the world saw was a fat girl. But honestly, why the hell should it matter either way? She had lost her dress size, not her abilities or her mind.

Was this going to happen everywhere? Claire's forehead knitted deeper in worry. Would she be stuck in some awful job forever because people assumed something about her that was utter nonsense?

She dried her hands on her pants and threw her hair up in a messy ponytail. She left the bathroom and found her platform. The train was already beginning to board. She landed hard in her seat and tossed her bag on the empty seat beside her. She leaned back, shivering slightly in her damp coat, wishing she had worn more than a tee.

When the train began to push forward on the track, she pulled out her cell phone and turned it back on. After the screen initialized, she pushed the speed dial for her mother.

"Hi, sweetie!" said Emily excitedly. "Out so soon? How'd it go?"

"You were wrong, Mom," Claire said harshly. "For once in your life, you were wrong."

"What happened?"

Claire was quiet on the other line, trying to keep her tears away. She couldn't decide whether she was more devastated or angry.

"Claire?"

"I got there; everything was fine. But the minute I went into his office something was off. He went from falling over me on the phone—for my first interview—to suddenly not wanting me there. He spent less than fifteen minutes with me. Maybe ten."

"What happened?"

"I had no idea until I left. I walked by this pretty boy," she said in disgust. "He looked at me like I didn't belong there. But I didn't think anything of it. I kept walking down the hall till I remembered I had forgotten my stupid umbrella for, like, the hundredth time today. I went back to get it, but that jerk was in the room—Chase's office. He called me 'that,' Mom. Like I was a thing. And then he told Chase, 'you promised you weren't going to hire any *fatties*.'" When she said the last word, she almost whispered it.

"Claire, I'm so sorry," her mother said sadly.

"*Fatty*. Nice, huh?" Claire said louder now. "Dad was right."

"What do you mean?"

"The other night he told me he'd noticed I looked different and that I had to watch it because I was going to get diabetes. And he said the world was going to judge me for being fat. How quickly the world forgets I used to be thin."

"He should have *never* said that."

"Why?" she asked defensively. "He's right."

Claire waited for her mother to say something, but Emily knew better than to argue with Claire when her mood had shifted. No logic could cure her and sympathy only made her angrier.

Claire closed her eyes as hot tears streamed from them. She turned her body to the wall of the train, embarrassed for anyone to hear her. "I don't want to be here," she whispered into the phone.

"It's OK, sweetie. You'll be home soon."

"No, Mom…*here!*"

Emily was quiet. Claire had asked her before—for permission to die. Emily could not hear this again, not now, when Claire was so far away from her. "*Claire.*" The word came out almost as a hushed plea.

Claire didn't say anything else. She did not ask again. Emily waited.

"Don't worry, I'm fine." Claire said more firmly, sniffling as she spoke.

"Claire, I don't know what to say."

"No, really. I'm fine," she said.

"I wish there was something I could do."

"But you can't," Claire replied sharply. She felt guilty the moment the words came out.

Emily sat quietly on the other end of the line.

"Sorry, that wasn't fair. I didn't mean…"

"I know you didn't. You know I worry so much about you."

"I know. I'm sorry for being me."

"Don't ever apologize for that. We all love you. So many people love you."

Claire sniffled again.

"You know that, don't you, Claire?"

She breathed deeply, in and out. "Yeah." She sounded unconvinced.

Emily was quiet then, unsure of anything else to say. She so desperately wanted to hug her daughter and take away everything that hurt her. "Text me when you get back to your apartment," she said fighting back her own tears.

"I will," Claire said. "I promise."

Claire was relieved that the girls had already left for winter break. They wouldn't be there to look at her, talk to her, or ask her questions. Claire had just walked in when Jill texted her from Colorado, wondering how it went.

Claire didn't want to talk about it; she didn't want to admit it at all. She just wrote: *Can't tell. Guess we'll see.*

Jill responded immediately: *I'm thinking good thoughts!!!*

Claire texted back a smile but her heart wasn't in it.

She then texted her mother before she forgot, or before Emily sent someone looking for her.

I might stay here tonight, Claire wrote.

I don't think that's a good idea, Emily responded.

I might lay down for a while, Claire lied.

Please call me soon.

I'm tired. Need to shower.

I'm worried about you.

I'm fine. I promise.

I love you.

I know. Love you too.

Then the phone was silent. Emily was likely a nervous wreck at home, but at least she stopped pushing.

A singular thought was on Claire's mind. She went to her room and pulled the insulin pen out from where she had stashed it. She wondered how it would feel. How long it would take. Was it fair to do this during the holidays? Should she do it in her bed? Lay down and just fall asleep?

She was still shivering from the New York rain. Her hands felt dirty. She stripped and walked naked to the bathroom. She stood at the counter, leaning over the sink, staring at her sullen face; white, stained with smears of black makeup; lips and cheeks void of pinkness. Her hair was matted down on her face.

What a grotesque sight you are, she thought. No wonder no one wants you. You're worthless.

In her hand she clutched the pen. Even as her fingers quivered—from doubt or chill—she pulled the cap away. She had watched her father prepare it a thousand times. Click, click, click out the dose and insert. It was that simple. The little silver needle was so delicate, like a strand of hair. Her father always said it didn't even hurt. For that she was thankful. She didn't deserve the pain. She pulled her robe from the door. She shouldn't be found naked. No one would want to see that.

As she held the pen, looking at its tiny little painless tip, she suddenly couldn't breathe. She couldn't see either as tears and thoughts of her mother blocked her vision.

"God, I hate you!" she called out, hoping she was talking to her mind and not her mother.

She hated how incapable she was of action; how weak she was; how childlike. She hated her fears and her sadness and panic. She hated how her illness stole her breath and her emotions whenever it pleased. Most of all, she hated how—at her lowest—the useless whim of hope glimmered. It was a charlatan and she believed it every time. It was all for nothing.

She lifted the pen up, her thumb poised on the flat head of the plunger, her fingers turning white under her quivering grip as her will to push it grew. Suddenly, as if her mother's hand rested on hers, her fingers spread open as she brought the pen down hard on the edge of the porcelain sink, smashing the plastic and glass. After she'd done it, recognizing the shattered plan lay in shambles, Claire began wailing in anger, knowing she had to go on—hating her life, hating herself—out of love for her mom.

She had failed again.

Hyperventilating, her forehead fell down into her hands as a child's might, covering its eyes to count in a game of hide and seek. But she pressed harder than for sport, her confining fingers cupped around the contours of her face to contain the tears. She pulled her hands away once she finally felt the warm blood touch her skin, and she noticed her right palm had been sliced by the syringe. It leaked quickly. Claire hadn't even felt the pain of the broken skin. She stared at it a moment, then turned, suspended from her senses, and twisted on the shower in a lifeless state. As the water warmed, Claire let the robe fall from her shoulders. Her face was blank of expression as her body moved by its own effort into the stall under the piping stream. Her eyes closed, pointed down.

The empty vial was left in pieces in the sink; her salvation seeping out.

The heat felt good on her skin so she kept turning the temperature up more and more. Her open palms were pressed out in front of her against the wall, diluting the blood trailing down the wall on one side. She never worked so hard to think of nothing—to forget tonight, to forget New York, to forget panicking about tomorrow. Then she stopped pretending. Sobbing breaths pulled in mouthfuls of steam that warmed her throat as she pounded her fists against the wall and cried out her frustration. The pain on her skin from the heat of the water felt good as it eclipsed the pain in her heart. She sank to her knees on the shower floor, shaking from nerves as the failure washed over her. She fell back and her hands rushed to her face, hiding her disgrace. The water hit her harder from the longer distance, plastering her hair around her head.

She fit uncomfortably at the bottom. The space was not wide enough to manage her torso and legs, and with her thighs pulled up to her chest, she barely had room for her sorrow. She shifted slightly, resting her cheek against the wall and sobbing softly.

As she lay there her figure blocked the shower drain, and soon she noticed the falling water was accumulating around her. Her mind was foggy from the steam and self-hatred as she watched the water rise, higher and higher. Through clouded eyes, she stared blankly at the glass and wished for the door to hold, promising to sit long enough to drown her problems away.

But as it inched up, she watched it start to leak out. It was a useless solution—like so many other things she tried. Claire finally shifted and the water rushed down the pipes. She leaned her head back against the wall and let the water pelt her, cleaning the blood and the memory of New York from her.

The heat made her dizzy. Her cheeks radiated the warmth and

her fingers wrinkled. Her legs fell open, dead, vulnerable weight. As she gazed up at the falling water, it all finally seemed like such a waste. She pushed herself up, shampooed her hair, and washed her body. She stepped from the shower feeling almost drunk and reached for her robe on the floor. Before she draped it, for the first time in a very long time Claire actually looked at her naked body in a mirror. Her fair Irish skin was deep red from the heat and she realized the irony of being burned twice in one day.

When she was dried and dressed, Claire pushed the clothes she had worn home into her laundry bag. She set the insulin pen pieces in the bottom of the trash and gathered the bags she had packed the night before.

She checked twice to be sure the door was locked and went back down to her car. The parking lot was mostly empty. Before she left, she texted her mother: *Decided to come home tonight.*

Emily's response came instantly: *Thank you.*

Claire wondered if she knew.

As she drove from Boston to Connecticut, drops pelted her windshield. When the rain eventually let up, her wipers only moved every minute or so to clear her view. Claire listened to the music, her face flat and unfeeling. Everything from the night seemed like a dream except for her train ticket on the seat and the cut on her hand.

Then home came into sight. She flipped on her turn signal and drove down the familiar street of her childhood. She parked in the driveway and turned off the engine, stepped from the car and pulled her bags out of the back. As she walked toward the house, the rain turned to snow.

"Mom, I'm fine," Claire said from the stairs when her mother called from the kitchen.

"Are you sure?" asked Emily, drying her hands to rush to help.

"I can do it. I'll be down in a minute."

Claire went to her room, but she didn't unpack. She had a new plan. She set up her computer on the desk and found the website where she could register for the GRE exam, finding an opening just before the end of winter break. She did not bother to ask her parents or pause to reconsider. She just typed in her profile information and her credit card number, and hit submit. Then she went to the AU Graduate School page and downloaded the application. She filled in the basic information and quickly read the prompt she would have to write, before closing her computer and setting it aside. She might not be ready to die, but she wasn't ready to live yet either.

She changed into a pair of gray fleece pants that fit her comfortably and went back downstairs. Her father was watching the news, mumbling something under his breath about a pundit who was speaking.

Her mother was in the kitchen unloading the dishwasher. "Hi, sweetie," Emily said quickly. She set the plate on the counter and hugged Claire a bit too tightly to her.

She lightly patted her mother's back, but barely put in any effort. "Hi," was her response.

"Do you want to talk about what happened today?" Emily whispered in her ear.

"No." Claire shook her head. "Not now."

"OK." Emily nodded her head, lingering her eye contact on Claire's face.

When she let Claire go, Claire pulled a bunch of green grapes from the fridge, resting just inches from her father's insulin case. She then joined him in the living room, slumping into a lounge chair, her legs tucked up underneath her. She began pulling grapes off the stem, eating them one-by-one. Her father glanced at her once and said "hello." She sort of answered him. He didn't say anything else. Emily must have told him.

When she went up to bed that evening, she noticed a missed text message from Kim. It said she hoped the meeting went well. Claire wondered what she should say in reply. For now, she didn't bother to answer. But once she dismissed the message, she forgot to respond all together. Kim never wrote back again during break, and by the time the girls returned to school for their final semester, not one inquired about New York.

CHAPTER 13

Kim reached the top of the stairs and turned left towards the girls' apartment. She sighed, seeing Claire's keys hanging from the door. Claire always did that when she fumbled to unlock the door with an armload.

"I think you forgot your keys," Kim called, as she walked into the living room. She could smell the makings of an Italian dinner and remembered Claire saying something the previous day about lasagna for the family dinner. Family dinners were not what they used to be since Kyra was gone. First semester she had spent most of her time at her boyfriend's apartment. This semester she was studying abroad in London. She had left a week before. At least Kyra's parents could afford to keep paying her rent, so her room became a moderately priced storage closet for Kyra, while giving Kim much-appreciated privacy.

Claire didn't answer until Kim appeared in the kitchen entryway. She saw Claire leaning over a white dish, laying down layers of ricotta cheese, pasta, and meat sauce. Kim secretly loved the meal but groaned slightly thinking of the calories.

"Claire!" She was almost shouting as she tried to catch her roommate's attention.

Claire turned around startled. "Hi," she said finally.

"Hi," Kim answered cynically. "You left your keys in the door, again."

"Oh, sorry."

Kim didn't think Claire seemed all that sorry. She watched as Claire sprinkled the last handful of mozzarella cheese on top and then slid the dish into the oven. Kim studied Claire's outfit as her roommate stood back up. "Claire, what's going on with you?" she said.

"What?" Claire turned once more to face her. She was drying her wet hands on a cloth.

"The clothes?"

Claire seemed perplexed, glancing down her frame. "What about them?"

"How many days a week do you have class on campus?"

Claire was even more confused. Kim knew full well how many times a week Claire had class. They had only been back for two weeks, but the girls had generally memorized each other's schedules. "Three," Claire said as though the question was stupid.

"And how many pairs of gray fleece pants do you own?"

Claire paused for a moment, staring at Kim, deciding whether or not to answer. She turned away. "Three."

"Exactly," said Kim.

"What's your point?"

"What is happening to you? You're wearing the same thing over and over again. And it's sleeping clothes. You never want to go anywhere or do anything, except what you have to do for school. And you've—"

Claire shifted her head sharply to the side, her eyes wider. "What?"

Kim stared at her silently.

Claire spread her arms—shrugging her shoulders—and said angrily, "Finish your damn sentence, Kim! You've obviously got something to say."

"You know what." Kim's voice and gestures were softer now, regretting bringing up the topic at all.

"And you've—what—gotten *fat?*" She emphasized the last word. "Right? Isn't that what you were going to say?"

Kim opened her mouth to reply but lost her nerve and closed her lips.

"Why are you suddenly bringing this up now? It's not like I wasn't fat yesterday."

Kim didn't respond.

"Besides, not like it's actually your business, but you know what? I wasn't always fat." Claire couldn't believe she was unloading like this. Today had been a pretty good day until now. "You all never knew me before college. Before my medications, I was as thin as you! I was still neurotic and really sad, which I still am, so I guess the meds aren't doing a damn thing besides making me fat. But what the hell else am I supposed to do?"

Kim had not expected Claire to open up like this, but once she started, it seemed she just couldn't stop. "I'm fat because I'm depressed and I'm depressed because I'm fat! Now you tell me, what the hell is fair about that?" Claire was hyperventilating, having barely breathed as she berated Kim for her accusation. She tried to control her tears but they overwhelmed her cheeks. "I hate this. And now I'm 80 pounds in! What the hell am I supposed to do?" She was yelling and shaking.

Kim stared at her.

"And you wanna know something else?" The tears started streaming down even harder. "I'm not getting that associate position in New York. Not because I can't do the work or wouldn't be a good employee. No! You wanna know why? Because I'm *fat!*"

"Come on," said Kim. "You don't know that. It's still early." She paused. "And what do you mean you won't get it because you're… because of your…" She couldn't find the right way to end the sentence. "You haven't officially heard, have you?

"Not officially. But I never told you what happened that day. The day of the interview, I left my umbrella in that jerk Chase's office. I went back to get it, but he was in there with someone else—this asshole who passed me in the hall when I left, who went scurrying into Chase's office when I was gone. The way he looked at me…" She paused to catch her breath. She shook her head as though trying to deny the memory.

"What?"

"He said to Chase, 'you're not hiring *that* are you?' And Chase made this awful huffing noise and then the other guy said Chase promised he wouldn't hire a '*fatty*.'" She used air quotes with the word.

Kim wrinkled her face in disgust.

"And Chase said there were others he was interviewing. As though telling the guy not to worry."

"Claire," Kim said more softly, reaching out toward her.

Claire put up her hand to stop the gesture. "He said it. And I left my umbrella, and I left the office and the city, and I came back here. Screw it. They're right."

"No, they're not."

"Yeah, they are. No one's ever going to hire me. I'm going to grad school. I already took the stupid GRE test."

"*You did?*" asked Kim, surprised. "When?"

"Over break. I'd already studied with Jill."

Kim shrugged approvingly. "Well, that's good. You'll do great in grad school."

"And then what?"

"What?"

Claire looked at her angrily, as if Kim had not been paying attention to any part of the conversation. She shrugged her shoulders deeply, thoroughly annoyed.

Kim shrugged back, softer than Claire. "Use the time to lose the weight."

"Oh, because it's so easy. I weigh 215 pounds!" Claire almost screamed. Then she took a breath to try to calm down a bit. "At least the last time I looked. I can't bring myself to look anymore." She wiped away her tears. "I love you, Kim, and I know you mean well, but have you ever been fat? Ever in your life?"

Kim seemed hurt by the comment, sensing it was an accusation. But what Kim didn't understand was that she could never understand. Because the answer was no, she had never been fat.

"It's totally different when you're fat. The world sees you differently. And it's so weird for me because I never was fat. Even now, sometimes I don't even think of myself as fat. Sometimes, I don't really see it either—even in a mirror. Isn't that strange?" she asked smiling, her face contorted by the illusion. "I mean, four years ago I was a size six. Even a four! God, sometimes a *two*! I had a great body." Then she muttered a snide chuckle. "But you know what's funny? I thought I was fat then." She laughed again, as though her youthful low self-esteem was somehow comical.

She took a moment to calm herself. She drew in quickened breaths as she sniffled. "It's the damn medication. And if I didn't have enough to worry about—hating myself with depression— now this," she said pointing to her body. "I feel like I'm suddenly seeing the world from a whole new perspective," she said. "People here at AU only know me fat. You only know me fat. And people I used to know somehow act like I've always been fat. It's not fair." She could feel the tears beginning to build in her eyes. "*I hate it.*" The last three words came out as a soft, shameful whimper, nearly a whisper.

Kim took steps slowly toward Claire and hugged her. This time Claire didn't fight. She just stood in the center of the room and cried on Kim's shoulder.

The only sounds from Claire were a few loud sniffles as she tried to suppress the tears streaming down her face, but Kim could feel the shuttering movements as she huffed and breathed, first letting out the emotions and then working to stop them. Finally, Claire pulled away gently from Kim and stared at her for a moment. Kim wanted to say something, but the girl who always had a comment ready for any situation was now left speechless. Claire smiled weakly at Kim and touched her index and middle fingers to the skin under her nose.

"I need a tissue," Claire said. She stepped to the side and started to walk past Kim. Then Claire paused and turned slightly.

She sniffled again, pulling gently at her pants. "I wear them because they're the only things that really fit," she said shamefully.

Claire went to the bathroom and blew and blew her nose. There was so much snot. She reached for the faucet and splashed handfuls of cool water on her face. Then she pulled the hand towel off the rack and drew it down her face, sopping up the beads of water that dripped from her cheeks and chin. She also wiped around the counter, trying to clean up her mess.

Claire stared into the mirror at the fat girl. She had smudged the little bit of makeup she bothered to put on today. She had saturated a few patches of hair around her hairline with water. Her face was deep red, almost feverish looking. She pressed her hand to her forehead, trying to push out the headache that had formed from the tears. She opened the medicine cabinet and pulled out a pain reliever. She tapped the bottle's neck on her palm and counted out the dose, secretly daring herself to triple it—or hell, take the whole bottle. But instead, she fit the cap back in place and returned it to the shelf. Then she left the bathroom and went to her room where she paired the pain pills with a small tranquilizer.

Claire climbed into her bed and pulled the covers up over her head. She didn't have anywhere to be, so she cried herself to sleep in the middle of the afternoon. At least she was already wearing sleeping clothes.

The next day, Claire got her rejection email. They thanked her for her interest in the job but they had hired *a more qualified candidate*. She promptly hit delete.

She didn't bother to think about Marshall's Creatives again. At least she tried not to. The few inquires she received made Claire curse herself for bothering to tell anyone about the interview. Janet had been the most shocked by the news. Even though the conversation had been via email, Janet wrote back uncharacteristically soon, asking why. Claire pretended she did not know, saying she had only received a form letter rejection. Janet wrote back yet again, asking Claire what was next. She seemed pleased to hear Claire was beginning a master's program in the fall and offered to help in any way she could. Claire thanked her, but secretly she wasn't sure she ever wanted Janet Ellis's help again.

By early spring, Claire checked her mailbox and found a thick envelope from AU's Bailer School for Communications. She was not surprised to be accepted. Although her overall GRE score was average, her verbal score had been relatively strong. Really, what point did the math portion have on her future? Combined with her undergraduate achievements, Claire was a natural graduate student candidate. Still, she remained concerned about the financials of this $36,000 refuge.

Two weeks later, Claire flipped through her mail and found another letter from AU. She pulled away at the sealed flap and flattened out the page to read it.

Dear Claire,

Adams University, Bailer School for Communications, is pleased to announce you have been awarded a Henry McConner Scholarship for Creative Excellence. Funded by the McConner Foundation, the scholarship is given to alumni who plan to further their education at the Bailer School for Communications in one of the five Graduate School tracks. The award is $5,000 per semester, which may be used for tuition, fees, and supplies.

To qualify for the scholarship, you must maintain a 3.4 GPA (grade point average), maintain full-time status (6 or more credits), and remain a student in the Bailer School for

Communications. If you meet these requirements, you are eligible to renew the scholarship for up to four semesters.

Please find enclosed a letter of acceptance for this scholarship, which must be returned by May 1. This packet also includes more information regarding the scholarship, for your reference. Please contact Melissa Bay at the Bailer School for Communications with any questions regarding this award.

Congratulations again on your high achievements! We hope you continue to excel as a Bailer graduate student and wish you the best of luck in your studies.

Sincerely,
Sally Patterson, Ph.D.
Dean, Bailer School for Communications
Adams University

Claire started to cry. She had only just read about this scholarship in the application paperwork, but you couldn't apply for it. The college reviewed all applicants and awarded the money based on the pool. She never imagined she would get one. Claire suddenly felt like a burden had been lifted. Her mind was set on graduate school, but her father had been lukewarm about paying another chunk of money for her education. He had not said "no," but he had not said "yes" either. She was already looking into graduate loans. Now more than half of her tuition was covered.

She called her mother to relay the good news. Emily was probably more relieved than Claire. John had been deeply on the fence about this whole experience. Sure, he valued education, but between tuition and living expenses, this was going to cost him another $60,000, at least. Part of him wanted to complain, but the other half wondered if things would be different for Claire without the mind he might have given her—one he feared passed on through his genes, from his mother. It was the family secret no one discussed. Out of guilt, he stayed silent, too.

During the next few weeks, John and Claire struck a deal. She would get a part-time job to pay her expenses and they would pay her rent and the remaining tuition. The compromise finally let Claire breathe. She knew she could not survive without them—and it was their support that mattered more than their money.

Then school was over. She walked across the stage at Commencement and tried to smile in the graduation photo—though made her mother vow never to buy it. The next day, she packed her major belongings up in her parents' car and sent them home, left alone to enjoy the last few hours with Jill.

"I'm going to miss you," said Jill in between sniffles and misty eyes. She had finished boxing up the last of her things and the movers had already come and gone. Jill's parents wanted to stay to help her move but she somehow convinced them to leave right after graduation. Now her flight home to Colorado was only a few hours away.

Claire smiled, holding Jill's hand. "I know," she said with a melancholy expression. "I'm going to miss you, too. I don't know why you have to go back to Colorado for graduate school. You should have stayed here. You could have been my roommate again."

"I know. But you know my parents. They won't even let me pick my own career. I'm lucky they let me leave for undergrad."

Claire nodded sadly.

"I can't believe you, *Ms. I'm So Not Going To Grad School*. I can't believe you beat my GRE score."

"I can," Claire said smirking.

Jill laughed. "Yeah, me too. What a stupid test."

"Well, what do you say?" Claire asked. "Should we go?"

"Yeah," said Jill. "I'm getting hungry."

She followed Claire out through the family room. They left their keys on the counter alongside Kyra's and Kim's. Kyra had never come back from London. Several weeks before graduation the girls packed up her things for her parents. She was staying for a full-time paid finance internship. Kim had said her goodbyes two days before and had gone to her parents' house. She already had three interviews set up in New York. Claire was heading home herself after she dropped Jill at the airport.

"What are you in the mood for?" asked Jill as she skipped down the stairs first.

Claire thought about it for a moment and then she smiled. "Italian?"

Jill looked back with a grin. "And then maybe a little gelato?"

Had they gotten the exact same table, the farewell dinner commemorating more than two years of friendship might have been the perfect stroll down memory lane. But Claire and Jill found they didn't need a view to mark the milestone.

"I know what I'm not going to get," Jill said reliving her first meal there.

"I think you should. Maybe you'll like it this time." Claire winked.

Jill wrinkled up her face, trying to remember the taste. "I think I'm going to go with a known winner."

"Lasagna?"

"Exactly," said Jill excitedly. She peered over the top of her menu. "What about you?"

"I'm still trying to decide, but I'm thinking the chicken and spinach stuffed ravioli."

"Spinach?" said Jill, making a disgusted face. "Ick."

"Oh, it's so good."

Jill shook her head in disagreement.

"It's good for you, too."

"So is cheese. Ooey, gooey cheese. Mm." She sighed under her breath as she closed her eyes, imagining her dinner.

Claire smiled. "Mine comes with cheese."

"And spinach."

The waitress approached them with their drinks. "Are you ready to order?"

"Yes! Lasagna," said Jill.

"And I'll have the chicken and spinach ravioli."

"Oh, that's a great dish," said the waitress enthusiastically. "Anything else? No? OK, I'll get this out as quickly as possible." She smiled and walked away from the table.

Claire smiled, staring at Jill. "Maybe I should have gotten fish with a spinach side."

"Oh, that's just disgusting."

"That would have been very good for me."

"Who cares about what's good for you when you're having a nice dinner out?"

Claire shrugged and spoke more seriously. "I do. I mean, I have to start doing something."

"About what?"

"The weight."

Jill seemed surprised to hear Claire say that. Claire had never once brought up the subject.

"I…" Claire paused, "…never really told you what happened in New York."

Jill tilted her head slightly. "No. But I know what happened," she said gently.

"What?"

"Don't be mad. Kim told me."

"Why would she—"

"No, I mean, she told me the *whole* thing; the fight and all. I think she didn't know how to help you or what to say. I think she wanted someone to tell her she hadn't been a bitch for bringing it up."

Claire was quiet for a moment. "Kim's been making comments for a while now."

"She didn't mean anything by them."

"No, I know she didn't. It just got frustrating after a while. I didn't do this on purpose."

"Of course not. Neither did I."

Claire looked at Jill as though she was selling herself short. "You're not as bad as me."

"Not by much. How much do you weigh now?"

Claire's face sank slightly. She wavered on answering, but then decided the question was valid. "Last count was about 215 pounds. I've stopped counting since."

"Wow, you don't even look it."

"Oh, please."

"No, I mean, yeah you've gained weight. But I guess because you gained it everywhere, it looks more like 180, 190 tops." She took a drink from her water. "I'm 170ish."

Claire sighed. So the weight on her face was that obvious? She didn't know why she kept denying everyone could see it all. Being fat wasn't something she just imagined. She was—in fact—fat.

"But I've been like this for years," said Jill. "Well, I've definitely put on some weight in college. But I've always had it."

Claire's expression softened now, never really comprehending Jill's struggle with weight. Sure, she was sort of heavy, but that was all Claire ever knew of Jill. Claire's mind instantly played back that thought as she realized how Kim must have felt. How others must feel about her—Claire. They reacted to what they saw. Suddenly, Claire wished she hadn't been so hard on Kim.

"The thing for me is," said Claire, "I haven't always had this."

Jill nodded. "I know. I've seen the pictures of you from high school. It's such an incredible change." She shrugged. "The short amount of time proves it's outside forces. Medicine, stress, all that stuff." She paused. "I wish I had a better excuse."

Claire looked hurt. Was she using excuses to validate the weight?

Jill noticed. "Sorry, 'excuse' was not the right word. Reason?"

Claire tried to smile, but she suddenly just wished they could change the subject. Yet Jill didn't seem offended, just matter of fact.

"I don't know if I'll ever lose it. But Kim was right. You should use grad school to reinvent yourself. Or restore yourself. Or whatever. Make you *you* again, in whatever form that may be."

"I don't know if the old me even exists anymore."

"Oh, of course she does. We all change, but we always keep a part of who we used to be. And we are affected somehow by the change itself. If you can't remember who you used to be, or you won't learn something from the new you, that's when you should start worrying." Jill took a sip of her water.

Claire sat quietly, trying to absorb Jill's words, and wondering what Jill's hopeful outlook on life said about Claire's more jaded one.

"But," said Jill, as she saw their waitress coming, tray in hand, "that Chase guy was an absolute dick for passing on you, and I know one day he'll come to regret it."

Claire smiled now, appreciating Jill's honesty, her support, and her ability to change the subject.

"Oh, that's beautiful," said Jill, as the lasagna plate was placed before her. Claire closed her eyes as she took in a deep breath of her own delightful dinner.

Jill cut a generous bite with her fork and slipped the food into her mouth, savoring the taste with quiet sounds and exaggerated facial expressions. "I truly don't care if this makes me fat. I love it."

Claire smiled again. She tasted her own and almost wanted to agree with Jill.

"And we're not," said Jill, pointing her fork towards Claire, "repeat not, skipping gelato after this. I'm not going to see you for a while. You can diet tomorrow."

Claire laughed. "Deal."

CHAPTER 14

Emily knocked softly on Claire's bedroom door. Claire lowered her book to her chest and invited her mother in. She had been a college graduate for just a few days, but sitting back in her childhood bedroom she still felt like a kid. At least her mother respected her enough to knock.

"Hi, sweetie, can we talk?"

"Uh, yeah. Sure." Claire slipped an index card into the book and sat up on her bed. "What about?"

Emily held a few pages of paper in her hand. She took a deep breath before speaking. "I've been doing some research and I talked with my doctor." She handed the pages to Claire. "I really want you to take this."

Claire stared skeptically at her mother and then took the pages from her hand. She turned them so that she could read the title at the top. *Bipolar Diagnosis Screening Test.* The confusion on her face deepened. "What is this?"

"You may not have just depression."

"You think I'm bipolar?" Now she stared at her mother as though Emily was the crazy one. "I'm not that bad." She held the test back out to her mother.

But Emily put up her hands. "Just read it. I thought I knew what 'bipolar' meant, too. I was wrong. You may not fit what people generally think it is—there are various types. I never knew that. You probably have more moderate mania, which is why you were misdiagnosed as having depression. Depression is your dominant symptom, but not your only one. From what I've read, that matters in treatment."

Claire sighed loudly, annoyed by her mother's suggestion.

"Just take it," Emily said more firmly as she stood up from the bed and left the room.

When she was gone, Claire tossed the papers on the floor, disinterested in anything the test had to say. She picked up her book again and opened to the white index card. But she found the story less interesting now, since she could barely keep her mind focused on the words. After rereading the same page seven times, she finally set the book down—wide open—and picked up the test from the floor. She grabbed a nearby pen and began reading the questions one by one, thinking honestly about the answers as she went. At the end, she graded her test and was stunned by her score.

Bipolar disorder? What the hell did that mean? She felt her breath tightening in fear as she suddenly became a completely different person in the matter of a moment. In hopes of making some sense of it all, Claire pulled out her laptop and searched for the topic on the web. Of course she had heard of bipolar disorder, but it was about out-of-control, even dangerous people who hurt themselves or others. They don't take care of themselves. They lived in institutions or on the streets. They're called "crazy" and "nuts" and "psycho."

She wasn't that. The wild fireflies came back to her stomach. She panicked more and felt faint tears welling at the corners of her eyes; terrified she would be trapped by something else that would keep her down, something else to hide.

As she wiped away the thick liquid uncontrollably streaking her cheeks—and tried to calm her breathing—she slowly read page after page on the illness. The tears continued, softer now, while she consumed the words and tried to make sense of the distant feeling of comfort that might live within them. Maybe her mother was right. All of the sites said there were two types of the disorder—and one was like her: mostly depression. She was also surprised to read about successful people—writers and actors she knew of and admired—who had it, too.

The calm began to settle more and her breathing became somewhat rhythmic as she slowly read the lists of symptoms, comparing resource sites and finding the same words, the same indications, traits, and concerns repeated again and again. Things she recognized. Could it be that the devastation, self-hatred, anxiety, and fear that had consumed her days and nights for these past years had a real name—a cause, no less? Not just a doctor stuffing her troubles into a diagnosis that might fit her—but finally one that did? It could explain why sometimes she still felt good, even on depression medications, and sometimes she still felt so bad, even on depression medications, that she wanted to die.

Did this mean it wasn't all her fault?

Hope, her fickle friend, tiptoed and teased as it always did. Then the reality came.

She typed into her browser the medication name she had read over and over again on all the sites. She had heard of lithium before without knowing anything about it. If it was the most popular drug for bipolar disorder, would she end up on it?

How would it change her?

And then the tears welled again as she read.

Third on the list of side effects, just after dizziness and nausea: moderate to extreme weight gain.

She hurried to other sites, searching the documents in a weak anticipation that the first source had been wrong. But the others parroted it; some even discussed the subject in greater detail, making Claire begin to feel dizziness and nausea without a prescription.

When would she ever escape this hell?

She glanced up and saw the senior year photo from her track team. Her face was so slender. Toned arms peeked out from her jersey shirt. You couldn't see her torso or legs from the back row, but her prom picture beside it told the rest of the truth. Claire was thin. That was four years ago. Now she sat oozing on her bed, stuffed in carbon-copied outfits—sleeping clothes, no less.

Claire put her computer away and turned back to reading her book. She barely made it through two pages before she slammed it shut in anger, unable to concentrate on a single line. Realizing she had forgotten to mark her space, she hurled it across the room. It hit the door and bounced backward to the middle of the room. Claire stared at it for a minute and then turned over on her side and cried softly into her pillow.

Why could nothing be easy?

Emily knocked softly about an hour later. It was dinnertime. She had called three times for Claire with no reply. She entered the room without Claire's permission and found her child sleeping in a ball on the top of her covers. She picked up a book lying on the rug in the center of the room and placed it on the desk by Claire's bed. Then she saw the quiz on the floor. She reached down and scanned the answers. When she flipped to the back page, Emily saw the score. Honestly, she was relieved to see they might have finally found the answer to this impossible question. But Claire's inaction and the test haphazardly tossed aside told Emily that Claire was resistant. Perhaps she didn't believe it. Emily, too, had been surprised at first by the notion. But then she did her research. She discovered much of what she assumed about bipolar disorder was not accurate. She learned that the illness affected everyone differently. It didn't mean anything until they could root out how it affected Claire.

Emily didn't regret bringing up the subject. Claire might be in her early twenties, but she would always be Emily's little girl. They had to start facing this. The gamble wasn't worth it.

She placed the quiz on the desk as well and lightly tapped Claire's shoulder. Claire jumped softly out of her slumber and rolled over to see her mother. She hadn't realized she was asleep and blinked for a moment to remember where she was.

"I guess you're back to being right, Mom," Claire said quietly when she saw her mother.

"About what?"

Claire looked down towards the ground for her quiz but it wasn't there. She turned her face up and saw it on her desk. She didn't remember leaving it there. But that was not where she left her book either. "Did you already see?"

Claire wasn't stupid. "Yes," Emily said.

Claire's face was unimpressed.

"It's good news."

"How is this good news?" Forgetting for a moment the stigma of the diagnosis, all Claire could think about was transferring from one weight-gaining medication to another. She had secretly hoped some day she would go off meds all together. Now she feared she might never be free of them.

"Isn't it better to have an answer?"

"What if you don't like the answer?"

"Those are two completely different things."

Claire exhaled loudly.

"Come on, Claire." Emily tapped her leg. "Dinner's on the table. Come eat."

"I'm not hungry."

Emily looked at Claire, tilted her head, and sighed. "I know you're upset. Just come eat a little. You need to get out of this room for a while."

Claire thought about it for a moment. "Fine," she said. She didn't want to go, but she feared being left alone. She would rather argue with her father about something or listen to her mother about anything than stay in her room and eavesdrop on her own mind.

A week later, Emily drove a reluctant Claire to a psychiatry appointment. She came along because she wanted to be sure Claire went. She also had lots of her own questions. But at the doctor's request, Emily waited out in the lobby while Dr. Ethan Blake spoke with Claire alone.

Dr. Blake was a kind-looking man dressed casually for a doctor. His khaki pants were paired with a pale blue Oxford shirt, which matched his eyes perfectly. The top button of the shirt was undone. Claire guessed he was in his mid-forties despite his forgiving skin warding off wrinkles. His full head of brown hair was well trimmed, his face was clean shaven, and just a faint hint of clean soap scent was present. On his bookcase sat a few photos of a sweet family, with three young blonde boys who resembled their mother more.

"Claire, I think you have bipolar disorder all wrong," he said.

"Oh yeah, why's that?"

"Because you think it's impossible."

She stared at Dr. Blake, wondering if her thoughts were that obvious. She tightened up a bit, trying to control her expression.

He smiled. "I'm not saying it's easy. I just mean it's possible to live a fulfilling life with this." He pointed at her. "Look at you."

She wrinkled up her face, trying to decide exactly what he was seeking to use as an example. Or worse, wondering which of her flaws he intended to discuss.

He raised his eyebrows and tilted his head. "What?"

Claire shrugged. "I don't know what you mean by that."

"I mean how successful you are."

She scoffed slightly under her breath.

"You don't think so?"

She shook her head.

"I do. You're a talented young woman. You've been successful in college. You are in control of your behaviors, for the most part. You don't abuse drugs or alcohol. You ask questions, you don't mask problems." He gestured toward the door where her mother sat outside. "You have a strong family relationship and you don't push that away. I don't think you understand how incredibly powerful and important that support system is."

She breathed more quietly now, listening to the words Dr. Blake was saying and trying to believe them.

"I sense something deeper than this diagnosis is troubling you. What is it?" he finally asked, noticing the bit of fear in Claire's face.

She shrugged.

"Don't, Claire," he waved his fingers gently, gesturing towards himself. "Don't hold it in."

She bit her bottom lip, contemplating whether she should be honest with him. He was still a stranger after all. "This isn't me," she finally whispered.

"What do you mean by that? What's not you?"

"This," she said, separating her arms out to reveal her body.

He stared at her confused. He never made guesses.

"*This,*" she said again, more forcefully. "*This body!*"

His lips and cheeks softened as he nodded his head, having registered her complaint.

"*Four* years ago," she held her fingers out for emphasis, "I was 80-something pounds less than this."

He pulled his lips in on themselves and continued nodding.

"I mean, sure I don't eat that well. Yeah, sometimes I eat bad things. I use chocolate as a substitute for my tranquilizers sometimes." She laughed cynically. "I don't know what's worse for me."

"Claire, it's not uncommon for some medications to cause weight gain. You're not alone there. Especially the last one you were put on. It would be a great drug if it didn't switch off the little lever in your head that says 'I'm full.'"

Claire looked away. "Well, I feel alone."

"I know."

She stared up at him, wanting to tell him that last statement did not make her feel better. It sort of pissed her off. "Why, are you mentally ill, too?"

He exhaled quickly, sort of smiling. "No." He shook his head. "I can't really understand exactly what you're feeling. But I've been doing this for a long time. I can see the pain. I know you're not making any of this up."

She was surprised by how moving that statement was. She actually believed him.

"What are you worried about the most?" he asked. "I can tell you have lots of questions…as you should. It just seems like something specific is heavy on your mind."

What a choice of words. She breathed out. "What do I have to take for this?"

"Treatment?" he asked.

She nodded her head.

"Well, therapy is always useful. You're going to have to learn what your symptoms are, how they affect you, and how you react to them. Then you will learn how to counteract them."

"That's it?"

"No," he said. "I also want to put you on a medication."

She groaned.

"What's that for?"

"This," she pointed at herself again. "This is from medication."

"So, that's what's bothering you? Claire, not all medications react the same for everyone. Unfortunately it's a lot of trial and error. It's a struggle for the patient and the doctor until we can find what works best for you."

She stared at him skeptically. "I don't want to go on lithium," she almost whispered. Tears were forming in her eyes.

He looked at her gently. "That's OK. I wasn't going to put you on it. Lithium isn't a bad drug. It brings a lot of comfort to a lot of patients. It has a pretty long history in this field, though it has its side effects." He paused. "But it's not the only one out there. And new drugs are developed all the time."

Claire's eyes looked at him sadly. His kind smile creased lines around his eyes, seeking to put her at ease.

"There are actually two types of bipolar disorder—or you may have heard it called 'manic depression,'" said Dr. Blake. "I don't know if you knew that. Bipolar I is defined by high manic and separate depressive episodes. Patients generally experience explosive energy, grandiose feelings of invincibility, and sometimes even psychosis—which is a break from reality. This can result in bad choices and sometimes painful consequences. Conversely, they experience periods of depression. Both states of bipolar I high and low mood shifts may leave the patient unable to function properly. It's the classification of the illness that the general public often thinks about when it hears the words 'bipolar disorder.' But even those presumptions aren't necessarily accurate. Violence, for instance, is not specifically part of the experience, but it's often thought to be." He took a breath. "The other type is bipolar II, which I'm sure you've deduced by now is what I am diagnosing you with. What bipolar I and bipolar II share is severe and sometimes debilitating depression. What separates them is the manic state. In bipolar II, patients experience hypomania, which is a lower form of mania. Hypomania can manifest somewhere on a long scale of severity based on the patient or even the episode, on what we doctors call a 'spectrum.' Symptoms can be some of the ones you've described: anxiety, less need for sleep, a more euphoric mood, or increased energy. Unfortunately, while both are serious conditions, bipolar II is often misdiagnosed, and patients are treated solely for their depression, like what happened with you."

He paused, looking to see if Claire was registering what he

was saying. While she was quiet, she seemed to be listening. He continued. "The problem is," he smiled softly again, "well, one of the problems, is that depression medications generally make bipolar symptoms worse. Depression medicines are designed to elevate a patient. You don't need elevating. Your moods need stabilizing. Unfortunately, because the manic symptoms of bipolar II can be less obvious than in patients with bipolar I—and this hypomania may even be considered a positive or *welcomed* experience if it leads to bursts of useful energy—then patients with bipolar II disorder may not discuss their elevated episodes with a doctor. Or, sometimes, the doctor just fails to ask. So, while your health care provider believes he or she is helping with depression treatment, it actually just makes the bipolar II symptoms worse, and the patient doesn't understand what has changed."

He smiled again at Claire, who looked at him wearily, trying to process the long lesson she had just been handed.

"That's one of the hardest parts of my job…"

Claire waited for him to continue—to lay the blame on his crazy patients.

"…when patients are too afraid to share their whole story because of the stigma of what they feel they have or who others fear they are. You are not a bad person if you suffer from a mental illness, Claire. It's a medical condition. No different from any other health issue."

Claire's face revealed a look of doubt.

"But you had been asking about treatment," he said, perking up. "I am going to start you on an antipsychotic medication."

Her eyes widened.

"It's OK, Claire. It sounds scarier than it is. You are not psychotic. Personally, I've never liked that term."

She was unconvinced by his attempt to reassure her.

But he continued. "And I understand completely that the side effect of weight gain is distressing to you. I can respect that. At this point, we'll work together, observing closely to see how you react to new medications. This one may or may not affect your weight."

Claire sighed.

"But if it does, we will watch for that. Medication is an important part of the process, but it does not have to be a detriment to your overall health." He stood up and walked over to the built-in wooden cabinet along his wall. "I'm going to give you some samples. I want to make sure you don't have any type of reaction to the medicine before you pay for a full prescription."

Claire was upset to be here now. Upset with her mother for making her come. Upset with Dr. Blake for not being able to suddenly make things better—to make her different.

He pulled out several small boxes and brought them back to her. She noticed they were varying doses. "First, you need to wean yourself off your anti-depressant. Cut the dose in half for the next week and then take just the morning dose for a week. After that, you'll start the smaller dose of the new medication for ten days and then begin the higher dose," he said handing her the boxes. "I'll write it all down for you before you leave."

Claire nodded as she somewhat listened to him.

"Once you start this new medication, you should notice any adverse reactions in that period of time—if you're going to have them at all. Make notes of how you feel while on this. Then I want you to come back in about six weeks and we'll talk again, all right?"

Claire was still nodding, trying again to hold back her tears.

Dr. Blake smiled at her again. "You're going to be OK, Claire." He paused. "Perfectly OK."

Claire stared to cry, soft tears that traveled gently down from the corners of her eyes and slipped beneath the curve of her chin. She couldn't say anything; she just kept nodding.

+ + +

When she got home that night, Claire took only one half of her usual nightly pills and she made a promise to herself that she would begin watching what she ate. Dr. Blake said this medication only might affect her weight. Maybe it wouldn't. And her medications were definitely not solely to blame for the weight.

The next morning, Claire started small. A low-calorie sweetener in her coffee and cereal instead of sugar, Dijon mustard instead of mayo on her turkey sandwich, more vegetables instead of potatoes on her dinner plate, and a tiny sliver of dessert instead of two large pieces. She also pulled out her sneakers that first day and went for a slow jog around the block. She was huffing when she came home but it felt good to be moving again for the first time in a long time. That night she rested on her pillow, feeling surprisingly relaxed and at peace. She couldn't help but smile at the slight ache in her leg muscles. That meant it was working.

During the next few weeks, Claire weaned herself off her old drug and nervously began the new one. She tracked her dosage and moods in a notebook, and she tried to stay busy to keep the worry away. Three days a week she tutored high school juniors in need of support if they hoped for a college acceptance letter. When she felt up to it, Claire jogged occasionally, each time going a little faster and a little farther. The sit-ups and stretching also became easier. Despite her efforts, she probably could have been doing more. But caring at least somewhat, and seeing somewhat of an improvement, was more than Claire had known in a long time.

On days she lounged around the house or exercised, she wore stretchy shorts or jersey Capri pants. When she tutored or went out in the real world, she hid behind forgiving summer dresses that fit loosely. Maybe it was denial or maybe it was hopelessness, but eventually she stopped paying attention to her weight, avoiding mirrors that revealed her form beneath her neckline.

She was too preoccupied to worry about it anymore as she slowly began to panic about the start of fall term.

Shortly before her next appointment with Dr. Blake, Claire lingered in front of her closet staring at her clothes, organized by size, not color or kind. She stood nearly naked in her panties and bra. As she slid the hangers from side to side, debating what to wear, she paused to notice her bare flesh. She pinched a clump of her belly fat. It was still fat—she was still fat, sure. But maybe she didn't seem as fat.

Was that possible?

She had been ignoring everything for so long that she skipped over noticing her dresses were somewhat more comfortable and her running pants no longer showed lumps or lines. When she undressed, her stomach was generally free from the unsightly marks caused by clothing bands fitting too tightly. It seemed absurd to hope—it had only been a few weeks since she went off the old meds and started the low dose of the new one. She had not been exercising that much and she still snacked.

Curiosity fueled her hand as she reached deeper into her closet and pulled out a shirt that had not fit in nearly a year. It was a size fourteen, which on its own was not amazing. She took it off the hanger and slipped it over her bare shoulders. The fabric met at the middle of her chest with enough give for the snap to close comfortably.

It fit.

Claire took a long breath as she turned to stare at herself in the mirror. There was only a small bulging space between the snaps and she could not see any rolls in the back. She tried not to get too excited, but she ran quickly to the bathroom. She peeled off the shirt and stood on the scale. She watched eagerly as the machine flashed three times and then the number appeared: 201 pounds. Claire had not been tracking her weight since the scale read 215 pounds. But after stopping the depression medication completely, she had lost nearly fifteen pounds! Claire's palm quickly covered her mouth as she registered the number. Hiding behind her fingers, she smiled.

Who knew such little pills could weigh so much?

<h1 style="text-align:center">CHAPTER 15</h1>

To his credit, Dr. Blake had not misled her—so far. The new medicine didn't seem to negatively affect her in any way. It was not halting the progress of her weight loss, though it did not seem to have a profound effect on her mind, either. Maybe she was expecting too much from it too quickly. After all, he said she would need to increase the dosage, which she had just done. In a few days she would be back on his couch for an evaluation. He had earned her trust with his honest and gentle tone. She liked him very much now. She truly believed, for once, that someone other than her mother cared. What she valued the most was that he listened and regarded Claire's own self-observations as vital to her care. Too often, doctors disregarded her expertise into the life of Claire Kelly.

It was after midnight that Thursday evening when Claire felt truly different. She had been erratic in her sleeping habits lately, which aggravated her father most of all. She was not trying to be difficult, but some nights she just wasn't tired. Besides, she didn't have to get up early for work like him. John often directed his daughter to go to her room just to find some quiet in his house. Claire sometimes complained and would not go to sleep right away, or at all until the early hours of the morning. Other times she would break him down until he grumbled and told her to at least keep the sound of the television low. She told him if he installed a satellite connection in her room, she would watch it there. He warned her not to push her luck.

But for the past few days they were gone on an impromptu trip to Maine visiting college friends. She was elated to have some quiet time, with the house to herself so she could make all the noise she pleased.

Tonight, though, she was restless and distracted. Her stomach fluttered. It was a relief no one was there or she might lash out in anger as her mood drew back in trigger tension. The one thing she craved was sleep, but it wouldn't come. Her mind was dancing quickly between thoughts of memories and thoughts of death, so simply as though they were all valid. It kept her rigid and her eyes taped open wide. Already dressed for bed, Claire finally clicked off the useless television and climbed the stairs to her room, but nothing there could distract her; not unanswered emails, a pending text, or the most recent paperback novel she had started. Not even her own writing could focus her. The memories were fading as the bad thoughts expanded their reach.

Your life is meaningless. You are nothing. Just die. Do it!

She climbed into her bed, now wishing her parents were there; someone was there. Someone to hear her still awake. Someone to ask her what was wrong. Someone to pry and push and stop her. Stop the thoughts. Someone. There was no one. No one who understood. No one could make sense of this nonsense. No one crazy was here but her.

She stared at the clock wanting to cry but she couldn't. She was too blank to make the sadness come. The void felt deep and wide. The not caring was hollow; the scariest of all. The clock read two o'clock. The moon was caught behind her tightly drawn shade, but she knew the nocturnal thinking meant she was reverting to the hovel of depression: awake at night and asleep in the day; the way she had been in high school those times when the depression was at its worst. The days she disappeared. The days she heard her mom cry and saw her dad's fear.

They couldn't understand; who could? No one normal could; not the people with complete brains and circuits that flowed straight and sharp. She needed the broken ones like her who knew how it felt to feel faulty.

She laid on her back and stared at the ceiling. She thought of nothing because she couldn't keep up with the thoughts. She let them race on their own and stood out of the way. If she closed her eyes tight, she could halt them slightly in concentration on her facial movement. But after a moment, the thoughts would catch their footing and start again.

She tumbled out of bed and clicked on the light, crawling on her carpet to the bookcase by the door. She realized she was crying slightly now.

Do it! Die! Nothing is worth this!

The thoughts were louder; so distinctly different from voices. They were her own inner voice barking orders.

Why? Claire wondered. Nothing had changed. She was fine. She was improving.

Her vacant look gazed forward as the tension in her mind began forming roots of a headache that sprouted in her forehead and traveled to her temples. The pain made her dizzy. The hot tears rolled down her cheeks in distinctive spheres, breaking halfway and following the canals of her face to her nose. It mixed with the thin snot that began running from her nostrils.

She was looking for nothing in particular as she pushed the physical books from side to side, staring blankly at their spines. Then she rested her index finger at the top of one and drew it out.

She opened the pages of *Ariel*, having never finished the book in her life. Tonight she envied Ms. Plath. Claire turned the pages trying to read, but each collection of words made her sadder without even comprehending them. She knew their meaning simply by knowing their creator.

The book quivered in her hands until she finally released it and it fell to the carpet, flipping closed. Claire pulled her legs up to her chest and began sobbing hard. Saliva filled her mouth, stitching together her lips by threads of spit as her mouth opened to release the sorrow. She rocked and wailed in the empty house. For once, she didn't even care about her mother. She cared about silence.

Something had changed. What had changed? How could a sea of possibility turn into a cliff?

Why did she care? How could it stop? How would she do it? Pills?

Pills!

Oh my God, she thought quickly. The pills!

She dashed from her bedroom floor, hastily wiping her warm tears and sticky snot. She breathed deep breaths as she ran toward the bathroom. Forcefully whipping open the cabinet, she snatched the boxes of samples from the shelf and tore open the sealed ends. She madly pushed the line of pills out of the foil until she had a mound of them on the counter.

She was still learning, but she couldn't do this anymore. She couldn't listen to Dr. Blake or her mother. This was right.

Pushing the pills into her hand, she paused for just a moment before wrapping her fingers tightly around them so as not to lose even one.

She was not a child. She was a grown woman still figuring out who the hell she was. Mistakes were mistakes. Fear was fear. Death might be peace.

But not tonight.

She tossed the little pills into the toilet and pushed down to flush them away. They might have helped—she might be too impulsive. But tonight impulsiveness was warranted because irrational thoughts were inching toward reality.

Shaking slightly, Claire went back to her room and picked up her cell. She hoped she had not been wrong. Dialing his office line, Claire left Dr. Blake a message. She tried to sound upbeat as she explained the episode, beginning with, "Don't worry, I didn't do anything…but I wanted to." She told the empty line that she knew it was a symptom. The only thing that had changed was her dose. "I'll see you Tuesday," she promised.

As Claire disconnected, she wondered two things. First, would Dr. Blake be mad at her for trashing the pills? Second, should she have saved them and gone back down in dosage?

Dr. Blake called her back first thing Friday morning.

"Claire, I got your message. Next time, you need to call the emergency line. That wasn't just an episode. It was a side effect. What happened could have ended very differently. You handled it, but it could have been worse. I need you to promise next time you won't try to do this alone. I said we are doing this together. On-call doctors are on call for a reason." His scolding was gentle but weary.

"I'm sorry. I thought I could handle it…I didn't want to have to go somewhere," she said quietly.

"I get that, but you have to be honest with me or we can't figure this out. I will trust you if you trust me."

"I'm sorry."

His concern was quite parental, and after he took a few breaths, he continued. "I want to push up your appointment to later today. You obviously have no pills left, so we need to get you on something to keep you stable. I can fit you in if you can come at two o'clock."

"Yeah, I can."

He breathed deep again. "OK, then we will continue our original plan. As I said so much is trail and error. We will need to switch you to a different medicine."

"OK."

He was quiet then, obviously regaining his composure. "You were lucky, Claire, and I don't like luck. But you were also observant. I like observant patients. You should be proud of your self awareness. Don't lose that, OK? Keep your eyes open for negative change. Medicine is suppose to help not hurt you."

She nodded. "OK."

"All right. Then I'll see you at two."

"I'll be there."

She was in his waiting room by quarter till, and he called her just before their appointment. As she sat on his soft leather couch, her fear of lithium resurfaced. She had worked so hard up to this point.

"Don't worry, Claire," said Dr. Blake, when she expressed the concern. "I'm still not going to put you on lithium."

"You're not?" she asked desperately, fighting back the beginnings of a panic attack.

"No, I told you, there are lots of other medications that I think will help you. Honestly, I would never prescribe lithium for you."

She sat up a bit in her chair. "You won't?"

He shook his head. "You've had problems with your thyroid in the past. Lithium can affect the thyroid, so it's not worth risking."

Claire stared at him nervously, listening intently to his words, fearful that the next option might be worse.

"I think it's time to try an anti-seizure medication."

Claire's face scrunched up.

"Yes," he nodded. "Some drugs have promising results for patients with conditions other than those the drugs were developed to treat." He headed to his locked cabinet, rifled through a shelf, and pulled out small packages again. "And I'm not making any promises," he said as he turned. "Because as I said, medications behave differently for all patients. But in my experience, this is a weight neutral drug."

"What?" Claire whispered weakly as she sat on the edge of the couch. "You mean it won't add weight?" Her tone was pathetic. She could feel a knot in her throat. She was almost afraid to believe him.

He nodded, handing over the new boxes of samples. Then he sat and jotted down for her the schedule by which to take them.

Claire's eyes were wide, her mouth covered by her hand. She was quiet, trying to register his words. With closed eyes, she drew in a deep cleansing breath and released it slowly, trying to convince herself to believe Dr. Blake's words as some of the tightness in her chest disappeared.

"I want to see you again in six weeks." He was writing down notes in her chart while she sat staring at him. He looked up when he finished and smiled. "And I want you to keep as vigilant as you have been, Claire."

She remained quiet.

"I'm here to help you through this. You are not alone. But no one is a better advocate for your health than you."

Unfortunately this new drug also caused an adverse reaction when she upped the dose—an overwhelming itchiness that might only be cured if Claire ripped off all of her skin and scratched.

She called him directly. "Stop the drug now," said Dr. Blake. "You probably have a sulfa drug allergy." He paused, obviously reading something on the other end of the line. "Let's see…we can switch your appointment to tomorrow instead of Friday. Would that work for you? Ten o'clock?"

"That's fine," she said. Her frustration was growing. Claire was exhausted by all of this. It wasn't Dr. Blake; it was her—her body, her mind, her bad fortune. But she went, somewhat against her will, because she had no other choice.

Claire's skepticism in finding something that would work for her wavered her faith, but she was calmed by her trust in Dr. Blake and his unwillingness to give up on her. His third suggestion, also for seizures, was recently approved for treating bipolar disorder. "But the results have been promising," Dr. Blake said.

Claire went home again with more small boxes of samples. During the next few weeks, she nervously took them, tracked them, and talked about them. The waiting was excruciating because all she expected was them to fail as well. She began to fear nothing would ever stabilize her.

Then the pills did something that none of the others had done before. They worked.

While her symptoms and her fears remained, the sharp edge of them lessened and no new ones occurred.

"They will never go away, Claire, you do know that, right?" Dr. Blake asked at their final appointment before school began. "Your symptoms, I mean. Our goal is to lessen and control them."

She nodded.

"Now you have to learn how the illness specifically affects you. Keep reading. Keep talking. And keep taking those," he said, pointing toward the written prescription in her hand.

"I know," Claire answered quietly.

During the last days of summer vacation, Claire tried to find some peace. Her anxiety was calmed somewhat as the details slowly fell into place for graduate school. She had secured an apartment just off campus and landed a graduate assistantship with the university's Alumni Association, working for the organization's marketing manger. As a private school, the post did nothing to help her tuition payments, but it alleviated the hassle of finding a job to pay her bills that would not interfere with her classes.

Probably most important in her twenty-something mind, Claire watched the weight continue to slip away, now that the old medication was far behind her. She had reached an astonishing 178 pounds. It was somewhat shocking to realize how much she had lost in a summer. She could not blame all doctors, but she could blame her doctors. How could they let this happen? She divided her anger between them and herself—she never should have accepted their answers. If not for her mother and Dr. Blake, where would she be? What life would she have?

Her mind was clearer and more steady, and the fat was disappearing, but it was heartbreaking to stare at the scars from it all. Faint red stretch marks along her hips, her stomach, her breasts, her arms, and the entire circumference of her thighs tarnished her delicate twenty-two-year-old flesh. She might be somewhat better, but she could never forget.

CHAPTER 16

When she moved back to Boston in August, Claire brought with her a collection of clothes that ranged in size from ten to fourteen, depending on the brand. She suddenly found herself with a wider range of options and a greater sense of worth. She still felt fat, but she no longer felt hopeless.

Living alone, she found herself eating less because there was less in the house to eat. She also didn't have to hide her eating, and as her shame diminished so too did her need to consume to calm her fears. When she found herself feeling overwhelmed, she took one of the new little white pills that Dr. Blake had prescribed for bouts of anxiety, and they helped.

The only thing Claire had a hard time cutting out were her frothy drinks at Solace. She still lived only a few blocks away and often found herself in an oversized chair in the corner, craving some type of human contact, even from strangers.

A month into the semester, Claire was cuddled there, blocking out the music and bustle with her devoted attention to Jane Austen, when she heard a quiet voice that broke her attention.

"Is this seat taken?"

Claire looked up to see a brunette with chin-length hair looking curiously at her. The short girl's eyebrows rose high, creating a look of sunshine to her face, while the tilt to her head suggested she might be shyer than she let on.

"Uh, no," said Claire, as she pulled her bag from the seat and placed it on the ground beside her.

"Thanks. I wouldn't have bothered you but this place is packed."

"No, it's fine," said Claire. She had tuned out the background so skillfully that she failed to realize the crowd. "It gets this way."

The girl nodded and sat down carefully in the seat, trying not to spill her tea. "Are you a regular?" she asked with a smile. She pulled her cup up to her mouth and blew on the liquid.

"I guess you could say that." Claire grinned, looking affectionately around the room. "I love it here."

"Do you go to AU?"

"Yup. You?"

"Yeah. I just started my master's program."

"Yeah, me too. But I also went here for undergrad."

"Oh, cool. I went to a tiny school in Rhode Island. I'm from Rhode Island." She shrugged.

"Connecticut," said Claire, pointing toward herself.

"I'm Ella Reed," said the girl, leaning forward and extending her hand.

Claire reached out and shook it. "Claire Kelly."

"What are you studying?" asked Ella, drawing the hot tea up to her lips for a timid sip.

"Master's in communications, specifically advertising."

"I'm in the communications program, too," Ella said once she had swallowed. "For PR."

"Oh, great," said Claire. "I guess we have a little something in common. How long is your program?"

"Two years. Aren't they all?"

"I guess, technically. But I was able to use some credits from undergrad since I went here as well, and by taking extra classes and summer school, I should be able to get out next August."

"You're ambitious," Ella said smiling.

Claire chuckled softly. "More like easily bored and over achieving."

Ella nodded, still smiling.

"Where are you living?"

Ella shrugged again. "I didn't know the area or anyone here, so I just did graduate housing."

Claire smirked. "How it is?"

"It's OK. More like a dorm with a kitchen. What about you?"

"I have a tiny place just off campus."

"Do you like it?"

Claire shrugged and smiled softly, too. "It's kind of like a dorm with a kitchen."

Ella laughed. "Any recommendations for fun close to campus?"

"That depends on your idea of fun. Bookstores, coffee shops, museums, even restaurants, I know. I can tell you a few bars, but not really from experience. As far as the big party scene, you've come to the wrong source."

"Because you're ambitious," said Ella smiling.

"More like a big nerd."

Ella nodded, accepting the answer. "I was looking for the other things anyway. I'm a big nerd, too. I guess we have two things in common."

Claire liked Ella instantly. She was smart and easy to talk to. Since most of her friends had up and left her—considering she didn't have many friends beyond her roommates—Claire figured she could stand to make a new one.

"I think you're right," said Claire. "Anytime you want to go out for a quiet dinner or bookstore browsing, you let me know."

Ella laughed. "That's sounds good to me."

Claire woke one morning toward the end of the semester, less hindered by a need for sleep, another positive change she had noticed since ceasing her depression medication. She readied easily and ate a small yogurt for breakfast. Then she slipped into her shoes, tugged her lightweight white jacket up over her shoulders, and grabbed her purse. The jacket had not fit since her second year of college, so wearing it now felt like another small victory. She had been forcing herself to go to the school gym occasionally, though she wished she could be more dedicated to the task. Unfortunately a *task* was exactly how it felt. She didn't enjoy a moment of it. Because she was still many pounds more than she wanted to be, she felt awkward and uncomfortable. She had to keep reminding herself that she used to be many, many, many pounds from where she wanted to be.

The first time she stepped into the gym, she surveyed the room and sensed the beginnings of a panic attack, as though everyone was watching her. Of course that was not the case. Yet, even as a size six, Claire squirmed a bit whenever she thought people were looking at her. She was no longer a size six, but despite her anxiety, Claire continued to exercise. The weight was coming off slower now, but that was her fault, not the medication.

She checked herself over quickly in the hall mirror before leaving for work and shrugged at the sight. She was getting there. She glanced down at her watch. She was late! She hated being late, yet somehow she always was. She rushed out the door and jogged down the stairs, debating whether or not to take her car. Since she didn't have class that night, she opted to walk to campus.

She shivered a bit in the breeze when she reached the street. But it was too late to change her mind. She figured a brisk pace would warm her against the cool fall air. She loved the sunshine on her face, and with each hurried step she felt a little warmer. She barely noticed the people she passed and soon she saw the gray stone building come into view. Claire looked at her watch again and released her rising tension with a deep breath. It was only 9:52 a.m. and she would be upstairs in less than five minutes.

She took off her jacket as she reached her floor and walked in as though she had intended from the time she woke up this morning to arrive at that very moment.

Aaron looked up from the front welcome desk. "Morning,

Claire!" he said with an enthusiastic smile.

"Hey, Aaron," she replied kindly as she passed. He was a sweet kid, though a bit needy.

She checked her watch again: 9:56 a.m.

Four minutes to spare, she thought proudly as she turned the knob to Amy's door and pushed, but it was locked. Amy wasn't there. Claire grinned at her stifled triumph of making it to work on time only to have it not really matter. But honestly, Amy never cared if Claire was a few minutes late. That was the advantage of being a graduate assistant. She hovered between a student worker and a full-time employee, with more responsibilities than the kids but less than the adults. Still, it didn't hurt that Amy liked Claire. She appreciated her drive, her creativity, and her willingness to pitch in, no matter the assignment. She even trusted Claire enough with a spare key to her office, which came in handy on mornings such as these.

Claire had been working on updating the Alumni Association's website when she left the day before, so she figured she would pick up where she had left off until Amy came back. Her work consisted of a range of marketing-related projects and odd jobs for Amy Dean, marketing manager for AU's Alumni Association. It was sort of an appropriate place for Amy, being an AU alumna with a marketing degree. She was in her early-thirties and had never left the campus. If she had her way, she probably never would.

Claire enjoyed the ease of her job, which paid her living expenses but never really expected too much; meaning the work she created was always met with delight. She wondered if that was an indicator of her exceptional abilities or lackluster former assistants. Erring on the side of optimism, Claire decided to agree with both assumptions.

She tried to remember if Amy had complained yesterday about a "week of wasted minutes." That was what she called busy times when she had more meetings than anything else. It happened every once in a while and she seemed to be particularly aggravated those days. Claire wondered if the week before Thanksgiving break would be better or worse for Amy.

Claire finally finished the last web updates and glanced at the clock. It was just before noon, which meant Amy would not be coming back for an hour. She was a stickler for taking her whole lunch break.

Claire bit into apple slices while she sorted Amy's stack of files. Her boss was annoyingly obsessed with paper and printing. Claire never understood why she wouldn't move things into digital folders, but Amy worried all the time that she would lose something. Claire shifted the documents back and forth among the growing piles, then punched holes at the long edge and put them into the massive binders. The ones for fall were already getting thick. She snapped the last set of rings shut and closed the cover, before heaving them back to the shelves. She quickly checked the closet to examine Amy's supply bin and saw the binder stash was gone. With nothing else to do, she walked down to Ann's desk to place an order on her boss's behalf. Claire had learned that Amy was notorious for forgetting to mind the little details such as supplies, but often developed an attitude when she did not have them. So far, Claire had only witnessed Amy's outbursts but was never the subject of her rage.

"Hi, Ann."

The office assistant looked up at her name. "Hey there!" Ann was always happy. Not an annoyingly happy person, just a happy person. Claire wondered if she was ever sad.

"Has Amy placed a supply order recently?"

"No," she said slowly. "Why?" She almost looked nervous. She was often someone who suffered when Amy was mad.

"Not a problem—yet," Claire said with a smirk. "So a crisis has been averted."

Ann breathed out quietly. "What's she need?" She was ready with her pen and a yellow notebook.

"Binders."

"Of course."

"She also seems to be going through a lot of sticky notes."

"Anything else?"

"I think the pad in her portfolio is low and I didn't see anymore of those either."

"Sure thing."

"That's probably it, for now anyway."

"OK. I'm happy you said something. I went to ask Amy this morning for a list because I planned to place an order today and was nervous when I realized she was out sick."

"She's sick?" said Claire. "I thought she had meetings."

"Nope."

"Huh… OK, thanks, Ann."

Now Claire had to figure out what to do for the last two hours. She looked down the hall and saw Laura's door was open. Laura had been at the university less than a year, managing outreach to major alumni groups along the east coast. Laura had not graduated from AU. She went to school somewhere in Maryland. Claire knew Laura had worked in public relations and marketing for a while in D.C. as well as New York. It was her husband's Ph.D. program at AU that brought her to Boston. Claire really liked Laura—the little she knew of her, anyway. Though Claire thought she was sort of quiet to be doing a job that required outgoingness—not that Laura couldn't talk to strangers; not that she was shy. She just seemed to be more of a thoughtful professor than a pushy communications staffer.

Claire stood by Laura's doorway and debated whether or not to bother her. She seemed to be staring intently at her computer screen.

"Damn it," Laura groaned quietly under her breath. She

banged her mouse hard on the desk in frustration, as if that might miraculously solve her computer glitch. She caught a movement in her line of vision and looked up.

"Sorry," said a sheepish Claire. She had never seen Laura get mad. "I was just…I didn't know if you needed help with something since Amy is out."

"You know anything about PDFs?"

Claire shrugged. "Such as?"

"I need to make a letter into a PDF and put it with all these other PDF forms, and then email the whole thing out," said Laura, distressed by the monumental task.

"Oh, that's easy," Claire replied quickly without thinking.

"Is it?" Laura asked.

Claire smiled softly, realizing she had inadvertently insulted Laura with her comment. "It just takes a second. I can show you."

"Please," answered Laura willingly. She pushed away slightly from her desk so Claire could reach the keyboard.

"I can do it, no problem, or I can show you if you want."

"Oh," said Laura. She seemed intimidated at the thought of technology.

"It's very simple, I promise."

"OK."

Claire walked Laura through the few steps in each program. "And that's it," said Claire, as the pop-up menu prompted Laura to give it a name.

"Wow, that is easy."

Claire grinned. "I told you."

Laura smiled a look of technology triumph as she clicked the keys to name it. "I wish these forms could be something people could type on." She looked up. "You don't know how to do that, do you?"

Claire nodded. "It takes a little more effort, but it's not hard."

"Really?"

"I can show you that as well, but it's somewhat more involved than a few clicks."

Laura wavered. "I guess not then, I have a meeting in a few and I have a lot of paperwork to do today, but I really want this out by tomorrow."

Claire thought for a moment. "If you don't need it this absolute second, I can do it for you today and then show you some other time."

"Really?" She was excited, probably more for the help than the lesson.

"Yeah. Like I said, I don't really have anything to do."

"Let me email it to you right now," she said clicking the keys on her computer to attach the file. "How long are you here until?"

"Usually three o'clock."

"Wanna do a little research for me as well?"

"Sure," said Claire enthusiastically.

"This is great! I need to figure out some venues for major upcoming alumni networking events. If I give you some areas, can you see what you can find out for menus, pricing, space…that kind of stuff?"

"Yeah. Of course."

"Oh, this is great! I'm so happy Amy's sick." She paused. "That came out really wrong."

Claire smiled. "I know what you meant."

Laura nodded. "OK, the PDF stuff sent. I'll email you some details on the events as well. Whatever you can find would be helpful."

"Sure thing." Claire waved quickly as she left and Laura thanked her again.

When she got back to her desk, Claire quickly fixed the forms and sent them back as individual files as well as one big document.

Then she began searching the web for restaurants in Boston and New York, following Laura's emailed guidelines. She gathered a long list of links for hot spots and methodically charted out their highlights. Before she left at three o'clock, Claire sent a four-page document that was organized, formatted, bulleted, and bolded.

She went from work to Solace for a few hours of coffee and comfort. She was nestled in her favorite chair at 5:22 p.m. when her phone dinged. She reached to check the message.

Claire,

You are in a word: Awesome! The forms are perfect (you're making me look good!) and the list is outstanding!!! Thank you so much! Come see me ANY time you are looking for things to do. I have plenty that can keep you busy!

Laura

Claire smiled as she typed a quick message back: *Happy to help!*

She was happy to help. She had a feeling Laura DeWitt might be a good person to know.

CHAPTER 17

Claire hated admitting when she needed things, but she was relieved to have found a friend in Ella. Sure, she had friends in her classes, but Ella was different. She was easy-going, easy to laugh, and fun. She had been a school spirit fan in college and had spent her last two years as an RA. Ella's generally upbeat personality reminded Claire of Jill, which gave Claire some comfort. She missed her undergraduate roommates, Jill most of all. She was the first to admit that realization shocked her. After all, during college Claire had wanted her own space. Now that she was alone, all she wished for was company. Ella agreed and the two cursed their leases.

"What are those?" Claire asked when she saw travel brochures on Ella's tiny counter.

They had just one more day of classes before Thanksgiving break and then a short leap until Christmas. This dinner was their celebration for making it through most of their first graduate semester and for having individually completed their final projects. But mostly, they just enjoyed cooking and not eating alone. Ella looked up from the stove. "I want to go somewhere for spring break."

"That's like five months away."

"I know. I'm just looking right now. I want to go somewhere fun. Somewhere far away—somewhere you have to take a plane to reach."

"Why's that a stipulation?"

"I've never flown before."

Claire was shocked. "Really?"

"I was one of five kids and I was the youngest. It was too expensive to fly all seven of us anywhere so we didn't. We always drove."

Claire nodded. "OK. That makes sense."

"And I've never gone away for spring break."

"Really?"

Ella chuckled. "I keep surprising you."

"No, it's just—no, it's not uncommon. I guess I take it for granted. I mean, I've never gone on big wild trips with friends, just away with my parents." She reached for the stack and sifted through the glossy pages. "London or Hawaii," said Claire. "Wow."

"What?"

"No, they're just really different."

"So, you've never been to either?"

Claire shook her head.

"Wanna come with me?" Ella nodded excitedly.

Claire look up at her and shrugged. She thought about it for a moment. "Sure, I'd love to go to either place. I just can't afford it." She paused. "How are you paying for it?"

"I've been saving a little every month for years. I knew I'd eventually have enough to go. Spring break is the perfect time."

Claire agreed and secretly wished she could go, too. Spring break had never really felt like spring break with her mom and dad in tow. Unfortunately, going to London or Hawaii was not going to be cheap. Her assistantship covered her credit card and some spending money. She tried to save a little each month, but it was precious little. She couldn't go blow the meager sum on a trip, and frankly, that sum would cover almost nothing.

"Would you at least think about it?" Ella asked, spooning the chicken and its sauce from the pan.

Claire looked down again at the brochures and then gently nodded her head. There was no harm in thinking. "Who will you go with if I can't?" she asked.

Ella placed the plates on the table and shrugged. "No one, I guess."

Claire was stunned by the answer. She would never go on a

vacation alone. What fun was a vacation shared with no one? The thought made her sad.

"So, you'll think about it?" Ella asked again gently, as she pulled out her chair and sat down across from Claire.

"Don't hold your breath," Claire said. "But yeah, I'll think about it."

Ella nodded. "I hope you like this dish. It's one of my favorites."

"It smells great," Claire said as she reached for her fork. She cut off a bite and ate it. She gave Ella a smile. "It tastes great, too."

Ella beamed. "I'm so glad you like it. But save room for dessert. Chocolate cake with double chocolate frosting!"

Claire smiled and struggled to contain her sigh. She had been trying so hard to watch her weight and now frosting was taunting her again. She ate her chicken slowly, straining to fill up on something not awful in hopes of having an excuse to give Ella that was not entirely false. But as she reached her last bite, Claire watched Ella jump up and snatch the cake from the counter. She proudly set it on the table and lifted the lid to reveal a lovely confection.

"It's my grandmother's secret family recipe."

Claire sighed loudly.

"What?" Ella asked, concerned by Claire's lack of interest.

"It's not you. It looks amazing!"

"But?"

"No, I'll…I'll have a piece."

Ella seemed offended now. "What's wrong?"

"It looks so good," Claire said finally, after staring at the pedestal.

"I've seen you eat desserty things before. I thought you liked chocolate?"

"I love chocolate." She paused. Claire wondered if she should say anything. If she were to estimate, Ella weighed 5 or 10 pounds more than Claire. But just a few months before, Claire had a good 30 on her. "I'll have a piece. I will. I want a piece. But I can't have a big one, OK? I'm trying to watch what I eat."

"Oh. Yeah, I should be doing that, too. It's really hard. I put on like 20 pounds in college and I've been too lazy to lose them."

Claire smiled. "I put on 80."

"What?" Ella exclaimed before she had a moment to think it through. "I mean—I'm sorry, but—what? How?"

Claire smiled. "It's all right. If you'd told me senior year of high school that my senior year of college I'd be 215 pounds, I would have had the same reaction."

Ella was shocked. "*Eighty pounds?* How is that possible?"

"The short version is I went on a depression medication freshman year. I put on about 30 or so pounds from that. But the medicine wasn't really doing anything except making me fat, so my doctor put me on a different depression medication, and then an additional supplemental drug that was supposed to stop the side effects of the other one. But those were even worse. The combination of stress, depression, eating because of stress and depression, and of course the meds themselves, meant in four years…well, 80 pounds."

"Four years? Jeez. How did you—I mean—what'd you weigh now? I weigh about 180. You have to weigh less than me."

"Right now I think I'm 171."

"Wow, 215 to 171," she said, mentally playing with the numbers. "That's 44 pounds. Obviously you stopped the medications. When was that?"

"About four months ago."

Ella was shocked again. "You lost 44 pounds in four months?"

"No, about 38 pounds in two months. The rest is just coming off a little slower."

"Two months? Jeez, I need your workout routine."

"But there's no routine. Like I said, it was just going off the medication, and maybe a little less stress eating."

"That's crazy!" Ella burst out. "So, you're not depressed anymore?"

"I was never just depressed." Claire paused for a moment, debating her next words. "I have bipolar II disorder," she said finally.

Ella seemed sort of confused as though the thought was impossible. "Oh," she said flatly. Then Ella remembered only a moment before she used the word "crazy" and she was suddenly very embarrassed.

Claire had heard it, but just smiled quietly to herself. The more she learned about the disorder, the more she realized it explained a lot of the things she had been feeling. No matter how stigmatizing the diagnosis happened to be, Claire was slowly becoming relieved by it and less embarrassed of it. She wasn't crazy. And each time she admitted it out loud to someone, it was easier to say. She would rather have a cause and regain some control over her life than live the life she was living before. "It's not exactly what you're thinking," she said.

"I'm not thinking anything."

Claire grinned. "Sure you are. And it's OK. There's a lot about mental illness that people don't understand."

Ella was listening intently as Claire spoke, trying to knit together everything she was hearing. She was certainly surprised to learn this about Claire. She seemed so normal.

"I'm perfectly capable of taking care of myself," Claire continued, "and of being successful in life. There are just things I have to deal with—like hating myself sometimes, sadness sometimes, lingering guilt, and occasional mood swings that the meds can't stop. The anxiety is the worst," said Claire. In a way, it sounded so contradictory. She said the words casually as though they were not hard. "What?" she finally asked, noticing Ella's face reacting to her.

"You have anxiety?" Ella paused, almost embarrassed. Finally she said, "I do, too. I have a pill I'm supposed to take when it gets bad."

Claire nodded, the corners of her mouth slightly curved in an understanding smile.

"I've never told anyone about it," Ella whispered.

Claire tilted her head and sighed. "That's part of the problem. No one talks about it and we're left thinking it's just us."

Ella placed her elbow on the tabletop and rested her chin in her hand. She was quietly thinking now, looking slightly off to the side.

Claire picked up her fork. "OK, I said I want a piece of your grandmother's cake and I meant it. Just don't make it a big one. The fat wasn't all the pills' fault."

Ella looked up and smiled. She rose and grabbed two small plates from her cabinet and a knife from the drawer. She set the plates down on the table and slowly pulled the blade through the center of the cake. She transferred a small slice to the plate and handed it to Claire. "My grandmother always said good things should be enjoyed in moderation," Ella said. "I guess that includes cake."

The next morning Claire climbed the alumni office stairs and wondered if Amy would be in. She wasn't. Claire considered pulling out homework or school reading, but she didn't really have any to do. Had she known the day would be empty, she would have brought her style guide and spent time studying. In truth, though, she really wasn't comfortable using work hours for personal assignments, even if everyone else did.

She checked her school email, but there was no message from Amy. Claire debated if she should bother her boss with an email when she really had no idea what was keeping Amy away. For all Claire knew, she was curled up in bed with a cold, hung over a toilet with the flu, or pampering herself with a faux day off. But Amy didn't seem the type to play hooky. Claire decided an email couldn't hurt. Amy didn't have to reply, but at least Claire would have made the effort.

Hi, Amy,

Sorry to hear you're still sick. I hope you're on your way to feeling better. I finished the web updates and the filing yesterday. Then I asked Laura if she needed help with anything, which she did. If you get this and think of something you want done before you get back, just let me know. Otherwise, I'll keep asking around the office.

Claire

She went out to the mailbox cubbies in the main office and collected Amy's mail. She returned and placed the envelopes in a neat pile on Amy's desk. Claire figured her boss would appreciate the gesture. Then she walked down to Laura's office. The door was open.

She knocked gently on the doorframe and Laura greeted her with sheer enthusiasm. "Amy's still out?" Laura heard her own voice and smiled sheepishly. "God, I keep sounding so pleased. I swear I like Amy."

Claire chuckled. "Yup, apparently she's still out. I have no idea what's wrong with her or if she'll reply to my email. I figured until she gives me an assignment, I'm available to help you."

"Are you sure you don't have any projects you need to get done for class?"

"Nah," said Claire. "My night class tomorrow was canceled and I have all of my other assignments done through the end of the semester."

Laura seemed impressed. "Nice. And you're going home for Thanksgiving?"

"Yeah."

"Where's home? When are you going?"

"Home is Connecticut, less than three hours away." She shrugged. "I was going to go after work tomorrow, but with Amy sick, I'm debating if I should come in tomorrow or not."

Laura scrunched her nose and shook her head. "I wouldn't. I'm not even going to be here tomorrow. I'm traveling to Maine to my husband's aunt's house. She suckered everyone into going up there." She rolled her eyes. "But she's getting older and he used to spend summers up there as a kid. He feels obligated to visit now." Then she brightened a bit and held up her finger. "Plus, letting him get his way for Thanksgiving means I get to decide our Christmas plans."

Claire smiled. "Where in Maine?"

"Bar Harbor."

"At least it's pretty up there."

"Yeah, I guess so. But it's getting cold."

Claire shrugged. "Unfortunately it's getting cold everywhere."

"That's true." Laura placed her open palms on her desk. "So, you're up for helping?"

"Sure, anything."

"Anything?" She looked somewhat devilish.

Claire nodded.

"OK. It's annoying, but I have filing that absolutely must be done soon. I'm months behind."

"Sure."

"And then I have these invitations that need to be done. Have you ever used a mail merge?"

Claire nodded. "A few times."

"Awesome. I think I'll set you up here at my desk for the printing because I have a meeting. If that's OK with you?"

"Of course."

Laura breathed a sign of relief. "This is going to be so helpful." She lowered her voice slightly. "I was going to ask Aaron to do it, but—and no offense to him because he's a nice kid—he's just a bit sloppy and absentminded. He did one other mailing for me recently and he got through the whole thing—printed, stuffed, and sealed—and then he realized he forgot to include the RSVP envelope! For the entire mailing! All 300!"

Claire covered her mouth with her hand. "Oh, no!"

Laura nodded, smiled, and raised an eyebrow. "Yup. I had to reorder all of the main envelopes, reprint them, and I took them home and did them myself. I'm just thankful I hadn't given him the stamps yet."

Claire couldn't help but laugh, which made Laura smile, as she shook her head.

"This new one's 500. I just can't risk it."

"Just to be safe, why don't you make up one sample packet for me," said Claire. "Just as it should be. And I'll follow it."

Laura nodded. "Good plan." She quickly assembled the pieces and then opened the computer file for the merge.

As the printer consumed the first crisp white envelope, Laura checked her watch. She turned to a box by the bookcase near her desk. Inside sat a pile of papers and various packages of colored stock. "I also need copies of these. I doubt you'll get to this, but since you seem interested in things to do, I'll keep you busy." Laura smiled. But as she looked over the individual pages, she seemed to almost regret mentioning the project. "I dunno, maybe this should wait. I mean, I want these things on different colored paper, and some are stapled to each other, but not all, and the packet itself is loose. You know, don't worry…" The sentence sort of trailed off and she seemed torn.

"You could do the same thing as the invitations…make a dummy set," Claire suggested. "I mean, if you want. You could use small sticky notes to indicate the colors and clip together the ones that should be stapled. Then just put it in the order you need."

Laura knew she could avoid the work if Claire had time to

do it. Besides, she figured she could trust Claire. She mulled over the idea for just a moment before quickly agreeing. "OK. This project is last—you know—if you have time." Laura gathered up the pages and marked their colors. Then she clipped together the necessary pages. "And these are the ones you staple."

Claire nodded.

"Of course, the paper's in here," she said tapping the box. "And then I guess you can just line them up as individual packets and make a big perpendicular pile," she said as she laid her hands on top of each other in opposite directions. "But like I said, don't overload yourself trying to get it done. I won't be back until after two o'clock because I have another meeting after lunch."

"OK."

"What time do you leave?" Laura asked.

"Three."

"OK. I should see you before then." She snatched her leather binder and placed a folder on top, grabbed her keys and small wristlet, and took a cleansing breath. "You're a huge help! Thank you so much." Laura smiled and gave her another devilish look. "I like Amy, but I'm really glad she's sick."

Claire grinned. "I'll be sure not to tell her that," she said as Laura waved and buzzed out the door. She watched Laura turn left down the hall and heard a final chuckle in the distance. Claire smiled to herself and secretly wished Laura was her boss; not that Amy was a bad supervisor or disapproved of Claire's work. Laura just seemed to appreciate her more. Even though Amy liked Claire and depended on her, she never once expressed interest in Claire's future. Deep down, Claire hoped that Laura might one day repay her kindness.

She loaded another set of envelopes into the printer's tray and punched holes in the final stack of papers to file. When the cabinet was again lined with neat displays of binder spines, Claire opened and checked her email. Still seeing no message from Amy,

Claire comfortably returned to her tasks for Laura. She laid out assembly piles on the floor and began forming a collection of invitation components, mindful of direction and quality. Three times she found cards improperly printed and set them aside in the discard pile. She hoped Laura had ordered a slight surplus.

Once she made a sufficient start to the project, Claire took a generous handful of printed envelopes. She kept a detailed eye on their progress as well to be sure the addresses were not crooked or upside down. She found only one mistake and placed it by the keyboard for reprinting. When the stuffed envelope pile began tumbling over, she knew it was time to seal and stow away.

Claire was pleased by her progress when she suddenly realized her shift was over. All of the envelopes were, at the very least, stuffed, and a third of them were glued. She decided anyone could finish this project—even Aaron would be hard-pressed to screw it up. As she wrote a note outlining what had been accomplished and what remained, Claire realized she had expected Laura back before now. After clipping the rejects together and placing them by the note, she checked her email one last time. Still seeing no message from Amy, she signed out of her account and shut Laura's locked door as she went.

Ann was standing in the hall. "Will you be in tomorrow?" she asked.

"I'm thinking no. I have a feeling Amy might not be in again and Laura already said she won't be." Claire shrugged. "When I mentioned it last night, my mom seemed to like the idea of having me home a day early."

Ann nodded and leaned in. "Good idea," she said. "I wouldn't come in either, if I was you."

"So, I'll say 'Happy Thanksgiving' now, I guess."

"Oh, you, too!" Ann chirped. "And then, in a few weeks, you'll be one semester done, right?"

Claire nodded. It seemed shocking and a great relief at

the same time. The idea of graduate school had initially been intimidating. On the very first day of school it hit her: graduate school was just a few more semesters of study, without the mandatory general electives she had never liked.

She was feeling more confident lately, even though the scale hovered in the 170s range. Changing her meds had taken half the weight, and Claire could feel a new lightness—not only in her body but also her mind. She didn't fear mirrors or people as much as she once did. She was even hopeful that she might soon fit into her former wardrobe—and maybe her sapphire ring. She could replace cheaper versions of everything but that. Claire wondered if her brighter outlook could be attributed to her new diagnosis and treatment, or to her slimming waistline. It was probably a bit of both.

Claire was a little disappointed to learn that her emotions were so intertwined with her appearance. She thought she was more evolved than that.

Perhaps someday I'll move beyond this, she thought. But in a society so dependent upon beauty, Claire couldn't fault herself too much for wanting to blend in. Especially since this whole experience had been thrust upon her in an almost forceful fashion, leaving her desperate for something more than air—it left her yearning for understanding.

As she closed her bag and pushed her purse up over her shoulder, Claire surveyed Amy's office one last time. Claire insisted that Amy's room should be in perfect condition for her return on Monday. She glanced down the hall as she walked away from the locked office; Laura still had not returned. Claire left holiday tidings unsaid and headed to class. She nibbled on a sandwich as she crossed the campus and finished her drink in her seat. She could have gone anywhere for the break before her class or she could sit in the room and think of absolutely nothing. For a mind that never slowed down, such a prospect was irresistible.

When her professor arrived, Claire was pleased to learn he had almost read her thoughts. The entire class vowed to stay on point and skip their break in order to get out at least an hour early. He kept his word. Claire was driving home before six o'clock, and to her great relief, snowflakes were her only distraction.

CHAPTER 18

"Tell me more about Ella," Emily said. She was standing at the stove stirring the gravy for their Thanksgiving dinner.

Claire sat at the kitchen counter flipping through the pages of a cooking magazine. She knew the low-sugar cranberry recipe she was making for dinner was somewhere in there; she had forgotten how much lemon juice to use.

"Well, I don't have any classes with her, but we've actually signed up for one together this spring."

"Do you do a lot together?"

Claire chuckled "She's boring like me."

"You're not boring."

"Yeah, I am. But it's OK. Maybe that's why we both have really high GPAs."

Her mother smiled.

"We talk about books. We go to movies. We've made dinner for each other a few times. We hang out at Solace. We talk shop, you know, because PR and advertising are similar disciplines. We keep saying we have to go workout together."

Emily looked up.

"Because we both want to lose weight. I weigh about 10 pounds less than she does."

"That's a great idea," Emily said. "A motivation buddy."

"Right," Claire continued. "But we've gone maybe twice. I guess we don't have enough motivation between the two of us to bother. I just hate going alone."

Emily was quiet for a moment. "How are you doing with everything else?"

Claire looked up from her magazine. "What—school or weight?"

Emily shrugged. "School, of course. But, yes, weight. Moods. Meds," she said gently.

Claire sighed. "Well, I'm a little stressed with school."

"Are you pushing yourself too hard with condensing the major and your assistantship?"

Claire shook her head. "No. I like my job. I think working in the alumni office could actually help me get some contacts after I graduate. I secretly search online for the names of alums who graduated with communications degrees, to see if they're big now."

"Found any?"

Claire smiled. "A few. Maybe at the end of the spring semester I'll see if my boss will let me email them." She shrugged. "Who knows? What some call stalking, I call networking."

Emily chuckled. "Are you maintaining the weight you've lost?"

"Mostly. I'm bad sometimes. But I try."

Emily nodded. "Your father and I are very proud of the progress you've made—with everything."

Claire shrugged.

"What's that for?"

"I'm still not where I want to be. It's not really anything to be proud of."

"Of course it is. You're making big efforts with the little things, which is how you're going to see big changes in the long run. You're thinking positively about the future, which I can tell you, you haven't done in a long time."

"Yeah—sometimes."

"Are you still depressed?"

"Sometimes."

"When? Are you writing it down?"

"No."

"You should be tracking that, Claire," Emily scolded. "You promised."

"I didn't really promise. It's all up here," she said tapping her temple.

Emily tilted her head disapprovingly. "You need to learn how the disorder affects you."

Claire gave a weak grin.

"What?"

"I just love when you call it a 'disorder,'" Claire said sarcastically. "I feel so crazy."

"You're not crazy. You have an illness. It's not your fault."

Claire looked up. "It's depression, Mom. Instant feelings of fault and guilt are prerequisites."

Emily's face softened. "Do you really believe that?"

Claire smiled. "It's a disorder. Belief is in the mind of the beholder."

Emily looked skeptically at her daughter.

"Don't worry," Claire said as she closed the magazine. "I've read all that stuff you and Dr. Blake gave me. I know it's not my fault. I know it's a lifelong thing. I know it will come and go. Blah. Blah. Blah. I'm rooting for more highs and less lows." She smiled. "I wish mine was the other kind and I had the wild sex stuff."

Emily looked at her with that disapproving tilted head again. "That's not funny, Claire."

Claire took a breath. "Sorry." She paused. "At least, I know now what it all means. That's half the battle, isn't it?"

Emily smiled and nodded.

"Or maybe a third of it," said Claire. "Knowing, accepting, and dealing. That's the process, right?"

Emily nodded again. "I think so."

Claire smiled.

"Have you told Ella?"

"Yeah. I told her that's why I'm fat."

Emily looked at Claire curtly.

"What?" Claire whined defensively. "OK, part of the reason."

"How did she react?"

"I don't know. What's she supposed to say? 'Oh my God, you're crazy? Um, maybe I don't want to be your friend.'"

"Claire," Emily said firmly.

Claire smiled. "She seemed surprised to learn I have it because I seem so normal."

Emily gave her another aggravated look. "Of course you're normal."

Claire shrugged. "She was also really shocked when I told her how much weight I'd put on with the depression meds. And she was impressed by how much I've lost."

"Well, why don't you two find a real motivation and push each other to exercise? What is something that could drive you both?"

Claire was quiet.

"What?"

"She wants to go away for spring break. She's never been. She's never even flown before."

"Really? Where does she want to go?"

"Hawaii or London."

"London in March?" Emily said dismissively.

"I know. I mean, I would love to go to London sometime. But it's cool there in the summer, isn't it? Let alone the end of winter or early spring."

Emily was quiet as she poured the gravy into a dish and set the pan in the sink to soak. "So, she wants you to go with her?"

Claire shrugged. "Yeah, she asked."

Emily was quiet. "What did you tell her?"

"That I'd love to, but I can't afford it."

John walked through the kitchen archway. "When are we eating?" he asked impatiently. "The smell is making me hungry."

"Everything's almost ready," Emily said. "The turkey just has to rest for about ten minutes. And your daughter has to finish the cranberries."

Claire jumped up from the stool and scurried to the stove. "It's almost ready."

"Well, get on it," he said. "I'm hungry."

"Then maybe you should be making dinner," Claire jested.

John looked at her with raised eyebrows. "Maybe you should be paying your own rent."

Claire smiled. "Rent for cranberries? I guess that's a fair trade. I'm on it."

John shook his head. Claire still had so much to learn. But he was ready to eat, so he figured the lesson could wait until later.

When Claire finally got the berries to the table, John was carving the bird. The juices ran slowly down the flesh of the turkey and puddled at the base. He served Emily and Claire before laying cuts of meat on his own plate. Then he helped himself to the rest of the sides. Claire's cranberries looked like a lumpy sauce with seeds in it. He missed the canned kind with the smooth wide waistband and the symmetrical rings. He missed spearing a slice and cutting it into cubes.

He tried to shield his expression as he spooned the goop onto the edge of his plate. She had made such a big deal out of eating healthier. He really didn't notice the potatoes were part cauliflower. The whole wheat rolls didn't taste that bad. And he promised not to butter up his vegetables. But for him, canned cranberry sauce was as much a staple of Thanksgiving as the turkey. He saw Claire looking at him and decided if he set expectations for her, he had to be an adult, too. He scooped the withered balls on to his spoon, the purple sauce tinting the silver. He pulled the bite up to his mouth and tasted it. He wondered how well he covered. The texture was wrong and the tartness was only exacerbated by the addition of lemon juice. He smiled weakly at Claire and swallowed quickly. He compensated with a big bite of potatoes and a sip of wine.

Claire was glad to see that her father approved of her dish—

one that limited his sugar intake while also helping to reduce her waistline. Claire tasted the cranberries herself.

"Ugh, Dad, these are *awful*!" she exclaimed. "Why'd you act like they tasted good?"

He set his glass back on the table. "I was being nice."

She stared at him bewildered. "Why do you bother lying about the little things? You say the big things to my face."

He scoffed at her comment, seeking to avoid confrontation and just enjoy his meal in peace.

"OK, just *stop*," said Emily. "Claire, they're fine. John, you don't have to eat them."

"I'm not eating them, either," Claire said, pushing the mound toward the edge of her plate with her fork.

"You made them," John said, suppressing a smirk.

"And you're supposed to eat them."

"Claire," Emily said in her warning voice.

Claire stared at her father, sensing most of his outrage was as false as her own.

John barely looked up at her. "A father doesn't always tell his kid the truth."

Claire smirked. "Only when it's convenient?"

"Only when it doesn't matter," he said more seriously.

Claire sat quietly then. John's sudden interest in his plate and his glass of wine meant he was done with their pseudo-debate. He had made his point.

They ate the rest of their dinner in silence. When John left to watch the news, Claire helped her mother clean up the mess. Then she went to her room with a book. She felt sleepy from dinner and before she reached the end of her chapter, Claire fell asleep.

She woke three hours later in a dark house. She considered rolling over and going back to bed, but she realized she hadn't brushed her teeth. The thought made her cringe. She reached up to the light with a heavy hand and pulled herself from the mattress.

After flossing and brushing, she washed her face, moisturized, and went back to her bedroom. Unfortunately now she didn't feel tired. She woke her phone and found it filled by her friends.

Help me! Why can't all holidays be on a leap year schedule? Can stand my family maybe once every 4 years. :) Hope yours is better! Hugs from Denver! xoxo

Claire chuckled at Jill and wrote back: *Things could be worse. Not sure exactly how, but must be something! Boring times here. Miss you! Come visit soon!!!! xoxo*

From Ella: *Happy Thanksgiving! Busy as usual. Hope your day was quieter. Missing Boston, you, and oddly enough, school. I guess that makes me a huge nerd, huh? See ya next week.*

"Aw," said Claire, typing back: *Same to you! Much quieter here… another word for boring? lol Looking forward to finishing the semester. Dinner when we get back? BTW, nerds are cool!*

She was particularly happy to see the final message. She had not heard from Kim in almost two months, but she missed her.

Hey girl! Hope grad school is awesome! When are you coming to NYC??? Job kinda sucks. Big news! Met a guy!!! Eli. Gorgeous, Ivy, banker! In love! Call me. Want to brag! ;) And want to hear what's going on with you!

Claire replied: *Hey there! Miss you! Guy sounds amazing! Where'd you meet??? Sorry the job sucks. How's NYC otherwise? I'll call you during break and we'll catch up. oxox*

Claire placed her phone on her desk and slumped back into bed. She shut off the light and lay still in the darkness. She tried to sleep but thoughts kept bouncing around her mind. It was nerve-racking, as one stream of consciousness flowed into another until she almost could not remember how her mind had gotten to where it ended up. She finally turned the light on again, fading out the neon green of her alarm clock. She reached for a book and rested her head on the pillow, the text propped up at an uncomfortable angle. Claire read a whole page before she realized she had not even paid attention to a single word. She sighed and scanned her eyes up to the top again. But it was no use. She was just in a thinking mood, about nothing in particular. She slipped an index card back into the pages and closed the cover, clicked off the light, and rolled over in the darkness to wait on sleep.

With her back to the clock, she couldn't tell how long it took her to drift off. But when she woke, it was daylight. She twisted back around to read the time and saw it was just before ten that morning. She slumped out of bed and grabbed a sweatshirt. She could hear her mother making noise downstairs. She found Emily in the kitchen putting away clean dishes.

"Hi, sweetie," she said.

"Morning," Claire replied sleepily as she poured herself a cup of coffee and added some skim milk. She smiled and lazily went to the couch and nestled into the puffy cushions.

Emily placed the last plate in the cabinet and then shut the dishwasher. She took her mug of tea by the handle and brought it into the living room with her. "How'd you sleep?" she asked Claire as she took a sip.

"It took me a while to fall asleep, but I eventually did."

Emily nodded and took another sip. "What do you plan to do today?"

Claire shrugged. "I dunno yet."

Emily took another sip. Then she sat quietly for a moment.

Claire tasted her brew. It was OK, but she wished it had cream and sugar instead of skim and fake sweetener. Sometimes she could really taste the difference. But her little efforts were paying off. When she hit 169 pounds, she was going to celebrate. She had to keep her momentum going. She looked over at her mother and secretly wondered what Emily was thinking. She hoped it was not another medical bombshell; one she was searching for the courage to mention. Claire's eyes diverted back to her cup knowing she couldn't handle anything big so early in the morning. Instead, she quietly sipped her coffee.

"So...," said Emily finally, "your father and I have been talking."

Claire looked up at her mom inquisitively, nervously. Oh, no, thought Claire. Here it comes. What'd I do? Claire rested her cup in her lap and braced for the worst. "About what?"

"I mentioned spring break to him."

Claire stared at her mother with a puzzled expression. "O…K," she said slowly.

"We are both so proud of you, all your hard work at school, your job, dealing with everything." She paused. "We know things have been really hard and you're really trying. We think you deserve something special."

Claire feared jumping to a conclusion, but she set her cup on the coffee table as she listened.

"It seems you would pick Hawaii out of the two trips, right?"

"In March?" she said sarcastically. "Are you kidding? Of course."

"What's a better motivation than bathing suit season?"

"Mom, what are you saying?" Claire's heart was beating faster.

"Plan it with Ella. Have a wonderful time."

"*What?*" Claire exclaimed. "Are you serious?"

"Don't go overboard with your plans," Emily warned. "And consider it Merry Christmas and Happy Birthday," she said softer. "But, yes. Go." Emily smiled.

Claire was baffled. "Dad's seriously OK with this?"

Emily smiled broader. "It was his idea."

Claire sat back quietly for a moment. She felt tears welling in her eyes. Finally she breathed. "Thank you, Mom," she whispered. She jumped from the seat and met her mother in a hug.

"You're welcome, sweetie."

"Is Daddy home?"

"No. But he'll be back later."

Claire was grinning deeply now. "I love you!" she exclaimed loudly as the reality slowly sank in.

"I hope you're not just saying that because of a trip," Emily smirked.

"No…but it helps." Claire winked.

"Go call Ella before I change my mind."

"Thank you!"

"Love you."

"Love you, too! For real," Claire called from the stairs as she dashed up for her phone. She pulled the cell from its charger and dialed Ella's number.

She answered her phone excitedly. "Hey, Claire!"

"Two things," Claire said quickly, cutting Ella off.

"What?"

"We have to go to Hawaii. I'm not going to London in March."

"What?" Ella asked again, this time confused but sensing the excitement.

"And we have to make a pact to work out. We have four months to look at least somewhat good in bathing suits."

"You're going?"

"We're going!"

"Oh my God!" she squealed. "I'm so excited! We have to book immediately."

"Yeah, I'm betting the good places fill up quickly."

"Probably, but I meant before you change your mind."

Claire smiled. "Don't bet on it. I'm motivated as hell right now."

Ella laughed. "What's your goal?"

"Until I don't feel fat."

"Claire, that's kind of an unrealistic goal."

Claire was offended. "What's that supposed to mean?"

"Size zero models feel fat."

"Ha!" Claire laughed out loud. "I'll never be a size zero. I meant till I don't feel fat anymore, or at least not as fat."

"OK," Ella said. "I'm in."

CHAPTER 19

Ella excitedly set out her mat on the floor of a studio in the university gym. Claire wrinkled her face as she repositioned her shoes next to her and wondered if she would be the only one still wearing socks.

"Come on, this is going to be fun! I did it a few times in college."

"Aren't you still in college?" Claire asked.

Ella smiled. "*College*, college," she said. "Undergrad."

Claire smirked. "Oh, right." She looked around and saw all kinds of people in the class. Most of them were women. A few men lingered in the back. She was surprised to see they were rather buff and one was even attractive.

Ella noticed her glance. "I'll bet they're athletes," she whispered. "I've heard coaches recommend yoga for athletes."

Claire nodded. She wasn't really sure if she could do this. "I'm not that flexible," she complained to Ella. "I used to have pretty strong cardio, but I've never been able to lay my palms flat on the floor and straighten my legs." She tried to mimic the move, but her hamstrings burned. She didn't even have the cardio she used to have, though since they started working out more regularly she had made a little progress on the treadmill.

"Well, maybe you will if you try."

Claire grumbled and rested back down on her mat.

"Hey, guys!" Claire heard a perky voice call from the back of the room. She shifted slightly to see a tiny blonde enter through the open door. The girl walked to the front and opened a door hidden in the wall. "How are you all doing?"

Collectively, the class said variations of "fine."

"Awesome," she said, as she tossed her bag in the closet and

took her shoes and socks off. "Welcome, to anyone who's new."
She gestured to herself, "I'm Abby, by the way." She placed her
phone into a speaker set. "I have a new music mix for you guys. I
hope you like it." She was smiling as she pressed play. The music
started blaring.

"Ah!" she exclaimed quickly as she reached for the volume.
"Let's turn that down a bit." Abby dropped the sound. "Is that
better?" she asked.

The class nodded and she stood to shut the door. "OK!" she
said with a little too much energy. "Let's get started!"

Claire groaned as she sat up on her mat. Pretty, perky, and
blonde—this was going to be hell.

"All right," Abby said. "Let's rest down on your mats and
breathe. We want to push the world out of our minds for the next
hour and just concentrate on yoga."

Claire sat back. She wished she could just sleep instead of
concentrating on yoga.

"Are you breathing?" Abby asked.

The class collectively nodded heads—palms, backs, and feet flat
on the floor. Claire smiled. "Let's hope," she quipped to Ella.

Ella's impatient hush was even more muffled than Claire's
sarcasm. Claire realized it was probably unfair to ruin the
experience for everyone in the class, including herself. She silently
pledged to set her judgment aside and try to find some good in
the hour.

Clearing her head of all thoughts proved to be as much of
a challenge for Claire as trying to touch her toes. But Ella was
encouraging, if not overtly expressive and supportive, nodding
each time Claire tried to contort her body into a pose until she
finally achieved some success. It left Claire thinking maybe yoga
would not be impossible. Abby's gentle directions eventually led
every movement Claire made, and she was surprised to discover
she had more inner goddess than she expected.

Inner peace might be harder to conjure up though.

"OK, now drop your body forward, rest your head on the floor, and just relax there," Abby said near the hour's close. "Let your body absorb the calm around you."

Claire surprisingly felt more at ease. She found that the deep breathing flowed fluidly through her body as it cooled her lungs and slowed her heart.

"Now, carefully rise up. Take as much time as you need," she said.

Claire was in awe of the difference sixty minutes had made to her mood. She suddenly didn't want to get up. She wanted to stay collapsed within herself and rest. She could not remember the last time her brain had been devoid of thought. It was a tremendous feeling.

"What'd you think?" Ella's voice came as an unwanted interruption. Claire could only nod her head, tucked between her arms. She didn't look over at Ella's eager glance, but Ella was pleased with Claire's apparent approval. She, too, turned back into child's pose and tried to escape the world, if only for a few moments more.

When Ella finally sat back completely and began stretching out her neck, Claire decided to give the world another try. She slowly lifted her body up from the mat, keeping her eyes closed as she straightened her back.

"So, what'd you think?" Ella asked again, this time more excitedly and impatiently.

Claire draped her loose arms over her bent knees and slowly opened her eyelids. She looked straight at Ella, who began to fear she had misjudged Claire's tranquility.

"I'm already dreading coming back next week to work out." Claire said flatly.

Ella's face fell.

"But I can't *wait* to do yoga again!" She gave a small wink and pushed herself up from her mat.

Ella rolled her eyes and breathed a sigh of relief as she secretly tried to hide her smile.

Once they had put their shoes back on, Claire grudgingly walked to the painfully bright hallway and followed her friend to the main gym. People of all sizes littered the room. Guys in sleeveless shirts wrestled with free weights, grunting and pushing up and up, trying to beat their personal best, while friends egged them on. Some showed signs of dedication—or maybe artificial bulk—while others struggled. She saw a lean guy with neatly trimmed dark hair push his glasses up the bridge of his nose, before lowering down to do another set with a heavily weighted barbell. Claire wrinkled her brow, wondering why he even attempted such a feat. But she was shocked when she saw his strength, how easily he thrust the barbell into the air. He lowered it and forced it up again—and again and again. It seemed impossible that his frame could handle the pressure or that his arms could provide the necessary support. But there he stood, mechanically moving, unwavering in his stance and form. Her prejudgment, as usual, was wrong.

"You coming?" Ella muttered, unaware that Claire was otherwise engaged.

"Yeah." Claire followed, turning her eyes downward to watch the path before her. She had nearly tripped on a mat.

If nothing else, Claire wanted to run. Not out of need or desire, but with a sense of obligation. She felt that cardio exercise was what would help her lose her remaining 20 to 40 pounds. Forty pounds was her goal, but 20 was more realistic—at least before Hawaii. If she could manage it, she would feel somewhat successful. The treadmills were all filled, so she agreed to begin on the weight machines.

You have to do this, Claire said to herself as she approached the first machine. She could see streaks of sweat smeared on the seat from its previous occupant and she wrinkled her face in disgust. She cleaned it with a paper towel and spray before sitting down—like that would really bring her peace of mind. She tossed her bag by the stack of weights and decided two things: commit herself to the goal and forgive herself if she didn't reach it completely.

CHAPTER 20

Claire turned in bed to hit the alarm, wincing slightly at the ache in her legs and arms. Her shoulders and calves felt tight. She sighed as she rolled onto her back and smiled. It was going to be a fabulous day. Her body surged with a warm flow of accomplishment. Yesterday had been her hardest workout yet. It seemed having an exercise buddy was the key to staying motivated. She and Ella had developed a solid routine since coming back from winter break. They did not go every day. They worked around their classes. But by early February, they had a steady, four-day-a-week rotation, including at least one yoga class. As March neared, they seemed more inclined to throw in an additional workout or two, and the results were showing. Yesterday, Claire had—without help, strain, or effort—stood up straight, leaned forward, and touched her toes! In nearly twenty-three years that had never happened. Yoga was amazing.

Claire stretched and tapped the snooze button a second time. She knew she had to get up. If she lingered much longer, she might not only be late—she might fall back asleep. She slipped out of bed and trudged to the shower. Surprisingly, she made it out the door ten minutes earlier than usual.

Although Amy had never returned Claire's pre-Thanksgiving email—which Claire noted was in sharp contrast to the complimentary messages Laura sent whenever Claire lent a hand—Amy did verbally apologize. She never explained her absence, but she commended Claire for her proactive use of time. She also remarked how grateful Laura had been for the help. In the following months, Claire worked increasingly for Laura during lulls, which she found to be a welcomed break from the same, often boring tasks she did for Amy. But Claire still worked for Amy, so whenever Amy had jobs for her, including busy work such as filing, she did it. At other times, Claire reveled in doing real work such as writing content for the website or consulting with Amy on language for a publication. Amy actually wanted Claire's opinion, jotting notes down on her impressions and reacting positively to her suggestions. Yet she never once invited Claire to participate in a marketing meeting or listen in on strategy sessions. She treated Claire as a lowly office worker, not a colleague; that became clearer by the day. Claire wondered if Amy even gave her credit for her input.

Laura was different. Laura was generous with praise and opportunities. Claire was quite shocked when Amy allowed Claire to assist Laura on a major networking event in New York. The look on Claire's face made Laura smile.

"She wasn't exactly thrilled with the idea," Laura told Claire. "Mostly because it wasn't her choice."

Claire looked confused.

"I mentioned your name to Ross Maynard and told him what a huge help you have been to me these past few months."

Claire's mouth gaped. She knew Maynard's name; he was Vice President of the Alumni Association. And now he knew her name? Claire was stunned. She assumed Amy had never even mentioned her name. Laura was giving her credit.

"I think I'm going to get a GA next year, which would be great. Too bad you're graduating." Laura winked. "So, anyway, I'm hoping you'll be OK with this new arrangement. You'll still work for Amy, so whenever she needs something done, you're hers." She paused. "That sounds so indentured. But I mean, filing, updating the website—anything like that—you work for her. But when I need you for the outreach work, especially the one coming up in New York, I can request your help and generally be assured of getting it."

Claire was speechless.

"Are you up for it? It actually means a lot more stuff for you. Well, at least a lot less downtime."

"Absolutely," Claire said excitedly. "I don't do well with downtime."

Laura smiled. "Great. OK, sorry to keep you. I don't want you to be late for class. I just wanted to explain this to you in case Amy hadn't told you everything."

"No," Claire said. "She didn't really tell me anything. I'm glad you did." She picked up her bag from the seat next to her and stood from her chair.

Laura rose as well. "By the way, I love that sweater."

Claire beamed. "Thanks. I just got it." She had almost fainted in the store when it fit. It was hot pink cashmere she had found on sale for an amazing price. It was a medium and fit her perfectly.

"It's adorable."

Claire wrinkled her face coyly. "I know."

Laura chuckled. As Claire slipped her jacket on, she watched Laura pull her own coat from the stand. "I'll walk out with you. I've got to leave early today for a dentist appointment."

"Oh, OK."

Laura locked her door and followed Claire down the hallway staircase. "Spring break is in a few weeks. Are you doing anything special?"

Claire beamed. "Big plans."

"Oh yeah, where are you going?"

"Hawaii."

"I'm so jealous!" sighed Laura. "I went to Hawaii on my honeymoon. I loved it. It's so beautiful there."

Claire nodded. "I can't wait."

"Have you ever been?"

"No."

"Are you going with anyone?"

"One of my best friends, Ella. She's a grad student here, too."

"Oh, you girls are gonna have so much fun!"

Claire smiled. "Yeah, I really hope so. We have lots of things planned. Actually, we only left one lazy beach day, and some wandering time the day we get there."

"How long are you going?"

"A week in Oahu."

"Ah. Nice. So you're doing the whole touristy thing, not just partying and drinking?"

"We're pretty much nerdy forty year olds."

Laura laughed out loud. "No. That's great! You can get drunk in Florida. Hawaii is about the island's history and culture."

Claire nodded.

"I think it's fabulous."

"Yeah, we just booked a snorkeling day at Hanauma Bay."

"That's awesome! We did that. It's breathtaking."

"It was on Ella's wish list. It's basically her trip. I'm just along for the ride."

Laura nodded.

"And then Pearl Harbor, Dole, the cultural center, and whatever else we find along the way."

"That sounds like an amazing trip."

"We hope so."

"Ah…now you have me wanting to go back." She smiled. "I wonder if my husband wants to go away for spring break, too."

"Well, he is in college," Claire joked.

Laura chuckled. "I'll have to tell him that!"

They had walked out in the cold to the center of campus. Laura's car was to the left and Claire's class to the right.

"Well, have a good class."

"Thanks. Have a good night…and dentist appointment. I'll see you next week."

"Sure thing." Laura waved a gloved hand as she left. Claire waved back as she watched her mentor walk away.

✛ ✛ ✛

Emily had immediately seen a change in Claire when her daughter arrived home for the winter holiday. Claire's face seemed thinner and her winter jacket finally buttoned all the way up. Emily also noted Claire's reasonable meal portions, her nightly jogs on the basement treadmill, and her sudden obsession with yoga. It had warmed Emily's heart to see her daughter making such an effort. It was never about a number. It was much deeper than that. Claire had to want to change. Without that, nothing she or John might say or do could have made an impact. Emily assumed, correctly, that if they had pushed, Claire would push back even harder. Emily knew people could change, but only when they wanted it for themselves.

During her phone calls with her daughter, Emily always praised Claire's efforts. Emily became more convinced that graduate school was a wise move and the Hawaii trip a valuable incentive. But the reward of spring break—her child's inherent craving for conformity in paradise—left Emily feeling ambivalent. Her concern for Claire's weight came from the purest of motives. And if Claire had even once hinted she was doing this wrong—a fad diet, intensive exercise, drugs, starvation, anything dangerous—Emily would have stopped her. The 80 pounds were never good for her body or her soul, but at least they weren't going to kill her.

Fortunately, Claire appeared to be doing weight loss right. Not only was she seeing slow, progressive results, but she remained eager to keep going. Emily noticed a renewed pride in Claire. She could even sense it over the phone. It was something Emily had not seen in a long time. It seemed as if Claire finally felt she deserved it, which Emily supposed to be a good thing. She also wondered how much of Claire's newly found mental wellness was helping revive her spirit.

Emily heard a sound at the front door. Claire was home. She had been rather cryptic on the phone about her reasons for the weekend trip, but Emily had sensed excitement. Maybe it was just about leaving for Hawaii the next week.

"Hi, Mom!" Claire called out from the stairwell.

"Hi, sweetie." She dried her hands and rushed to the family room just as Claire darted up the stairs. Emily was on edge, hoping it was happiness she had sensed from her child, not anxiety. Often with Claire, you never knew. Some days, sarcasm masqueraded as humor, leaving Emily generally unwilling to commit to a conversation with Claire until she saw her daughter's face.

"How was the drive?" Emily asked loudly enough for her voice to carry from the base of the staircase.

"Fine," Claire called down from her room.

Ah, *fine*, Emily thought, an answer that said nothing at all.

"I'm happy you came home this weekend," Emily continued. "I figured we wouldn't see you until after your trip."

"I had to come home," Claire's voice trailed from the upstairs hallway.

Emily's brow ruffled. Was she being sarcastic? Did she feel obligated to come home? What was her face saying that Emily couldn't see?

Claire bounded down the stairs with a spring in her step. "My summer clothes are here."

Emily's eyes opened wide at the sight. Claire's face certainly said it all. It conveyed confidence and joy. She smiled, which only further accentuated the skin along her high cheekbones. Her dimples, once consumed by her face, dented each side of it just as they used to. She wore a hot pink sweater that clung to a slender torso and rested comfortably just above a waistline that revealed not even the slightest bulge. Emily was in awe.

"Look," Claire smiled as she held up her right hand and wiggled her fingers. "It fits." The sapphire and diamond ring she had received on her sixteenth birthday shimmered as it caught the light. Of all the things that had become too small for her, Claire had missed it the most.

"Look at you!" Emily blurted out. She felt her throat catch at her sudden emotion and she moved forward to hug her daughter. As she gripped her child's body tighter, she closed her eyes and released a breath of relief. Emily almost felt silly by her reaction, not wanting Claire to assume any meaning.

"Hi, Mom," Claire said with a chuckle as she tried not to fight her mother's close grasp. She felt quiet sighs from her mother's chest. "Are you OK?" Claire asked, somewhat worried. She had not expected such a response.

"I'm sorry," Emily said, hesitant to let go. "You just…"

"I know. How about that?" Claire asked, turning slightly to model her figure.

Her mother shook her head. "Claire, you look lovely. Beautiful!"

Claire smiled. "Thanks, Mom. I've still got more to do. I'm at, like, the low 150s. But—"

Her mother cut her off. "Oh, please. You look perfect!"

Claire shrugged. "I'm not back into everything yet."

"Claire, you're healthy. That's all that matters. I just want you feeling OK." She paused. "Are you—feeling OK?" She paused again. "You…seem OK." Emily looked at her cautiously.

Claire grinned. "Well, I don't hate myself right now, if that's what you mean."

The words made Emily cringe. She couldn't imagine such feelings. Everyone loved Claire. How could she hate herself?

"I'd like these to be a six or four," she said casually, gesturing toward her pants. "But I'm really proud they're single digits again."

"What have I always told you?"

"I know. Wear your size…" Claire said somewhat sarcastically, trailing off the sentiment once the point had been made.

Her mother touched her face. "And you're proof. An eight is perfectly healthy for your shape and height. Don't ever feel bad—"

She cut her mother off. "No. I don't. *Really*," Claire said seriously. "I feel great and I know I look great." Then her face fell just a bit. She pulled off her sweater. "I just hate this," she said lifting her arm and motioning toward the skin inside her bicep, revealing faint stretch marks. "And it's just on the left side. That's so weird."

Her mother smiled kindly. "I would have never noticed."

Claire sighed, shrugged, and straightened out the sweater to slip it back on again. She pulled her neck through the hole and smoothed it down over her torso. She had been rubbing her arms, her thighs, her stomach, and her hips incessantly with expensive cream since she started losing the weight, and she had to admit the color was fading a bit. But the stretch marks remained, and she knew she'd never be rid of them.

"Come on, have something to eat," Emily said. She gestured for Claire to follow her into the kitchen. "I made chocolate chip cookies." She was smiling proudly. Emily picked up two and handed one to Claire. "I think you deserve this."

"Mom, what are you doing?" She set the cookie on the counter and Emily ruffled her brow. Claire stepped over to the cabinet, pulled out two small glasses, and poured two cups of ice-cold milk.

"Calories must be enjoyed completely." She toasted her mother and bit into the cookie. It was still warm. Claire rolled her eyes slightly. "Totally. Worth. It."

Claire stayed the night. Her father was away on business and she was sad to miss him. She assumed what his relief would have been, had he been there. She was out of the risk zone for diabetes and she could no longer be judged wrongly by her outward appearance. No one could say she would be attractive "if…" She was attractive, and for the first time in a long time, even she believed it.

Claire enjoyed the time with her mother, and Emily was sorry to say goodbye so quickly. But Claire had always planned to head back to the city by mid afternoon. She needed to pack, vacation-prep her apartment, and get a few more hours of sleep.

She stowed a collection of outfit treasures that fit again into the back of her SUV. The fact that her efforts had reclaimed them made her love them all the more. She was particularly shocked to discover the navy blue cocktail dress she had worn at sixteen was one of them. It had been gently folded and placed among the many flowing skirts and dresses she had found in the plastic bins at the back of her closet.

Claire was grateful her mother had stopped her raging outburst that night many years ago, when she tried to throw them all out. "That's a lot of expensive stuff," her mother had said, trying to get Claire to be reasonable. "You're not throwing them out. I might want something in there, if you're so convinced you'll never need it again." The suggestion irritated Claire, thinking of her forty-something mother taking her wardrobe. Claire stuffed the things back in, paying little attention to neatness. Years later, the untouched items were sufficiently rumpled. She cared for them gently, washing, ironing, and steaming out the wrinkles to prepare an island wardrobe. She packed her toiletries in their quart bag for the plane and stashed her cell phone charger in a pocket of her suitcase. She didn't need them now, but her sunglasses were gently resting inside the case, tucked away in her carry-on bag. She finished packing with a beach towel and her tankini. She didn't love the new suit she bought last week, but she had tossed her older ones in a previous fit of anger, before her mother had interfered.

Whatever, Claire thought. I'll replace it soon enough.

Ella's ringtone chimed. "You ready?" she asked Claire over the phone.

Claire smiled, thinking of the many outfits she planned to start wearing on the island the next day. Claire was certainly excited to visit Hawaii, to enjoy the beach in March, to have a week away from classes and Amy. Ella, however, was elated. The trip had great meaning for her. It was something she had worked hard to afford, a luxury she had never known before.

Perhaps Claire had earned it, too. Vacations were not unfamiliar to her, but this time it was very different from an escape.

CHAPTER 21

They saw the island long before they touched its land or smelled its air. Ella had woken Claire; she tugged her friend's arm excitedly, gesturing toward the view outside the window—one only slightly obstructed by the wing. If they turned their heads to the proper angle, between wisps of clouds they could see it—paradise.

The water beneath them was cobalt blue, deepened in parts by shadowy masses under the surface—lightened in others by streaks of teal. As they drew closer to the ground, the ocean faded to exquisite shades of turquoise, draped loosely around the shoreline like a hand-painted shawl of silk.

Claire was relieved to see Ella had calmed down since they had boarded the first plane hours ago in Boston. The girls had arrived at the airport in the dark by taxi. They both agreed splitting cab fare was cheaper and smarter than parking a car in the long-term lot. This trip was already costing a small fortune. Claire wondered if her dad might re-categorize it as Happy Birthday and Merry Christmas for the next few years. But she didn't care. She felt energized and—dare she say it—attractive. Never before in her life had Claire Kelly ever believed she would experience joy and satisfaction from a scale that said 152 pounds. But she had, earlier that morning, when she read the scale by the light of her bathroom vanity.

Sixty-three pounds lighter.

It almost seemed unreal some days—how the years of struggle and self-hatred had been wiped away so quickly. Claire had almost forgotten what she had looked like then—she only had a single photo to remember it by. But it was not so much about moving beyond being fat. Claire was grateful to have only stumbled upon a temporary weight problem. It could have been a lifetime struggle. From the experience, she had gained a deeper understanding of those locked in a constant battle with their weight. She had also developed great respect for their courage. This world is hard and judgment is blind. Weight gain is never a goal; it is a torment that clings to you, dragging everything down. For Claire, it was an unintended circumstance that changed her in so many ways; some that she accepted and others that left her scarred. She would never be happy to have had the experience, but she would not waste it either.

Losing the last 20-something pounds by herself—during a five-month period of sweat and grit—left Claire with an odd sense of pride. She was no longer in double digits, which relieved her. But Claire was surprised by the epiphany that followed. In high school, at 135 pounds, she sometimes felt fat—OK, more than sometimes. She often stared at her classmates, her friends, the strangers around her and on the covers of magazines, and wondered: why can't I look like that? She pondered what she could be *if only*. What did it feel like to be a size zero? She dreaded her hips; she hated her ass. Why weren't her breasts bigger if she had curves? She worked out and ate sensibly.

Why was she fat?

Now she was somehow satisfied to be at 152 pounds. Sure, she wanted to keep going. Sure, she had even bigger plans for herself. But here, sitting next to her jittery friend, just minutes away from the source of her motivation, Claire Kelly felt content.

It was a tremendous feeling. She only had recollections of teenage joy—she almost couldn't remember moments unaffected by melancholy. It was not that the years of her youth had been bad, but the depression had dragged her down and tainted her memories.

Claire sensed excitement in the air. She could feel the plane starting to descend and she realized Ella was no longer a flight virgin. Ella had not seemed to appreciate Claire's harmless jest at

Logan about it being Ella's first time at an airport. "I have been to an airport before," Ella remarked almost aggravated; as though picking up or dropping off was the same as flying. She certainly was not starting small with air travel—taking a commuter plane to D.C. or jetting down to Florida; that was a reasonable first flight. No, Ella was flying from coast-to-coast across the United States, with the final leg of her trip taking her partway across the Pacific. Claire understood and was willing to indulge Ella's agitation.

Personally, Claire loved to fly. She had flown up and down the east coast many times, had been to Mexico once, and twice to Europe and back. She especially loved turbulence, when it forcefully tossed her in her seat, sometimes hard enough to lift her slightly off the cushion. She had never experienced any real danger in flight, though; if she ever did, she assumed her feelings would change. But sitting beside Ella, Claire was the strong one, the one in control, the one who knew what to expect. She liked that feeling—it didn't happen often.

The plane jostled roughly as it finally touched down. Ella clutched her armrest with a white-knuckled grip. "I'll never get used to that," she complained, mostly to herself.

Claire smirked, still straining to see the view from the aisle seat. She could almost feel the warm Hawaiian breeze as she watched the ground crew at work in shorts out on the tarmac.

"Welcome to Oahu, ladies and gentlemen," the captain's cool voice flowed from the speakers. "The temperature outside is 76 degrees. The weather is sunny."

Claire closed her eyes and sighed.

"Thank you for flying with us today," the captain continued. "We hope you have a safe and wonderful trip here on the islands, or wherever your final destination may be. Mahalo."

They disembarked, and after claiming their bags, they received an official Hawaiian welcome from local women dressed in long floral garb. Claire envied their lovely complexions. She wondered how long it would take her and Ella to sunburn. She leaned forward to allow a small woman to place a lei of delicate orchids around her neck.

The girls then headed outside the terminal for a coach bus to their hotel. "There it is," Claire said as she grabbed her bag by the handle and started toward it. Ella trailed behind, taking photos of everything: the locals, visitors, vehicles, plants, and the airport itself.

"Are you coming?" Claire called playfully. After all, Ella had paid good money to be a tourist in Hawaii, and she had paid it all herself.

"Yeah, coming," Ella called, her back still to Claire. She focused her auto zoom lens on a white flower with delicate petals, so perfectly formed they almost resembled clay. Ella snapped no less than ten shots of it, at slightly different angles and distances. Then she joined Claire in line.

"These are so pretty," she said fondling the flowers around her neck. "I'll bet they won't survive the trip home, huh?"

Claire nodded in agreement. "They probably won't last till tomorrow night. But you're right...they are beautiful," Claire said. She gently brought her lei up to her face with both hands and breathed in the intoxicating fragrance.

Ella smiled again, tilting her head to the side to smell her flowers as well.

"Aloha!" burst the loud voice of a large man in a black Hawaiian shirt tiled with pale pink hibiscus.

"A-lo-ha!" Ella replied excitedly to the driver, drawing out the word.

"Welcome aboard," he said as he took their bags and hoisted them effortlessly into the belly of the bus. He chatted with the visitors and mentally noted his route as they shared their hotel names. Once inside the coach, he introduced himself as Ray and asked everyone to take their seats. The bus turned out of the lot and pulled into traffic. Tiny storefronts and weathered homes soon dotted the roadside. The sights were not at all what Claire expected, imagining the postcard views of the coast. But the closer the bus pulled toward Waikiki Beach, the busier the roads and sidewalks became, the larger the storefronts and homes—until finally, everything was beautiful.

The bus stopped several times en route to their hotel. When it passed by the International Market Place, Ella pointed excitedly. "Oh, that's where I want to go tomorrow."

Claire wondered how much Ella had researched this trip. Claire wanted to hit the highlights: Dole, Pearl Harbor, and the beach, while the island's largest flea market and Hanauma Bay were on Ella's to-do list. It all sounded good to Claire, except maybe the flea market.

Ray pulled hard on the wheel to take the corner, slowing the coach for center barriers and tourists cutting across the street wherever they fancied. As the beach grew in the distance, Claire's excitement rose. The hotel had not lied about its access to the sea. When Ray pulled up to the curb, he leapt from his seat faster than the two girls, and hurried down the steps to start unloading bags.

"The black one with the pink ribbons," Claire said directing Ray to her suitcase.

"And mine are the green ones," Ella said.

Ella—in Claire's opinion—had over packed for the weeklong stay. She brought several changes of clothes—outfits for all temperatures. She also brought too many accessories: her laptop, her pillow, and a bath towel. Claire's single case was a bit smaller than Ella's main bag. Claire had packed light. In fact, her suitcase was a quarter empty. She didn't know what she would buy, but she was experienced enough to know a few things: you can always purchase necessities on vacation if you forget something, hotels come with bath towels and pillows, and you will always find things along the way to bring home.

Claire wondered if she should help Ella with her luggage, but she decided it had been Ella's decision to bring so much—she could carry it.

"Got it?" Claire asked anyway.

"Yup," Ella said, somewhat out of breath as she pulled her wheeled bag behind her up the steps, while keeping the duffel bag in place on her shoulder. When she was partway up the stairs, a bellboy came around the corner and scurried down to assist her. Ella gratefully relinquished control of the suitcase handle and thanked the attractive young man. He lifted the bag effortlessly, careful not to damage it. At the top of the stairs, he rested it on its wheels again and offered to help the girls to their room, reaching out for Claire's bag as well.

"No, thanks. Really. We still have to check in," Claire said. "We're fine. So long as there are no more steps."

"No, there's an elevator." He smiled softly. "Enjoy your stay." He turned to walk away.

"*Mahalo!*" Ella called out somewhat pathetically.

He turned and grinned again. She smiled back and leaned in to Claire. "Oh my God, he's so hot!"

Claire smiled. "Yes, he is."

They checked in at the front desk and followed the woman's directions to the elevator, reaching their room with little trouble.

"Not bad," Claire said after surveying the space. Sure, their view was a parking lot, but they planned to experience the beach firsthand versus paying to see it by moonlight.

"This is great!" Ella burst out as she hauled both bags through the door. "Oh, look at the quilts!" she said longingly. A mix of white and faded coral fabric was patched together to form a pineapple. "I love these," Ella said, gently fingering the stitching. "You think they sell them?"

"I'm sure someone does," Claire said. She didn't have the heart to ask how Ella would get it home. Maybe Ella would leave her pillow and snag the quilt.

Claire's stomach rumbled. There was still part of a day left, but the girls were exhausted and hungry. They promised each other to be reasonable about what they would spend on food, but they agreed to one nice night out. Claire was specifically looking forward to that evening—not so much for the food or the atmosphere, but the attire.

She was still technically a size eight, but somehow she fit into the navy dress she had worn on her trip to Mexico nearly a decade earlier. At sweet sixteen, she was at most a size six. She was not fat then, so she wondered how the dress could fit her now—not that she was fat now. She assumed the empire waist made it more forgiving, though she had grown a cup size bigger since then, too. When she tried the dress on last week at home—convinced it was not going to fit—all she discovered was cleavage. She could live with that.

"You wanna get something to eat? Look around a little?" Ella asked.

"Absolutely. Can I unpack a few things first?"

"Uh, yeah, sure," Ella said, sounding deflated. She was eager to get out and explore. She was also ready to eat.

"It'll only take a minute," said Claire, changing into a comfy pair of flip-flops and a jersey skirt. Before she went, she hung her navy dress in the closet by the door.

CHAPTER 22

They wanted to make the hours count in Hawaii and were out of their room early the next morning. "Let's walk around and find a place to eat," Claire said when Ella asked about breakfast. They could have gone to their hotel, but they wanted to sample Waikiki beyond the lobby. Their short walk the evening before had taken them down the block to the main drag, parallel to the ocean. They had heard the waves crashing in the distance and could faintly see the outline of the shore from the road. Today, after they ate and shopped, they would go see the beach.

Turning left out of the lobby, they wandered a few minutes past people and places. Small storefronts displayed mostly clothes and gifts. As they glanced around, the only eating establishments were chains. Somewhat disappointed, Claire spotted a wooden sign out on the sidewalk ahead: *Fresh juice! French Toast Special! Eggs cooked to order!*

"What about there?" she asked.

Ella examined it. She was hungry and finally shrugged. "I guess so."

They went up the stairs leading to a wall of glass, which was partially blocked by bamboo curtains. The girls could see wooden chair legs beneath the curtains.

A smiling woman greeted them. "Aloha. Two for breakfast?"

"Yes," Claire said.

They sat on formal chairs with white linen tablecloths. Claire thought it seemed nice, but Ella was skeptical.

"What's wrong," she whispered across the table.

Ella raised her eyes from the menu. They were stiff and wide.

"What?" Claire asked again, her brow creased in confusion.

Ella was so quiet Claire could not hear a word.

"What?" she asked a third time.

"It's really expensive," Ella said.

Claire relaxed a bit, nodding her head as she leaned back. She glanced down the line of prices, bobbing her head more expressively as though she was empathizing. She didn't want to be condescending, but nothing was going to be cheap.

"You're right. I'm sorry."

Ella shrugged.

"Look, this place was my pick. How about I treat?"

Ella didn't specifically object, but weakly shook her head. "No. I can't let you—"

"Come on. I insist. We'll find a different place tomorrow. One with grass-skirt tablecloths, not linen ones," she smirked.

Ella smiled. "OK…then it's my treat."

"Deal."

With the dilemma solved, Ella happily ordered the French toast and a large glass of orange juice. Claire craved fresh pineapple juice and paired it with two eggs. To her dismay, it also came with two strips of bacon and two pieces of thickly buttered toast. She resisted to the best of her ability, eating just part of the second piece of bacon and two halves of the bread to soak up her yolk—only after she had scraped off most of the butter. Ella ate every bite of her meal, commenting repeatedly how good it tasted.

As Claire paid the bill, she wondered why Ella had been so surprised by the prices, which were only somewhat higher than Boston brunch. The quid pro quo deal for tomorrow's breakfast left Claire a little worried about which venue Ella would pick.

"Ready?" Ella asked cheerily. A savory, free breakfast sat well with her friend. Claire held up a finger. Her flute of chilled fresh pineapple juice had just been replenished on the house. If Claire had to slide a spoon around the inside of the glass after she chugged the drink, she would consume every last drop of its sweetness.

"Are you gonna eat your last pieces of toast?" Ella asked.

"Nah," said Claire pausing mid-drink. "You can have them if you want."

They collected their purses and Claire followed her friend down the stairs to the street. "I think it's this way," Ella said, directing them. They were starting small, venturing just blocks away to the Marketplace. It lived behind a manmade wooden structure; its name blocked out in letters constructed of tiki-inspired font.

Claire wrinkled her nose at the commercialism, but today they were tourists. They had a schedule for the rest of the trip; this was their lazy day.

"Look at these," Ella cooed, slipping into a stand with jewelry that masqueraded as being made in Hawaii. "I think my sister would like this."

Claire nodded, trying to hide her sarcasm; then stupidly realized Ella had lots of people to buy for and not a lot of money to spend. "It's really cute," Claire said, genuinely agreeing this time. As they moved from booth to booth, even Claire made a purchase: Hawaiian shirts for her parents.

"This place is great!" Ella said again, stuffing another small white plastic bag inside her others. Claire smiled and nodded. Ella looked around and recognized they had come full circle back to the entrance. "Wow," she said glancing down at her watch, "we've been here for a while. Wanna see what else is around?"

"Lead the way."

They left the walls of the Marketplace and popped in and out of stores lining the path back to their hotel. Claire bought little else as they wandered except a long-sleeve shirt for herself with the name of the beach in small letters across the chest. It was simple, soft, and a medium. As noon neared, they stopped by their hotel to drop off their spoils, then left the lobby and walked straight for the beach. Claire heard Ella make a slight squeaking noise in her throat as she saw the beach come into view. She thought her friend's excitement was sweet. They were still in their street clothes and without even a towel to dry themselves off. But the sand stretched out before them; they could not resist darting over to take a peek.

"You're sure you don't want to just skip the shopping and go grab our towels?"

"Nope," Ella said shaking her head. "We'll check out the rest of the shops on this side and then come back here for a little while after the hot part of the day."

Easily slipping off their sandals, they scooped their shoes up in their fingers and ventured between the towels. "That's probably a good idea," Claire said as she surveyed the packed beach. She hoped the crowd would thin out later.

She watched girls her age walk by laughing, comfortably parading through a busy mess of people with almost nothing on. She envied their ease, thinking sadly that she used to look just like them but hid her body from view.

Despite their hard work, Ella still brought a one-piece bathing suit and Claire had her cheap tankini. They were covered. But as the girls continued by, Claire could not stop thinking about getting a new suit. For the first time in her life, she was not mortified by the concept of a bikini.

The idea seemed foreign to her. Five years ago in Mexico and Bermuda, she chose tanning spots tucked away from other beach goers. In Italy, she shrouded her figure behind a towel. Here in Hawaii, nearly twenty pounds heavier—less muscular, more jiggly, and physically scarred at her hips, thighs, and stomach—she suddenly did not care…as much. It was not that fewer strangers would be sitting around her. She just didn't weigh 215 pounds anymore. She didn't even weigh 175 pounds. She weighed 152. Here in Hawaii was the first time Claire had ever been on vacation with an actual understanding of what thin meant.

"OK, OK, we have more stores to go to before we hit the

beach," Ella said. "Plus, I'm getting hungry. Let's do that, then do that, then do this."

Claire nodded.

"If we're back by one thirty or two o'clock, we'll still start our base."

Claire shrugged. "All right, let's go." She followed Ella back to the sidewalk and knocked the sand off her legs.

"Wanna go in there?" Ella asked, pointing to the first store they reached. Peering in, they saw clothes meant for middle-aged women with large wallets. Claire shook her head at the second and third doorways as well.

"Here?" Ella asked at the fourth.

"Yes!" Claire exclaimed darting inside. The shop was lined with all sorts of colorful bathing suits. Claire smiled at the friendly clerk behind the small counter and immediately started sifting through the racks.

"Are you gonna get one?" Ella whispered. She had already looked at the price tags for a few of them and held in her gasp.

Claire smiled. That cheap tankini didn't suit her. She bought it because she had a poor selection and short notice. Claire looked devilishly at Ella and smiled, confirming she had seen the prices. "I don't know yet. I have to look around."

"What colors are you thinking?" Ella asked. Claire looked pretty great, despite her occasional off-handed comments about wanting to lose fifteen or twenty more. Ella's goal was Claire's current weight; she only had thirteen pounds to go, and Ella was shorter than Claire by at least two inches. But Claire said her goal casually, comfortably, as though she knew she would get there eventually, but it did not have to be tomorrow.

Claire reviewed the selection, picking through rows of suits. She stuck to the two-pieces, smiling secretly at her conviction. She felt as if she was doing something wicked and it felt good. She was ignoring her own instincts and realizing how wrong she had been all these years. It was hard battling yourself—and Claire was just getting used to it. As she pushed another line of hangers back to flip through its contents, she promised herself she was not only going to leave Hawaii with a bikini—she was going to leave with tan lines from the suit.

The old Claire would have been mortified.

"Do you like this one?" She turned and saw Ella holding up a pink leopard print.

Claire grinned, half laughing at the joke and half wondering if it was meant in jest. She was relieved when Ella winked and put it back. Claire draped two possibilities across her arm and kept going. The two suits Claire held were solid colors—black and hot pink. She feared the latter might be too bright, but the black one—while cute—was just a bit boring. She moved to the rack in the back by the dressing rooms.

No, she thought, pushing them away. "No. No. No," she muttered quietly to herself. Maybe this was not going to be easy. As she was about to give up looking and try on the two she held, Claire saw another suit deep in the back. Her eyes widened as she reached for the neck of its hanger and gently lifted it up from the metal bar. She took the second one behind it, too, a size up.

"*Oh, that's pretty*," Ella cooed, admiring its simple yet stylish look. The two-piece suit was a navy blue with dark teal cording coiled in mirrored patterns along the small of the back and the two bra cups. It reminded Claire of something inspired by a western or Celtic design. The bottom was a solid piece; the top tied at the back and the neck.

Claire's smile partially expressed her excitement. Her eyes sparkled. She hoped she had found it. "In here?" Claire directed the question to the doting employee, obviously eager for a sale. The woman nodded vigorously, pulling away the curtain of the dressing room. Claire hung her bag on a hook she found inside and pushed the hangers on after. She tossed her dress on a small chair that barely fit in the space.

"Try on the others first," Ella called through the curtain. She figured she knew the one Claire would buy, if she bought any. She wanted a big reveal.

"OK," Claire said, having intended to all along. She pulled the black top off the plastic form and slipped her arms through its straps. The demi cups were cut sharply and as she bent down to slip the bottom on over her panties, she felt her right breast pop out slightly. Claire repositioned her flesh, but wrinkled her nose when she pulled open the curtain. She smiled doubtfully at the saleswoman, who shook her head disapprovingly at the selection. "That's not you," the stranger said flatly.

"Yeah. Not good," Ella chimed in.

The suit was a large—the only one on the rack. Claire was nervous for the next one. The hot pink set had been her least favorite and it was a medium. She timidly pulled off the black top and hung it on the hook, the same with the bottom. She untangled the pink suit—string top and bottom—from the hanger. She had to close her legs tightly to keep the crotch of the bikini from falling as she tied the sides at the hips. Before she had even gotten the bottom fastened in place, she already hated it. It was not that the medium didn't fit, exactly. It just didn't fit comfortably. After pulling on the matching bra—which she discovered had unnecessary cup padding—she tightened the thin strings around her neck and back. Claire grudgingly opened the curtain.

She felt fat in this one. It showed too much.

"Nope," Ella said quickly.

Claire rolled her eyes as she nodded in agreement. Pulling the curtain back in place, Claire slowly took off the suit, delaying the disappointment she might experience with the last option. She took time to return both suits to their hangers. Then she halfheartedly pulled the medium navy bottom off the hook and stepped into it. Regardless of wearing underwear, the bottom fit snugly—too much for the money. There was a huge distinction between wishful thinking and denial. The medium bottom leaned toward the latter. Claire scrunched her face up and sadly pulled it off.

"How's it going?" Ella called.

Claire secretly wished they were not out there. She felt a flood of failure mounting as she pulled the large off its hanger—not disappointment from wearing the size, but from fear that the bigger size might not fit either.

"Fine," she called faintly.

She stooped to pull on the bottom, then paused, turning to judge herself.

She smiled. It fit.

Renewed in spirit, she pushed aside the medium top. She was a D cup; if either piece had to be a large, let it be the top.

Claire held the fabric in front of her, examining the construction. She wrinkled her brow, pondering exactly which way it was supposed to go. She turned it several times, continuing to expect the new angle to be more accurate, but both ways looked wrong. Finally, Claire just spread it across her chest and struggled to tie the strings in place. When she was done, she surveyed her work. It was really cute, but she wasn't sure she liked the way it fit. She pulled open the curtain and stood waiting.

"Oh!" Ella said instantly before she had had a chance to really take it in. Claire's face was more doubtful.

"I like it!" Ella announced. "What's wrong?"

"I like it, too, a lot. It's just, I don't know if I like the way the top fits," she said, trying to reposition her breasts a bit beneath the fabric.

Ella tilted her head and examined the issue. "Uh…oh," said she. "Well…"

Claire shrugged. "You see it?"

Ella nodded.

"Maybe if you…" said the saleswoman, trying to fidget with the top. "Wait," she paused standing back. "Oh…" she grinned, "it's on upside down."

Claire's eyes widened a bit as she smiled. "Oh… really?" She turned to the mirror and saw it instantly. It was so obvious.

Ella chuckled. "And we're in graduate school," she quipped sarcastically.

Claire smirked and whipped the curtain closed. The saleswoman smiled proudly and waited while Claire quickly flipped the suit and tied it back into place. When she pulled the makeshift door to the side again she was beaming.

"I'll take it."

"I love it!" Ella said.

Claire redressed quickly and met the woman at the counter. Ella stared on with awe as Claire slid her card across the glass counter. This was something Claire would be paying for herself. She had spent months earning it.

Though self-esteem was certainly priceless, now and then you could attach a number: $167.96 and worth every penny.

CHAPTER 23

"Isn't this great?" Ella said the next morning as they walked through the archway to their new breakfast find. Ella had spied the venue the day before.

Claire was instantly dissuaded as she watched two children feed a bird at their table. How charming, she thought, wildlife directly inside the establishment. "Great," she replied weakly. She followed Ella to the cafeteria buffet and picked up a faded maroon tray. She flicked her hand quickly to shoo away another bird.

Ella spooned a serving of scrambled eggs onto her plate, a small helping of fruit, toast, and two sausage links. Claire perused the food before taking a bowl and a box of cereal.

"That's all you're getting? Remember, it's my treat."

"You know I'm not big on breakfast."

Ella seemed skeptical but served herself a glass of juice from the machine. Claire did the same, filling a second cup with milk for her cereal. While Ella paid, Claire took her tray to gather silverware, napkins, and a packet of sweetener for her meal.

"Good?" Ella asked as she ate her own. Claire nodded. Cereal was cereal. She glanced down at her watch.

"How much time do we have?"

"We really should finish up in about ten minutes. The bus leaves at nine o'clock."

Ella started eating faster.

Claire stared at her. "Don't make yourself sick."

Ella took a few more bites and then swallowed it all with a gulp of orange juice. "OK, I guess I'm ready."

"But you didn't finish it all."

Ella's shrug surprised Claire. They took their trays to the trash, food-court style. Claire looked at her watch again. "We should go."

Ella nodded. They darted through the new crowd of diners—grateful they had come early. "You didn't like it, did you?"

Claire looked at Ella. "No. It's just…"

"It's OK that you didn't like it."

"I told you I'm not big on breakfast. Even after that place yesterday, I felt sort of sick in the heat. I guess I'd just rather spend my money on things versus food."

"But we have to eat."

"I know."

They turned the corner by the ABC Store—a local market-meets-drug store. They had poked around it the day before. "Do you like cereal?" Claire asked.

"Of course."

"Maybe tonight or tomorrow morning we can grab a box of something and a small thing of milk there." She pointed. "We have the mini fridge in the room. It might just be easier and cheaper."

Ella paused. "That's a brilliant idea."

Claire smiled. "Well, I am in graduate school."

"Aren't you special," Ella said sarcastically.

They hurried between tourists, scurrying back to their hotel. The bus for the Polynesian Cultural Center would arrive soon. A small group of people waited outside. When it pulled up to the curb, they were welcomed aboard the coach by Mack, an exceedingly attractive man of Hawaiian heritage. They found seats together toward the front of the bus; Ella took the window.

"Everyone comfortable?" Mack asked. The bus load nodded.

"Are you all excited to see Hanauma Bay?"

Their faces contorted. "I thought this—" started one whiny woman in the front, frowning under her flamingo visor.

"I'm kidding," Mack said, with a dimpled smile. "Though, I highly recommend you go there."

As the bus pulled away from the curb and weaved through the

streets to the last few hotels, Mack began talking, and he didn't stop talking for the entire ride. His commentary was peppered with interesting tidbits of Hawaiian history, contemporary facts, and only a few more lame jokes. The day was beginning to warm as they got off the bus just outside the center. Ella was already taking photos. Hosts in costume welcomed the group while they waited for Mack to fetch their tickets. Inside the wooden walls, the group moved through the displays for nearly two hours. From structures for living, learning, and worship, to cooking simulations and tool displays, they paused in unison for various lessons on Polynesian culture. They passed around replicas of jewelry and housewares, and looked at examples of building construction. Mack stood off to the side at each location. He was not the educator, just the chaperon.

"This is so cool," Ella said as they wandered away from a schoolhouse. She paused to snap a picture of the garbage can with the word Mahalo (*Thank You*) written across its hinged door. Claire nodded, hoping Ella meant the center not the trash.

They sat down for a lesson, which would yield a small green fish woven from a palm frond. "Nice job," the instructor told Claire as she easily maneuvered the leaves. "And you finish like this." He tore away half of two long strips on his sample, forming rustic points that resembled feathery fins. Claire ripped hers carefully then looked up at him with simple delight. He winked at her and moved on to another guest. She helped Ella finish hers, just as Mack leaned down and pointed toward a small food stand where they could start on lunch. After paying, the girls found seats at the waterfront in anticipation of the cultural show Mack said would start at the top of the hour. Suddenly, music and excitement filled the air. The girls were nearly at the tail end of the river, so they waited patiently for the commotion they could only hear at first. From around the corner, they saw wooden floats approaching. On each, women and men dressed in matching ceremonial costumes performed highly stylized dances. Display followed display until, finally, the music faded away, and Mack wandered through the crowd gathering up his people.

When dusk came, they were ready to eat again. Torches lined their path as Mack led them to their final show of the evening: the luau.

"Is this bad for us?" Ella asked holding her plate of food with one hand, while the line of people halted in front of her.

"I guess it's sort of fattening," Claire said. "But it's slow roasted pig in the ground, not a deep fat fryer. And fresh fruit and vegetables. It's not that bad." Claire speared chucks of pineapple with a large serving fork.

"You really love pineapple, don't you?"

"You have no idea. I can't wait for Dole."

Ella smiled and took a spoonful of potatoes. "What is that?" she said as a new dish caught her eye.

Claire tilted her head to see the cause of the exclamation. "Oh my…is that roll…*purple*?"

"Uh…I think it's a roll. It's definitely purple."

A server smiled. "It's taro. Taro root. A favorite in Polynesia," she said proudly. "It's very good." She took the tongs and held one out to Ella's plate.

"Sure," Ella said shrugging.

"It's so pretty." Claire eagerly accepting one as well. "Mahalo."

The woman smiled again, nodding her head kindly.

The girls took their feast to the family-style tables, and even though the pig was greasy, it was delicious. No matter, thought Claire as she enjoyed the fare and then the show. It's the habits you have to mind, not the occasions.

Chapter 24

The next morning they took a taxi to the airport and Claire signed for a rental car, a small white compact.

"Take a right here," Ella said, pointing to the exit as she held the GPS in her hand. Claire drove nervously until she saw the signs for Pearl Harbor. They found a spot in the lot to leave the car and gathered up the few items they thought they might need. Claire slipped her credit card and some cash inside her pocket and took her camera from its case. She glanced at her watch. They had about an hour until the tour to the memorial. Under the open-air roof of the center, they asked a guide where they should start. They picked up their boat passes and went to the museum to explore the exhibit: scale models of the USS Arizona, photographs of the attack, artifacts, and multimedia displays.

"Interesting, huh?" Ella remarked somberly.

Claire nodded. She looked back at her watch, noting their boat would be leaving in about thirteen minutes. She held out her hand toward Ella. "Think we should go get in line?" she asked.

Ella was intently reading a scripted letter. "Yeah, in a sec," she said without looking up or barely hearing the question. "Aw, that's so sad," she said when she reached the end. "It's a love letter."

Claire arched her neck slightly in an attempt to see the note. She nodded.

"What'd you say? Sorry, I was reading."

"The boat. Should we go get in line?"

"Oh, how much time do we have?"

"About eleven minutes now."

"Oh, yeah, probably. I'll follow you."

Claire saw a line forming by a small dock where a single boat bobbed gently in the ocean. The craft had just pulled up to the metal frame floating in the water and a group of people disembarked from its stern. The girls joined the line and waited, wondering how they would all fit on board. But from the corner of her eye Claire saw another vessel approach, returning back from the massive white structure in the bay.

When the crew invited those in line on board, the girls took two seats apart, giving them each a place at the edge with a perfect view of the memorial: long and white, slightly bowed in the center, with an American flag swaying proudly on the top in the soft island breeze.

Once the seats were filled, the boat pushed away from the dock and sped out to the wreckage. Only from the photos in the display on shore did Claire know the memorial ran perpendicular to the battleship below. Just a rusted circular tube protruded from the surface. At the smaller dock alongside the memorial's entrance, another line of people waited to leave. They did not push or really even speak. They waited silently to go. Claire held her camera close to her body as she stepped off the boat and up the ramp.

Sunlight spilled through the large cutouts in the ceiling down the long, straight tunnel. Its clean white walls were disturbed only by a series of uniformed breaks guarded by gates to stop a fall into the ocean. Claire peered down over the metal rail to see rainbows in the water from fuel. Bobbing between the reflective sunshine, hovering solemnly above the massive sunken ship, were tributes of bright flowers gently floating in the salty sea.

Claire paused at the eerie beauty of them and zoomed in to capture the moment. Then she turned and continued down toward the back wall. She could see its end, with black lines running side to side, stacked upon each other. As she stepped closer, she realized those lines were text, names chiseled into the white stone. Columns marked the massive causalities, protected by velvet rope chains held up by metal stands, adorned with flowered wreaths and leis.

She had forgotten to note the time when they reached the dock, but glanced down at her watch to check it. Claire turned and looked for Ella. She found her friend bent over a gate, photographing the water as well. Claire snuck through the mess of people and came up behind Ella. "What'd you think?"

"It's so surreal," she said in wonderment. "It's almost hard to comprehend what happened."

Claire nodded.

When another boat docked to deliver a new group of visitors, Claire and Ella took the shuttle back to land. They poked through the gift shop for a short time and bought some postcards. Before leaving, they each slipped a few dollars into the donation box and returned to their car. The day would be a span of sentiments, a somber experience of history before a commercial swap meet at the nearby football arena. They barely talked on the way to the stadium.

A swap meet was probably the furthest thing from a good time that Claire could imagine—especially on vacation. Wandering around cheap junk in the hot sun sounded like a mild form of torture, but in many ways she considered this trip Ella's adventure. And since Hawaii's largest flea market was something Ella specifically said she wanted to see, Claire didn't argue.

The parking lot was already packed by noon. Claire tucked her camera under a jacket in the car and grabbed the small bag with her wallet. She didn't expect to buy a thing, but she figured she might want a snack. Vendor tables stretched almost beyond view. The market quickly enthralled Ella; Claire followed her through successive tents of random stuff. Ella paused to examine so many things she did not need or would ever buy. Claire finally wandered ahead because she was not sure she could take the cooing another moment. Three tents beyond Ella, Claire found a woman's handmade jewelry and she was intrigued. The crafter smiled at Claire and offered to answer any questions but otherwise left Claire alone to browse. The pieces of jewelry were not cheap, but they were well made. This piqued Claire's interest, and finally she came across a necklace that embodied her idea of Hawaii. It was a short, delicately woven rope, looped twice around a carved abalone shell. The inner part of the mollusk's casing was a single swirl, bluish-green in tint. It shimmered and moved like the waves.

The woman watched Claire and encouraged her to try it on, holding out a mirror. A small ball slipped through the loop to close the circle of the string around her neck. The shell landed just below the hollow curve in the center of Claire's collarbone. Only months ago that clean line of her body had been hidden from sight, washed away by her own flesh. Delicately now it anchored her, and Claire reached up gently to touch the pendent. The simple attention it drew to the newfound part of her femininity made Claire breathe quietly with relief.

"Oh, that's so pretty," she heard Ella say.

Claire turned slightly, smiling. "Isn't it?" She kept staring at herself.

"It looks great on you," the seller said. "You have a beautiful neckline."

Claire looked at her, beaming gratefully. The woman smiled unknowingly, never realizing the value of her simple compliment. Though it might have been just a pitch to sell a necklace, Claire accepted it.

"Do you have any more?" Ella asked.

The woman handed Claire the mirror and moved toward Ella. "There are others. None of them are the same." She showed Ella the different ones she had left, but the design and length of them failed to form the perfect effect of the one Claire held firmly, but gently, in her fingers. Ella looked down at it again, warily. "Gee, I like that one the best. I don't know what's different. Maybe these others are just bigger?" Ella was disappointed, but Claire was secretly pleased hers would be unique.

Claire paid for the piece and the woman offered to wrap it up. "I think I'll wear it."

"Perfect," the artist said, handing the necklace back to her. "I hope you enjoy it."

"I will. Thank you," she said.

As they left the tent, Claire rubbed the shell with her thumb and index finger. She smiled when she saw Ella sneaking another glance at it. She had left the tent empty-handed. Claire left with not only new jewelry but also a renewed sense of beauty.

As the sun reflected off the blacktop, Claire was relieved to finally find a food vendor with things other than junk. Ella relented and bought a hotdog because she was too hungry to wait. Claire could not stand the thought. She did not eat hotdogs. She settled on an overly priced container of fresh fruit and a bottle of water.

"God, you're so good," Ella said almost bitterly.

"I'm just not that hungry. It's the heat." She was sort of lying. She could have eaten more but it was already after one o'clock. Tonight was their special dinner out—the night for which she had brought her size six navy dress all the way to Hawaii.

Claire meandered after Ella as her friend explored the rest of the tents. She poked the sweet fruit slowly with her plastic fork, the bottle of water tucked tightly under her left arm. She savored every bite of the natural fare and noted proudly to herself that she was being good. It was about the little things.

Tonight, she said quietly inside her head, I'm having dessert.

Around three o'clock that afternoon Claire parked their tiny white car in the garage under the hotel, and they went back to their room and dumped their things on the beds. Ella had some little trinkets to put away and Claire set her camera to charge. Then she went to the bathroom and put on her new bikini. She slipped into it, feeling almost guilty. She still could not get over the cost. In a way it was stupid, but somehow symbols could not be foregone. This was the first time she would wear it in public. She was nervous. Maybe it was not the price tag that scared her. Maybe it was the lingering feeling that she still did not look good enough to pull it off—that she might never be and it was a waste because she would never wear it.

She turned in the mirror and watched herself. Her body was nothing like it once was, despite her effort. Her breasts were hoisted up to their youthful position only by fabric that cradled their mass. She was too young to have them sag naturally, but they did. Along her hips, white squiggles bore the marks of stretched skin. They marred her torso and the inside of her left arm as well. Certainly they had faded from care, but they lingered nonetheless, reminding her of it all. Her inner thighs quivered as she moved. No matter how many reps she endured, they were not bouncing back. On some level her labor seemed futile. She was only twenty-three and her body would never be young again. She cursed the meds, the doctors, and the mind she had been stuck with. She would never be able to forget it. She would always be scarred.

She suddenly resented buying the suit. It was $167 wasted, wasn't it? Dabbing her eyes with a square of tissue, she finally gulped in air and breathed out long and hard. She stared in the mirror and saw a pretty face in the glass. "OK, it is what it is," she whispered quietly. "It's better than nothing." She nodded her head weakly, nibbling at her lip, trying to convince herself to leave the room. Finally, she turned, pushed the latch down to release the lock, and stepped out into the room.

"*Ah, you're wearing it!* The Hawaii bikini!" Ella called excitedly. Her outpouring of glee made Claire smile and lessened the memory of her moments of doubt. She was not done, after all. She would keep going. She would keep losing. It was not over yet. Claire chuckled softly, grateful for her wonderful friend. She shrugged and curtsied, modeling the suit.

"It looks so great on you! I'm so happy you got it," Ella said. "I guess I'll go put on my boring one." She grabbed her one-piece and headed toward the bathroom.

Claire didn't know what to say, so she just smiled.

On the beach, Claire reluctantly removed her cover-up and laid it on the sand by her shoes. Ella seemed even more uncomfortable, but did the same. The other beach-goers were busy, ignoring the two pale girls as they darted towards the surf in their suits. The water was tepid but comfortable. They waded quickly out to their waists where the sea would shield them. But as they trekked deeper, they noticed the soft sand beneath their feet turning to rough rocks. They lifted their legs and let the buoyant water keep them afloat. Claire was surprised that a renowned coast could be so painful on her feet, but the view was impeccable so she could not complain. She only hoped the ground would be more pleasant at Hanumana Bay.

They said little to each other as they bobbed in the sea, and Claire was not sure how long they had floated. But as her fingers pruned and her stomach began to rumble, she looked at Ella. "Are you getting hungry?"

"Yup."

"Are you ready to go?"

"Yeah, I guess so."

They paddled until there was sand beneath them, stood, and fought their way to the shore against the current. They dabbed their skin to sop up water before slipping back into their covers. The dip had been refreshing, but Claire's eyes burned from the salt. She could not wait to take a shower.

Claire offered the first shower to Ella and went out on the

balcony to keep her bed from getting damp. The view from their room really was terrible. Below, a parking lot stretched away from the building and other tall structures stood in the distance. Only if she tilted her head could she see even a sliver of the sea. It didn't matter, though. She could still hear it.

Ella finished quickly. They switched and Ella put on her dress while Claire washed away the day. She stood under the shower head, the water only somewhat warm; she was still hot. She could have stayed there for hours, but Ella was waiting on her. She finally twisted the knob off, stepped over the edge of the tub, and dried off. Outside, she found Ella applying a small bit of makeup to her face. Her dress was a simple sundress, but it looked nice on her, and its length gave the otherwise casual outfit a more evening flair. Claire knew her dress was far dressier, but so what? They were on vacation, on an island of strangers. It didn't matter how they looked to others.

Claire dug a pair of panties and her strapless bra from her suitcase, and pulled her dress from the closet. She was eager to get into it and twirl. The flouncy wave of the skirt was ideal for movement. She stepped into the body and pulled the fabric over her torso. Then she rubbed the water out of her hair and gelled it. She applied a dab of light moisturizer to her face—noting the sun-kissed look on her cheeks—and only touched up her eyes, lining the bottom lid with a black pencil and coating her lashes with a layer of mascara. She would finish with her tinted lip gloss, but that was outside in her purse.

She turned around to open the door and paused to notice herself in the mirror. She smiled at the sight, surprised by how adorable she looked. If anything, the dress somehow fit her better than it did when she was sixteen. It was probably her chest. The fullness of her breasts rounded her figure nicely, and the remaining pounds she wanted to lose were comfortably hidden beneath the empire waist of the forgiving design. She stepped outside and scooped up her navy sandals, slipping into one and fastening it around her ankle, then the other. When she stood and turned, Ella's mouth hung open. "Wow, you look amazing! I love that dress!"

Claire was flattered. "Thanks. I've had it for years. I'm just thrilled it fits again. That makes it better than new."

Claire transferred a few items from her casual vacation purse to a dressier one that matched her outfit. "OK," she said. "I'm ready when you are."

They went down to the front desk to inquire about restaurants. They were most intrigued by one several blocks away and many stories up. The restaurant revolved. The front desk clerk promised it was a fabulous experience, and the girls wagered it would be.

They walked parallel to the ocean as the sun hovered in the sky. That meant they were eating unfashionably early, but that also meant they would have a pinnacle view of the setting sun. They passed by people on the street and Claire swore some were looking at her. She wondered if she and Ella looked silly all dressed up for dinner while it was still light out. But they were hungry and they had another long day ahead of them. She was already tired. From across the street she heard a loud whistle of two flirtatious keys. She tilted slightly at the sound and saw an attractive man in a group of attractive men watching her pass. She felt mixed emotions of mild embarrassment, slight paranoia, and flattery.

She looked at him sideways, nervous to make eye contact. He smiled and waved. She looked covertly toward Ella who was grinning at her. "That guy is totally hitting on you. I told you that you looked hot." Claire tried not to smile, but couldn't help it. The outfit never got that kind of reaction at sixteen—nearly 20 pounds lighter.

Forget the dress—it had to be the breasts. Maybe fat wasn't all bad.

CHAPTER 25

In the morning it was drizzling. They hoped it would not last long, but their drive to the Dole Plantation was peppered with raindrops. By the time they arrived, that part of the island was a soggy mess. Dole was good on a good day, disappointing on a wet day. At least dampness meant the tour line would be shorter. They bought cheap plastic ponchos before climbing on the train that meandered through the fields. Claire imagined every pineapple enthusiast had to come here at least once, but she soon wished the tour would end. When the train rolled back to the station, the girls hopped out and hurried inside the store.

Claire was freezing. She hadn't bothered to bring a jacket to Hawaii. She found a simple brown sweatshirt embroidered with just a small pineapple and the word "Dole" practically hidden in thread that matched the fabric. It was unassuming, something she could see herself wearing again. Unfortunately it was a size large and it was snug. Had there been anything else remotely better or at least equivalent, she would have bought it instead. Grudgingly, she paid for the tight top and vowed to cut the tag off when she got home. She slipped it on over her summer dress and rubbed her arms to warm herself while Ella shopped.

Though rain had dampened the visit, Claire's attention perked up as they approached the cafeteria. "Does that sign say 'pineapple ice cream'?" she asked.

"It does," Ella grinned.

Claire ordered a cone. The woman pulled the lever and out pumped a soft serve ice cream tinted a pale yellow. She filled the cone with it and finished it off with a pretty spiraling mound on top. "I hope you enjoy it," she said as she handed it to Claire.

Claire went back to Ella and smiled nervously as she took

a small bite. It was incredible. The pineapple flavor was deeply infused in the frozen cream. It went down smoothly, with just the right amount of sweetness. Claire's rave review inspired Ella to try one as well, even though she really didn't love pineapple. She agreed it was good. Before Ella had gotten through even a third of hers, Claire went up for seconds without a speck of guilt.

Having nothing more to do in the rain, the girls headed back to their hotel, hoping the weather there had cleared up. It had. With several hours left in the day, they sunned at the beach. When the dinner hour arrived, they had a simple meal at a small restaurant, and Claire found herself yawning.

"Getting tired?" Ella asked.

Claire covered her open mouth with her hand. "Isn't that pathetic?"

"Don't forget we're six hours behind. We can go back to the hotel if you want. We probably should. Our shuttle leaves early tomorrow."

They certainly needed the rest. They were inching toward needing a vacation from their vacation. At least they woke mostly refreshed for their last day. No more rushing around. After quick showers and even quicker bowls of cereal, the girls stood outside the front of the hotel to catch a ride to the beach. Claire had never even heard of Hanauma Bay before Ella mentioned it. It took her several times asking Ella to repeat it before she remembered how to pronounce it. But it took only one look at a photograph online to want to go.

Claire secretly smiled knowing her Hawaii bikini was under her black sundress. She didn't want to bother fighting her way into it at the bay, though the bulky string bow tied across her back left a lump in her cover up. The driver wished them a good morning as they climbed in the small shuttle van. Along the bench seat in the back sat three young men. Claire and Ella took the seats in the middle row.

"Just one more stop," the female chauffeur said. The girls nodded. The boys stared out the window and then toward each other, whispering quietly.

"Sorry to interrupt," the driver said. "So, you boys are Navy?"

"Yeah," replied the sailor in the middle, then they were quiet again. The driver didn't continue her line of questioning, responding instead to the road as pedestrians darted in front of her. Claire smiled at the sailors. They could not have been more than eighteen, though they looked more like twelve.

The passengers traveled for a few minutes without talking until the sailor in the middle made casual eye contact with her. "Are you stationed here?" Claire asked—kicking herself as the words came out. It felt like a stupid question, but the silence was killing her.

"No," he said. "We're here on tour. We're in the Navy choir."

"Oh." Claire nodded. She didn't know what else to say. She had never thought about enlisted men serving musical duty, but she could not envision any other armed forces role for them besides choirboys. They seemed so innocent.

"We're the best in the world," he paused. "Well, one of the best."

She nodded again. "I would imagine."

He smiled shyly.

Claire was sitting awkwardly with her back against the window of the van, the seat belt fastened loosely around her waist. She could converse with him more easily, but given her position, she doubted the belt would save her life.

"Are you here on spring break?" he continued.

"Yup." Claire noticed a kindness about him, but also hints of a comical spirit, despite his serious crew cut. The others seemed aloof and bored. Having them behind her—staring at her, maybe making or thinking comments about her—made Claire uncomfortable. She remained in the risky position to watch them and shifted on the seat to pull her beach cover into place. Even shrouded with a dress, Claire felt exposed.

"From college?" he asked.

"Yup. Adams University in Boston," Ella chimed in.

He nodded recognition. "Are you from Mass?"

Both girls shook their heads in unison.

"Rhode Island," Ella said.

"Connecticut," Claire added.

His eyes perked up a bit and he moved to speak as the driver took a rough turn into the third hotel. "Sorry about that," the driver apologized. "I almost missed the driveway." Claire jostled a bit and decided to straighten out in her seat.

In front of the ritzy building stood a father and two girls who appeared to be in their teens or early twenties. Claire felt an abrasive air the instant they climbed onboard. Their aggravated scowls almost made them look ugly. They probably resented being packed in tight with college girls and teenaged boys with military cuts.

The guys seemed intrigued by the attractive young women, obviously ignoring the princesses' disinterest in everything around them. The sisters were likely used to the attention, even though they seemed oblivious to it. Their father appeared to be equally indifferent, but he at least acknowledged the other passengers, tipping his head and smiling somewhat. "Hello," he said flatly.

"Hi," Claire said while Ella grinned weakly.

The boys leaned forward and awkwardly tried to reply, but the family had turned forward in their seats. The sailors leaned back again. The bookended two resumed their stares out the window while the inquisitive one in the middle returned to Claire. "So, you're from Connecticut? My dad was stationed there a while ago, in Groton."

"At the sub base?"

"Yeah."

"My grandparents used to have a boat in the area."

"Oh, cool," he said, suddenly more interested in her. "Yeah, I'd like to do sub training eventually."

Claire nodded warmly, still seeing the young boy in him. "That's a long time under water."

He shrugged. "It's in my blood."

They chatted for the duration of the ride about nothing in particular. The sisters seemed to look back every once in a while, probably irritated at having lost the stares, and even more so at overhearing his invitation, asking Claire and Ella to a party the next night. Claire was sorry to say, "We'll be back in Boston by then."

He nodded.

When the van pulled into the lot for Hanauma Bay, the family got off first, despite the natural flow of the side door exit allowing either the first or second row to leave comfortably. Not even the father waited. Claire glanced sideways at the boy with wide owl eyes and a sarcastic smile. He suppressed a laugh in his arm, rested along the back seat of the girls' row. The boys left last and his friends pulled the sub boy away. He gave a wave and smiled as they left. She never got his name.

Claire and Ella followed the crowd toward the entrance of the bay. After watching the mandatory film on the rules of the bay and renting their snorkeling gear, they opted to trek down the massively steep road on foot, which would take them to the shore. A tram drove passengers up and down the hill, and fare was cheap but the line was long. It was not necessary for the way down; the trip up might be a different story.

The horseshoe-shaped bay contained some of the clearest water Claire had ever seen. Its varying depths appeared tie-dyed in shades of fading turquoise to cobalt to navy blue. They repeatedly admired the view below, trying to brace their steps down the sharp road while barely watching where they were walking. Ella stopped often to snap photos, interrupting beach goers behind her who also were not paying attention.

At the bottom, they weaved in between tourists, finding a

more secluded spot far off to the end where they left their towels and bags on the sand. Claire realized she was glancing to the side slightly, a bit nervously, as she slipped out of her dress. But around her, people with bodies of all shapes and sizes lay sunbathing, and no one was looking at her. Her Hawaii bikini sat low on her hips, well suited to the natural curves of her figure.

Still, her arm rested nervously across her stomach, hiding the faint stretch marks that made her self-conscious. A battle raged inside her. The slightest movement of her skin as she walked on the sand made her feel insecure. But she also felt proud of her efforts to slim down. Whatever her size, at least *this* Claire was willing to venture beyond the security of her towel. That clearly demonstrated personal growth. Besides, it seemed silly to worry about strangers' eyes when they had such spellbinding sights to look at around them.

Ella put on her mask and stared at Claire with a cocked head and goofy eyes that made her laugh. Ella pointed at her.

"What?" Claire asked.

"You match," she said, moving her finger from the teal and navy suit to the teal and navy bay.

Claire nodded, smiling. "I do. Come on," she said, dropping her hand away from her body and trudging toward the water. She sat in the gentle waves and slipped on her flippers before shuffling backward into the sea. Ella followed. Claire swished her mask in water and spit into it.

"Ew!" Ella exclaimed. "What are you doing?"

"It keeps it from fogging up." She rubbed the mess around with her finger and rinsed it in the water again.

Ella skeptically mimicked Claire, hoping the person before her had not done the same thing.

Claire fixed the rubber mask to her face and shifted the snorkel into position before waving at Ella and slipping down beneath the turquoise blue. They dove in the shallow water for hours, shadowing marine life, avoiding other snorkelers, and snapping cloudy photos with cheap disposable underwater cameras. When they returned to the surface, the masks had indented their faces, and the rhythmic huffing noise of their breath through the snorkels still seemed to ring in their ears. They swam then without gear before returning to shore and toweling off. The salt on Claire's skin felt unpleasant as it dried in the air.

Ella checked her watch. "Should we head back soon?"

"Yeah, probably."

After the active and well-deserved week, Claire and Ella slowed down a bit, choosing a small local restaurant with an unencumbered atmosphere. It served fresh seafood, strong drinks, and an ocean view they could almost touch. In the early morning they rose for their flight. The last thing Claire packed was her still-damp bikini, which she tucked into a pocket of her bag. She tossed the last of the cereal into the trash, piled the wet towels on the bathroom floor, and told Ella one last time she couldn't take the pineapple quilt when she left.

<h1 style="text-align:center">Chapter 26</h1>

Claire returned to work before the semester started. She was disappointed that Amy almost forgot to ask her about her trip. Sure, most of her mild tan was hidden beneath clothes that kept her warm from the winter air, but her face and hands were certainly a different shade than when she had left, and Claire had been gone from work for a week.

Amy seemed a bit distant but finally asked her a few questions about Hawaii. Claire's responses matched Amy's interest. She dealt with filing the backlog that had built up during the past week, made some website edits, and finished a few other routine chores. After nearly two hours of feeling tension between her and Amy, Amy called out to her. "When you finish that, Laura wants to see you," she said flatly. "You're gonna be doing some stuff for her as well as me for a while. I think she already told you something about it."

Claire spun around in her chair. She could see the quiet disdain that Amy tried to hide while she clicked away at her keyboard. Her lack of eye contact would have been somewhat insulting had it not been sad. But Claire's vacation mood persisted and Amy's challenged authority was not going to bring her down right now.

"She mentioned something," Claire said casually, working hard to cover her annoyance. Even though Amy was not looking at her, Claire wagered an eye roll would be seen. She waited until she spun back around for that.

Claire watched the clock and waited almost fifteen minutes before finding a convenient place to stop. She began to say something before she left, but Amy had already turned and started sifting through her files. Claire rolled her eyes again as she slipped out the door. Five offices down across the hall, Claire knocked softly on Laura's office door.

The tiny brunette looked up and smiled. "Hey! Welcome back! How was the trip? Didn't you just love it there? I can't believe you bothered to come back!" she said, chuckling.

Claire sighed dramatically. "It was amazing. I loved it. I almost didn't want to come back."

"What was your favorite part?"

"Well, it might sound lame, but it was all pretty wonderful. I mean—Hanauma Bay was gorgeous and so relaxing. The Polynesian Cultural Center gave a lot of interesting background on the island, and the luau and fire show afterward were fantastic. We had really bad weather at Dole, but it was still cool to tour, and I'm officially obsessed with pineapple ice cream." She paused to breathe and think. "Oh, and of course we went to Pearl Harbor. That was so eerie and sad. I almost felt like I was disturbing a sacred site just by being there." She shrugged.

Laura smiled softly. "We must not forget. That's why it was important to go."

Claire nodded. "And, let's see, we also did the beach, some shopping, and wandered around a bit."

"So, a good time overall?"

"A very good time."

Laura's smile widened. "My husband will be so jealous. I told Kevin about your suggestion that he take a spring break trip, too. When I told him where you were going, he complained that he wanted to come."

Claire laughed.

"So, I suspect you're here because Amy freed you for a little while?" Her tone filled in some of the mood that lingered in Amy's office.

Claire responded with wide, exaggerated eyes and a slow nod that required no words.

Laura shook her head. "As I thought. OK, come in and let's get started. And by the way, if this gets too tense for you, please let me know."

Claire was surprised that the comment was even necessary, but nodded affirmatively.

During the next few weeks, Claire worked less with Amy and felt relived to be in Laura's presence. Claire happily occupied herself with the little details of the event: the mailings, guest lists, menus, and name tags, and soon learned her obsessiveness was well suited for event planning. Laura made the same observation, but relayed the sentiment more delicately.

A few days before the event, Laura turned to Claire after she had slipped on her jacket to head home. It was much later than Claire normally worked, and today was not the first day she had stayed beyond her regular hours. Laura had insisted Claire take off Thursday, hoping to even out some of the time.

"I've been meaning to ask, would you be interested in coming down to Manhattan for the event?" Laura asked casually, but Claire sensed there was something more to the question. "My budget could swing your ticket down and back, if you would agree to count just the time at the event as working hours. I don't know if I could convince my boss to pay you for all the travel time, unfortunately."

Claire went to speak, but Laura interrupted her.

"And then," said Laura, "if you could somehow swing the cost of lodging somewhere in the city that night…"

Claire looked at her silently, now knowing she was trying to get something out, but stepping lightly. Claire was curious.

"There's someone I'd really like you to meet."

Claire was stunned and intrigued. She finally asked the obvious question when it seemed Laura would not offer up the last delicious detail without prodding. "Who?" Claire had wondered who would be helping Laura on-site since she seemed to be single-handedly overseeing the entire event. She thought perhaps someone else from the Alumni Association would be going. Maybe someone still would, since Claire suspected if she went, it would be a favor granted by Laura more than a favor asked.

Laura smiled deviously. "Eve Staunton is a very dear friend of mine. We went to college together in Maryland and have remained close since then, despite not getting to see each other as much as we'd like. I've known for a while you two had to meet. She was actually supposed to come up here a few months ago, but that fell through. Now that we have a reason to be in the same city, we have dinner planned. And if you want, I'd like to bring you."

Claire was dumbfounded and confused by the blatant insistence that Laura's student worker crash a quiet get together between girlfriends.

But Laura was still smiling. "You see, Eve owns a—be it smaller—creative agency in Brooklyn."

Claire's eyes widened in disbelief; her mouth opened just a bit.

Laura kept smiling as she spoke, with gentle motherly eyes. "Her firm began in Baltimore and moved to the city not quite three years ago. It's still growing," she said, holding her hand up in caution, "but Eve is amazing, smart, and sassy. She's actually a designer—well, a designer and now a CEO. She's down to earth but not a pushover. She's very honest, which is why she probably hasn't made it as big as some others. But she has a real reputation for solid hard work, and I think she just prefers the environment of a more intimate operation." Laura smiled. "I've talked about you a few times when I mention work myself, and I told her a bit about what you're interested in. I hope you don't mind that I shared with her a few of the details you told me about your experience with Marshall's Creatives."

The mention of the name made Claire's face wrinkle a bit.

Laura laughed. "Well, that's pretty much how Eve feels about them." She paused as though in contemplation. "Actually, maybe twice your dislike would be more accurate."

Claire grinned.

"Anyway, I sent her your website and she loved what she saw."

Claire was soaring with excitement. "Oh my God!"

"I am not saying she'll offer you a job or anything. But if you are serious about moving to New York and working as a copywriter, she might just be a brilliant place to start."

Claire drew in her shoulders inadvertently as she covered her mouth with her hands. She could barely contain her giddiness. She let out a little squeal and jumped up to hug Laura.

Laura laughed and patted Claire on the back softly. "So, you think you can finance a night in the Big Apple for the chance at a big opportunity?"

"One of my best friends lives there. I've got a couch for free. I don't even have to ask."

"Holy shit! Of course, sweetie," said Kim when Claire called that night. "You've got a place anytime. Eli will be out of town on business, which sort of sucks because I'd love you to meet him. But it's perfect timing because we can have a real girls' weekend. What day are you coming? I'm not usually home until seven o'clock most nights, but I might be able to leave work a little early."

"Well, the event is Friday night till later anyway."

"Oh, perfect. Then if you get here early enough, you can drop your stuff at my place. My doorman, Carlos, is a trip. He'll keep it safe."

Claire was comforted to have plans falling into place, despite the chaotic feelings that still lingered about thoughts related to

New York. Maybe that explained her hesitance every time Kim asked her to visit.

They chatted for a few minutes more and then Claire said she hated to go but had dinner plans. Kim seemed happy to hear Claire was not spending the night alone but did not go so far as to say the words. She wished her a "good night," and sent hugs and kisses to Boston.

As Claire hung up from Kim, she checked her watch because she had promised to call Ella about dinner. Claire felt bad she had missed yoga again this week. At least Ella went without her, with Claire's blessing. Ella had texted back that she couldn't wait to hear the news Claire promised to share over dinner, and to let her know when she had finished her important call. Claire swiped the wake-up button on her phone almost at the same time as it started ringing.

"What?" exclaimed Claire alone in her apartment, smiling at the photo the phone revealed. "Hey, stranger!"

"Hey, yourself. How are ya? Anything new and exciting going on?"

"Well…" and Claire proceeded to tell Jill the possibility of New York.

"Oh my God, that's amazing!" Jill said when Claire paused for a breath. "I think you're probably more ready for it this time."

"I think you're right."

Claire sensed Jill had exciting news of her own to share. "What about you?"

"Who, *me*?" Jill asked.

"Yes, *you*."

"Well, I've had several chats with Marian and Donald, and somehow—*who knows how*—I've finally explained to them after all these years that just because they've lived their own lives pretty successfully up until now, that doesn't mean they know everything about life. I'm not saying they don't have an idea about what the general template of life is, but you know I've always hated that they pretend to know everything about mine. And I suppose I've hated myself on some level for letting them dictate it."

"What are you saying?" Claire asked. Something big lingered in her dear friend's far-away voice.

"I'm coming back east."

"What?" Claire exclaimed again.

"Well, hopefully. I'm waiting to hear back from some schools, but I've officially applied to four grad schools for a Ph.D. in clinical psychology!"

"Oh my God! Please tell me that at least one of them is in New York."

"Two, roomie."

CHAPTER 27

Claire took a train to New York by herself. She had planned to go with Laura, but that fell through at the last minute when prior commitments kept Laura in Boston. She asked Claire to go ahead and make sure the site was ready. Laura and a colleague would follow later. In a way, this worked to Claire's advantage, giving her extra time to drop off her bag at Kim's banker boyfriend's apartment.

Carlos was, in fact, a trip. Claire gave him permission to give Kim the bag if she came home before Claire's event ended, which it seemed would be the case.

When she arrived at the venue, the staff was friendly and hard at work. Laura had briefed the manager a few days prior, and he showed Claire around the site to make sure everything was set. Claire called Laura to report and reassure her that things were going smoothly. She set up several signs that Laura had provided and handed off the alumni banner to the restaurant crew. Then she left for a nearby coffee shop to relax until the others arrived. With an ebook, an iced coffee, and an uncut bagel, Claire happily found a wide chair in the back, slipped in her earbuds to drown out the ambient noise, and nestled her phone by her leg on vibrate. It went off when Laura arrived.

Laura was in full event-mode when Claire caught up with her. She gave orders directly, with less of a smile and more determination than normal. Claire happily obliged. She quietly unpacked the few boxes Laura had shipped, unloaded the rolling case she had brought on the train, and laid out name tags, papers, and branded gifts according to her boss's specifications. They finished more than an hour ahead of schedule. Laura breathed a sigh of relief and flashed her usual smile. She patted Claire on the shoulder and invited Claire and her co-worker, Wendy, to join her at the bar for dinner.

The three ate tavern food, talking and laughing over the quiet lull of a ball game playing in the background on the flat screen TV. Laura periodically checked her watch and took a last sip of iced tea. "We should probably think about getting ready for it."

The three manned the door and soon after began greeting arriving AU alumni. The trickle gradually turned into a crowd of nearly 150 eager people, all linked by a shared college experience at AU. Claire handed out name tags, directed guests inside, and answered questions. No one lingered long enough to notice the graduation years on her name tag. The Alumni Association Vice President walked by without pausing. But she forgave him; his support had indirectly brought her to New York.

Laura had encouraged Claire to mingle, pointing out that she was an AU graduate, too. But Claire preferred to stay at the check-in table with a virgin drink in her hand, occasionally snagging an appealing hors d'oeuvre that passed by. The party rumbled on in the private room as Claire watched covertly from the outside, quietly wondering if she could make it here.

Just after nine thirty, the group started to thin out. The music had slowed, the stationary food had been replenished twice, and the bar had moved well beyond the complimentary first hour of drinks. Claire looked down at her watch, bobbing softly where she stood as she cursed her high heels. She should have known better. But they paired perfectly with her skirt and top. Her hair was far shorter now than it had been in her early years of college, and she pulled it back after it had fallen into her face one too many times. The few strands that had escaped her ponytail curled softly around her face and the nape of her neck as if deliberately placed there.

"Long day?" she heard a warm voice ask. Claire looked up to find herself face-to-face with a tall, quite gorgeous man. He had dark hair, trimmed facial hair, and smart, thin glasses covering steel blue eyes.

Claire smiled weakly. "Very long."

He chuckled. "I'm Wes Elliot."

"Claire Kelly."

In the same motion he shook her hand and also peered at her tag. "Ugh, I feel old. I've got seven years on you." The skin by his eyes and mouth creased as he smiled, suggesting the gesture came easy to him.

Claire chuckled. "Age is just a number. You don't look old. Do you act it?"

"Never."

She touched his arm. "Then I think you're safe."

"So, what's your field? Is that the communication college?" he said peering again at her tag.

"Yup. My field is, as you said, communications. My focus is advertising and writing."

He nodded his head. "Do you work in the city?"

"Actually, I'm still at AU. I'm finishing my master's degree this summer."

"OK," he said still nodding. "I did both there as well. Engineering."

"And I'm assuming you work in the city?"

He chuckled. "Yup. I'm a bit of a nerdy geek."

She touched his arm again, drawn to the thought of a handsome nerd. "Well, you don't look old or nerdy."

He smiled sheepishly. "That's a relief." His nervousness was almost sweet to Claire. She never imagined it might be her.

"Well," he said after a few moments of quiet, "I'm late for a drink with friends. But if you end up in the city after the summer, or before then, you should give me a call." He handed her a business card he had pulled from his pocket. She took it with a coy smile herself. She was too surprised to say anything but "OK," and nodded her head softly. Fireflies fluttered wildly in her stomach, and she felt her body warm as blood rushed through her veins and dizzied her shy mind.

"OK…well, bye," he said with a wave and a final grin that creased the lines by his eyes again. She barely managed to say the same.

Claire stood stunned for a few moments more, forgetting to say goodbye to more alums who passed her. Laura snapped her attention back. "How's everything going?" she asked. "Ah, I see you made at least one connection." Claire nodded, still holding Wes's card in her hand.

As the hour approached ten, the last of the group left. Claire helped pack up and then asked Laura if there was anything else she needed her to do.

"Nah. Go back to your friend's. Enjoy the rest of your night. I'll see you tomorrow at the restaurant at seven thirty. Do you have the name?"

"Yup. It's in my email. It's actually pretty close to Kim's apartment, which is great."

"Wow, she's in a *nice* location."

"She has a *nice* boyfriend."

"Ah. That helps."

Claire smiled.

"Great job, again. Thanks for all of your hard work, on everything for tonight. Ross was thrilled."

"It was a perfect event. I was happy to be part of it," she said smiling.

Laura nodded. "All right. See you tomorrow."

"Sounds good."

Claire grabbed a cab to Kim's place. She was not wandering New York's streets aimlessly at night. She had texted Kim that she was on her way. Kim used several exclamation marks to note her excitement and told Claire the doorman had already handed over her bag. Claire's poor feet were officially in pain when she finally knocked at apartment number 342. Kim whipped open the door and stood in disbelief. Despite Claire's tired exterior, she made a stunning image. Her loose curls, her form-fitting skirt, and her heels displayed a confident woman. Kim's expressive face failed to hide her utter shock at the shape of this Claire, whom she had never seen before in person.

"OH. MY. GOD! Claire! Look at you!"

"I need to sit down," Claire said with a halfhearted smile.

"Shit! Yeah, come in. But…I can't get over it. You look AMAZING!"

"Thanks, dear." Claire sounded old.

"Sometimes I couldn't really believe your photos from high school. Now I can."

Claire was somewhat flattered and somewhat annoyed. She could have been offended, but she knew Kim didn't mean it that way. If she did, she would have said it outright. Claire took it as the compliment Kim meant it to be.

"How was the party?" Kim said finally, realizing she might be taking it too far. "Sorry I didn't come myself."

"Oh, that's fine. It was great. But I wore the wrong shoes."

"No, honey. Those look perfect. Sore, maybe, but they look killer."

"They feel killer."

Kim chuckled. "Here, take them off. I'll get you a glass of wine and then you can take a long hot shower, slip into some pjs, and we'll lounge on the couch. I'm too tired to go out. I hope you didn't want to."

"No!" said Claire.

Kim smiled again as she handed over a large goblet.

The wine was drier than Claire would have liked, which just meant she sipped it slower. Her feet loved the freedom of being bare, and she massaged them softly, tucked up under her body. She yawned and set the glass down on the table. "I might take a shower now and then we'll talk."

"Sure thing. There are towels and soap and everything in the shower. Feel free to use anything you find in there."

Claire smiled. "Thanks."

"No worries."

Fifteen minutes later, Claire emerged, soft and pink, with wet hair and cotton pants. "So much better."

Kim grinned. "I'll bet. So…tell me more about everything," she said in a motherly tone. "I haven't talked to you in forever."

Shortly before seven the next evening, Claire put last-minute touches on her face and checked her dress once more in the mirror. Kim had dragged her all around the city starting with morning coffee at her favorite shop, just a block from the apartment. Claire was impressed by the luxury lifestyle Eli and Kim enjoyed, yet Claire knew if anything worked out with Eve, hers would be quite different. She was grateful that Eve's place was in Brooklyn. Despite the supposed stigma of a borough, Brooklyn had become quite trendy, if not somewhat more manageable for living. Claire kept hoping Jill would be accepted to one of the schools in New York and would transfer there. That seemed to be her plan.

"I'm sorry that my dinner tonight will cut into our time together," Claire had said earlier but Kim immediately waved away the notion.

"Come on," she had said, "this is a potentially amazing opportunity for you! If anything comes from it, we can have nights out whenever we want!"

Claire emerged from the bathroom all dolled up, ready for her night out. Meanwhile, Kim was in the small living room, slumming it in yoga pants.

Kim smiled proudly and shook her head. "I'm sorry. I don't mean to harp on it, but jeez, honey, you look a-maz-ing!"

"Thanks."

"I love that dress. I might have to borrow it." Kim winked.

Claire chuckled as she picked up a light dress jacket and her purse, slipped on a pair of tall boots, and bid her friend farewell. She apologized again for abandoning her.

"Oh, stop. Have a fabulous night. I could use an evening in. Good luck!" Kim exclaimed, tossing her arms around Claire, positioning them just so as to not disturb Claire's hair.

Claire took a cab to the restaurant to avoid any chance of getting lost in New York. At least tonight, unlike her dreary trip to Marshall's Creatives, she moved with confidence. This time, everything just felt right. Claire was waiting at the bar when Laura arrived.

"Don't you look nice," Laura said, reaching out to squeeze Claire's arm. "You're gonna love Eve."

"I'm dying to meet her."

Laura smiled. She felt like she was setting two people up on a blind date. "Eve texted me a few minutes ago. She's not too far away and told us to get a table. They shouldn't have a problem seating us. Apparently, they know Eve here."

"Fancy."

"I know, right? Anyone who meets Eve never forgets her."

Claire followed Laura and the hostess to a small table by the far window, tucked away in a quieter nook, if that was at all possible in the loud space. They chatted and ordered wine, and waited on Eve. Claire knew she had arrived by the smile on Laura's face. Eve wore tall boots with a flowing black skirt and a bright purple shirt tucked in at the high waistband. It called attention to her upper torso, but was sheltered with a delicately painted scarf that fell as it pleased and a long layered necklace of silver chains. She was of average height with mid-length dark wavy hair and softly applied makeup. The slight fullness in her face and hips did nothing to detract from her positively lovely appearance as she swooped into the room. Laura jumped up and embraced her, marking the time since they last met in person.

"Look at you!" said Laura, pulling back and touching her friend's hair.

"Oh, yeah, I cut it. You like?"

"I love!"

"Well, you haven't changed a bit, still so damn skinny. I'm jealous."

"Oh, please," said Laura, sheepishly waving her hand away.

"How's Kevin?"

"Great. Avery and the kids?"

"Doing well." Eve turned toward Claire, who had not wanted to interrupt the friends' reunion. She started to stand now and held out her hand with a smile.

"This beautiful woman is a fatty? God, they're more deluded at Marshall's place than I thought."

Claire couldn't help but chuckle slightly. Not so much at the slanted truth behind Eve's first impression, but more so at her blatant dislike of the agency.

"Well, if they even deserve a defense," said Claire, "I was definitely heavier then."

Eve shrugged. "Eh, they're still a bunch of asses."

"I won't argue that point."

Eve chuckled. "You're right, Laura, I like her already." She pulled out a chair, slung her coat on its back, and settled in, turning specifically back to Claire. "Tell me, which little weasel called you a fatty?"

"I have no idea. Some attractive grown man in a superhero t-shirt."

"Oh," she said expressively, pulling back slightly in her chair and nearly tipping the ice water at the table, "that could be any one of them. He has interchangeable minions running around for him."

Claire found Eve's distaste for Marshall's Creatives' crew refreshing.

"I still can't believe the remark," Eve said.

"Well," Claire hesitated slightly, "I did weigh a little over 200 pounds." The words seemed somewhat impossible to comprehend and she found herself rounding down.

Eve seemed taken aback. Her eyes initially widened somewhat in disbelief at the number, but then Eve was genuinely disappointed by her own behavior once recovering from the surprise. "I'm sorry," she said. "That was so rude. I'm just a little amazed. You can't be more than—"

"One hundred and thirty-three," Claire said proudly.

"That's almost 70 pounds in a year."

"The last time I stepped on a scale then, it said 215. So, I've lost about 82 pounds."

"Wow!" Eve seemed intrigued more than surprised. "That's amazing. How'd you do it?"

Claire paused for a moment, but finally decided honesty and bravery were more freeing than hollow success. "Well…I was this size when I was younger." She chuckled and repeated the word *younger*, making silly air quotes with her fingers. Eve and Laura laughed. "And of course I thought I was fat then. But I went on a depression medication in college, which didn't work very well. Then I went to a different one that was even worse. We eventually discovered I actually have bipolar II disorder and my doctors took me off everything. Now I'm on a mood stabilizer that works great. A big part of the weight was the original meds. When I went off them, I lost about 40 pounds in less than two months."

"Jeez! That's incredible. And the rest was just diet and exercise?"

"Not so much diet as less frosting and brownie mix."

Eve and Laura laughed out loud again.

"Life is far less enjoyable without frosting and brownie mix," said Eve.

"True. I make exceptions from time to time," said Claire.

"Well, mine's the result of beating cancer but losing half my thyroid in the process," said Eve, motioning towards a small scar at her throat. "Add to that two wonderful children and being a decade or two older, and…I just don't worry anymore. I have too many other things to worry about."

Claire smiled.

"And as long as my husband loves me and my children love me…" she looked up toward Laura, "…my friends and my clients love me, hell, I think I'm doing all right."

"Well, I think you look stunning," Claire said.

Eve smiled. "Thanks, dear. So, everything is good with you now? You're feeling good?"

"Great. The best treatment is knowing what's going on…whatever it is. It sounds lame, but knowledge really is transformational."

Eve smiled expressively, nodding her head in agreement. "No, that's so true. My aunt actually has bipolar disorder, too. She was much older than you before she found out about it, and she had a really difficult time until she learned what was going on, how to deal with it, and more so once she accepted it. You're very lucky. You're honest, too. I like that."

Claire smiled outwardly, breathing a sigh of relief.

"And honey," Eve said reaching out to gently touch Claire's hand, "no matter if you weighed 200-anything, you're talented. If they didn't hire you because of your dress size, they are bigger idiots than I thought."

Claire smiled and nodded slightly. She had almost forgotten that no defense was deserved at all.

CHAPTER 28

Though Eve didn't offer Claire a job that night, she gave Claire plenty of hope. "I'm chasing a new account, which, if I get it, I will definitely be looking to expand my crew." Eve smiled at Claire when she said it.

Claire nodded and smiled back. She casually asked for a few particulars, trying to appear interested without being nosy. It was an organic beauty and cosmetic company, which piqued Claire's interest. She sometimes wondered what types of accounts she would have worked on at Marshall's Creatives.

"I might even be looking for some freelance pitch ideas." Eve winked.

"I'd be honored."

Eve liked that response. She preferred knowing who she was getting before she hired. She already liked what she had seen from Claire so far. The young woman's enthusiasm to prove herself was promising.

The next morning, Claire and Kim enjoyed a leisurely brunch and some window shopping. "I can't wait for you to move here," Kim said excitedly. "Wouldn't it be fun to have us all back in the same city? Well…" she paused, "except Kyra, who's probably never moving back." Their jetsetter fourth had eloped last winter with a man she met in Paris.

"I know. I really hope Jill gets into school here. I don't see why she wouldn't. Her second try on the GRE earned her a pretty impressive score, despite all of her griping."

Kim grinned, remembering the study sessions back in Boston that she had avoided by hiding out in her room. As she sat by Claire now, she also noted to herself how different Claire seemed. She didn't actually have a job in the city yet, but she seemed to think it was possible this time.

"And my friend, Ella, might move here in a year, too," said Claire. "She's doing AU's PR program right now. It'd be great to have her close. And maybe if I'm settled in business, I'll be able to help her find something."

Kim nodded. "It sounds like you've got it all figured out."

Claire smiled. "Not even close."

Kim laughed. "Hey," she said, tugging Claire's arm. "Want a cupcake?"

Claire was stunned.

"What?" Kim asked.

"*You?*" Claire asked. "You want a cupcake? Especially after brunch?"

Kim laughed. "A little one," she said, holding two fingers just an inch apart. "They're amazing."

Claire shrugged. "OK, a little one."

They picked out their treats, paid, and went back to the sidewalk to eat them.

"How is it?" asked Kim, licking the frosting away from her lip after a bite of her tiny dessert.

"It's great!" Claire smiled secretly to herself; happy to learn Kim could eat a confection—no matter how small—and enjoy it.

"So…you're good then?" Kim asked warily, finally toying with the point she had been too nervous to make all weekend.

Claire grinned awkwardly at Kim, as though she were about to laugh.

"Come on," Kim whined. "I'm your friend and I care about you. I know what happened the last time I brought it up, obviously ineloquently. I just want to make sure you're OK. I mean—you've gone through a lot of shit these past few years."

Claire smiled again, a bit softer this time. She sampled another taste of frosting from the tip of her finger and savored its sweetness. "Yeah, I suppose," she shrugged. "I guess it's just life.

My life. I wouldn't wish this on anyone but it's treatable, if you let it be. I guess I'm proof of that. But I know I have my family, my doctor...and of course my friends to thank for that."

Kim smiled. "You have yourself, too."

Claire chuckled. "Yeah, I guess. And it wasn't all bad."

"No?"

Claire shook her head. "I lost parts of my life, and almost even my life itself, but I learned compassion. I hate the stretch marks and I totally wish my boobs were back up where they started, but I found beauty."

Kim smiled even as she looked like she might cry.

"And I've come to know that nothing in this world happens without some type of reason, and I'm not talking the lame motto 'all things happen for a reason.' That's ridiculous. It's more like you never know what's going on in someone else's world. I'll bet most strangers would have never guessed why I was fat. That I was dying inside. People just make that first judgment and nothing else matters. And because I already felt like it was my fault—with everything that was going on—I let them judge me. But there's always a backstory to everyone's life." She paused. "I think that's why it's still hard to let go of what happened at Marshall's Creatives. It wasn't even the words the guy used. It's what he meant by them. I was fat therefore was I stupid and useless. It couldn't be anything else."

Kim tilted her head slightly, not knowing what to say.

"But he's really not the only one." She shrugged. "The world looks at overweight people and passes judgment like it did in my case. Yet no one seems to care about the reasons behind the fat. They think you're just lazy and worthless—that you sit around all day aimlessly eating. And I'm not saying extra weight is a good thing, but it doesn't make you a bad person. And it's not a choice, not really, anyway. It could be medical—like me; emotional—like me; metabolic—which isn't me yet, but I'm still young." Claire winked and Kim laughed. "What's worse though is if Chase knew the real reason for my weight, he probably would have shoved me out the door instead of just waiting for me to leave. You know, because I'm *crazy* and all."

Kim shook her head.

"That's why I told Eve from the beginning. It was risky but worth it. Lying is so exhausting. Now I don't have to be anyone other than myself—the good and the bad. Eve's an amazing person to see there's more good to me. I really admire her for that."

Ella picked Claire up at the train station back in Boston, eager to hear how the event and business dinner went. Claire was tired from three busy days of travel and activities, and really just wanted to go home, but she felt she had ignored her friend for weeks now, and was obliged to accept Ella when she asked to go out.

"Eve is awesome. I love her. Even if she doesn't get the account, I think there's something there for me. I feel like I could have two mentors now, which I know sounds silly, but…" she trailed off, shrugging her shoulders.

"Not at all. I'm really envious that you've put yourself out there."

Claire looked up softly at Ella's admission. Ella smiled. "And you had a good time with your friend, Kim?"

"Oh yeah. We didn't have that much time together because I was busy most of Friday and then went out without her on Saturday night, but she's really excited about the idea of me moving to the city."

"I'm sure. And it'll be fun if your other friend goes, too. You'll be with your old group again."

Claire made a sad face. "Do you think you'll come eventually? I told Kim we might have a fourth for our group again, since Kyra went off to Europe, probably forever."

Ella perked up at the thought. "Well, I'd love to do an internship there the last semester of my program, so maybe. Actually, I've been thinking—and I talked the idea over with my advisor—that I might go to summer school, too, and finish in December. I still have time to sign up for classes. Not much time, but some."

"I think that's a great idea. The sooner you can get out, the better. And summer school is a shorter semester, so there's usually less busy work. It's more to the point."

Ella seemed far away and nervous. As Claire's life began to find its direction, Ella was somewhat lost. But there was not much Claire could do now besides being supportive. Once her life was more settled perhaps Claire could offer more help.

"It'll all work out. You'll be fine," she said, patting Ella's hand.

Ella smiled and nodded. Claire wasn't really sure Ella believed her though.

That night, Claire searched for Eve's agency, Muse 9, and perused the pages of creative content. She scanned through the company's gallery of work, studied its philosophy, and read the bios of its core staff. Each person's name had an embedded email link. Claire copied Eve's and typed out a message to her. She kept it short but wanted to say something. She titled it, "Dinner with Laura," hopeful that it wouldn't be deleted as spam.

Dear Eve,

Thank you again for welcoming me at your reunion dinner this weekend. I was thrilled to meet you and hear more about your company. I am so impressed by your business, its goals, and its clients. If any opportunities arise, I hope you will keep me in mind. I'll certainly be checking your job site. If you have freelance work, please do not hesitate to contact me. I would be eager for the chance to prove myself.

Best,

Claire

She felt the message covered all that she wished to say without dragging on. After a final review, she pushed send, and then whined nervously and popped a tranquilizer to calm the anxiety that was building as graduation day neared. She knew it was a mix of excitement and fear, but it was making her sick. It also was keeping her up. She tried to sleep that night, but words kept flashing through her mind. She wrote prolifically in her journal, jotting down random thoughts and two poems; one that she finished and another that remained a skeleton of an idea.

The next day brought no word from Eve, not that she expected it. Per Laura's request, Claire skipped work to even out the hours she had put in at the event. She could not surpass her allowed maximum. Claire wondered if most of her time would revert back to Amy, and if so, how would she take it. It had been a few weeks since Claire worked steadily with her former boss. It would likely be awkward going back. Claire welcomed the idea of avoiding the office altogether. Instead, she focused on the last class project of the semester, which was mostly finished and was not due for two weeks.

That evening, like the one before it, Claire studied the clock. She finally turned it around and watched the flashes of lights that came through her window and danced on the ceiling.

She awoke after 10 a.m., showered, dressed, and walked to Solace, hoping to find just that. She ordered her favorite iced coffee and opened a very large classic. She just couldn't find the power to concentrate, and instead read the same page three times. She finally rested it in her lap—still open—and gazed at the people milling around the shop. Her phone dinged, announcing an incoming email. She opened the message and held her breath at the subject line, which read: "Re: Dinner with Laura."

Dear Claire,

Sorry for the delayed response. I'm usually quite prompt with email, but things have been busy. It was a pleasure having you join us. Laura has spoken so highly of you these past few months, and I can see why.

I was very serious about freelance opportunities. In fact, we are working on that new prospect I mentioned. We're on to some ideas. And though we have a few strong ones, I thought I would throw out the assignment to you for another take. I've attached an overview of the client's needs and wish list. I'll need your ideas this week. Sorry for the tight deadline, but you asked for real world experience. You're on, if I can have your thoughts by the week's end.

-Eve

Claire was shaking at the prospect of doing actual work for Eve. What if she failed? What if she succeeded? Both outcomes terrified her.

Now she truly couldn't concentrate. Since her phone offered little help to thoroughly view the attachments, Claire finished the last quarter of her coffee quickly, ordered a second one to go, and scooted back to her apartment. Sitting cross-legged on her couch, she brought up the email and opened the linked files. They were images from an existing campaign, a strategy report for the new one, and some photos unmarked with words, likely tentative imagery from the team's brainstorming. The word *natural* jumped out at her, as did *personal connection, the individual,* and *clean.*

Ideas instantly came to her. She jotted them down and immediately started shuffling them around like a puzzle. She was adamant that *nature* or *natural* be part of the five-word statement that sold the brand. After ten minutes of concentration, a thought popped into her head and she couldn't let go of it.

"That could work," she said out loud and jotted it down on a sketchpad. But Claire knew better than to stop at an early idea, even if it ended up being the best. Instead, she replied quickly to Eve's message, thanking her for the opportunity and promising to come up with some interesting concepts by the deadline.

Now, Claire couldn't think of anything but the project, and was grateful that her schoolwork was done. Even as the message consumed the rest of her day, she found herself continuing to come back to that first note she had made. She thought about it at dinner. She returned to it at midnight watching a sitcom, trying to clear her head. And she thought about it at 2 a.m., while she watched the clock.

She dragged herself out of bed at eight thirty the next morning and arrived at work by ten o'clock. Amy had some assignments for her and the transition was not as painful as Claire feared. When Amy left for a meeting across campus, Laura popped her head in the office. "Thanks again for everything!"

"No, thank you. Eve is such a sweetheart. She actually gave me a chance to help on the pitch for that new account."

"She did? That's awesome! She mentioned she would. I'm so happy to hear it worked out. Who knows?" said Laura excitedly, shrugging her shoulders.

"I know. I really can't thank you enough."

Laura waved away the comment. "You earned it. And not just by helping me. You really deserve this opportunity."

"I'm so happy I've had the chance to work with you—Eve or no Eve."

Laura smiled sweetly. "Aw, thanks. Me too. You better keep in touch when you leave."

"Oh, I will. Maybe you'll find me at Muse 9."

"Definitely!" Laura said.

That night was too much like the prior one. The insomnia was exhausting. Claire took another tranquilizer before bed, which seemed to calm her down a bit. She eventually fell asleep sometime after 1 a.m. By morning, the project was gnawing at her mind again. She couldn't let go of her good idea but felt guilty, thinking that it came too easily. She wondered if it might not be good at all.

She finally decided the only way to find peace was to send it and let it go.

Dear Eve,

I'm a little ahead of deadline, which I hope will not be perceived as rushing through this incredible assignment. I feel strongly that this creative message could meet the needs of your client. It is two complementary statements that match the goals of the strategy and could stand as one cohesive thought or alone if needed. As a complete statement, it says the brand comes from nature, but also that the products are so natural they are practically equal to a person's own skin.

Creative message: Built by nature. Like you.

Thanks again for including me on this. I hope your team likes it… and your client!

Claire

When it was gone, Claire finally breathed freely. She stood by it. She hoped Eve would as well.

Eve wrote back after lunch. The short response left Claire wondering.

Thanks, Claire. I'll take this to the team. Wow, you're fast!

Three short sentences. Nothing more. It wasn't elation, but it wasn't rejection either.

CHAPTER 29

It had been ten excruciating days and still nothing from Eve. Claire began feeling like a failure who had wasted almost five years of her life on an aspiration that did not match her talents. Her classes for summer started next Tuesday, and as she paid the fees for the semester and purchased the books, she was sick.

She shuffled around her apartment, disinterested in eating, disinterested in talking, disinterested in being awake. She tossed her feet up on her small coffee table and watched the television without interest as well. She stared at it and wanted to cry.

Her phone vibrated and she saw a text message from her mother: *Text me or I'll call Ella.*

That was Emily's veiled threat, which arose when her depression symptoms returned and Claire avoided answering the phone. Her mother didn't trust Claire to be alone when she got like this. Claire wagered if she didn't reply, Emily would indeed call Ella, or worse.

I'm alive, Claire texted back.

Want to talk?

Not really.

OK. But I'm here.

I know. Thanks.

Claire put her phone down by her side and turned her attention back to the show. She couldn't really follow it. She felt exhausted even after sleeping until 11 a.m. She was taking her meds but sometimes they just couldn't ward off the flood of symptoms.

Her phone started ringing. "God, Mom!" Claire grumbled loudly as she looked down, but the song's ringtone was wrong. It was an unfamiliar number. She rolled her eyes, wondering who was bothering her now. She debated about answering it. Below the number read the words: New York. Kim? Maybe it was the boyfriend's number.

She sighed, straightened her back slightly, and mustered a normal tone. "Hello?" she asked.

"Hi, Claire?" The voice sounded oddly familiar.

"Yes." Claire pushed herself up more on the couch.

The caller's voice was warm. "It's Eve."

Claire's heart stopped. She sucked in her breath. "Hi," she said again, softer and calmer. She stood up from the couch and walked into the kitchen. "How are you?"

"I'm great. You?" Eve sounded easy and confident.

"Good," Claire lied. She started pacing around the apartment in an infinity twist.

"So, I wanted to follow up with you about your concept. Is this a good time?"

"Of course."

"OK. Great. We've been so swamped here these past two weeks, I don't even remember when I've had a real night's sleep." Eve laughed.

"I'm sure," Claire said sympathetically.

"But it was for a good reason."

"Good news?" she asked hopefully.

"Great news. We pitched yesterday and they loved it."

"Wow, congratulations."

"I didn't want to bother you too late, but thought you'd like to know that it was your line they fell in love with."

Claire was silent for a moment. "What?"

Eve chuckled. "Yes. Yours. The one you sent—before deadline, I must add."

"Seriously?"

Eve chuckled. "Yeah. How long did it take you to come up with that?"

Claire's mind was foggy. "The truth?" she somehow managed to say.

"Why?"

"Ten minutes."

Eve was quiet for a moment. "You know what, Claire? That just means you're good."

Claire thought she might start crying. She hated needing words like that. She nodded, but realizing Eve couldn't hear a nod, quickly said, "Thanks."

"I mean it. I don't say that casually. That's also why I'm calling. I'm wondering what your schedule looks like the next week or so. I know it's pretty short notice, but I'd like to have you come meet the team, and we can talk about the account and the firm. If you're still interested, that is."

Claire was speechless.

"I hope you are," Eve said.

"Of course. I'm just a little overwhelmed."

Eve seemed relieved. "I like your honesty, Claire. You'd never have liked Marshall's place. You'll do well here."

The words said so much to her in such a short statement. "I think you're right," she said finally. "So…" Claire paused, trying to get her mind on track with her mouth, "when did you want to get together? My classes start Tuesday…I should probably be around for them," she said playfully. "But I am free on Monday or Friday, definitely."

"Monday could work. What time were you thinking?"

"I'd probably come Sunday and stay over at my friend's place, so really, anytime would be OK."

"Oh, that's perfect. Maybe get here at 10 a.m.? You could meet everyone and get a feel for the place."

"That sounds perfect."

"It's a plan, then."

Claire hung up and held the phone in her hand for a moment,

wondering exactly what Eve meant by everything she had just said. Was this a job offer, a potential job offer, or just a thank you? Either way, it was more than she could have imagined ten minutes before. Claire shoved her face down into the toss pillow on the couch to muffle her scream of excitement.

"Mom! Guess what?" Claire almost yelled into the phone.

"What?"

Emily breathed a sigh of relief as Claire relayed the conversation almost word-for-word. "I told you that you deserved it, sweetie—that it would happen."

"I know, Mom. It's just hard to believe, sometimes."

Claire eventually got off the phone, despite wanting to talk for hours. She needed to text Kim to see if she could crash at her place again. She hoped it would be OK, even if Eli was around.

Then Claire took off the bedclothes she was still wearing at noon and took a shower. She had nowhere to be that day, but she felt the need to leave her apartment and go somewhere— anywhere. Coffee would do.

Kim said she could stay, of course. And Claire finally got to meet the famous Eli. He seemed nice enough, Claire supposed. He was certainly attractive, but he didn't say much to her or Kim. He spent the night on his plush couch playing on his tablet and watching bad TV. Claire thought it was interesting that Kim pulled her into the other room to chat. It was as if Kim felt uncomfortable having Claire in his presence, as if it might upset him.

Eli and Kim were gone early the next morning, giving Claire plenty of time to prepare for her day at Muse 9. She was wildly nervous about what to wear, realizing this was still a job interview. She didn't want to be over- or under-dressed. But she could only choose from what she had brought. Yesterday, a knee-length black dress and gray suede Mary Jane pumps seemed appropriate. She paired them with a smart gray blazer and thought she looked a lot more put together than she felt.

Kim had convinced her a cab ride to Brooklyn would be ridiculous. The subway, she had said, was her best bet. "It's not that hard." Claire swore Eli made a snotty noise with his throat and she knew she didn't like him.

Using Kim's directions, Claire found her way to the correct station stop without trouble. The tranquilizer Claire had taken with her morning pills certainly helped. Then the GPS on her phone brought Claire across the street from the office, where she looked up at the second-story windows. It was far different than the view she imagined in college, the view she ended up finding at Marshall's Creatives. This was a simpler sight; one she was slowly realizing fit her better. The street was quiet, clean, and quaint. Light poles and trees dotted the sidewalk. Families and singles walked by her, the scent of coffee and pastries lingered in the air. Maybe she didn't need that extra pill after all.

The caffeine drew her to it, and she sat by a bright window with her cup, flipping through an ebook on her phone until a few minutes before ten o'clock. She popped into the bathroom before she left, swished mouthwash around to freshen her breath, and checked herself once more in the mirror. She was nervous but she was ready.

She walked up the stairs to the second floor and opened the door labeled Muse 9. Inside, a young woman welcomed her. No frantic calls demanded her attention like the receptionist at Marshall's place. She asked Claire for her name and said to wait one moment. Eve was walking by just as the receptionist pushed the button to call her.

"Claire," Eve called out happily. "Great to see you!"

"Hi," Claire said approaching Eve, who looked striking in a long red dress and black-rimmed glasses. Claire expected to shake her hand. Instead, Eve hugged her. Not a wide, motherly embrace, just a quick grasp with one arm. But it was comfortable and inviting.

"Did you find us all right?"

"Oh, yeah. I had a cheat sheet for the subway, but at least I didn't get lost."

Eve laughed. "That's all that counts. Come in and meet the team."

She had gathered her crew in a room at the other end of the lobby. The space had cozy chairs and a long center table that was low enough to have been in someone's private living room. Laptops, tablets, and cups of coffee sat on it. So did a vibrant bouquet of fresh flowers. Claire recognized a few of the faces from the Muse 9 website page listing senior staff, but she felt nervous among strangers. Most of them were chatting in pairs or groups of three. A few looked up at her and smiled. She smiled back and nodded her head politely. Claire wondered if they knew she was coming.

She sat to Eve's right in a hot pink seat. It was even softer than it looked. She fidgeted with the pen in the leather portfolio on her lap. Claire glanced around. She clearly was the most dressed up of the group, and she was glad she had fought the urge to wear a full suit.

"Good morning," Eve said with a grin. "How was everyone's weekend?"

The group murmured a mix of "goods" and light-hearted "not long enoughs." Eve chuckled. "Elena, did the event go well?"

"Perfect. Everyone loved it."

Eve turned toward Claire. "We had a marketing event for one of our clients this weekend. Elena…" she gently pointed toward her colleague with an open, upward palm, "came up with the concept and ran with it. It was interesting and a new project for us." She kept her attention on Elena. "Will it work well in the future?"

"I think so. The client already called today to thank me again and to talk about what's next."

Eve nodded. "Fantastic. We'll debrief more this afternoon."

Elena nodded.

Claire noticed eyes shifting between Eve and herself. She felt exposed and nervous, wishing she were not sitting so centered in the room, even though the team was seated in a circle. Eve turned toward her again, smiling excitedly. Claire knew she should be listening to what Eve was saying, but all she heard was "…a big reason we got Décor, Claire Kelly."

The team smiled and clapped gently. Everyone was staring now. Claire knew she should acknowledge the introduction even though she missed most of it. She smiled and nodded kindly. "Hi," she said, waving slightly, trying to sound contained. What an impression she just made for herself, the so-called wordsmith. Maybe she did need that pill. Maybe she needed another one.

"So, I've asked her to come meet you all and chat." Eve was speaking to the team, but glancing back at Claire every few seconds.

"I'm thrilled to be here. Thank you for having me." She was grateful to get the sentences out, but Claire hoped she wouldn't have to say anything else for now. To her relief, it seemed Eve had invited her to the meeting just to be introduced. She was able to listen quietly through the rest of the hour as the team discussed new ideas, new projects, and new business.

"Anything else we need to cover right now?" Eve asked.

They shook their heads and reached for laptops, tablets, and empty coffee cups.

"OK. Carry on." Eve smiled and turned toward Claire as the group dispersed. "What'd you think?"

Claire didn't know what to say. She still wasn't sure why she was here. Was Eve looking for an intern, a freelancer, or an employee? Or did she just want to show off her place? Did she remember Claire wouldn't be free for at least a few more months?

"They seem great."

Eve beamed. "They are. We were very careful about how we constructed this team." She picked up her own tablet and rose. Claire followed. "Knowing people is really important to me." Eve walked back through the lobby as Claire kept pace beside her. "This place is my life," Eve looked around gently. "It's my second home. Surrounding myself with people I trust is the only way I really know to do business."

They had entered an office, Eve's office, no doubt. It looked like her. A bold paint color, vintage photographs and advertisements mounted on the walls, wooden sayings with fading lettering interspersed between the frames, oversized pillows on the furniture, and a busy print on the throw rug. It was just a bit excessive, yet chaotically styled. It was her. Claire liked it instantly.

"Sit," Eve insisted.

Claire lowered herself onto the curved faded chocolate leather sofa that hugged the corner of the room. Eve sat across from her in a complementary chair.

"I meant it." Eve was more serious.

Claire looked at her curiously. Her brows rose slightly, but she hesitated, not wanting to ask a stupid question.

Eve smiled. "I truly believe you are why we got the Décor account. And it was a big one for us."

Claire's expression softened. "Thank you, Eve."

"You're thanking me?" Eve chuckled. "I'm thanking you!" She picked an envelope up off the table in between them.

Claire had not even noticed it was there.

Eve handed it to Claire. "Open it," she said.

Claire lifted the unsealed flap and pulled out the paper inside. She tried to contain her surprise but failed miserably.

"That's the high end of what we'd pay a freelancer. Right now, that's what we've been using because we hadn't committed to another full-time copywriter yet. But in the next few months, I'd say around early August," she smiled, "we'll be completely ready to hire."

Claire looked up at her, not wanting to speculate.

"I'm talking about you," Eve said with a slight laugh.

"I'm sorry," Claire said somewhat embarrassed by her stunned appearance. "It's just…"

"Don't apologize. I never actually told you why I asked you here. So, are you interested?"

Claire was at a loss for words, which was an inopportune reaction to a job offer for a writer. "Um…" she was dying. "God," she said, trying to start over, "absolutely. I'm still just…"

"And I'm hoping you'll still have time during your last semester of school to do a little more freelancing," she said kindly.

"I'd love that," Claire replied decisively this time and with excitement.

Eve smiled contentedly. "Super!" She sighed. "Well, then the big things are figured out. The little things can wait." She looked down at her watch. "I guess we'll spend the next few hours getting you better introduced to the place and everyone. Lunch should be here around noonish. It's from this great deli around the corner. Everyone likes you already because you're the reason for lunch today," Eve teased.

Claire waited through the rest of the afternoon with Eve; she waited through a cab ride and a train ride back to Boston; she even waited through her car ride home. She needed time to herself to really absorb what had happened today and a quiet place from which to make the call, in case she started screaming out loud with excitement.

"That's great, kid," John said. He had been holding the phone up to his ear for what seemed like several minutes now, waiting patiently for his daughter to finish her incessant, rapid talking. Emily puttered happily, putting away dinner dishes after handing him the receiver. Claire's good news had put her at ease. She didn't have to see Claire's smile to sense it. Tonight, Emily would rest easy.

"I told you I knew you could do it. I've always known you could," John said.

"I know," Claire replied sheepishly, still wondering if she really believed it. "I mean, I don't officially have a job," she sounded less secure again, thinking of the crash that could come from being too hopeful.

"No. But you're closer to one now than when you started."

Claire shrugged.

"And you seem more ready for it. Like you want it more."

She wondered how she could have wanted Marshall's place more. Maybe hanging aspirations too high on one thing was her problem. She waited for it. This time, fate wanted her. Now if it would only follow through.

"Claire?"

"Yeah?"

"Oh, I thought I lost you."

Just to my thoughts, she said in her mind. "No, I'm here."

"Well, kiddo. I think this place sounds better for you, anyway. You need that type of environment. The other place seemed to have a bunch of assholes running it. You don't want that."

She smiled. "Yeah. I think so, too."

"And this Eve sounds like she knows what she's doing. I mean, she's smart enough to hire you."

Claire's eyes welled just a bit, but she chuckled and swallowed the tears. "Thanks, Dad."

"What are you thanking me for?"

She smiled more. That's true. Her father never feared telling the truth or faking a compliment.

"OK, kiddo. I've got some work to finish up. You want your mother or are you done?"

"Just a quick second!" said Emily, spinning quickly for the phone. "Congratulations again, sweetie!" She was Claire's cheerleader. She kept Claire grounded. But mostly, she kept Claire going.

"Thanks, Mom," Claire said softly. She would cry if she said any more. Emily deserved the hug she would have reached for had Claire been standing in front of her. They could both use one. Instead, Claire bid her mother "goodnight."

She had another message to send, this one to Jill. A text had rumbled her phone moments before and across the top of the screen were plastered two words: *Guess what???*

Claire hoped it was an acceptance letter or two from New York schools. The only way this would really work was if she had a roommate and a friend by her side.

Chapter 30

Somehow it seemed *too good to be true* might finally be true after all. In the months following, Claire got to know her future colleagues through phone calls, video chats, and occasional trips into the city, and she handed in her employment agreement before she submitted her thesis.

It was hot that summer when she, Jill, and Ella searched for an apartment together in New York. Jill's parents reluctantly agreed to her choice of an east coast grad school, and she flew in for a weekend to tour the town and commit to a place. Ella had found a paid PR internship in the city for her last semester, with a little help from Eve.

On Claire's last night at home, John came into her room and leaned on the edge of her desk. She was cross-legged on her bed, looking more like his little girl than his grown daughter. John was quiet, staring somewhat at the floor before he looked up. Claire wondered if he was going to tear up.

"Daddy?" She said it gently with concern.

John searched for his resolve because emotions indeed lingered too close to the surface, and he didn't like emotions. He feared them.

"I, uh…just want to make sure you're all set for tomorrow. Everything's packed, right?"

"I hope so. The apartment's not that big." Claire smiled.

His face was weak. His mind was heavy. He didn't want to be sitting here saying these things but he couldn't not say them. He nodded to buy time.

She looked at him with raised brows, wondering what was bothering him.

"I, uh…just wanted to tell you how proud I am. You…got handed a lot these past few years. And you really…" He paused.

"You really handled them well."

She smiled, hoping her father wasn't going to cry because then she would.

"I know I'm hard on you sometimes. I just want what's best for you."

"I know that. I'm sorry I'm hard on you, too."

The idea of it made him grin softly. He nodded his head and he actually sniffled a little. "Before you leave, I just wanted to…" He took another breath. "Well, I wanted to apologize."

"You don't have to."

"No, I mean…it's all my fault, really."

"What is?" she asked curiously.

"Your mind. Everything that's happened."

She stared at him in confusion. "What are you talking about?"

"Genetics. Your grandma had it, too. Nobody ever really talked about it, but that means you got it from me."

"Oh my God, Dad! Don't." She leapt from her bed and threw her arms around his neck. "I know about Grandma and I loved Grandma." Her hug lasted long and it was strong. His arms found their way around her waist. She didn't sense tears but she sensed regret and pain. When she pulled away, she looked him square in the eyes, ones that looked tired and sad. "Besides, Dad, life isn't easy. You know that. I've learned that. And guilt gets us nowhere. If there was no Grandma, there would be no you, and there would be no me. And where would the world be without us?"

Her smile was the brightest he had ever seen. His eyes closed for a moment as he nodded his head. Then he kissed her on the forehead. When he had swallowed the emotions caught in his throat, he opened his eyes and smiled at her. "When did you get so smart?"

"I take after my dad."

His laugh was subdued, but genuine and grateful. He hugged her again and took a cleansing breath. "All right, well, we should all get some sleep. Big day tomorrow."

"Scary day."

He smiled. "I'll always be there if you need me. You know that, right?"

"Don't worry, Dad. I'll never stop needing you."

His hand dropped down to hers and he squeezed it once before leaving. She went to bed that night feeling more at peace than she had ever felt in her life.

In one day's time, the moms and the dads left their daughters in a cozy three-bedroom Brooklyn apartment. Claire was back with roommates and she was happy about it this time. She knew the companionship was more important than the shared utility costs. New York was not a forgiving city, especially for a single girl who rarely forgave herself.

Claire seamlessly started full time at Muse 9 and Eve formally paired her as a creative partner to Abe. He was the thirty-something photographer and art director who had led the Décor account. His work uniform consisted of expensive sneakers, designer jeans, a button-up shirt or t-shirt, and a blazer, which he rarely wore inside the office. Most of the time, he worked in rolled-up shirtsleeves. She found Abe's combination of good looks, talent, and husky voice almost intimidating. But Abe was also funny, easygoing, and somewhat shy until he got to know you. They quickly established a genuine relationship, and Claire was grateful that Abe welcomed her ideas and didn't laugh if she said something stupid. Claire realized having a willingness to be wrong freed her. Her career was turning into a second education—but one that paid.

"Did you hear?" Abe said excitedly as he came into their office one morning nearly a year into their partnership.

"Um…apparently not," Claire said, glancing up from her tablet. She had been reading a writer's blog while she waited for Abe to get in. He set two coffees down on her desk and dropped his bag onto his own desk. He pulled the tablet from her hand and typed into the browser. When he returned it, the Alster Diamonds website was on the screen. She looked at Abe with a knitted brow. "And?"

"They're looking around."

Claire sat forward. "Really?"

He nodded. "They're one of the biggest jewelers in the business. So, you'd think they'd want a big ad firm, right?"

"Of course."

Abe smiled and shrugged his shoulders. "Well, that's what they thought, too. Then they discovered that their 'big' agency had been massively overbilling them for years; they're making a change. It's a real opportunity for a firm like us."

"Did Eve get—?"

He nodded. "She did. And it's all hands on deck. I mean, if we could get this account…"

"*We*," she repeated, nodding and wagging her index finger between the two of them.

He smiled. "Precisely."

The whole team heard the news at their impromptu staff meeting. "I'm opening this up to everyone," Eve said. "I want you all to think about nothing but diamonds. Liesl Alster will be in town two weeks from tomorrow. Figure out your calendars and get working. We've got a week to come up with something special. Liesl took my call because—although we're small—she knows we can think big, like we did with Décor. But I also want you to spend some time today evaluating your other accounts. We care about all of our clients, millions or no millions." She paused and looked around seriously at her employees. "But, damn, the million would be nice."

Everyone chuckled.

"We can order from Magnolia today, on me," Eve said. "Let Kelsey know what you want before eleven o'clock, OK?" she glanced at her assistant, who nodded and smiled.

When the meeting ended, Claire and Abe talked as they walked back to their office. "How are we going to split this up?" she asked him.

"What do you mean?"

"Well, if Eve wants us to do the *boring* account review and still be *brilliant* for Alster Diamonds…"

He smiled at her and cocked an eyebrow "You want it, don't you? You want the glory and to stick me with the grunt work?"

She shrugged innocently.

He pursed his lips. He knew he worked well under pressure. He could give her a day. "OK. I'll do the boring review. You can have a day. *One day*. Deal?"

Claire smiled. "Deal."

She brought up the pages about Alster that she already had bookmarked and some information about Liesl, too. Alster's thirty-six-year-old owner had inherited the company less than three years before from the grandfather who raised her. She believed in love and forever, or so she said once in an article. She said diamonds were enduring symbols of love, no matter where a woman wore them.

Liesl was a striking blonde, who had been raised in Germany. Her mother was American, her father a German. Both parents died in a plane crash when she was seven. Of all the things she wished she had of her mother's, she said it was her engagement ring. It was a beautiful antique Asscher cut that had been her grandmother's. "Everlasting and timeless," Liesl said. "It lives on forever, somewhere." She said she once considered replicating its design, but somehow it seemed wrong. "It should remain lost with her."

Claire was struck by Liesl's connection to the past and her insistence that all love was eternal. Ideas played through Claire's mind, but they all sounded too close to existing campaigns. She shook her head after nearly two hours of concentrated effort toying with words and concepts. She was not yet ready to share her thoughts with Abe. He looked over at her a few times during the second hour. "Whatcha thinking?"

"I'm not there yet."

"Care to share anyways?" he said impatiently.

"No."

He rolled his eyes and went back to reviewing their current projects.

"Lunch is here," said Kelsey popping her head into their office at noon, "Come eat."

Abe turned to Claire. "I'm pretty much done here. When we get back, we're either discussing the client list or Alster. And before today is up, you're bringing me up to speed or I'm taking over. Diamonds might be a girl's best friend, but we—*you and I*—are going to lead this account *together*. I just gave you a head start because I'm nice." He said it sternly but with a smile. She was grateful that he always gave her leeway to think. She knew he found her process frustrating sometimes, but she also knew he put up with it because she made him look good in the end.

Claire nodded as they left their office and went to the casual seating area where staff could work or eat together. Claire had ordered a cranberry mayo and turkey croissant with just a little greens. And she didn't feel even a little bit bad about the mayo. Abe licked dripping salsa from his fingers and she chuckled at him. She handed him a napkin, motherly like, and he smiled as he wiped the last little bit away on the brown paper. "It's too good to waste."

"I know the feeling."

Out of her left eye, Claire caught Dana scrunching her face up as she looked at them and picked at her own lightly dressed tossed green salad. Dana was the young intern with a seemingly perpetual bad attitude, who had joined the team that fall. Claire wondered how Eve could make such a hiring mistake until she learned that Dana's uncle was one of Eve's friends. The decision still seemed out-of-sorts considering Eve's stated managerial philosophy. Claire eventually grew to feel sorry for Dana and her lack of imagination, especially seeing her eat the bland salad. Magnolia was known for its sandwiches, soups, and salads, but Dana's seemed completely run-of-the-mill. Dana's avoidance of calories, her faithful exercise routine, and her designer clothes outside a waifish figure, left Claire fearing the girl might face a battle of her own inside.

But Claire said nothing as usual, and just turned back to her meal and ate in silence beside Abe. The room was decidedly quieter than normal. Gone were any traces of the usual clever banter. All minds were focused on Alster. The Muse 9 creative teams appeared to be almost as obsessive as Claire, if that was possible. Today, small talk was limited to a few brief conversations: Abe, Milton, Gabe, and Chin briefly discussed a technology event scheduled for the next month. Mia and Elena compared notes on a new sushi restaurant. She thought about how Jill would cringe and smiled to herself.

Claire never saw Kelsey duck out, but when Eve stood up at the far end of the table, Claire noticed that Kelsey now held a white cardboard box. "I know you're all still finishing up," Eve began, "but today we have dual reasons to celebrate. The food is for the pitch." Then she turned towards Kelsey. "And this is for Claire." Eve looked up and smiled. Inside the box was a lovely white cake with delicate white accents. "Happy birthday, Claire."

Claire smiled, blushed, and covered her face with one hand. Abe nudged her with his elbow. "Thought you'd get away with not telling anyone, huh?" he chuckled. "You know Kelsey is kind of a birthday fanatic. She marks it down from your personnel records."

"Oh, jeez. Thanks, everyone," Claire said sheepishly. "You're not going to sing, are you?"

The table laughed.

"No," Teri, another writer, quipped. "The song is copyrighted."

"Exactly. So it would be illegal," Claire chuckled.

"I'll just set it over here," said Kelsey. She put it on the sideboard by the door. "Help yourselves." She left napkins, small plates, and a long knife beside it.

Abe cut two slices and put one on Claire's plate, next to her sandwich.

"Aren't you a gentleman?"

He grinned.

Claire left the last few bits of her bread. She would rather have carbs from the cake. She stole a clean fork from the center of the table and cut through the small slice. It was by far one of the best cakes she had ever tasted. It was moist and sweet, with just a hint of almond. "Kelsey, you are a genius for picking this out," she said. "And thank you so much for going with buttercream. I hate whipped-cream frosting."

Kelsey beamed. "It's my favorite bakery. It's just down the street from my house. It's sort of dangerous."

Claire smiled and ate the rest of it in silence, except for a few quiet sighs. When she finished, she scraped her fork across the plate for the last remnants of frosting. Then she stood up and went to the trash with her dirty plate. She dropped the bread and its wrappings into the bin and pivoted for another slice of cake. Dana came up quietly and tossed a quarter of her salad away.

"Aren't you going to have some?" Claire asked. She smiled and pointed at the half-carved cake. "It is my birthday, after all."

"It's empty calories," said Dana snidely without thinking. "You're just gonna get fat from it."

Claire's widening eyes shushed the girl, who stood staring at her hesitantly, wondering if the bossy copywriter might go tell on her to Eve.

But Claire unexpectedly laughed. "Are you kidding?" The hushed words stumbled out quickly, tight-roping somewhere between aggravation and amusement. Her eyes narrowed and her brows rose.

Dana looked sideways uncomfortably before making eye contact with Claire again.

"You *are* serious? Oh, Dana, an itty, bity piece of cake won't make you fat. Don't you work out like *hours* every day?"

"So?"

"So, you are seriously worried that you can't even have something bad for you every once in a while?"

Dana seemed resentful of the question.

"OK," Claire held up her hand and relented. "You know what? I'm not judging. I guess you have to do what's right for you. But honestly, if I had to choose between being super thin or having a slice of birthday cake on my birthday, I'd rather be fat."

The comment seemed absurd to the intern.

"Just do me a favor," said Claire. "Please don't toss the 'f' word around. You obviously have no idea what 'fat' means." She started to turn from the stunned Dana, but paused. "And by the way, this is my second slice," she said, pointing her index finger toward the plate. "And I, my dear, am not fat."

Chapter 31

The Alster account grew in Claire's mind. Eve had not assigned it to Claire alone but it felt as though she had. Claire was quiet as she followed Abe back to the office again, and they spent the next several hours reviewing pending projects. It was a spring-cleaning of sorts as they trashed old materials and made notes about their priorities. By 4 p.m. they had mapped out what was coming.

"All right," Abe said as he clicked the buttons on his keyboard to clear his screen. "Now it's your turn. What are you thinking about?"

Claire suppressed a smile, realizing that sounded very much like a statement a man in love might say to a woman. Their relationship was strictly platonic. He had broken up with a long-term girlfriend a few months after Claire started at Muse 9, and to Claire's knowledge, he had not dated seriously since. Abe never really talked about his ex. Claire had never even seen the woman's face until she found a photo accidentally, several months ago. It had fallen behind a bookshelf they decided to move just after the New Year. The dusty, black and white image rested face down on the tweed carpet. Claire had picked it up and looked at the face for a moment. The woman was striking: long hair, a flawless smile, and delicate features of golden ratio perfection.

"Is this a model from your portfolio?" Claire had asked casually as she handed the photo to him.

She remembered Abe staring at it, unable to take it from her.

Claire had looked at him curiously then, and tilted the image just a bit to look back at it. The haunted expression on Abe's face clicked the connection in her mind. "That's Sara, isn't it?" she had asked.

His eyes shot up to Claire's as though he had forgotten she was in the room. He simply nodded. She turned it away from him and stared at it herself. Keeping the face from him, she asked, "Do you want it?"

He looked at the white back of the paper as if the face was still reflected in it. "No," he said finally.

"Are you sure?"

He nodded.

Claire remembered wondering if Sara had ever not been beautiful—wondering if her beauty was what Abe missed. She also wondered, probably most of all, why Abe left Sara.

Claire had placed the photo gently in the recycling bin that held all of the other papers they tossed that day.

He never spoke again about Sara or the photo. But when Claire pawed through the blue bin the next day to find a scrap page she had accidentally recycled, she saw it was gone.

"Well," Abe asked again. "Your thoughts?"

Claire blinked, returning from the memory of the day. "I'm not happy with any of my ideas yet. But..." She outlined her research, her thought pattern, and her notes. He liked where she was going, but he agreed the idea was not quite original enough to stand alone.

"OK. Why don't you forward me what research you have and I'll look through it to see what sparks. I don't want to overlap where you've already gone."

She sent him the leads and then set to work expanding her search from business to family to personal, stumbling across an article about Liesl's engagement from five years ago that she broke off after learning of her fiancé's infidelity. "I guess he just didn't love me enough," she was quoted as saying.

Claire stared at the lines of the piece and eventually forwarded it to Abe. It chimed through his email, but he didn't say anything about it. Claire wondered if he had not read it yet, or if he read it but it hit too close to home.

The details of Liesl Alster's life filled her mind until Claire sensed a headache inching in. She felt useless and tired after staring at a screen all day. She thought about her little college daydreams of what work would be like, twenty stories up and working long nights on major campaigns. It was dinnertime. Sunlight still came through the window, and her view was a small street, other modest brick buildings, and a few tree branches. She smiled at the reality of her life and how she preferred it to her dream.

"Are we done for today?" she asked, rubbing her weak eyes.

Abe seemed a bit surprised. "It's not even seven o'clock yet."

"I know."

"Don't you want this account?"

She was annoyed by his guilt. "Yeah," she said flatly, "which is why I need to get out of this box and let my subconscious do some thinking for me." She smiled softer, hoping she was not aggravating Abe too much. She could tell he was somewhat irritated, but deep down she knew *he knew* she was right. She needed a little room to breathe.

"All right. Tomorrow we make magic?"

Claire chuckled. "Deal." She scooped their accounts report off his desk. "I'll take this to Eve."

"Claire," Abe said, taking her wrist gently.

She stared into his serious eyes.

"I want this."

She smiled. "Me too. I promise. Magic."

He let her go, and as she walked out the door she tapped the folder on the open door. "Tomorrow, coffee's on me."

He bobbed his head softly in response and she hoped he was not mad at her.

All of the other doors were closed and the pairs were working over pads and screens. Words and pictures littered the walls and floor. She wondered if she should feel guilty but she didn't. She hoped Abe would go home, too.

She reached Eve's door and saw her at her desk, with her glasses on her nose. She looked up at Claire, whose purse was hanging from her hand. "I wanted to give you our evaluation of our other accounts. We've got notes and timelines for them. We checked in with Paige and Elena about two that might be somewhat affected, but they didn't see a problem. They're going to follow up tomorrow with the clients, so we should be in good shape."

Eve took the folder and flipped through the pages while Claire talked. She looked up when she finished and saw Claire appeared ready to leave. "Heading home?" she asked inquisitively.

Claire wondered if she was wrong, if Eve would fire her on the spot for her lack of dedication or seriousness. She hoped she had not miscalculated Eve's faith in her. "I have Liesl Alster in my brain. I've been looking at her all day. If I stay here for the night, I'll be of no use tomorrow."

Eve nodded. Claire could not read her.

Finally, Eve closed the folder. She didn't seem mad or happy. She picked up the report and put it to the side. "I said you have a week to form your pitch. How you spend that time is up to you." She pulled her chair forward a little. "Thanks for the client review. Have a good night, Claire."

Claire nodded somewhat timidly. "Goodnight, Eve."

Her boss had already turned back to her computer. Claire left her office and passed Kelsey's desk. The assistant was gone for the evening, but it seemed no one else had left. Maybe Claire was blowing it. She had the pinnacle opportunity of her career and she was tossing it aside for a headache. But she pushed the door open anyway and walked out toward home.

❖ ❖ ❖

Ella was working late, when Claire and Jill heard a knock at the door. They looked at each other. As Jill stood up to answer it, they heard a pathetic whimper of "Claire" through the door.

Claire, who had been reclining on the sofa with a glass of chilled cheap sweet wine, sat up quickly. She really shouldn't have been sipping wine on top of the tranquilizer she took on her way home. Eve's stale reaction and Abe's aggravation had caused a minor panic attack as she left the front door of Muse 9. Jill had ordered a pizza and Claire had not objected. She had taken a hot shower after eating and wondered if she should text Abe, but she decided on wine instead. The pill, along with the booze, had calmed her worries, and now a crisis waited behind her door.

Jill peered through the hole before grabbing the chain quickly and pulling the door open. Claire jumped up at the sight of Kim.

Makeup streaked down her face, her hair was in a messy ponytail, and she wore yoga pants in public. "Oh my God, Kim," Claire said. "Are you OK?"

Jill took her arm and rubbed her back with an open palm.

Kim was trying to speak while gasping.

"Honey, sit down," said Jill softly, leading Kim to the sofa. She plopped down in the center. Jill went back to close the door and noticed a bag dropped in the middle of the doorway. She pulled it inside, pushed the door shut, and hurried back to the couch. Claire crouched in front of Kim, trying to calm her. "Honey, what's wrong?"

Kim was attempting to compose herself. Jill picked up her own glass of wine and held it out. Kim grabbed it and tossed its contents down her throat. Claire and Jill exchanged glances.

"He broke up with me!" Kim finally blurted out. "I thought the bastard was going to propose to me and he dumps me! What a prick!"

"Oh, sweetie," said Jill reaching down toward Kim, who handed her the glass instead. Jill snatched it before it fell.

"What happened?" Claire asked.

Kim's forehead was down in her open hands, hiding her face. She looked up. "What do you think happened? He said he doesn't see a future for us, doesn't want to get too serious, and though he really likes me, he just doesn't love me."

Claire pressed her lips together, feeling void of appropriate experience to offer any real help. Jill sat down beside Kim and began rubbing her back again. "What an asshole. How could he say that?"

"I don't know!" Kim sputtered. "I thought he did. We've been together for two years! I've wasted two years of my damn life on a lie. He lied to me!" Now she was getting angry.

The door opened as Ella came home to Kim's commotion. The three friends looked up at the bewildered Ella, who had gotten to know Kim pretty well during the past year. "What's wrong?" she asked genuinely concerned.

Jill waited for Kim to speak, but she was sniffling into her hands again. "Eli broke up with her," Jill whispered.

"Oh, Kim, That's awful! You'll stay with us as long as you want."

Kim had always been halfhearted about Ella, but looked up gratefully at her and smiled; the smile quickly turned into sobs again.

"Of course," Claire and Jill chimed in, echoing Ella's first reaction. They had not even gotten that far. "You can share my room," Claire said, holding Kim's hand. Kim wrapped her own grip around Claire's and squeezed tightly. Claire patted the embrace with her free hand, mostly for comfort and concern for Kim, but also in the hope of slightly loosening Kim's painful grasp. Kim finally looked up at Claire and nodded. She tried to breathe deeply and calm herself.

"Here," said Ella, handing her another glass, this one full of wine. Kim happily took it.

"Slowly," said Jill, pulling back on the stem of the glass that Kim had tilted fast to her lips. "You can make yourself drunk without making yourself sick."

That made Kim laugh. Maybe it was the irony of Eli already having made her sick that night. She took another moderate sip and then set the glass down in her lap. "You don't mind?" she said to Claire through a sniffle.

"What?"

"If I stay with you?"

"Of course not!" she replied quickly. "I'd mind if you didn't stay here."

Kim nodded.

Claire smiled softly. "But I'm afraid your commute just grew exponentially."

Kim laughed again. Claire chuckled with her.

After a hot shower and one of Claire's tranquilizers, Kim settled into Claire's queen size bed. The sheets were cold and she shivered a bit. She was tired and she knew she had to get up at least an hour earlier the next day to make it into the city for work. She wished she could call in sick. She hated Eli for springing this on her in the middle of a workweek. Didn't she at least deserve a weekend to start moving on? The more she thought about it, the angrier she got, but then she thought about moving and realized she had to get all of her things out of his place. *His place.* The thought made her start to cry again.

"Kim?" Claire whispered into the darkness of the room. She knew asking what was wrong would be stupid. But she didn't know what else to say.

"He told me he loved me, you know?" Kim said, as though Claire might not believe her. "He used those stupid words all the time, like they meant something."

Claire laid there quietly, listening.

"He didn't mean them. He just said them because they were easy. And I believed him. I gave my life over to him. I paid bills there; I cleaned that damn apartment; I did his laundry. And now I'm homeless. I have *nothing*. Why did he say he loved me when he didn't mean it?"

Claire didn't know how to reply. She wasn't sure how to help. "I wish I could tell you something that would make you feel better," she said finally, matter-of-factly, "but no man's ever told me he loved me."

Those innocent, honest words seemed to affect Kim more than Claire knew. In the dark room, Kim's look of realization didn't reach Claire. But she felt Kim's hand slide across the sheets searching for hers, and when she found it, Kim squeezed. "I think you're the luckier one," Kim whispered. "Next time, I won't believe just words."

Claire smiled but Kim couldn't see. They just lay facing each other, the sheets far less cold with the warmth of two people; both quietly wondering which one was better off.

Claire was awake for a while more, but as she drifted close to dreaming, a thought came to her, and she felt the excitement rise up that comes with a good idea. She toyed with the words in her head for several minutes before she quietly grabbed the pad that she kept by her bed and scribbled down the words in the darkness. Then she set both the pen and the page back in place, nestled deeper into her pillow contented, and easily drifted off to sleep.

In the morning, Kim seemed calmer and more herself. Claire wondered if her friend had some amazing revelation that night, or if it was really so easy for Kim to separate her personal life from the demands of her professional one. She was dressed in a tight gray suit with a pencil skirt and black patent leather pumps. Claire imagined, in the light of day, Eli regretted losing her.

Claire rose with Kim, even though her friend insisted she

should not get up for her. But Claire left the bed anyway, pulling the sheets and quilt tightly into place while Kim readied. She bid Kim a good day, gave her an extra-long hug, and waved her friend off to her extended commute. Claire sat out on the couch by the window with a cup of coffee in her hand until her own alarm would normally chime. She had turned it off forty minutes ago but felt oddly awake, despite the early rise.

She left the house early as well, and picked up more coffee and cinnamon rolls for her and Abe. Inside Muse 9, she was one of the first to arrive. Eve saw her through the glass of her office, noticing Claire's pleasant demeanor as she bid Kelsey a happy morning.

She drank a quarter of her coffee and nibbled a few bites from her roll before Abe arrived.

"Morning," he said. He tossed his first empty cup of coffee into the trash and reached into his messenger bag for his tablet. He was ready to share the ideas that had started to form for him at home around midnight. He looked tired compared to Claire's more refreshed face, and he definitely needed extra caffeine. "Thanks," he said, reaching for the cup she had placed on his desk. From the paper heat cuff, he pulled a sticky note and read it. He looked up at her and smiled.

Claire leaned back in her chair, feet crossed on the desk. "Magic," she said grinning, and took a long sip of her coffee to wash down the cinnamon taste.

Chapter 32

They spent the next two days moving the idea forward, with words and pictures littering their walls and floor. Eve checked in on them the third day. "How's it going?" She smiled sweetly but Claire could sense a tiny bit of apprehension in her voice.

Claire was relieved to say, "We're mostly done."

Abe's nodding head seemed to intrigue Eve. "Really?"

"Want a sneak peek?" Claire asked.

Eve was tempted but she promised to give all of the teams a fair shot at the lead. "I'll wait for the pitches, but I have got to say I'm so proud of you two. Everyone's exceeding my deadline. We may be talking about these come Friday. Think you'd be ready in a day?"

Abe looked at Claire, who looked back and nodded. "Absolutely."

Eve smiled, glancing at Claire. "Maybe a good night's sleep was worth it."

By Friday morning, Claire and Abe had the framework of their campaign set to pitch. Eve wanted to meet with each team separately, as if they were pitching Liesl Alster, not their boss. Claire teetered between nervous and confident. She felt uncomfortably warm and dizzy, and feared she might throw up. She fought her first urge to take a tranquilizer, but in the end she snuck one from her purse and swallowed it dry. Unlike her, Abe seemed at ease. Claire was envious of his comfort and wondered if the presentation might benefit from it. In a way, she wanted to present what began as her idea. But she felt they both owned it now, and she thought Abe's self-assurance might play better.

"I think you should do it," she said quickly in the hall as they walked to the conference room.

"No way. You're doing it," Abe insisted. "You know it better than I do."

"Oh, you're fine. You have better composure than I do."

"That's bullshit and you know it."

"I really think—" she could feel her jitters taking over.

"Don't be crazy, Claire."

An unfortunate phrase, it seemed. But it was just a word. Especially since Claire had slowly confided almost everything to Abe during their year together. He was never swayed by her confession. It explained many of Claire's idiosyncrasies. She preferred it all to be known; it made panic moments unnecessary to explain.

"If you're not part of the pitch, what's Eve going to think? There's a very good chance we'll pitch this to Liesl herself. Who do you think can sell this?"

She knew he was right. It needed to be a woman's voice. Claire nodded her head. Maybe nerves were a good thing—maybe it meant she wanted it?

When Claire pushed aside the glass door to the conference room, Eve and her husband, Avery, sat waiting at one end of the table. Avery was a well-established photographer, and though he didn't work for Muse 9, his influence was there. Often too, he could be found around the office. Many times, he had his and Eve's two children with him. But today, he was childless, sitting at the end of the table as Eve's collaborator. Eve set great stock in his judgment, so Claire wasn't surprised to see him there.

"Come in," Eve said, more like a client who was making time than a boss who paid them to be there. Claire nodded, remembering this was practice. Sometimes she thought Eve was silly in her need for realism, but somehow it made the experience more immediate. Claire was instantly relieved for her chemical calm.

"Thank you for coming."

Claire smiled. "Thank you for having us."

Eve nodded her head politely and asked them to get started. Claire took the projector remote in her hand, drew in a calming breath, and started speaking. Her scripted words began spilling from her mouth as though they had been thought up on cue. Abe sat silently by her side, turning casually to watch Eve's head bob and Avery smile softly.

Abe only winced at one line. "Women know guys sometimes lie," Claire said, then paused and smiled, "to get what they want from us."

Claire couldn't see him. She was invigorated by the moment and realized the churning in her stomach had dissipated somewhat. It was replaced by a cooler excitement as she delivered the last line and set the controller back on the table.

They both looked at Eve, who was writing down notes. Avery nodded, seemingly impressed. But he was always easy to please. He was too kind sometimes, which made him hard to read.

When Claire finished delivering the concept, Abe pushed typed notes across the table to Eve and Avery, which outlined the finer details of the idea. Eve was more critical than normal, which made Claire nervous, but Abe seemed unfazed as he tossed out quick answers to her concerns. Eve nodded along the way and Claire noted that Avery was still smiling. Claire hoped that was a good sign.

"How do you think it went?" Claire asked when they turned the corner from the heavy glass conference room door.

He nodded. "Really great. I think we have a shot at this."

She sensed he only mostly meant it.

"What?" she said.

He looked at her. "What? Nothing."

Claire reached her arm out to stop him. "No, it's something. What's wrong? Did it not sound right? Did I miss a line?"

"No," he said, shaking his head. "You got every line." He started walking.

"Abe," she said, reaching out to stop him again. "What is it?"

"Nothing," he repeated. "Just drop it."

"*Drop it?*" she said strongly. "Drop what? What's 'it'? It's *something.*"

"It's the 'guys lie' line," he said suddenly. "Finally, hearing it up there…"

She was surprised by his aggravated tone.

"What's wrong with it?"

"Look, I know this idea all started because of what happened to your friend. And I'm really sorry about that. But not all guys lie about love, that's all." He started to walk away.

"Whoa, wait a minute." She jumped ahead of him and blocked his path.

He stared at her, looking hurt. But he didn't speak.

"Where's this coming from?" she asked. Then her face dropped. "Sara?" she asked quickly. His eyes momentarily flashed anger. "This is about her, isn't it? What happened with her?"

He shook his head stubbornly. "Just drop it."

"No. Sara is 'it.' That's what's wrong with the line for you. Did you ask her to marry you?" She looked hard at him.

He seemed to blame Claire for putting the name back in his head. But she knew it was there all along.

"That's what happened, isn't it? You loved her. You asked her to marry you. And she left you. She said she didn't love you anymore, didn't she?"

Claire didn't want to force him to answer, but she was driven to know the truth.

He stared at Claire; sorry he brought it up at all. "Before she left, Sara said she'd never loved me. She was just trying to make her ex jealous."

As the words left his lips, Claire was stunned. Gorgeous, lovable, successful, Abe? She reached out to touch his arm instinctively. "I'm *so* sorry," said Claire, almost in a whisper.

"Why?" he said flatly. "You didn't lie to me."

"No." She shook her head. "I forgot women break hearts, too."

His lips softened into a half smile. Then he perked up. "Is that ours?" he asked, looking toward their office where a phone was ringing.

Claire listened. "Yeah, I think so."

Abe suddenly looked hopeful. "Eve?"

Claire shrugged and jogged down the hall to grab it. "Yeah," he heard Claire say. "OK. Sure thing."

Abe waited by the doorway. Claire looked up. "Eve's in five."

"Eve's in five," he repeated happily.

Their boss was alone when they knocked at her door. "Come on in," she said. "Sit down." She was always serious at this point in the creative process. She hated giving anything away. "Great job, again, you two. I loved your ideas."

Abe leaned back. He sensed a "but" coming.

"The meeting is Thursday at two o'clock. Liesl moved it up, so you'll have to be ready by then."

"Us?" said Claire.

Eve nodded. "Yes," she said smiling. "Congratulations."

They almost couldn't believe it.

"Now let's get started."

After a strategy session, Eve called the meeting. Claire was following Abe out the door when her boss called her name.

Claire spun around to meet Eve's eyes. "Yes?"

"I want you to give the pitch on Thursday."

"*Me?*" Claire stammered.

"Yes. I think Liesl will find you…charming…and fresh."

"But…I—"

Eve interrupted her. "By the way, I just found out we're one of four firms pitching. I thought you'd like to know that one of them is Marshall's Creatives."

Claire's eyebrows rose angrily.

Eve smiled at her fire. "I hear he's going himself for the pitch. He called to wish me luck, in the way only Marshall can."

Claire shook her head. "He's a class act, isn't he?" she said.

Eve chuckled softly. "I just thanked him for his well wishes. I'm not worried, Claire. We have the better campaign because we have the better people." She paused. "And besides, it never does any good to tell a man like him that he's wrong. That's why you have to show him."

The meetings were to be held at Alster Diamond's New York corporate office. Eve was pleased to learn they would pitch last. They were each given their own conference areas in which to prepare, and then wait their turns. When she finally came in, Liesl graciously shook Eve's hand and nodded as the Muse 9 crew was introduced. "Thank you for coming," she said politely, with a perfect American accent.

Claire was slightly amused, remembering Eve had said the same thing when they pretended to pitch.

"Let's get started, shall we?" asked Liesl.

"Absolutely," said Eve, wanting to make every minute of their time count. She turned to Claire.

And Claire was on.

She could see out the window between the slotted blinds. They had to be twenty stories up, with a perfect view of the city skyline. The sight made her smile; remembering this is where she once wanted to be. And now, here she was. She nodded at Eve as she stood to speak and the words came out effortlessly, despite the fireflies fluttering.

"Diamonds," said Claire confidently. "What do they say?" she asked. "To me, diamonds often say a relationship that may lead to marriage, hopefully for love. Making a commitment to just *one* person." She smiled, holding out her index finger to emphasize the word. "For some people, it's easy to say 'love' and not mean it."

Abe perked up as Claire went off the script they had reviewed so many times in their office, so many times in Eve's office. She had it down perfectly. Now she was improvising. Abe watched Eve's eyes widen a bit but she controlled her emotions. He could do nothing but hold his breath and listen.

Claire paused and smiled again. "But a diamond? Now that's a real investment in a future. That says something."

"A woman," said Claire, clicking the presentation through its pages. "She's in love, but she's been hurt before. But this time, this man, the words seem more real to her. She believes them more. Yet she wonders how she can trust this time. But when she sees a box from Alster Diamonds, she begins to cry. She smiles and kisses him when he slides the ring on her finger. It's not even about a diamond; it's what this particular diamond means. Because she knows what we know—with an Alster diamond, this time it's real."

Claire clicked the button and advanced to the final page. "Alster Diamonds," said Claire again firmly. "A promise more than words."

The lights came up. Liesl pressed her left arm across her body, while her right hand covered her lips. Claire couldn't tell if she had just sold the deal or blown it.

Liesl pulled the hand away and touched her chin. Everyone was looking at her but she stared exclusively at Claire, as though she was the only person in the room. "Why should this be the new message for Alster Diamonds?" she asked pointedly.

Claire set the remote on the table and sort of smiled. "Because I know that girl—the girl who's heard those words before and worried if she should ever believe them. I know a lot of women with the same fear. I know men with it as well." She paused. "Alster Diamonds is already known for quality and style. We think it should be synonymous with true commitment and enduring love as well."

Claire thought she saw a small grin from Liesl, who nodded softly and began asking questions. Together, Eve, Abe, and Claire shared the layers of their integrated campaign for the Alster brand until Liesl turned to her team and then back to Muse 9. "I believe we've heard what we need to know to make this decision. I want to thank you again for your time. We'll be in touch soon." She rose, as did her team, and shook hands before leaving.

Abe and Claire followed Eve to the elevator, and Abe touched the button for the ground floor.

The moment the door closed, Eve turned quickly to Claire. "I trusted you with this pitch and you changed it." Her face was tense. "That was so risky. Why did you do it?"

"I'm sorry," said Claire in a mild panic. "The words just kind of came out."

Eve was silent. She stared at Claire, waiting for more of an explanation.

"I thought the original pitch was good," said Claire, "but it felt a little unfair to men. Arguably, they're the ones who will buy the diamonds. We shouldn't blame them all because some men are jerks. Besides, sometimes the story relates to the guy more than the girl."

Eve stared at her for several more moments. "Make it a habit," she said finally.

"What?" Claire throat was dry and her nerves brewing.

"Following your instincts. I told you they were strong."

Claire's mind registered relief, and she slowly breathed out and nodded her head; descending from the dread of being fired. The door opened and another handful of people came on. From the far corner, Claire saw Abe catch her eye. He was smiling.

When they arrived back at the office, it was difficult to work. They loitered around the office until later than normal, just waiting for word. Claire and Abe sifted through nearly a year's worth of files and notebooks, purging scraps and reorganizing ideas. They moved the bookcase back to where they originally had it months ago and shifted around the seating area to the other corner. Eve popped her head into the office a little after seven o'clock.

"I see you've been busy," she said smiling. "Are you up for dinner?" They both stared at her, searching for a hint of news. "Well?" Eve pressed.

Claire paused. "Uh…yeah, sure. I'd love to."

"Yeah, that would be great," Abe said.

"Eight o'clock, D'Lano's."

"Eve?" Claire asked as she turned to leave.

Her boss smiled. "Don't worry, everyone's going. This is a team celebration after all."

"We got it?" Claire asked.

"Of course we did." Eve said it controlled and contentedly with just a slight twinkle in her eye. "Liesl doesn't waste time."

They didn't bother to be fancy. That was not how Muse 9 functioned. D'Lano's was a fantastic local Italian restaurant with splendid food, wine, and service. Claire sat between Abe and Eve, and laughed so hard they quickly forgot the stress from only hours before.

Claire knew she would never have had this at Marshall's place. Maybe it was just the wine making her emotional, but she stared at Eve and then leaned in and touched her arm.

"I'm so grateful to you, for everything, Eve. I couldn't imagine being anywhere else."

Eve smiled and hugged her loosely as she had the first day Claire stepped into the office. "I knew you were something special even before I met you. I guess I owe Laura dinner or something for sending you to me."

Claire chuckled. "Oh, Laura! I need to call her. When's her baby due?"

"Three months. Did you get the invitation to her shower?"

"Yeah. I'm definitely going."

"I'm hoping my schedule is free. I'd be so sad if I missed it. I'll let you know, but we should go up together."

"That'd be great."

"By the way…" said Eve. She pulled out her phone and touched the screen for her schedule. "What are you doing…not this Saturday but the following one? The seventeenth?"

"Uh," Claire pulled out her own calendar to check. "Nothing, I think. Gosh, that sounds so lame."

"Well, barring any major fires, I'm going to P.J. Nair's birthday party. He's turning seventy-five."

"Who?"

"Nair Communications."

"Oh!" Claire said suddenly, realizing Eve meant the largest media mogul in the U.S. "*That* Nair."

Eve smiled. "Avery doesn't want to go. He hates things like that. Would you want to be my plus one?"

Claire was shocked. "Wow. Yeah, I'd love to."

"One stipulation."

"OK?"

"If I introduce you around New York, you can't leave Muse 9."

Claire laughed. "I promise."

CHAPTER 33

The next day Claire had only a slight headache from the wine, or maybe it was the late night. Either way, Eve had suggested they all take an early weekend. Claire wondered if she suspected the team would be somewhat hung over or if Eve just wanted an extra day with her kids. Monday morning, she vowed, the real work would begin.

Claire didn't argue with Eve, nor did she argue with Jill, who badgered her to meet her in the city after she finished teaching her morning freshmen seminar class.

Claire would have rather slept in and enjoyed the bliss of a free day, but she knew she had been neglecting her friends for the past two weeks. After her subway ride, she received a text from Jill: *Running twenty minutes late!*

Claire desperately needed caffeine now. *OK,* she texted back, and then slipped into the first coffee shop she found.

She was digging through her purse when she looked up and saw him. His hair was different and so was his outfit. But that face and its usual expression were exactly the same. Not quite three years had passed and he had not changed. Apparently, she was unrecognizable.

"Erik," she said. Claire had heard his name when his coffee was called, so she knew she was right.

"Yeah?" He turned, expecting to know the person who had just said his name with a familiar tone, but he stared at her as if she was a stranger. His eyes squinted slightly as his mind scanned through names and faces of people he knew he should remember. But he did not know this lovely young woman, even though she obviously knew him. It seemed awkward for him, and Claire somewhat enjoyed the discomfort she was causing. She wondered if she should feel bad about that, but she didn't.

Finally, he half smiled and began to admit his ignorance. "I…" The sentence trailed as the barista called out her drink. "Claire."

His face pulled toward hers ever so slightly as his catalog of memories narrowed to that name. "Claire…" It came from his mouth first as a faint question, but then the tone turned to recognition and shock as he found her last name. "*Kelly?*" he said with awe.

"Hi," she said quickly with a deep smile, before she turned and walked the few steps to the small counter for her cup. He followed, standing beside her, almost baffled.

"Wow! You…" She waited for him to say "look different" or "lost so much weight" or "have changed," but he did not say any of those words. He stopped himself, and in the pause regained his thoughts. "*How are you?*" He said it with overemphasis or perhaps flirtation.

Claire was truly enjoying this. "I'm good. How are you? Do you live here? I thought I heard you were at Georgetown?"

Her line of white teeth showed more than Erik had ever seen; confidence exuded from her face. He never remembered that about her.

"I am," he said finally. "I'm a summer associate for a corporate firm here." His tone changed. "You know, pick the city you want to work in…" He trailed off.

"Ah, gotcha," she said nodding. "You look different," she added, laughing inside at the irony of her words. "You cut your hair," motioning to her own.

"Oh, yeah." He seemed clumsy in his response. "Have to be grown up now."

"I guess. It has some advantages, I suppose."

"Sure," he said quickly. "And you…look *great!*" He accentuated the last word, which she loved even more. It was a good way for him to handle what was obviously making him tense.

"Thanks. I feel great. Things are great."

"Yeah? What are you up to? A copywriter, right? At a firm?"

She was impressed that he remembered so much. "Well, I actually didn't get that job." She chuckled.

"*You?*" he said expressively.

"I know, right?" she replied sarcastically.

"No. I mean it. Who wouldn't want you?" He seemed serious.

She smiled. "Well, it really was for the best. I actually stayed at AU for my master's."

"See, I told you," he said smiling, pointing.

She laughed. "You did. You called it. And it ended up being the best move on so many levels. I eventually did get a job as a copywriter, at a different firm, a smaller agency with more potential for opportunities. And I'm grateful to my amazing boss for giving me her faith and those chances." She smiled coyly and lowered her voice just a bit. "I actually just landed a major new account for us."

"Wow! Congratulations."

She nodded. "Thank you. And the best part…"

He leaned in as though it was a secret.

"I beat out the agency that didn't hire me when I won it."

Erik pulled back and laughed at her smug face.

She was nodding proudly. "It was fun."

His jovial expression turned to more of a gentle smile. "I guess you showed them what they missed out on."

She looked at him wondering exactly what he meant by that, besides the obvious. Then she grinned. "I guess I did."

They stared at each other awkwardly again. Her phone vibrated; it was probably Jill. "Well, it was really great bumping into you, Erik. I'm happy things are going well."

"Yeah, me too."

She could tell he wanted to say more, but didn't.

"Maybe I'll see you around," Claire said as she turned to leave.

"Claire!" he called out. She turned back.

"You have to let me take you out to celebrate."

Her brow ruffled. "Celebrate?" she asked.

"Your account, for..."

"Diamonds," she replied, filling in the word he didn't know.

"*Diamonds*," he repeated, even more impressed.

"Engagement rings, specifically."

He smiled wider, but softer. "Yeah, for that."

"You don't have to..." She was shaking her head slightly.

"I really want to." He stepped closer to eliminate the space she had put between them when she turned. "Please?" He gave a pathetic smile.

She chuckled and rolled her eyes. "Oh, all right. If you really want to celebrate my account, I won't say no."

"Great," he replied proudly.

She slipped her hand into an easy pocket of her purse and pulled out a business card. "Here," she said handing it to him. "My cell is on the back." She didn't want to be the one to make the call.

He took the card, watching her eyes. He smiled. "Are you free this weekend?"

"I might be. I'll check my schedule and let you know." She felt exhilarated by setting the rules.

"I'll call," he said.

"Sounds good," she replied sweetly as she turned, waving slightly with her free hand as she left with a musical "bye."

She took out her cell and caught his stare through the window as she walked by. Smiling, she motioned another casual wave with the fingers not holding her cup. He pulled his own free hand from his pocket to wave back.

The message was indeed from Jill. She was almost ready and asked if Claire wanted to meet at the coffee shop on campus.

Already have a cup, Claire texted.

K. I'll get one and meet you, Jill wrote back.

When Claire arrived, she saw Jill from a distance leaving the doorway of a café. Claire had a smile plastered on her face that set Jill's mind speculating. "What? More news on the account?"

"More news from the past," said Claire.

"Huh?"

"Guess who I just ran into?"

Jill was stunned and reveled in the moment as well, even though she had never met Erik, or even seen him before. "And he looks better?"

"Oh my God, yes. Men always get better with age."

"Age! Come on. He's twenty-four."

"OK. Well, he's not nineteen anymore."

"All right. That's true. So, what are you going to do?"

"What do you mean?"

"Are you gonna go for it?"

"Dinner?"

"*Not dinner.* I know you're going for dinner. Are you open to more from him than dinner?"

"Sex?"

Jill rolled her eyes. "No! Jeez. For someone so smart, you can be so daft at times."

"What are you talking about?"

"Would you *date* him?"

Claire shrugged. "It was a stupid meeting in a coffee shop. He didn't ask me out on a date."

Jill balked. "Oh my G—*what?*"

"What?" Claire complained.

"He. Just. Asked. You. Out. On. A. Date." She cupped her hands together over her mouth as she spoke. "Under the guise of 'congratulations.' It's not your account he wants to get to know better."

"I know," Claire said shyly. "This is new for me."

Jill softened. "I know, sweetie." She rubbed Claire's back. "And it shouldn't be. You were beautiful then just as you're beautiful now. He should have seen it then."

Claire was quiet. She shrugged. "I guess."

"You guess?"

"I don't know. I just wonder if it's fair for me to judge him for not seeing it."

"Why?"

Claire turned her face up towards Jill. "I didn't see it either."

Jill smiled. "Sweetie, he only knew what he took the time to see. I knew you then, too, and to the outside world, you might have been shy, but you were lovely."

Claire grinned.

"Except maybe the gray fleece pants," Jill added.

Claire laughed. "Yeah, that year was not my best."

"Not so much 'best,'" said Jill. "Just every day was always painfully the same."

Claire smiled softly. "Yeah, that pretty much describes depression, too."

Erik did call. He called later that day, in fact. His turnaround time had improved greatly since college, when his text messages came within days not hours. Claire always knew she had no specific plans for Friday or Saturday. When he called, she lied. "Not tonight, but I might be free tomorrow."

He seemed eager to meet her for dinner then, and she agreed to the restaurant he suggested. She knew the atmosphere and showed up in a gray cocktail dress that would befit the wife of a corporate lawyer. That thought crossed his mind too as she walked up to him at the bar. Her hair looked stunning in a controlled mess of chaotic curls, with a few hanging down at the nape of her neck. Others wisped softly around her face. He would have never guessed the look took just a moment and an elastic band. Her makeup was subtle, which he liked as well. Only her eyes were somewhat emphasized. He had never looked close enough before to see their shade of hazel green. He almost couldn't handle the sight of her.

"Hey…you look amazing," he said, reaching out for her waist and softly kissing her cheek.

Claire hated that his gesture made her nervous. It was so unfamiliar, from any man. In a way, she somewhat blamed him for being part of that absence of knowledge. He had been in her life then, when she thought she should be forming those memories of young love. Her fear and sadness started in high school, so maybe she should blame those boys, too. They never tried either. She already blamed herself.

But she let him kiss her anyway, her cheek at least. And she fought the shyness toward his touch. She was still exceedingly attracted to him, and now, he was to her as well. She wanted to be fine with this, to be all right with his change of heart. She was different, wasn't she—beyond the scale or the dress size?

"Sure," she said, when he asked if they should sit. The hostess led them through a busy room of people. She noticed glances up and glances down, both men and women. They stared at her. They stared at him. They stared at the charming couple.

She loved it, in a way. Being special. Being normal. Being part of the lovely crowd. There were beautiful people here tonight and she was one of them. She might need a mirror to prove it to herself, but she was.

She was sad to know the change had come again. She was sad again.

Maybe it was the stress of seeing Erik that shifted her mood tonight. Maybe remembering her former self from when she knew him made her sad tonight. Here she was, a beautiful person among the sea of beautiful people in a beautiful city with a beautiful job and a beautiful life and a beautiful new account. Sitting across from a beautiful man now, she felt awkward, like that girl who pretended to be comfortable in the library as she set up her laptop for an advertising project. She was actually living that life now, the one she pretended to live then, but at the restaurant table she felt nineteen again.

He was talking to her about something. He made a gesture up with his hand. She tried to listen but she wasn't really hearing him. It was not the lull of the restaurant talking to her; it was her mind. They were not voices; they were thoughts; memories and a realization that things would never be normal for her. She would always be Claire: quiet, except when she was loud; attractive and sometimes thin; smart but self-loathing; creative but paranoid; doting but shy. She was far from average, and that was all she ever would be.

He was telling a joke and she felt she should laugh, but she was hazy from the panic.

"Is our waiter coming back?" she asked finally, touching her throat. "I could use some water." Claire felt like she was suffocating.

He stared at her. "Yeah, I just…called him."

"Oh, sorry." He must have said that when he motioned up with his hand.

"Are you all right?" he asked.

"Yeah," she smiled genuinely, finally seeing him. "I'm just tired. It's been a long few weeks." She kept taking deep breaths.

He sighed expressively. "I know the feeling."

She forced a grin. "And it'll only pick up for you from here."

"I hope so. I'm ready for it." Erik smiled, reaching for her hand. "I'm really happy I ran into you, Claire. It's nice to see a familiar face." He touched her fingers lightly. "I'm glad you stopped me."

She chuckled softly as she found herself pushing back against the fear.

"I almost wouldn't have recognized you. You look so different."
He paused. "So beautiful."

Maybe she shouldn't have judged him. Maybe she should've stopped him. She wished he hadn't said that. "You know, it's a shame," Claire said sadly.

"What's that?" Erik asked gently, leaning down to listen.

"You never had the luxury of knowing me thin—the first time, I mean."

"What?" His face fell a bit, wondering where she was going.

"I looked like this my whole life. I was always fit. A medication caused all that weight in a matter of a few years, and then, suddenly, I was a fat girl to everyone at AU. That's how you knew me. I never really knew myself like that. Not really. I almost can't remember it."

He seemed confused.

"I liked you a lot then, Erik. I don't know if you remember any of the times we ran into each other, but I remember every single one of them. And you never kissed my cheek "hello" or touched my hip. Not once."

He pulled his hand up, hovering uncomfortably above her fingers.

"You never touched me once."

He was tense and silent.

She breathed deeply and smiled gently, more so than she expected. But she had to talk or she would scream. "When I was fat in college, you and I were acquaintances, at best. You always just seemed to be passing by. Now you're finally taking the time to stop. I'm suddenly different?" She paused. "We both know only one thing has really changed."

He stared at her. Anything he said would be wrong.

Claire reached for her purse.

"Please…" he said suddenly. "Please, don't go." He looked at her with his charming eyes and she almost couldn't help but smile.

"I'm sorry, Erik. But you're about five years too late."

"Can't it just be the stupidity of youth?" he asked weakly.

She looked at him, chuckling slightly. "It wasn't *that* long ago," she said more playfully.

He smiled and placed his hand on hers again. For a moment his touch felt nice, but she gently pulled it away completely and he realized she was serious. She shrugged, wondering deep down if maybe his answer might surprise her. "Did you ever once want me then?" she asked pointedly, hopefully. Some part of her wanted to stay.

He looked away awkwardly and then met her eyes again with remorse.

She continued thinking maybe he would make some grand gesture. "If you can honestly admit that you saw me—not a fat girl in your class—even just *once* when we knew each other, then maybe I'll reconsider."

She waited but he did not lie to her. She smiled again and nodded her head softly as she rose, taking her purse in one hand. She backed up her chair. He didn't try to stop her. She really didn't think he would. She left the seat pushed out and began walking by their small table.

But as she passed him, she paused. Without deliberation, she suddenly turned behind him, reached out her hand, and slowly slid her palm down over the curve of his shoulder toward his chest. His loose muscles tensed at the touch of her soft fingertips through his shirt. Excitedly, he tilted his head slightly as he sensed her face hovering by his right ear, eagerly convinced Claire had changed her mind.

"Take this as a life lesson," she whispered. "Even if people change, the past always stays the same."

He sat there comprehending her words as blood rang in his ears. When he turned his head, he saw just a final glimpse of her leave.

She passed by them again, the people glancing. She forced
a smile as she went, putting on that outward show she was so
practiced at performing. But some of it was real; some of it was
because of Erik. She did not pause to see if he watched her exit,
but just a part of her delighted in knowing that twice now—in all
the years she had known Erik—she was the one walking away.

Had she bothered to give him a second glance, she would
have seen him watching, still shaking his head, but this time at
himself. He was thinking back to the day in the library, way back
to sophomore year. It was the day he stopped to realize Claire was
beautiful and never said a word.

CHAPTER 34

She tossed in bed for hours that night, stomach tight, mind full, wondering, worrying.

Maybe she had judged him too quickly. Maybe Erik could have meant more to her. He was, after all, an immature man when she knew him. She had changed—could he?

Claire agonized about forfeiting her chance with him after wanting him for so long. But at the restaurant, standing before him, feeling his touch, watching his smile fall to her, she had realized she couldn't let go of the hurt. Maybe she was no better than he was.

The panic had not subsided once she got home. Now alone in the cool sheets of her bed, thinking about the man whom she had pined after for so long, it made her dizzy and short of breath. In the darkness, she again felt insecure. She hated it.

Damn him, she thought, for ruining the glory of her Alster win.

Maybe damn her.

He had done nothing but appear. She was the one who lived with this mind, the one who let it drown her in worry.

She was back here again. This moment proved it—happiness was fleeting for her. This hateful illness.

She reached for the bottle by her bed and took another tranquilizer to dull her senses. She had to get to sleep. On days like this—she never knew when they would come—her mind would not stop replaying the minutes of the night and the week through her consciousness.

Damn it, for its persistence.

She pulled her soft eye mask down over her lids again, shoved the pillow to the side, and somehow coaxed her brain to rest.

By the morning, she was somewhat brighter. Or maybe it was the haze of exhaustion and lingering chemicals. Back in her office Monday morning, the energy of Abe, Eve, Paige, and the team helped divert her thoughts from the anxiety that remained. She soon fell into the new routine of their dynamic firm, which was transformed by the acquisition of the Alster account. Liesl had wanted a smaller agency with more character, but by simply bringing her business to Muse 9, the agency grew. Still, it was not so much about the size, as Eve reminded them. It was about the people. They were the inspiration and the soul. But with this account, Eve was more hands-on than ever; she never had so much to lose.

Claire let herself get caught up in the excitement of the week and was eager again to rekindle the thrill of the victory. Yet she still felt cheated out of real rest. She craved it. After nearly three weeks on edge, she longed for the silence of the weekend. She wanted to go home, shove her roommates out the door, and just stand in a hot shower for hours thinking of absolutely nothing, if that was possible.

"Are we still on?" Eve asked after their Wednesday morning staff meeting.

"For?" Claire said.

"Saturday."

"Oh, right, of course," she said, hoping she had covered well.

"Yeah. I'm not sure if I ever officially confirmed with you."

"No, but I figured we were going until you said otherwise." She had actually forgotten about the party. "I knew I'd have to check with you eventually. I don't even know where it is."

Eve smiled. "I reserved a car. We'll pick you up at your place at seven o'clock."

So much for a weekend to herself; maybe she would have a good time.

✤ ✤ ✤

Saturday night, Claire waited at her curb, decked out in a black evening dress that she had also rescued from her high school toss pile. It had been a beloved favorite, and tonight, it fit her just as it had at sixteen. She breathed calmly, and she had to admit she actually felt almost beautiful in it now, more so than before.

When they arrived at P.J.'s building, she followed Eve up to the penthouse. Inside the party, surrounded by a din of voices, Eve gestured a phantom glass to her lips. Claire nodded as her boss motioned the number two with her fingers. The bar was at the center of the room, shielded behind a mass of people all waiting to drink on P.J. Nair's dime. A single body maneuvering through the line likely had a greater chance of reaching the front. But once Eve left, Claire felt awkward and alone again in the middle of the crowd. She fidgeted a bit with her purse and rubbed her chilled, exposed arm with her free hand.

"Should I be offended?" Her glance shot quickly to the warm voice beside her. Claire looked around inquisitively, wondering if the comment had been intended for her.

As the crowd shifted, just a foot from her stood a familiar face, a gorgeous nerd in a tailored black suit, with steel blue eyes and thin glasses. She felt her stomach knot a bit when she placed him from the alumni event. "Wes," she said quickly, somewhat embarrassed but relieved that she remembered his name.

He smiled. "At least I'm not totally forgettable."

She tried to compensate, hoping she sensed humor in his tone. "No, you're not…"

He bent his head down toward her slightly and gently touched her bare arm as he whispered in her ear. "Claire, I'm teasing you."

"Sorry," she said weakly. His demeanor and eyes calmed her. "I'm not used to this," she said finally. She still didn't feel like a New Yorker. She probably never would.

"Yeah, it's something," he said, glancing around at the glitz.

Her brow knitted now, confused by the sight of him, somehow just comprehending that he actually stood before her. "What are you doing here?" she suddenly blurted out.

"You really didn't look at my business card at all, did you?" he said.

She hoped he was feigning the offense. She sighed loudly. "It had been a long night." She shrugged and looked him right in the eye. "And…" She stopped, hesitating to say the truth, not wanting to admit that she had not thought enough of herself to believe he really meant it.

He tilted his head, waiting for her to finish. She loved his gentle and concerned look, even though she was still a stranger to him. She felt safe around him, relieved to be talking to him. Forgetting about her self-consciousness, she looked at him more confidently. "Wait. You didn't answer my question."

He chuckled softly. "Which question?"

"Why you're *here.* I never imagined running into you here of all places."

"New York's really not that big," he quipped playfully. "Honestly, I think everybody's here."

She laughed out loud and that made him smile more. "Besides, what are you doing here?" he asked in a toying, sarcastic tone.

"My boss invited me. I'm a plus one."

She could see his face change.

"Her husband didn't want to come," she quickly finished.

He seemed relieved. She was deeply flattered—and terrified.

He nodded, just staring at her.

"I have to ask *again?*" she said.

"Ask what?"

Her eyes widened and her face fell in faux disbelief. "New York's not that small."

"*Oh.* I work for him. Nair," he said.

Claire was surprised. "I thought you were an engineer?"

"Computer engineer. I oversee his global network."

"*Oh—wow*," she stumbled, feeling fooled by her assumption. He was so young. She didn't speak for several seconds, unsure of what else she would get wrong.

But he was not swayed by her reaction. He was fueled by it. "And you? Where do you work?"

"Um…a creative firm in Brooklyn."

"Oh, fantastic. I live in Brooklyn."

She smiled. "So do I."

"Well, that makes it easier."

"What?"

"Dinner."

She blushed.

"And I'm going to need your number, since you obviously can't be trusted with mine."

Claire studied him for a minute, grinning. She pulled a business card from the back of the small case in her purse, one that had her cell on it. She coyly hesitated handing it over. "I'm a bit of a handful," she said, somewhat seriously. "One might even say unique."

He chuckled. "I have no doubt," he answered, plucking the card from her fingertips.

She let it go. Maybe she could be happy?

"Business?" said Eve, holding two flutes in her hands and sensing she was interrupting.

"Pleasure," Wes replied, keeping eye contact with Claire until she broke it out of unease.

Eve's eyebrows rose. "Even better," she said quietly, knowing she was interrupting. But just as she moved to excuse herself away from their obviously private conversation, a woman called his name.

"Wes, can I steal you for a moment?"

He turned, recognizing the voice, and was slightly aggravated to be called to work. "Sure, Cindy," he said, covering for his true reaction. "Cindy Malay, our CFO."

He had noticed Claire's quick response, seemingly nervous about a new woman touching his shoulder. He liked that. Claire softened once the truth registered and the introduction had been made.

"I just need him for one minute," Cindy said.

Claire nodded. "Oh, of course. I'll be around," she said, directing her eyes to him.

He held her card up between two fingers. "I know where to find you. Unlike you, I'm not tossing this."

Claire failed to suppress a smile as Wes followed Cindy away.

"Who is that?" Eve asked when Wes was out of earshot.

"A classmate."

"Oh, I think he's more than that."

Claire grinned and took a sip of her champagne. It had a faint coral hue to it and she tasted sweetness interspersed within the bubbles.

"Apricot Bellini," Eve said when Claire turned to her pleasantly.

Claire took another sip. "It's delicious!"

"Ms. Staunton." They heard Eve's name called coolly from the crowd, and when the speaker stepped forward, Eve fought an eye roll.

"Chip Marshall." Eve's response was sweeter compared to his cocky tone. Hers would have seemed subordinate had she not already been the victor. Or maybe it was the Bellini?

"I haven't had a chance to congratulate you on Alster."

She looked at him, trying not to laugh at his pathetic attempt to prove he was comfortable losing. "Well, thank you," she replied smoothly.

Claire watched him glance over at her, running his eyes down her body. She stared back at him unmoved, determined to ignore the underlying intimidation she felt. She also wanted to avoid, at all costs, looking at the man by his side.

"But I actually…" said Eve, pivoting slightly, "owe it all to this woman."

Chip shot his eyes to Eve and then back to Claire. "*Really?*" He held out his hand to Claire. "I don't think we've met."

Claire sipped the drink again and then offered hers. "Claire Kelly," she said with false composure. It would be such a shame to waste the Bellini all over his face.

"How long have you been with Eve?" he asked.

Claire looked at her boss. "A little more than a year?"

"Yeah, that sounds about right. It was last June that you wrote for Décor."

She nodded as she looked back at him. "Over a year."

"Well," he said, "when you're looking for a change—"

Before he could finish, Claire chuckled dismissively and shook her head. "No. I'm exactly where I was meant to be."

He didn't seem to know what to say. Most people begged for his number.

"But it was nice meeting you." Her eyes roamed to his shadow. "Chase," she said quickly, with a slight tilt of her head, finally admitting he was there.

Chase stared at her awkwardly, fiercely trying to place her. He frantically searched in the distance of his memory for how he had met her. He could feel Chip's piercing eyes turn to him and he wondered what he was missing.

Claire desperately wanted to ask for her umbrella back. She wanted him to know her, to remember her. But she expected such a subtle reference would escape him, so she said nothing.

She didn't know that Chip Marshall never missed a gesture and he never forgot a name. His secretary found *Claire Kelly* in the company's HR database the following Monday morning. But since *fat* wasn't an acceptable reason for dismissing a candidate, it was not there in the notes. Chase struggled to remember the woman, as he stood before Chip's desk, unable to answer for her rejected application more than two years ago and the subsequent loss of a multi-million dollar account at present day.

But Claire didn't need to know what happened that morning in Chip's office because they didn't matter anymore. Instead, she excused herself politely and walked away from him, with Eve by her side, silently hiding a smug smile in a sip of her Bellini.

Claire smiled, too. It was not about proving Chase and Marshall wrong. It was not even seeing Wes in the background, holding her card up again as he caught her eye. She smiled out of relief; of the things she had learned, things outside of school that only living can teach. She smiled at the solace she had found, despite her limitations, from the strength that endured within her even at her weakest. She smiled at her judgments, her assumptions, and her perceptions. And she smiled knowing that it didn't matter—worrying about what others think. Because what lives outside, the things so easy to see, are so easy to get wrong. It's what's beneath the surface, where it is hard to reach and quick to bruise, that truth exists. She smiled knowing that although life would not always be easy or happy for her, between the sadness dwelled the good days, the days to live for.

www.ingramcontent.com/pod-product-compliance
Lightning Source LLC
Chambersburg PA
CBHW031213120726
47905CB00002B/317